How DARK the LIGHT Shines

M.J. Bell

Cover art by Aria Keehn

Interior format by The Killion Group
http://thekilliongroupinc.com

Thank you.

Dedication

For Connor, Brendan, Ben, Sam, Sofia, Ethan and Joey
And for Daniel, my genius, who never gave up on me.

Chapter 1

The darkness was gaining strength. Margaux could feel it in her bones and in the cold that gripped her heart; and for the first time in her life, the optimism—that which had gotten her through so many tough times in the past—was gone. Gone like her dream of living a care-free life with the fae in Tir na-nÓg; all because Grossard and Mordred had made off with the Shard of Erebus. In that one day, everything changed: Keir was gone, Deston was avoiding her, and the fate of the world was unknown. She couldn't imagine things getting any worse. Yet, she sensed they were about to.

She shivered and swallowed back the wave of nausea that had been a constant ever since she woke up in the infirmary with broken ribs and a torn tendon in her ankle. Her sick feeling wasn't just because she missed Keir so very much, or because the doctors didn't know if her unborn cousin would survive the trauma of its mother being stabbed. While that all added to her stress, the main factor pressing heavy on her mind and heart was that Deston had been avoiding her since their return from the temple. She realized he had been hurt, too, and was laid up the same as she, but he could still talk to her telepathically if he wanted to, or answer her when she attempted to contact him. Four days had passed without a word from him and the silence hurt worse than her broken bones.

The silence also gave her way too much time to think about what had happened to bring them to their current juncture. As much as she hated to admit it, it was all her fault. She should have just stepped into the portal with Deston instead of going back into the temple to get Caluvier. She was a firm believer in the theory of nothing happens by chance, but she didn't believe it was true in this case. Her stupid move had changed the course of events and cost her everything: Keir was dead, Grossard had the Shard, and Deston hated her.

Half hidden under the canopy of a giant leaf, Margaux stared unseeing at the rainbow colored flecks of the fish darting amongst the rocks and water lilies in a pond. She had come to the secluded outer circle of the palace's floating gardens because it was seldom visited, especially now that the majority of residents of Tir na-nÓg were out dealing with the destruction and havoc Grossard and the Shard were generating across the globe. She had hoped a change of scenery would help to calm her mind, but not even the serenity of the water, the lotus blossoms and the bright colored day lilies surrounding the pond could do much to soothe the turmoil roiling inside her. She had failed Deston, and the date when Grossard would reverse the earth's magnetic pole and open the portal to bring the god of darkness into the world was growing nearer. The world would literally be turned up-side-down and she didn't know what she could do to fix it.

"I spoiled everything. No wonder Deston hates me," she whispered to the air. She gulped back a sob and swayed with the pain that sliced through her mid-section.

"Margaux? Is that you, ma chérie?" NiNi exclaimed, breaking into Margaux's solitude. "Oh my … it is," NiNi continued, pulling the leaf that partially concealed Margaux out of the way. "What a pleasant surprise. I did not expect to find anyone all the way out here in my little patch of sunshine."

Margaux lurched up and jumped to her feet without thinking, which triggered a double dose of pain from her ribs and her ankle. She grimaced and sputtered, "I'm so sorry. I didn't know this part of the gardens was yours. I wouldn't have intruded if I had. I was just looking for a place to—" She left her words dangling and bent to pick up her crutches, hoping to hide the blush she could feel warming her cheeks. "I should be getting back," she added, adjusting the crutches under her armpits.

"Non, non. You are not intruding. I call this my garden, but to be truthful it is not really mine. I have just added my own little touches to it to remind me of home. Please stay and keep me company. I have wanted to hear how you are doing and there is no better place to talk than out here with all this beautiful nature. We can sit and you can tell me how everything is going with you." The laugh lines in the corners of NiNi's eyes crinkled as she tilted her head and studied Margaux. "Hmm … you have some color back in your cheeks. That is good to see. How are the ribs? Do they still give you pain?"

"Sometimes, when I forget and take too big of a breath, or if I try to walk too fast with the crutches. The healer thinks I should be able to walk without them tomorrow and that should help."

"It never fails to amaze me how quickly you fae heal. If only us poor old humans could do the same. Heaven knows if it were me, I would be down for months with the kind of injuries you have suffered," NiNi remarked, her penetrating gaze locked on Margaux's face.

Margaux fidgeted under NiNi's scrutiny and tried to look away, but she was caught. Her cheeks turned a deeper shade of pink.

"I am sensing there is another pain, one you are trying to hide. The healers cannot help you with this kind of pain, but maybe I can. Will you tell me what troubles you so?" NiNi prodded.

Margaux squirmed and adjusted her crutches under her arms. Deston had told her that NiNi could read thoughts, but she hadn't experienced it for herself until that moment.

Seeing Margaux's hesitation, NiNi added, "You are young and your body will heal nicely, but your body is not the issue here, is it? It is your heart that is broken and that is another matter altogether."

Without bidding, the tears began to well behind Margaux's eyes. She did her best to hold them back, but they came of their own free will. Before she realized what was happening, she was wrapped in NiNi's arms, sobbing big gulps.

"I know ... I know," NiNi whispered as she held Margaux tight and patted her on the back. "Your heart wants what it wants, but sometimes fate does not agree and takes us where we do not expect or want to go. I know it is not easy to accept, but you must have faith that it will work out as it should—as the Universe has set in motion."

Margaux pulled back and shook her head. "But Grossard has the Shard—how can it work out? He's going to destroy the whole world."

NiNi smiled tenderly and tucked a piece of Margaux's hair behind her ear. "Non, that will not happen. Oseron and Deston will see to it. I have no doubt about it. But the fate of the world is not all that bothers you. Tell me ... why such big tears?"

Margaux sniffed and dropped her head. "It's nothing—"

"Phew! You do not hide out in a garden that no one visits for no reason. I can see a deep sadness in your eyes. I know something is wrong. Come ... sit here beside me and share your burden. It will do you good to talk about it," she took Margaux's arm and guided her to a bench in the sun.

Margaux let NiNi lead her and sat down without protest, but instead of speaking, she lowered her head and wrung her hands. No one but Deston knew they had kissed or that she was the reason Grossard had gotten away with the Shard. She would have liked nothing better than to confess and relieve her burden, but she was too afraid of what NiNi would think of her if she heard the truth.

NiNi sat silently and waited. She sensed Margaux wanted to talk, but something was holding her back. She cleared her throat and decided to try another approach. "Deston's leg seems to have healed nicely, from what I hear. He was lucky the arrow missed the bone."

Margaux flinched and her chin sank further into her chest.

NiNi's brow rose and her head nodded in understanding. "I fear he is going to overdo and harm himself again with all his scampering about. I know he is fae, but a wound like that needs time to heal. I wish he was not so stubborn and would heed the healers' recommendation. He should be in Tir na-nÓg where there are people to look after him. If he reinjures his leg, he will not find as good of help in the lower realm if that is where he has gone." NiNi stopped abruptly as Margaux's head jerked up and her mouth fell open.

"Deston has left Tir na-nÓg?"

NiNi was seldom taken off guard, but Margaux's reaction truly surprised her. "Why yes. He left before light this morning. Did he not tell you?"

Margaux's face lost all color. "No, I ... I haven't talked to Deston since we came back from the temple. I guess ... I, um—" her words trailed off.

"Ah, ma chérie," NiNi cooed, reaching out and pulling Margaux into her side. "Deston has been through a lot over these past few months. Give him time. He has much on his mind. Do not feel bad that he did not tell you. He did not even tell his *maman* he was leaving. He left her a note saying he would be back and not to look for him. I am sure he thought we would all try to stop him from going if we knew of his plan, which of course we would have. You know how he can be when he sets his mind on something."

"Yes, I'm sure that's what it is," Margaux responded pulling back and getting to her feet. "I'm sure I'll hear all about it when he gets back." She fidgeted with the crutches, knowing that may not be true. "I better be going. The healers want to check my ankle this afternoon. I will see you later," she added and hobbled toward the gate.

"Give him a little time, Margaux. He is battling his feelings as much as he is battling the darkness," NiNi called out after her.

Margaux nodded her head in response without turning around and picked up her speed as more tears threatened to fall.

Chapter 2

The early morning fog shrouded the tree tops, leaving the Great Bear Rainforest in an ethereal glow, halfway between dark and light. It wasn't raining, but the heavy amount of moisture in the air had Deston's hair plastered to his head as he clung to a tree branch as if it was his lifeline in a raging sea. His hands were sweating, even though there was a chill in the air, and his arm muscles quivered with fatigue, but no way was he going to let go until he achieved one more chin up. With a loud yell, he pulled up with a final heave. The second his chin brushed the rough texture of the branch, he let go and dropped the four feet to the ground.

As his weight came down on his injured leg, it buckled beneath him and he fell back on his butt. Unconsciously, he rubbed the puckered indention on his thigh where the arrow had pierced it. In the early morning chill, as well as right before it rained, the spot bothered him the most, but he didn't let the ache keep him from his rigorous exercise routine. And after two weeks of self-inflicted, torturous workouts, his thigh was no sorer than all the other parts of his body. With a swipe of his hand across his eyes, he brushed his hair back and flopped to his back to do stomach crunches.

"Exhausting yourself isn't going to change what's happened, you know," Zumwald stated from the trees on the other side of the area Deston had cleared for his camp.

Deston paused half way up and looked over at the old man. Then without saying a word, he returned to his crunches, blowing short puffs of air out through his clenched teeth each time he came up.

Zumwald squeezed the grip of the bow he held in hand until his knuckles turned white, wishing he had a magic spell that could help the boy. But magic cannot take away heavy guilt, especially when one was holding onto it so tightly. Silently, he counted as Deston came up again and again. He had reached seventy-five before Deston collapsed on the ground, panting to catch his breath.

"How d'ya find me, Zumwald ... or should I call you, Merlyn now?" Deston asked once his breathing had slowed enough for him to speak. "Do you have someone spying on me?"

Zumwald—Merlyn—didn't react to Deston's attempt to rile him, but waited patiently until Deston looked up before answering. "Your whereabouts was never a mystery to me, and I have kept that knowledge to myself. I would have come sooner, but I thought you could use some time alone to work through your grief and come to terms with what has happened." He cocked his head and searched Deston's face. "I may be a bit presumptuous here, but I'm going to say you still haven't made much headway in that respect. Nor have you worked through much of anything as yet. Am I correct?"

Deston's lips curled as he sat up. "Work through what? The fact that I let Grossard get away with the Shard, or the fact that Keir is dead because of me?"

Zumwald's shoulders slumped and he shook his head sadly. "I know you don't believe that in your heart, so I'm not going to justify it with a response. However, I must say that what you're doing ..." He lifted his arm and pointed to the tree branch; then swept it down to the ground to indicate the sit-ups. "... this over-extending your body and mind before they've had the time to properly heal, will not help you get prepared to face Grossard and Mordred again when that time comes. And it will surely come sooner than you may think, I'm afraid."

Deston's face turned scarlet at the mention of those two hated men. Scrambling to his feet, he clenched his fists. "Yeah? Just what d'ya think I've been doing here? Don't worry about me. I'll be ready when I see Grossard again, and I'll make sure he doesn't have a chance to hurt anyone ever again!"

Zumwald's hand came up and though Deston's mouth continued to open and close, no words came out. Realizing Zumwald had blocked his speech, Deston pursed his lips and glared at the old man.

"I, too, have lost friends—some by Mordred's own hand, as a matter of fact—so I am perfectly capable of understanding how you feel," Zumwald said, ignoring Deston's scowl. "But wallowing in pain and self-pity does nothing to honor those who have been lost. Nor does it help you or the fae resolve the new problem at hand."

Deston blew a breath out through his teeth. Zumwald had a habit of showing up out of the blue and drawing Deston into his schemes, which usually resulted in Deston and his friends risking their lives. He grabbed the towel that was hanging over a low branch of the tree and wiped his face; then ran it over his head, hoping the old man would take the hint and go away.

"Correct me if I'm wrong, but I'm detecting you have had a change in focus. It seems to me you are more about seeking revenge than you are about finding and destroying the Shard." He looked at Deston from under a pair of bushy eyebrows. "Revenge is the typical human response when one feels another has harmed them, and I am well aware Grossard and Mordred have done you great harm. But you are *not* a typical human." He paused to let that statement sink in.

Deston narrowed his eyes and turned his back on the old man without responding.

Zumwald breathed a weary sigh and looked up through the tree branches. He had told Oseron he would find Deston and bring the boy home. He had thought it would be a simple matter once Deston understood the scope of work that still needed to be done. But Zumwald hadn't taken into consideration that even though Deston was extremely gifted, he was still an adolescent and his emotions often overruled rational thought. That became apparent as soon as he arrived on Swindle Island in the Great Bear Rainforest and he saw how Deston was still battling his grief. He had stayed in the background and waited, in hopes Deston would be able to put it behind him quickly, but two weeks had already gone by in the lower realm and Deston didn't seem to be any closer to a resolution than when he arrived.

"They killed Keir. How am I supposed to forget that? Macaria is going to grow up without a father." Deston plopped down on the ground and dropped his head into his hands. "I grew up without a father. I know what it's like. It isn't fun and it isn't fair. That knife was intended for me. I should have been killed. Everyone would be better off if I had."

Deston's voice was so low, Zumwald shouldn't have been able to hear, but he did. In less than a heartbeat, the old magician was standing in front of Deston.

"If you had been killed, where would that leave the world? There would be no one to stop the darkness from taking over and devouring the light. Everything you know and love would cease to exist. Can you look me in the eye and truthfully tell me you'd prefer to have your friends and family contend with that madness without you by their side?" Zumwald's voice boomed through the trees and shook the branches. A flock of birds took to flight, squawking their annoyance at being disturbed.

Deston flinched at the harshness in Zumwald's voice. Tears pooled in his eyes, but he gritted his teeth and refused to let them fall, just as he had been doing ever since Keir's death.

"You've been greatly blessed by the gods and they have been extremely patient with you, but they will not and cannot wait forever. They can rescind your blessings at any time they please, and do not think for a moment that they will not go to those measures." Zumwald paused and then continued in a softer tone. "I know you've been through a lot and a lot has been asked of you. It's natural for you to think that unfair. But might I ask you to stop and think how unfair it was for the gods to flood the earth long ago, leaving but a handful of humans to carry on? And how unfair was it to let Christ be crucified, or for one third of the population of Europe to die from the Black Death? I could go on and name hundreds—no, tens-of-thousands of events that were deemed unfair at the time they took place. Now that time has passed and we have gained a different perspective of those happenings, it is easier for us to see that, even though they were horrific, they needed to happen as they did in order for the world to progress and bring about a better present day. If the gods hadn't flooded the earth, darkness would have ravaged everything long before now. This world would not be a fit place for man or beast to live in. If Christ had not been crucified, his teachings of compassion, humility and forgiveness would not have spread and made the impact it has on so many lives. Do you see? We can only understand and accept the reasoning for all of it because we have witnessed the results over time. The good that has come about is as clear to us as the bad, just as someday you will be able to understand and see the good of why you were led here to this moment.

"There are no coincidences in the Universe, Deston. Everything happens for a reason ... including your being born in this time. That is a Universal truth you must learn to accept. The royal blood of the fae flows through your veins and for this reason much is expected of you. But you also have human blood within you, and it, too, is there for a reason."

A long pause followed before Deston finally mumbled to the ground. "Why does it have to be me?"

Zumwald's face crumpled in anguish, but he kept his tone even as he replied, "Because you're a being of two worlds. You have the compassion and light of the fae within you, but you also have the attributes and darkness of the human race. The latter is what is going to provide you the necessary means to do what the fae cannot—that is to kill Grossard and Mordred."

Deston's head jerked up and he gawked at Zumwald, his exasperation plainly etched on his face. "You can't be serious? Back when you were training me in the forest of Avalon, you told me I needed to do whatever I could to resist my human nature. You said it was holding me back, and if I didn't let go of it, it would become dominant and I'd never be able to access my fae powers. Now you're telling me to forget all that just because you want me to be your hired assassin?" He sighed in disgust and shook his head. "You're freakin' crazy ... you know that?"

Deston's words stabbed at Zumwald's heart, taking away what was left of his energy. He sagged against the tree and slid down to the ground, letting his head fall back against the trunk as his eyes closed. The sound of song sparrows, chickadees, and red-breasted sapsuckers battled each other to be heard over the other, filling the air with a cacophony of sound, but it was only white noise to Zumwald as he sent a silent plea up to the gods.

"I've lived with the inhabitants of this planet for more centuries than I care to count. I've done all that has been asked of me, and in all that time I've never made a request of you before now. However, I cannot let this matter of the boy pass without asking you to rethink your decision. He's too inexperienced for an undertaking of this magnitude. I fear he won't be able to tap into the power to dispel the darkness once he opens that door. And my even greater fear is he may not be able to return from the darkness once it finds him. That would be a great loss to all humanity." He let out a sigh. *"Please ... I ask you to take my request into consideration. There is surely some other way, some other person more experienced and better suited to handle the situation than this boy."*

He held his breath and waited, praying against the odds that the gods would listen to his appeal. After several excruciating seconds, a stern voice spoke inside his head, stating the answer he dreaded.

"He is the one that has been chosen. We expect you to carry out your instructions as given. Do not disappoint us, Myrddin," the voice rebuked.

Zumwald exhaled his breath and swallowed back the resentment that stuck in his throat. He shook his head sadly and replied, *"Your bidding will be done as it always has been. But I want it written in the record that I disagree. This time I believe you are making a grave mistake."*

Dropping his chin to his chest, Zumwald gathered the strength to force the words out and do what was expected of him. "Maybe I was wrong. Maybe we've all been wrong," he mumbled softly.

The words were barely audible, but they got Deston's attention and his head snapped up.

"The boy is conflicted ... too unsure of his abilities and strengths. That is to be expected, I guess. He was not raised with the teachings of the gods, and he did not choose this battle. It was put upon him. Who am I to say he should take up the fight if he doesn't want to?"

Deston pressed his lips together and clenched his jaw, but remained silent.

"Too much has already been asked of Deston," Zumwald continued softly. "He is too naïve and not equipped to stand up against the darkness of the Shard. Even if he agreed to pick up the mantle at this very moment, I don't know if there is enough time for him to get prepared." He expelled a big breath through his mouth. "I'm afraid it's time to look elsewhere for a champion and leave the boy be. Too much is at stake. We need someone who is willing and ready to do what must be done."

A heavy silence grew between them and the sting of Zumwald's words pricked at Deston's heart. He rested his forehead on his knees, feeling the weight that Atlas must have felt while carrying the world on his shoulders.

I'm not a great magician like him and Mordred. I'm just a kid from Pennsylvania. I didn't know about magic or the fae until a few months ago. Now I'm supposed to just instantaneously know all about fighting the darkness and how to become a hero. As his mind roiled with thoughts, his old anxieties slowly stirred back to life and replaced the resentment he was feeling. *Maybe Zumwald's right. I can't be who they want me to be. I'll only let them down like I did Keir and Lilika. Then I won't be able to face mom and dad, or ... or Margaux ever again.*

Zumwald could feel Deston's distress radiating off him and it took a great deal of effort to turn away and not interfere. He got to his feet with a soft groan and a heavy heart, picked up the bow and shrugged the leather quiver off his back. "Lilika asked me to give you these," he said, holding the bow and arrows out for Deston to take.

A flash of recognition crossed Deston's face as he looked up and pain shined in his eyes, but he didn't make a move to take the offering.

"Typically, a warrior's bow and sword are sent with him into the next life, but Lilika held these back for you. She thought if you carried this piece of Keir with you, it would help you to stay focused and his hand would always be there to guide yours." Zumwald paused to give Deston a chance to say something.

Deston blanched and lowered his eyes.

"You may not realize it, but it is a great honor to receive a gift such as this. Rarely has a warrior's bow been given to someone outside of the family, especially after his death," Zumwald continued when he saw Deston was not going to respond. "Lilika is not only being incredibly generous, she is sending you a message. I hope you reflect on that message and take it to heart." He laid the bow on the ground next to the base of the tree and stepped back, his heart aching as he looked down on Deston. "Your path was laid out for you long before you were born. That does not mean you don't have the free will to choose a different path if you so wish. You were raised in the lower realm, so it would be easy for you to go back and live there as a normal human if that is what you prefer—although life in the lower realm as you remember it may not last much longer if Grossard gets ahold of the book. Nonetheless, you do have choices. You must understand, though, once you start down a path, it will be yours and there can be no turning back."

Deston stared at the ground for a long moment before looking up, his eyes glassy with his despair. "You say it's my choice, but is it really? From the beginning I've been a pawn in this little game of yours, and we both know pawns are dispensable. It seems to me that the gods have already laid out my whole future. What does it matter what I want?"

"Everything matters ... especially what you want. No one, the gods included, can force you to do something you don't wish to do, or that is against your nature." Zumwald paused and a jagged spark of light in the shape of a lightning bolt flashed through his right eye. "I've given you much to think about, so I'll leave you now to contemplate your future with this one final piece of advice. Follow your heart and be prepared to embrace wherever it leads. Most of all have no regrets."

Zumwald turned to leave. As he was about to step into the trees, he stopped and looked back over his shoulder. "One match is all it takes to drive away the darkness, Deston. You may be the match, but this battle is not just *yours*. You are not alone, nor will you ever be—unless that is what you wish. I give you my word on that." Zumwald nodded his head, sealing his words, and stepped into the shadows.

Deston didn't acknowledge Zumwald's last words, or even that the old man had left. His eyes were locked on the bow and his mind was in such a state of turmoil, everything else around him faded out, including the large black crow with a white tuft under its beak that circled overhead. The crow made several passes before it came to rest on a high branch and looked down on the clearing below.

Chapter 3

Deston's eyes shot open and he reared up out of a deep sleep. His senses were fully awake, but his brain was still in the fog of sleep and the sight of the dirt walls momentarily confused him. As he stared, trying to place where he was, a loud squawk, just like the one that woke him, floated in through the cave entrance, jolting him out of his stupor. In a flash, everything came back. Assuming Zumwald had ran back to Tir na-nÓg and told Oseron where he was, he twisted around expecting to see a giant hawk glide by, but the only thing outside the cave opening was blue sky.

With a disgusted sigh he collapsed onto his bedroll, closed his eyes and tried to go back to sleep. All night long he had tossed and turned as visions of Keir and Margaux took turns badgering his dreams. He breathed in deeply and held it in his lungs before blowing the air out through his mouth, hoping sleep would come again, but it wasn't to be. Grudgingly, he opened his eyes and stared up at the earthen ceiling.

It had been over three weeks in the lower realm since he arrived after sneaking out of Tir na-nÓg without telling anyone. But in the high realm it had been only a few hours since he left and it was possible they didn't even know he was gone. Although Deston figured Zumwald should have made it back to the high realm by now, and he was sure the old man would have gone straight to his parents and informed them as to his whereabouts. He cringed at the thought of how furious his parents were going to be. No doubt he'd be grounded for the rest of his life. Still, he didn't regret leaving. He couldn't stand to see the pity in everyone's eyes when they looked at him, and he felt like he was suffocating with the healers constantly hovering over him and his mother treating him like he was something fragile. It had been a rash decision to leave as he did, and he had had no plan or destination in mind. He just knew he had to get away from there.

With a groan, Deston rolled to his hands and knees. The small cave in the side of the bluff that he used as a bedroom wasn't large enough for him to stand up in. But it did provide him shelter from the rain; and as an added bonus, it was twelve feet above the ground so he could sleep without the worry of an errant bear or wolf happening upon him in the middle of the night.

Pulling the blanket around his shoulders, he crawled out onto the narrow rock ledge that ran horizontally across the bluff. The sun had finally come out and burned away the gray that had shrouded the landscape and muted the sky for over a week. The water droplets that hung from the needles of the trees sparkled in the sunlight, adding a magical light to the ocean of green that stretched out before him. Deston closed his eyes and turned his face into the sun. It seemed like it had been ages since he'd felt its warmth on his skin. He stood and let it soak it in until the cold in his bones started to melt.

Sighing with contentment, Deston opened his eyes and gazed out at a wispy white cloud, the only blemish in the otherwise startling blue sky. He followed its path as it lazily floated along, stretching and shifting into the shape of a bird's wing. The wing brought Keir back to mind and shattered his moment of serenity. He shivered as the cold in his bones returned, and with a scowl, he turned away and transformed into a kestrel to fly down to the ground.

His morning ritual had become a routine of starting a fire and putting on a pot of water to boil to make his breakfast, which consisted of a kind of oatmeal type dish that he had learned to make while training with Zumwald. Mechanically, he stirred the ashes in the fire pit and rose to get the wood he had gathered and stacked under a lean-to that was topped with several layers of hemlock branches and ferns fronds to keep the wood dry. As he turned, his gaze landed on the bow Zumwald had left at the base of the tree. A bitter lump rose in his throat, but he slowly moved toward the bow as if he was under its spell. Sitting back on his haunches, he stared at it for several long minutes before reaching out and running a fingertip across the wood of the grip where it was darker and shinier from the oil of Keir's hand. It felt warm as if Keir had just released it, but he knew that was only wishful thinking on his part. *I wish he would have taught me how to shoot,* Deston thought, itching to pick the bow up, but at the same time feeling it would be sacrilegious if he did. He breathed a heavy sigh and stood. "One more thing I didn't do that I should have," he muttered under his breath.

There was a sudden movement out of the corner of his eye. He flipped around, half expecting to find Zumwald standing there, but it wasn't Zumwald. It was a bear—a white bear. Years ago he had read a book about the rare breed of white bears that lived in the Great Bear

Rainforest. The bears had intrigued him, because unlike most other species that produced a white offspring, these bears were not albinos. They were an actual subspecies of the black bear that had a special recessive gene, which gave them their white fur. The local Native Americans call them 'spirit bears' and believed them to be reminders of times past. They were quite reclusive and seldom seen by man, but as luck would have it, there was one sitting at the edge of Deston's camp, grooming itself and seemingly not in the least bit interested that he was standing a few yards away.

Deston held his breath, afraid that even the sound of his breathing would draw the bear's attention to him. *Stand still or run? Stand still or run?* That question ran through his head as he tried to recall what to do in the case of a bear encounter, but his mind was as frozen as his muscles were and he just stood there and stared with his mouth hanging open.

After standing as still as a stone pillar for what seemed like an eternity, Deston took a chance and ventured a step backward. The bear didn't take notice, but as he lifted his foot to take another step, the bear raised its head and looked at him for the first time. Deston froze again and got ready to run if the bear decided to attack. The bear stayed where it was and just stared at him.

"I'm not here to hurt you, bear," Deston spoke softly, so not to spook it. "I'd appreciate it if you didn't hurt me, either ... okay?"

Deston had the ability to hear and converse with animals, but the bear didn't seem to be in a talkative mood and offered no reply. Deston nervously licked his lips, but his mouth was so dry it didn't help.

"Why don't you just move along and go on home? It's a big forest and there's lots of other food out there. I don't think you'd find me very appetizing, anyway, so shoo ... go on and get out of here."

The bear yawned and scratched its ear, but it made no other move. Sweat broke out on Deston's forehead and palms, and he didn't move, either. Another long, agonizing minute passed before the bear let out a snort and pushed up to all four. Deston sucked in a hasty breath and took a step backward. He was just considering changing into a kestrel to fly away when Keir emerged from the trees. Deston's eyes bulged and his mouth fell open, and his thoughts were no longer centered on the bear.

Keir had appeared in Deston's bedroom shortly after his death, but Deston had been pretty out of it at the time and had come to believe it was just a dream. This time, though, Keir looked nothing like an apparition. He looked solid and real, and he held a bow in his hand. The only thing that looked off about him was the glow that surrounded him. It was a soft white glow, as if his body was a star throwing off light. Deston had witnessed the silvery glow around a person under an invisibility and cloaking spell, but he had never seen a white glow like this before.

A crow suddenly cawed out loudly, startling Deston out of his daze. He glanced over his shoulder and when he turned back, Keir was gone. "Keir," he cried out and started forward. The bear gave a snort and stopped him in his tracks.

"Why didn't you take off too?" Deston grumbled. The corners of the bear's mouth stretched back and if Deston hadn't known better, he would have thought it was grinning. *I must be losing my mind*, he thought and turned to walk away. He looked up and came to an immediate halt at the sight of Keir standing beside the tree where the bow lay.

Deston looked from Keir, down to the bow on the ground, and back up. Keir inclined his head toward the bow and then moved into the center of the clearing. He purposely position his feet shoulder width apart with his left leg slightly forward. He then reached behind his back, drew an arrow from the quiver and nocked it. After hooking three fingers of his right hand around the string, he raised his left arm up in slow motion and pulled the string back until his right hand was beside his cheek. He held that pose for several seconds before letting go. The arrow sailed straight into the trees and there was a soft thump as it pierced its mark. Keir looked at Deston, inclined his head toward the bow by the tree again, and repeated his movements, starting with repositioning of his feet, placing three fingers on the string, pulling back and firing.

After watching Keir go through the motions three times, Deston went to the tree and picked up the bow Zumwald had left him. It felt strange in his hand, but he lined up next to Keir, mimicked the warrior's stance and nocked the arrow. His arm quivered a bit as he pulled back on the string, but he kept pulling until his hand was beside his cheek and then he let go. The string slapped painfully against his forearm and with a loud howl, he dropped the bow, bent over, and vigorously rubbed the red mark to relieve the sting that ran all the way down to his fingertips.

"You locked your bow arm," Keir stated, breaking the silence.

Surprised to hear Keir speak, Deston flinched and looked up. "Huh?"

"Your elbow on your bow arm was locked. Rotate it just a bit to the left. That will help."

Deston blinked at Keir. *Is this really happening?*

As if Keir knew what Deston was thinking, he pointed to the bow Deston had dropped. "You can't get better if you don't keep practicing."

Deston's brow rose, but he quickly picked up the bow and held it out in front of him, rotating his arm as Keir had instructed.

"That's too much. You need only a slight rotation," Keir added.

Deston corrected his form and Keir nodded his approval.

"Now relax and breathe. Lock in on your target."

For the next two hours, Deston and Keir stood side by side, shooting arrows, as the white bear lounged at the edge of the clearing not in the least bit interested. It took Deston a dozen or so shots before any of his arrows actually made it all the way into the trees, but by the end of the session he was happy, and more than a little amazed, at his progress, especially considering he had never fired a bow and arrow before in his life.

"That's enough for today," Keir stated, noticing Deston's arm was trembling with fatigue. Without saying anything more, he slung the bow over his shoulder and walked to where the bear was waiting.

"Hey," Deston called out after him. As Keir paused and looked back over his shoulder, Deston was suddenly at a loss for words. There was so much he wanted to say, but he didn't know how. "Will you ... are you going to come back?" he finally stammered out.

"I will come back and be with you for as long as you need me," Keir replied and then walked off into the shadows. The bear opened its mouth in a loud yawn, stood and followed Keir into the trees.

Deston stared into the darkness long after Keir disappeared. *Am I dreaming again?* He looked down at the bow and then at the large purple bruise on his forearm. There was no doubt the bruise was real—it still ached. A smile slid over his face and he lifted his eyes to the heavens. "I will always need you, Keir," he whispered.

For the first time in weeks, Deston felt at peace and there was a skip in his step as he loped off to collect his arrows.

The rest of the day was a blur, and that night Deston slept through the hours without a single nightmare. When he awoke the next morning, the clouds speckling the sky were streaked with pink and the birds were singing their morning song. Without hesitating, he threw the blanket back, flew to the ground and hurriedly dressed. After wolfing down a cold breakfast, he wrapped a piece of cloth around his forearm for protection and sat down to wait for Keir.

The minutes dragged by and the sun sluggishly crept higher in the sky. Anxious to get started the minute Keir arrived, Deston laid his arrows out on a blanket and rearranged them several times to bide the time. The minutes slowly turned into hours and when the sun was directly overhead he finally gave up the wait.

"He said he would keep coming for as long as I needed him. I guess he lied," Deston grumbled despondently, looking down at the arrows lined up on the blanket. *But who says I need him? Margaux practices on her own all the time.*

He picked up the bow, positioned his feet and nocked an arrow. As he lifted his arm and pulled back on the string, his shoulder and back muscles screamed out in protest, but he clenched his jaw and ignored the pain. The second he let go, he knew it was a bad shot. The string not only slapped into his arm again, igniting the pain from the previous day, but the arrow fell far short of the target. It was the worse shot he'd taken yet, and his bow arm and shoulder were aching as bad as his forearm. He groaned in frustration, dropped the bow and stomped away, vowing to never touch it again.

The following morning Deston was aroused from his sleep by a loud squawk outside the cave entrance. He pushed up to his elbow and turned to look out as a silhouette of a large bird streaked by the opening. His brow furrowed and he gritted his teeth against the ache in his heart. No matter how hard he wished, he knew it would not bring Keir back. Swallowing the lump in his throat, he crawled out onto the rock ledge, surprised to see the sun was already high in the sky.

"I was beginning to wonder if you were going to sleep the day away," a voice called out from within the shadows of the trees.

Deston jumped and his foot slipped off the ledge. His arms flapped about as he teetered on the edge, but as soon as he regained his balance and got both feet back on solid rock, he looked down to see Keir and the white bear at the edge of the clearing. He stared for a moment and shook his head, thinking he was imaging it, but Keir was still there when he looked again.

"I ... um ..." he stuttered, not knowing what to say. "You didn't come yesterday, so I thought ... I didn't think you were coming back," he stammered once the shock had worn off.

"I said I would come back. I didn't say it would be every day. You're a novice and your muscles aren't conditioned for the demands archery requires. You needed a day off between lessons to give your muscles time to repair. A good warrior always respects his body; otherwise, he ends up hurting himself along with his form. But yesterday is gone and I am here now. The day is wasting away. Are you going to come down or shall I leave?"

"No! I mean ... yes, I'll be right down. Don't go."

Deston flew down and in a matter of seconds had pulled on his boots and tunic and grabbed up the bow.

The second session went a lot smoother than the first and Deston was ecstatic that he hit the target tree more than half the time. However, all too soon, it was over and Keir prepared to leave. As Keir walked toward the trees, Deston called out, "Keir, wait."

Keir halted and looked back. Deston felt the heat spread across his cheeks, but he charged on. "I was wondering if you would also teach me how to use my powers. You know, show me the spells like the one you used at the temple to protect us from Mordred and Grossard's magic," he rushed out, and then held his breath in anticipation of Keir's answer.

Keir's eyes drilled into Deston's. "So you have decided to pick up the mantle and see this situation through to the end after all?"

Deston's face paled. Then just as quickly, his temper flared and his face turned red. "I should have guessed this was all Zumwald's doing. He'll stop at nothing to get me to do what he wants," he spit out with a harsh laugh.

"My being here has nothing to do with Zumwald. I came of my own free will because you have much to learn and little time in which to do so," Keir replied.

"It's the same thing. You're here to persuade me to kill Grossard and take up Zumwald's battle, right?" Deston challenged.

Keir turned and his presence seemed to suddenly fill the clearing. "This is hardly Zumwald's battle. And of course I hope you'll take up the cause to stop Grossard. I'm a fae the same as you. It has been our duty to thwart the darkness from the time the gods brought us to earth. As far as killing Grossard, I do not know what Zumwald has asked you to do, but to intentionally take a life is not the fae way. We soldiers have all had to take a life at some time in our career, but it was in battle and could not be helped. It still comes with a great price even then.

"One thing I do know is Grossard must be stopped and the Shard must be destroyed. It is the only sure way to guarantee my loved ones' safety. My duty to take care of my family transcends every plane of existence and I take that obligation seriously. Do you not feel the same way about your family?"

Deston swallowed hard at the mention of Keir's family and his exasperation lost its steam.

"I know you. What's more, I believe in you," Keir went on. "You're the best chance the fae have of defeating Grossard, as there are only a few things in this world he fears. You are one of them and that is where your advantage lies."

Deston lurched back and his eyes grew wider.

Keir's brow creased and his head cocked to the side. "You did not know that? How can you have Oseron and Oberon's blood and be so naïve?" His eyebrows suddenly rose in question. "You do know how to neutralize Mordred's magic powers … do you not?" The confused look on Deston's face gave Keir his answer. He rolled his eyes to the sky. "Gaia help us." He wiped his hand down his face. "Do you see the etched line there in the wood of the bow right above where your hand grips it?" Deston's eyes flicked down and right back up. "It pulls apart at that line. Inside the cavity is dirt from King Arthur's grave. Throwing that dirt on Mordred will neutralize the dark energy that fuels his magic."

Deston ran his thumb over the groove and gawked at Keir in total awe. "You know where King Arthur is buried?"

"Of course, his grave is in Avalon. Everyone—" Keir saw Deston's eyes widen and amended what he was going to say. "Most everyone knows that." He paused and studied Deston, who was looking down at the bow with a glazed look on his face. "You are aware that water does the same to Grossard. It will diminish his powers in the same way."

Deston's head jerked up. "It does? Plain old water?"

Keir shook his head. "You have much to learn and Grossard is getting closer to his goal every day. You're going to have a hard enough time defeating him as it is, but if your heart and head are not fully committed to the cause, all will be lost for certain. I don't believe you want to do that to your family and friends." He suddenly clamped his mouth shut and stood a little taller. "I've said too much. Do not let my words sway you. The decision is yours and yours alone. You need to follow your own path." He held Deston's gaze for another moment; then bowed at the waist, turned and melted into the trees as Deston stared at the bow in his hand and mulled over Keir's words.

As soon as Keir left, a large crow lifted from its perch and soared across the sky toward the gateway.

Chapter 4

"Let go of me! Do you not know who I am?"

The screech could be heard throughout the desert compound. As it leaked through the crack under the door of Grossard's chamber, Grossard smiled to himself, but he didn't make a move to help remedy the situation. Several minutes passed before a knock sounded on his door and a hairy pooka guard tentatively stepped inside the room and bowed low.

"Master, the sorcerer has arrived and insists on seeing you. He claims you sent for him."

Grossard didn't look up from his prone position on the overstuffed lounge, nor did he answer. He took a bite out of the bloody piece of meat he held in his hand and chewed leisurely.

The guard stayed in his bent position, waiting for instructions. There had been no orders to keep Mordred out, but there had been nothing said about letting him in, either.

In the hallway, outside the door, Mordred fumed at the indignity of being ignored. With each second that ticked off, his temper swelled. It had taken him over two years to find Grossard's new compound after Grossard had stepped through the gateway in the wall of the temple and took off with the Shard of Erebus. Mordred had barely made it through the same gateway before it closed, but he was still too late, as Grossard had already vanished.

Mordred let out a disgusted sigh and shook his head. It had been a mistake to involve Grossard in his plan to retrieve the Shard in the first place. He hadn't wanted to and only did, because at the time, he thought he had no other option. He had discovered the Shard's location—in the temple in the city of the gods under the ice of Antarctica—but Grossard was the one who knew where in the temple Olcas had left the Shard and how it was disguised. If only the Oracle had told him the boy would get to the temple and locate the Shard first, it would have saved him the misery of having to deal with Grossard. It would have also saved him the effort and time of hunting Grossard down to get what was rightfully his back.

Mordred's mouth twisted into an ugly sneer at the memory of Grossard stepping out of the shadows at the temple. All his plans and efforts had gone to waste at that moment, but he wasn't out of the game yet, for he still held the trump card. He had the *Book of Tenebris*, which contained the incantation to unlock the Shard's full powers. He was also the only one in the world who could interpret the ancient, lost language the incantation had been written in. That meant Grossard would never be able to obtain the power he craved unless he started cooperating with Mordred. Mordred, on the other hand, only needed to touch the Shard to unleash its full power, for he had the incantation memorized.

Mordred looked up at the closed door and his resentment doubled. *How dare he treat me in this fashion.* With a disgusted exhalation, he gave the guard blocking his way a push. A second guard grabbed his arms from behind and roughly pulled him back.

"Get your hands off of me," Mordred ground out through clenched teeth.

The guard screamed out in pain and jerked back as the skin on his hands smoked and bubbled up red and raw as if doused in acid.

A wicked grin replaced Mordred's sneer as he adjusted the cuffs of his Luigi Borrelli shirt and brushed the desert dust from the shoulders of his custom-made cashmere jacket. Then, with his head held high, he marched into the room with no further interference.

As he passed the guard, who was still bent in half waiting for orders, the creature flew backward out of the room. The door slammed shut behind him with such force it rattled the paintings on the walls.

"If you care anything at all about your drudges, I suggest you let it be known that if any of them ever lay a hand on me again, it'll be the last thing they ever do," he stated, making his way straight to the back of the room and the intricately carved French Renaissance sideboard on which several liquor bottles sat. Without asking permission, he poured himself a drink. As he reached out to pick up his glass, a sparkle of color caught his eye. He glanced over and did a double take at the magnificent pink diamond ring sitting regally on a velvet cushion not more than a foot away from his hand. Recognizing it as the famous twenty-four carat Graff pink diamond that had been reported stolen a few months back, he let out a small gasp before he could stop himself. He cleared his throat, hoping to mask the faux pas, and lifted the glass to his nose, inhaling the woody scent of the expensive liquor as he turned back to face Grossard.

"I'm glad to see your taste has become somewhat more refined, if not a tad garish," Mordred commented, casually lifting the glass in a salute before taking a sip and perusing the lavish décor of the room.

The floor was covered with a rare silk Isfahan rug and the walls were adorned in rich, dark damask and gold-leaf crown molding, which provided the perfect backdrop for the beautiful landscapes, nudes, and other well-known pieces of art, including a Renoir, a Van Gogh and a da Vinci. Ming vases, Faberge eggs, and marble, bronze and stone sculptures were scattered around the room and all cast in the light of an elaborate Murano glass chandelier that was the size of a small pond and sparkled from the high ceiling as brightly as the light bulbs themselves. It was a far cry from the dreary cave Grossard formerly occupied and Mordred couldn't help but feel a twinge of jealousy.

Grossard turned his head and looked at the visitor under half-closed eyelids. "I created this fortress out here in the desert and put up a cloaking charm to avoid unwanted guests. And I don't recall sending for you, Mordred."

"Hmmm … is that a fact? I'm sure that was just an oversight on your part," Mordred replied, lifting the glass to his lips. He really wanted to rip Grossard's heart out and shove it down the imbecile's throat, but instead he took another sip of the fifty-year-old scotch. He needed to bide his time a little longer, just until he discovered where the Shard was hidden. The full lunar eclipse was coming up on the winter solstice and if he didn't have the Shard by then, he'd have to wait another ninety-five years for the next one to come around.

Grossard harrumphed and went back to his meal as if Mordred wasn't there.

Mordred's gaze didn't leave Grossard, but his hand inched along the edge of the sideboard. He held back a smile as his fingers closed around the diamond ring and shoved it into his pocket with the stealth of a professional pickpocket. He then sauntered to one of the antique baroque chairs across from Grossard.

"I must say it looks like you've been keeping yourself rather busy. This is quite a nice collection of antiquities you've got started here. The news articles documenting your escapades have not done you justice." Mordred continued as he made himself comfortable and scanned a duo of Monet paintings that had also recently been reported stolen from the Musee d'Orsay.

Grossard threw the piece of raw meat on the silk rug and pushed his bulk up to a sitting position, wiping his hands on the velvet settee. He no longer needed Mordred's potion to sustain his strength and bolster his appearance—he had the Shard for that. However, much to his exasperation, he had discovered he still needed the *Book of Tenebris* and the key it held to renew the Shard's powers and summon the dark energy of the Universe. The ring idea had come to him after being unsuccessful in tracking Mordred down, but he had yet to figure out a way to get the ring to Mordred. It was his good fortune that Mordred had shown up out of the blue, for it solved that little problem; and instead of wondering how the sorcerer had found his desert compound, Grossard's thoughts were on whether to just go ahead and kill Mordred or let the sorcerer take the ring and leave.

"As I said earlier, I don't believe I sent for you. And I don't particularly enjoy having uninvited visitors drop in. So, might I suggest you leave while I'm still in a forgiving mood?" Grossard replied, resisting the urge to look at the sideboard to see if Mordred had picked up the ring.

Mordred bristled and set the glass on the small marble table beside his chair to free his hands. "I don't much care if you wish to have visitors or not. You may have thought you could elude me by cloaking this compound, but as you see, I will always find you." He smirked arrogantly and then sighed. "We're well past the point of playing games, and since I don't enjoy your company any more than you enjoy mine, I'll get to the business of why I'm here. Although you should already have a good idea, since you absconded with *my* Shard and have been draining its powers with your foolish escapades." Mordred lengthened his neck and gave Grossard his best condescending look. "Of course, the Shard won't be of use to you much longer without the incantation to renew its powers. I assume you have already figured that out for yourself, have you not?"

Grossard narrowed his eyes and bared his teeth.

Mordred's elated grin spread across his face. "Ahh, so you have!" he giggled. "I bet you have also surmised that the key is in *my* book, along with the incantation that calls Erebus forth. And that, my sorry friend, leaves you in the same predicament you were in before—having to rely on my help to get what you want." He shook his head and feigned a look of pity. "It's a shame you didn't know the Shard's darkest powers could never be yours without the book before you double-crossed me." He laughed outright at the menacing look that flashed across Grossard's face.

Grossard ground his teeth together. "As usual, you're putting too much credence on your importance. I don't like to repeat myself, but this I don't mind saying again ... your mother was a lot shrewder than you and a lot more powerful, and yet, look where she ended up."

Mordred sobered. "If you think you're—"

"I don't think anything ... I know," Grossard shouted, cutting Mordred off.

The room was suddenly infused with the smell of rotten eggs and in the blink of an eye, Grossard was on his feet, hurling a fiery ball of energy straight at Mordred.

At the same moment, Mordred jumped up and released his own ball of energy. As the two came together in the middle of the room, a deafening boom rippled the air and bounced into the walls. Large fissures spider-webbed up the plaster and across the ceiling, and with a resounding crack, great chunks of plaster fractured and rained down like hail stones. Furniture shot across the room and crashed into walls, knocking the paintings off their hooks. The intricate gold-leaf frames shattered as they hit the floor, tearing through the priceless canvases as if they were tissue paper and reducing them to worthless scraps in a matter of seconds.

Mordred and Grossard's hands remained outstretched and the energy continued to flow, but within seconds Mordred could feel Grossard's power taking over, driving him back. A small sense of panic began to nibble at the back of his brain for the first time since he had faced Arthur in battle. He hadn't thought it possible for Grossard to gain this much power from the Shard without the help of the spells.

As his strength continued to weaken, and he realized he was about to lose the battle, he drew his hand back, vanished, and reappeared behind Grossard. Grossard didn't miss a beat and twisted on the spot, throwing a ball of fire toward the back of the room. Mordred dove to the floor just in the nick of time and the sideboard took the direct hit. With an ear-splitting boom that shook the room, the sideboard, along with the crystal containers sitting on top, were reduced to a million small splinters that jetted out in every direction and impaled everything in their wake. One of the small projectiles took a small slice out of Mordred's ear before he was able to react and erect a protective shield around him.

The tiny missiles were the least of Mordred's worry, however, for Grossard was suddenly in front of him and had him by the throat before he could get to his feet. Grossard's double-row of shark like teeth flashed in the light as he lifted Mordred off the floor and pushed the sorcerer's back up against the wall. Mordred gasped and grappled to get free, but he was no match for Grossard's brute strength. His face turned pink, and then a ruddy shade of purple and the words to his magic floated away in a spinning gray fog. As a last resort, he dug inside his cloak for the dagger he had hidden there. A cloud of unconsciousness hovered at the edges of his vision and Grossard grotesque face became a blur as his fingers closed around the hilt, but he was able to pull the dagger free and he pressed its blade against Grossard's heart.

"Enough! I will pierce your heart with this blade before you can squeeze the life out of me, and neither of us will win the day," Mordred

screeched telepathically, as he didn't have the air to push the words out vocally.

The shrill voice slicing through Grossard's head jolted him out of his blind rage. He blinked Mordred's blotched face into focus and for a split second was shocked to see his hand around the magician's throat. He stared transfixed and watched Mordred's struggles grow weaker. As Mordred's mouth formed the words, 'the book,' a glint of comprehension finally flickered in Grossard's eyes. With a silent curse he threw his hands up and took a step back, but he held his glare, daring Mordred to try something else.

Mordred slumped over, coughing, and with great gasps, tried to fill his lungs with air as he rubbed his throat.

Satisfied he'd shown his prowess, Grossard popped to the center of the room as the settee flew in behind him. He threw himself backward with a grunt, stretched out, and closed his eyes in an attempt to demonstrate he wasn't worried about what Mordred would do. But truthfully, the strength of the sorcerer's power had surprised him. Though Grossard had told Mordred many times he wasn't as shrewd as his mother, it was a deliberate lie. Mordred was not only as shrewd, he was ten times more calculating—the proof of that was how he had managed to keep the book hidden for the better part of two years, even though Grossard had tried every way he knew to find it. It infuriated him that he needed the book to fulfill his dreams and he trembled with hatred for Mordred, and for the fact that Mordred was the sole obstacle blocking his victory.

"Since you are so eager to prepare for Erebus' return, I assume you have brought the book with you," Grossard stated, nestling his head into the shredded cushion of the sofa.

Mordred gasped in another breath, his eyes shooting daggers at Grossard from beneath his brow.

"Need I remind you that without me you have no way of possessing the full strength of the Shard's powers? Any wise person with that kind of knowledge would show respect, and as much concern about keeping their benefactor alive, as they did about the whereabouts of the book," Mordred spat once he had regained his composure. "But no one has ever accused you of being wise, have they? So let me put it in simple terms for you … the book is *mine* and I have it well hidden, as you already know. What that comes down to is I'm the only one who has the means to reverse the magnetic field and open the portal to renew the Shard and bring Erebus back. Without me, you have nothing but a used up piece of crystal. So whether you like it or not, I'm the quintessential element in you achieving what you want. It would be to your grave disadvantage if you lay another finger on me or upset me again."

Grossard looked down at his fingernails, trying to decide whether to tell Mordred he had no intention of bringing Erebus back. He had come to that decision after realizing it was so much more appealing to be a god versus the minion of one. It was true that without Erebus he would not be able to bring the ultimate darkness into the world, but all he actually needed to reign over both realms was the book and the spells to fill the Crystal of Light with darkness. That, along with the powers of the Shard, would be enough to force the fae and humans alike to bow down to him. He would live like a god and be the supreme dictator of the earth for all eternity.

"The only reason you've gotten as far as you have is because of me," Mordred continued, struggling to keep his composure. "Our agreement was fifty-fifty, which means I should have the same access to the dark energy as what you have. Your actions have made it perfectly clear to me that you aren't willing to share and so I have come to take what is rightfully mine."

Grossard looked up ready to throw back a verbal jab, but instead he burst out in a loud chortle at the righteous expression on Mordred's pale face. "We truly are made from the same cloth, you and me," he said between fits of laughter. "It seems we both have the same ploy in mind as well." His laughter died, but his mouth remained twisted in a malicious grin.

"I don't know what ploy you're referring to," Mordred replied, straightening his spine and doing his best impression of being indignant.

The smile slid off Grossard's face. "Don't play me the fool, Mordred. Do you think I didn't notice the Oracle you had with you at the temple? Your intentions were as clear then as they are now. You have every intention of taking the Shard and bringing Erebus back, so he will favor you and help you do away with me." He half expected to see a glimmer of guilt on Mordred's face, but the sorcerer was a master of the blank stare and gave nothing away. "Lucky for you I'm feeling generous today, so I'll make you a proposition … acknowledge that I am the master of the Shard and my powers are far greater than yours, and give me the incantation I need, or you'll find yourself sharing Morgane's current sleeping quarters."

Mordred tensed and the veins on his temples bulged like worms under his skin. "Are you threatening me?" he said in a deadly tone.

Grossard sat up slowly. "You can take it as a threat if you wish. The message is what it is, however you want to interpret it."

Mordred's hand balled into a fist as he glared at Grossard. "We had an agreement. We were to share the power of the Shard equally. I demand you give me access to it immediately or you'll be the one sleeping with Mother, not I."

Grossard jumped to his feet and in the next instant was standing inches in front of Mordred's face. "You don't want to start up a war with me, sorcerer," he hissed, bathing Mordred with his spit and the putrid scent of rotted meat.

Mordred sneered, but didn't back down. "I had not intended on doing so, but since you are shutting me out and refusing to cooperate, I don't see how that can be avoided. I am, however, willing to give you one more opportunity to make it right, as war is time consuming and will give neither of us what we want or need. To succeed we must cooperate and work together. So bring the Shard to Viroconium in five days. Be there at midnight and come alone. Midnight," he reiterated, "and not one second past, or a war is exactly what you'll get."

Mordred turned to leave, but Grossard caught his arm. "You're so insistent on getting access to the Shard, but you keep avoiding the subject of the book, which you have been keeping from me. As I recall, that was a part of our original fifty-fifty agreement. So, as a good faith gesture, you could show it to me right now and prove to me you still have it. How about that?"

Mordred put his hand over Grossard's and a charge of electricity shot from his fingertips, scorching the flesh on the monster's arm. Grossard felt nothing, but he jerked his hand back to let Mordred think he had the power to hurt him.

Mordred took a step back. "Do you really think I'd be fool enough to bring the book with me? It is safely secreted away in a place you will *never* be able to access. A location I alone know. So unless you provide me with my rightful share of the Shard, you'll watch that precious piece of crystal turn into a useless piece of glass." His eyes glittered with insanity.

"You may be able to hide the book from me, but you cannot hide it from the obsidian skull," Grossard fired back.

Mordred flinched and his eyes briefly widened. He then tsked tsked and shook his head. "You expect me to believe you have retrieved the skull from Tartarus? I suppose you also want me to believe the gods told you where the entrance lies, as they are the only ones who have that knowledge." He snickered. "I dare say if you truly did have the skull, you would not be standing here talking to me right now." His grin dissolved into a sneer. "You have less than a week. If I were you, I'd use that time and that infinitesimal brain of yours to rethink your position. Even you should be able to see you'll never defeat Oseron without me. The power you have gained from the Shard is not enough and will only diminish over time if not renewed."

Grossard glared back, but held his retort. He wanted Mordred to leave so he could track the sorcerer to the book through the ring.

"I look forward to our next meeting, then," Mordred added, unconsciously patting the diamond in his pocket as he strode purposely across the room. He paused at the door and looked back over his shoulder. "Don't try to double-cross me, and don't bring your men with you. I can and will destroy the book if you make a single move toward me." He pushed the guard aside and slammed the door behind him with such force, more of the loose plaster rained down from the ceiling.

"I expect you to come alone too, Mordred, or you can forget about getting your hands on the Shard," Grossard yelled after him. He stared at the door, waiting to see if it would reopen. When it didn't, he turned back to the settee with a satisfied smile.

Mordred had taken the pink diamond just as Grossard knew he would. He was just as confident the sorcerer would put it on his finger, and the minute he did, Grossard would have a direct channel and be able to see everywhere the sorcerer goes. He rubbed his hands together in glee. The book would be his even sooner than he thought, for once he fails to show up at Viroconium, Mordred will be forced to retrieve the book to get the curses in order to wage war. He won't have the faintest clue that he's leading Grossard right to the prize or that he's digging his own grave.

"I guess this proves who has the brains and who is more powerful ... doesn't it?" Grossard chuckled to himself.

"Master," the pooka guard spoke from the doorway, interrupting his thoughts.

Grossard's expression immediately hardened and he turned a steely gaze on the guard. "I thought I had made myself clear that I wasn't to be disturbed today. This is the second time you've shown your face. Unless you wish to be separated from that head of yours, you best not disturb me again," he grounded out through clenched teeth.

"I'm sorry Master, but you wanted to know when news of the boy came in," the guard answered back brazenly.

Grossard tensed with anticipation. "Go on."

"The scouts have not been able to locate the prince after he crossed into the new world. They believe he might have left the lower realm," the guard answered.

Grossard reared up. "Of course he's still in the lower realm," he screamed. "I would know if he returned to Tir na-nÓg."

His temper, which had already been elevated by Mordred's visit, erupted. His lips stretched into a thin line as he turned his hand palm side up and squeezed it into a tight fist.

The pooka's eyes went wide and his hand went to his throat as his tongue began to swell. He gasped and gagged, his tongue growing bigger with each tick of the clock. Foam dripped from the sides of the guard's mouth as his tongue reached the size of a mini-loaf of French bread.

Then with one small squeak, he doubled over, fell to the floor and didn't move again.

"Someone come and get this moron out of here," Grossard yelled out through the door.

Two guards immediately appeared in the doorway and grabbed hold of the dead man's arms.

"Inform the search party to keep searching until they find the prince. Tell them I will not accept failure," Grossard added.

With a nod of their heads, the guards backed out of the room, pulling their colleague with them. Grossard waited until the door clicked shut and then settled back onto the lounge, staring up at the newly exposed ceiling beams. He was certain beyond a doubt that Deston was still in the lower realm, but how the boy was able to hide so well puzzled him. Even more puzzling was the question of why Oseron would let Deston leave Tir-na-nÓg in the first place. It was a bit too obvious to be a plan to lure Grossard out into the open.

"I bet the prince thinks he is capable of locating the Shard again, but he has no concept of how ill-prepared he is to play with that kind of fire," Grossard scoffed. "There will be no glory for him this time. My day will be here sooner than he thinks. Then he and his father will pay dearly for the suffering I've had to endure. I will rule this planet and make the fae my slaves." His chest bounced up and down with his chuckle that rapidly turned into a full-blown laugh and shook his entire body.

Chapter 5

The floating gardens that surrounded Oseron's palace on three sides were legendary for their beauty and the variety of plant life they held. Every species of flora that had ever existed on the earth lived in one or more of the layered sectors, even those thought to be extinct and never seen by modern man. The gardens were open and available to all residents of Tir na-nÓg to enjoy, except for the section adjacent to Oseron's private library. Oseron kept that one piece of the garden to himself and it was partitioned off from the rest by a nine-foot-tall hedge. The only way in and out of the private sanctuary was through the library—unless you were a giant wolf who had very long, sharp claws and could dig a hole under the hedge, that is.

Rellik paced restlessly between the rows of jasmine bushes inside the private garden, caring little that he was leaving a trail of mud clumps all along the mosaic walkway. He kept a wary eye out for the appearance of another and his muscles were taut and ready to lunge into the foliage if anyone other than Oseron showed their face. He was no longer considered an enemy of the fae and could come and go through Tir na-nÓg as he pleased, but he didn't have the time or the patience to go through proper protocol to request a private session with Oseron. The information he had recently uncovered was time sensitive and he figured stealing into the garden was the fastest way to get the audience he desired.

It was a new experience for Rellik, and a somewhat awkward one at that, asking for help from the fae, especially after having spent seven years working with Grossard to destroy the high realm. If Grossard hadn't attempted to kill him and his family—not once, but twice—he'd more than likely still be at Grossard's side. But Grossard had tried to kill him and would have succeeded if the fae hadn't brought him to Tir na-nÓg and nursed him back to health. Nursed him back the best they could anyway, considering his injuries were far too severe for even fae magic to cure. The healers hadn't said as much, but he was fully aware his time left on this earth was down to a few months, or possibly less. That was the reason he was so determined to find and kill Grossard. It was all that kept him going. Unfortunately, Grossard had become somewhat of a ghost and none of Rellik's sources had heard so much as a whisper of where his former master was hiding out.

Mordred had also mysteriously gone underground. Though Rellik had no quarrel with Mordred per se, he was convinced the sorcerer had knowledge that would lead him to Grossard. For that reason alone, he had extended his search to include the sorcerer. But as with Grossard, Rellik had been unable to gather information on Mordred, until yesterday, when he learned the location of where the sorcerer would be in one week's time. Upon that discovery, Rellik hastened to the palace to ask Oseron to provide him with a glamour. It was the only way he could travel through heavily populated human areas without causing a major ruckus.

Rellik continued to pace up and down the garden path, even though he was bone tired and would have preferred to rest. But he was afraid if he stopped, his muscles would grow stiff and he didn't want anything to slow him down now that he was so close. As he made another pass by the open window, the sound of an angry voice blasted out from within. His whole body tensed and his ears perked up. He did a quick look around and then crept between the bushes that hugged the palace wall to peek into the library window and see what was going on.

~~

Tiff hummed to herself as she flew along the tall hedge that walled in Oseron's private garden. She had completely recovered from her injury, but had opted to stay and help-out at the palace instead of going out to search for Mordred and Grossard as so many of the others were doing. She told everyone it was because Lilika needed someone to look after her, but in reality, she wanted to be there to be close to Deston.

However, when she made the decision to stay, she hadn't taken into consideration how boring life in the palace would be, especially with Deston locked in his room and refusing to come out. So to fight boredom, she had started volunteering for every task that came about, even the smallest ones such as fetching NiNi, which was what she was on her way to do. As she had spent the morning laying out herbs to dry, she elected to take the long way around the outer-edge of the gardens to clear her head. She knew the way well as she'd come this way many times before, but this time, as she flew along the meticulously sculptured hedge of the private garden; she noticed a large mound of dirt piled up at the base of the greenery. Mortified that someone had the audacity to dump their dirt this close to the palace, she darted down to take a closer look and to see if she could determine who had committed the heinous crime. As she drew nearer, her indignation turned to alarm, when she saw it wasn't an act of vandalism, but a hole someone had dug under the hedge.

Without a single thought of alerting the guard or of the danger she might be putting herself into, she swooped under the hedge. The ever-blooming garden was breathtaking in its array of colors and smells and would have normally been too enticing for her to ignore, but she barely noticed it as she hurried to the closest jasmine bush. She burrowed in amongst the star-shaped flowers and peeked out to locate the perpetrator. The thick foliage provided her cover, but also severely limited her line of sight. She had no trouble seeing the trail of mud Rellik had left behind, though.

Tiff's wings fluttered faster and her heart pounded in her chest as she stared at the trail. Again, she had no thought of going to find the guards. She flew out of the jasmine and followed the trail up to the shrubbery that lined the palace wall. Just as she approached to do a closer inspection, Rellik's head poked up near the window. Her hand flew to her mouth and she sharply sucked in her breath as she ducked into a hydrangea bush.

She had heard rumors floating around the village that Rellik was helping the fae, but those rumors also said he'd left the city. Yet, he was here, sneaking into the king's private garden. Why would a friend of the fae be doing that?

The hydrangea was worse than the jasmine as far as blocking Tiff's view, for the blue blossoms were huge and she couldn't see Rellik at all or what he was doing from the bush. Fearing he was there with sinister intentions, she zoomed into the air to get a better view. As soon as she spotted Rellik again, her eyes locked in on him and she wasn't aware she was flying straight toward a crape myrtle tree. The trunk of the tree was just two feet in front of her when she finally realized it was there. Her response was instantaneous and she went into a twisting dive to avoid crashing into it, but her wing still got caught up in one of the spindly branches and she plopped down hard on a lower branch with a rustle of leaves. Hurriedly, she sat up and pushed the hair out of her eyes. Then ever so carefully, she parted the leaves and peeked out to see if Rellik had noticed. Fortunately, he was only interested in what was going on inside the library and not what was going on in the garden. She heaved a sigh of relief and moved up to a cluster of blossoms to see what was going on.

~~

Oseron stood behind his desk in the library, his jaw clenched tight as he fought the urge to throw Merlyn out. "What do you mean you didn't bring Deston back?" he yelled. "By the gods, that's the only reason I let you go alone. You were in the lower realm for weeks, which was surely enough time to convince him to come back with you." Oseron turned and walked away a few paces and then whirled back. "The darkness is spreading faster than we can keep up with. We're already spread thin searching for the Shard and managing the catastrophes and chaos Grossard is perpetuating. I don't have one extra man available to go and guard Deston. One man wouldn't be enough anyway. I recently learned Grossard has been searching for the entrance into Tartarus. If he finds it and gets its open, what kind of chance will Deston have going against an entire horde of demons?" He glared at Merlyn, and then with a disgusted snort stormed to the door, grabbed the handle and gave it a yank. The door didn't budge.

"You're walking a fine line here, Merlyn. Release this door immediately," Oseron ground out through his teeth without turning around.

"I will open the door once you have listened to what I have to say," Merlyn replied calmly.

Oseron begrudgingly turned, the deep dimple in his cheek twitching furiously.

"You are correct in what you said. I did extend my visit longer than I had originally planned. I felt it was necessary to do so once I arrived at the Great Bear Rainforest and realized Deston needed more time to come to terms with all that he has recently endured. For you to think I would leave him on Swindle Island without adequate protection offends me deeply. More than sufficient precautions have been put in place, so you can rest assured he is as safe in that forest as he would be here in Tir na-nÓg with the army to protect him.

"You are also correct when you say I could have forced him to come back with me. But what would be the point of that if he turned around and ran away again?"

"He would *not* run away again. I'd make sure of it. I'd attach a guard to him twenty-four hours a day to follow his every move. Or I would just lock him in his room. I would do whatever it takes," Oseron shouted.

Merlyn held up his hand. "You are thinking as a king, who demands complete compliance from his soldiers. Deston is not a soldier. He is your son, and I can tell you with complete certainty that if you were to employ those kinds of tactics with him, it would end any future relationship the two of you might have. You already missed out on fourteen years of his life, so I know you do not want that."

He walked across the room, passing several chairs before wearily collapsing into the one closest to the open window. "I'm asking you to step back for a moment and look through his eyes." His voice rose to carry across the room. "Deston wasn't raised with the training and guidance you and the others were privy to growing up here in Tir na-nÓg. This is a strange new world to him and nothing like what he is accustomed to. He is frightened, confused and angry and needs time to sort through all that's befallen him, as well as all that is requested of him. Isn't it enough to know the gods are watching over him while he is in the Great Bear Rainforest? If you do not trust me, you should at least trust them."

Oseron sat down in a chair and buried his head in his hands as he mulled over Merlyn's words. He knew what the magician said was true, but that didn't make it any easier to accept. Merlyn obviously knew his son better than he did, which hurt more than a little bit. With a heavy heart, he wiped his hand over his face. "What am I to tell Joliet? She is expecting him back. She won't be happy to hear you left him out there alone." His words were muffled as he stared at the floor.

"Tell her nothing," Merlyn stated casually.

Oseron's head snapped up. "It's apparent you have never been married or you would know that is no option. I have to tell her something. She's going to want to know where her son is, and she has every right to know."

"No … you don't have to tell her a thing. And in this, you must not." Zumwald's voice was hard and commanding. "The retrieval of the Shard and the defeat of Grossard and Mordred depend on Deston more than you know. If Joliet or you interfere in this matter, it could jeopardize the continued existence of this realm. Knowing you as well as I do, I know you will be tempted to step in when Deston and Grossard face each other again. I am telling you now that you *must* hold back. It will be hard for you to do so, I know, but for once in your life, this is not a problem you can take care of. The gods have determined it is Deston's fate. He alone must deal with it. You are going to have to put your faith in them, as they have put their faith in you. It will all be as it should be in the end, but only if you let the Universe play it out as it was designed back at the beginning of time."

Oseron stared at the old magician for several long minutes before he shook his head wearily. "I don't know where Grossard is and Mordred has eluded my men again. Every time we think we're getting close, Mordred vanishes before the men can get there. I fear Mordred is searching for Deston now, the same as Grossard."

"On that I can ease your mind. Mordred has no interest in Deston. He is single-minded in his desire to get his hands on the Shard. That has been his sole vision for centuries. He will not waste one ounce of effort on anything that isn't tied to that piece of crystal."

Oseron buried his head in his hands again. "I command legions of men, but I'm at a loss at how to deal with my own wife. She is not going to like that I am keeping her in the dark."

Merlyn rose and walked to the door. "I suggest you find a way." He pulled the door open and started through, then stopped and looked back over his shoulder. "It is true I have never been married and have no experience with a wife, but I do know Joliet is strong. She loves you and you love her. You'll find a way to work it out," he added with a sympathetic smile and left Oseron to figure it out on his own.

~~

A dozen thoughts pummeled Rellik's mind as he eased backward out of the bushes. He could barely contain his excitement. *Deston's in the Great Bear Rainforest all alone.* The unexpected piece of news was dizzying. *Is it possible? Is good fortune finally coming my way?* A grin lifted the left side of his mouth as a new plan began to take shape.

He ran back to the hedge, his step much lighter, and wiggled through the hole. If he could get out of the village and make it to the gateway into the new world without being questioned, it would be a simple task to find Deston. Then, all he'd have to do was talk the boy into helping him get to Mordred. That shouldn't be hard as Deston wasn't as experienced or as adept as his father at detecting lies. And from the sound of it, Deston was fighting his own inner battles, which Rellik could also use to his benefit.

Rellik almost felt like his old self again as he turned into the foliage at the side of the road and raced away from the palace, knowing for sure that no ogre was going to screw it up for him this time.

Chapter 6

Tiff had just parted the cluster of pink flowers for a better view when Oseron's voice bellowed out through the open window. She had never heard Oseron raise his voice in anger before and it suddenly dawned on her what she'd done and how much trouble she was going to be in for eavesdropping on the king. She reared back and covered her ears with her hands, but Oseron and Zumwald were both speaking so loudly she could still hear everything they said. Her wings buzzed excitedly as she looked around for another place to hide. But then she heard Deston's name mentioned and instead of moving farther away, she inched out on the branch so she wouldn't miss a single word.

Her reward came seconds later when Zumwald disclosed Deston was staying on Swindle Island. She had to stop herself from squealing out in delight and jumping up and down on the branch, but her joy was short-lived when she looked down and saw a grim smile slide across Rellik's face. A kernel of panic instantly blossomed like a rose in the pit of her stomach and both of her hands covered her mouth.

That smile means nothing, she told herself, shaking her head side to side in denial. *Rellik is on our side now. He's just happy to hear Deston is safe.* She really wanted that to be the case, but as she watched Rellik rush to the hole in the hedge and slither out, her gut told her it wasn't.

Rocketing off the branch, Tiff followed and soared through the hole in the hedge in time to see the tip of Rellik's tail disappear into the foliage alongside the road. Wringing her hands, she looked back over her shoulder at the palace unsure whether she should follow Rellik or go alert the guards. The problem was she had no proof Rellik was going after Deston. If the guards didn't believe her and took the time to check out the hedge for themselves, it would give Rellik a huge head start. He'd be able to escape through a gateway and there would be no way of finding out where he went.

Scrunching up her nose, she looked back at the underbrush Rellik had slipped into. She was the only one who knew he was there. It was her duty to follow him and at least see which gateway he took. That would give her the proof she needed, or she would find out her suspicions were wrong.

"Please don't let him be going after Deston," she whispered and darted into the leaves.

Tiff zipped through the boughs faster than she knew was safe, but she had lost Rellik's trail and her only option was to get to the gateway into British Columbia before he did. Her head was in a constant state of motion, pivoting side-to-side in search of a sign of Rellik's passing. As she darted under a leafy limb and came up on the other side, a red head was suddenly in front of her. She only had time to issue a small 'oh' of surprise before smacking right into Margaux.

Though Tiff was a small sprite, the force of the impact was enough to throw Margaux off balance. She fell backward before she could catch herself. Tiff was also thrown back, fell into a bush, and bounced off.

Margaux immediately pushed herself up and scowled at the sprite. "Tiff, what are you doing? Don't you know you could hurt someone zipping around like that?"

Tiff blinked, as surprised as Margaux was, but in the next instant, she realized Margaux was just the person to help. "Margaux, thank goodness I ran into you. I looked everywhere for you earlier, but couldn't find you. Where were you?" Tiff exclaimed, rushing up to Margaux's face.

Margaux rolled her eyes and brushed Tiff to the side as she got to her feet. Tiff had become an even bigger nuisance than usual, ever since they had come back from the temple, and had stayed glued to Margaux's side much of the time. "I already told you Deston hasn't contacted me. You need to stop following me—" Margaux started, but Tiff cut her off.

"Rellik is going after Deston."

Margaux's back went rigid and her brow shot up. "What did you say? Is Deston back?" There was both a hint of excitement and trepidation in Margaux's voice. Even though she was upset with Deston for leaving without telling her, she very much wanted to see and talk with him so she would know one way or the other if he could ever forgive her.

"No, Deston's not back," Tiff answered, shaking her head so fervently her whole body bounced back and forth. "But Zumwald went to see him and he told Oseron where Deston is staying."

Margaux perked up for a moment, then just as quickly her head drooped and she shrugged her shoulders as if it didn't matter. "Well, that's good. I'm glad Zumwald's been in contact. I'm sure Oseron was happy to hear Deston's safe," she mumbled, her voice catching as she said Deston's name.

"You don't understand. Deston is in the lower realm ... in Canada, and Rellik knows that. He was there, too, and overheard the same thing I did. Then he left in a real hurry. I think he's going to go after Deston," Tiff exclaimed, zipping around Margaux in her agitation.

Margaux's head snapped up. "What do you mean, Rellik was there? Where were you when you heard this?"

"Zumwald and Oseron were talking in Oseron's library. Rellik was spying on them from the bushes outside the window. They didn't know he was there and they don't know he heard where Deston is staying."

Margaux's eyes widened. It was hard to understand Tiff sometimes when she got this excited and Margaux wasn't sure she heard had everything right. "But Rellik is on our side now. He wouldn't want to hurt Deston. I'm sure you've got it wrong," she replied, knowing Tiff had a tendency to jump to conclusions.

"You wouldn't say that if you saw the look on his face. If Rellik is on our side, why did he sneak into the gardens and listen at the window, and then run off like that?" Tiff countered to fortify her suspicions.

Margaux's head was swimming and Tiff was making it worse with her flitting about. Reaching out, she caught hold of Tiff so she could look into her eyes. "Tell me everything you saw and heard."

Tiff recounted her story. As Margaux listened, the blood drained from her face. Once Tiff had finished, Margaux let her go and walked a few paces away to think through what the sprite had said. Her mind reeled with the same reservations Tiff had, but at the same time, it didn't make sense. Why would Rellik go after Deston? He was supposed to be working with the fae. A feeling of dread slowly crept up Margaux's spine and she suddenly had trouble catching her breath. It was very possible Rellik hadn't changed at all. The whole time he could have just been stringing them along until he had the chance to strike.

"We've got to warn Deston," Margaux said, testing the words on her tongue. She looked up to see if Tiff agreed.

Tiff nodded her head up and down. "Yes, that is why I was following Rellik when I ran into you. But maybe we should go back and tell Oseron what's going on?" she added as an afterthought.

"NO," Margaux yelled out and then anxiously looked around to see if anyone heard her. "We mustn't tell anyone," she lowered her voice to a whisper.

"But—"

"Think about it, Tiff. Rellik's already got a head start. If we go back, we'd have to wait to get in to see Oseron. By then Rellik will be through the gateway and he'll get to Deston before we even leave Tir na-nÓg."

Tiff's mouth and eyes formed 'o's, but she then shook her head. "But the king ordered us to stay within the city limits. Are you saying we should go against the king's command?"

Margaux ground her teeth together to keep from shouting out her frustration. "Look Tiff, every second we delay gives Rellik more of a chance to get to Deston before we do. We need to leave right away. You said you heard where Deston is. If we hurry, we should be able to fly there faster than Rellik can run. So I guess my question to you is ... how willing are you to risk Deston's life on a technicality?"

Tiff winced and her bottom lip quivered.

"Okay, so let's go," Margaux said and took off at a run, thinking Tiff would be right behind her. When she looked over her shoulder a few seconds later, she saw Tiff hadn't budged an inch.

"Tiff, come on. There isn't time to waste. Rellik already has a head start on us," Margaux called back telepathically.

"The king's orders are not to leave the city. And Lilika told us that if we ever took off again on our own, she'd lock us up in a dungeon until the mountains crumble into the sea. That's a very long time. I don't want to live in a dungeon for that long."

Margaux let out a disgusted sigh, knowing there wasn't time to argue this out. *"Fine, stay here. I'll go by myself. They can do whatever they want to me, but I'm not going to sit back and let Rellik sneak up on Deston and deliver him to Grossard. Just tell me where Deston is."*

"Grossard?" Tiff whispered. *"Do you think Grossard is behind this?"*

"I don't know who's behind it, but can you think of another reason why Rellik would sneak out, as you say, after he heard where to find Deston?"

In the next second, Tiff was at Margaux's side. "So you think Rellik is going to deliver Deston to Grossard?"

"I just said I don't know. I'm not willing to take that chance, though ... are you?"

Tiff looked appalled. "NO, of course not. Deston is my prince. As a citizen of Tir na-nÓg, I am bound to protect him."

"Then come on. Help me find him before Rellik does," Margaux pleaded.

Tiff pressed her lips together and nodded her head, but then added, "Wait ... we have no weapons. Shouldn't you take your bow? What if we have to fight Rellik, or there are others with him?"

Margaux halted in mid-step. Tiff was right. If Rellik was determined to take Deston, there may be a fight. Reluctantly, she turned back. "You're right, but we must hurry. And we can't let anyone know where we're going. If someone stops you, tell them we're just thinking of going out to do some practice shooting. That's all. Got it?"

Tiff nodded again, but Margaux could see in the little one's face that she would never be able to pull off a convincing tale.

"Oh please let us get in and out without being seen. And please don't let Rellik get to Deston first," Margaux silently prayed as she raced back toward the palace with Tiff speeding ahead of her.

Chapter 7

Oseron's mind was occupied with a dozen different things as he sat at his desk going through the daily stack of reports. Darkness had spread fast through the lower realm—the rash of mass murders, growing violence and increased tensions and threats of war between the nations attested to the onslaught of darkness. Even the earth had been infected and the number of natural catastrophes had tripled. If the darkness continued to grow at the rate it was going, a time would come in the near future when he wouldn't have the resources or strength to stop it.

He dropped his head into his hands. How was he ever going to stop Grossard if he couldn't find him? As distracted as his mind was, he still sensed Joliet the second she entered the room.

"Joliet," he said under his breath as he rose. It was the first time they'd been in the same room since Deston left and he was surprised to see her there.

Hearing Oseron say her name, Joliet's heart flipped and she almost came undone. She hadn't expected him to be there. She thought he'd be off calming some disaster somewhere and she had planned to just leave him a note. She paused inside the door to regain her composure before moving into the room and stopping in front of him. She bowed low, her hands clasped together in front of her in the formal greeting.

"I didn't mean to bother you, my king. I was going to leave you a note to inform you of my intentions," she said as calmly as she could, but her voice betrayed her and shook with the raw emotion she could barely hold inside.

Joliet," Oseron whispered again, taking a step forward and reaching out for her. She deftly stepped out of his reach.

"I wanted to let you know I was leaving, so you wouldn't send men looking for me. The army has more important issues to take care of at present and I am perfectly capable of taking care of myself," she responded, trying to keep her face neutral, but failing miserably.

She looked up and immediately realized her mistake as the pain that washed over Oseron's face cut through her heart like a knife. She steeled her jaw and quickly lowered her eyes to keep from losing her nerve. "I'm going to find Deston and bring him back. I know you sent Merlyn after him. I also know Merlyn has come back and you met with him today. I'd appreciate if you'd share with me the information he gave you and save me the time of searching needlessly." She was going to say more but her voice cracked, so she lifted her chin and pleaded with her eyes.

Oseron's heart plunged to his stomach. He had no idea what to say, but he knew he couldn't lie to her. "Joliet, please ..."

Joliet read his face and knew he wasn't going to tell her anything. She straightened her back and squared her jaw. "You know where he is, don't you?"

"My love, listen to me," Oseron replied, taking a quick step forward and encircling her in his arms before she could move away.

Joliet didn't pull back, but she closed her eyes and remained stiff in his embrace.

Taking that as a good sign, Oseron pulled her in tighter. It felt so good to feel her heart beat against his chest and her breath upon his skin. He loved her so much. "I know you hold me responsible for Deston's injury. I accept that blame. I made you a promise and I let you down. I should never have let him go into the Sistine Chapel alone, and I should have realized he'd try to find the Shard on his own." He paused. "There are many things I should have done differently, and I don't fault you for being angry with me."

Joliet felt his chest heave and she could tell he was struggling with his emotions as much as she was hers. She looked up into his eyes, which were glistening with his pain, and some of her anger melted away. Tentatively, she reached up and placed her hand against his cheek. His gaze lowered to hers and their eyes locked.

"Will you ever forgive me?" he whispered.

A tear escaped Joliet's eye and ran down her cheek. Oseron brushed it off with his thumb and she sighed and leaned her forehead against his chest.

"Someday ... maybe, but not until I find Deston and know he is safe," she mumbled.

He squeezed her tighter. To his relief, she hugged him back. He savored the brief moment of reprieve, knowing it wasn't going to last.

"I cannot tell you where Deston is, nor can I allow you to go searching for him." He closed his eyes as she stiffened once again in his arms. She tried to pull back, but he held her tight. "Hear me out ... please." He waited until she stopped writhing to escape before he continued. "Deston made it very clear in the note he left that he wanted to be left alone. Merlyn reiterated that request when I spoke with him. You have to understand that Deston has been through more than most men have and he is still only a boy. He's struggling to process all that has happened. You can't really hold it against him for needing time to himself."

Joliet's head snapped up. "So I was right ... Merlyn *has* been to see him?"

"Yes, he has, and has reported back that Deston is well," Oseron replied. "I know you want him home, and you believe you know what's best for him, but in this, you don't."

"How can you say that? I've lived with him for fifteen years, fourteen of those I was on my own. No one knows him as I do," she fired back.

"He's a teenage boy, my love ... no one really knows him."

Joliet started to protest again, but he cut her off.

"Much has been asked of him; more than what is fair, I'm afraid. That choice has been neither his nor mine. The gods are directing this play and we have no say over what is or what must be. But Deston is strong. I've seen that strength—the strength you gave him. You did an extraordinary job raising him, but now you must step back and let him discover the warrior and leader he was born to be. It is for his sake, as well as the sake of Tir na-nÓg and the earth. I cannot guarantee you he won't get hurt again. We're in the midst of a war and causalities are one of the many misfortunes of war. But I swear to you I will give my life to protect him. That is the only promise I can make you."

His chin came to rest on the top of her head. "It pains me to the depth of my soul when you're angry at me, my love, but I can't let that change what must be done. Deston is the key to our success ... the gods have ordained it to be so and have made it clear I cannot interfere. Despise me if you will, but know that I love you and Deston with my whole heart. I will do whatever is in my power to keep you both safe."

Oseron expected Joliet to start yelling her protest, but instead she lifted her head and looked up at him with puffy red eyes that were hard as steel. "I told you once before that if anything happened to Deston you would not see me again for a very long time. I meant that. I understand it's his destiny and he has to be involved, but he's not ready for all of this. You're asking too much of him."

"How can you say that after witnessing him faceoff with Grossard?"

"What I saw then was a scared little boy, who—"

"No, you're wrong. Deston may not have been fully aware of what he was doing at the time, but he had the courage and instincts of a true fae warrior," Oseron cut in, his voice strong.

"You don't know—"

"I *do* know. What's more, the gods know. Deston is no longer a naïve boy from Pennsylvania. He's the Prince of Tir na-nÓg. Trust me and trust the fae power within him. He is resilient. I'm confident he'll rise to whatever challenge is thrown his way."

Joliet pulled away from Oseron's embrace. "You have an unfair advantage over me. As the king, your words cannot be disregarded and my wishes are lost. But as Deston's mother and as your wife, I demand one thing of you. If the gods persist in using him, than I insist on being there, fighting the battle at his side."

Oseron tensed and opened his mouth to protest, but Joliet held up her hand, silencing him. "There's no room for discussion on this, Oseron. Either I'm involved every step of the way, or I will find Deston and take him back to the lower realm. You'll never see either of us again."

Oseron took a sharp intake of breath. "Joliet—"

"I mean it. I'll not give in on this. You'll use both of us, or you'll use neither. That's more of a choice than what the gods have given me or him."

Oseron let out a heavy sigh and closed his eyes. One of the things he'd always loved about Joliet was her commitment to those she loved, but this time she was taking it too far. She didn't have the training or the powers to face the darkness of the Shard. He couldn't risk losing both his wife and his son. But as he looked down into her eyes and saw the resolve on her face, he knew there'd be no talking sense into her. He had lost, at least for the moment. "You don't know what you're asking," he breathed.

Joliet pressed her lips together and held her glare.

Oseron sighed. "There is nothing more I can say. It's in the gods' hands. I'll do nothing to stop you, but I cannot guarantee that they won't." Joliet lifted her chin higher. "Well then, let's hope the gods know better than to stand between a mother and her son."

She turned on her heel and left Oseron standing alone in the middle of the room.

Chapter 8

Shades of gray had commandeered the sky and a light rain was falling, but Deston didn't notice. He sat on the wet ground and stared at the bow.

Why does it have to be me? I am nobody. I know nothing about fighting magic. He shook his head in misery, closed his eyes and flopped to his back. *I've already failed once, why do They keep coming back to me? My powers aren't strong enough. I don't know if they'll ever be strong enough. I'm just going to cause the fae more trouble and someone else is going to get killed because of me.*

"You are not the cause of anyone's trouble, Deston, but you could be the answer," a voice said inside Deston's head.

Deston reared straight up. *"Who is that?"* he asked, looking around the clearing until he saw his grandfather, Oberon, standing on the bank of the stream.

"I can't begin to tell you how proud I am of you, my boy," Oberon added with a smile. *"You've already accomplished so much in your short life. It is a real testament to your fortitude that Grossard considers you such a threat."*

Deston could feel the blush creep up his neck, but he didn't look away.

Oberon moved into the clearing and sat down on a makeshift stool, leaning his elbows on his knees so he and Deston would be at the same eye level. *"I told you once before that I'm part of you and you're part of me. Because of this, I can feel the turmoil and sorrow that is holding you back. I wish I could do something to take your pain away and give you peace, but that would be a great disservice to you. Even though it is hard for you to cope with, it is a necessary element to your development. It will build your character and give you the drive you need for the next vital juncture of your life. But I can give you one small nugget of comfort ... there is no such thing as death. Your loved ones never leave you. The life energy departs from this plane of existence and moves on to the next, but we're still very much available to you. You'll always be able to count on me and Keir to lift you up whenever you fall or whenever you need us. You have already seen that to be so with your own eyes. The knowledge and wisdom you seek is ours to share. We are happy to help you prepare for and overcome the challenges that are ahead of you ... if you'll allow us to."*

Deston stared at Oberon for several long minutes, wanting to believe him, but afraid to. "What makes you so sure I won't fail again?"

The blue flakes in Oberon's silver eyes sparkled. *"Because you are my grandson and the blood of many a great fae runs through your veins,"* he stated plainly. *"But beyond that,"* he went on. *"I know because I've already seen what you're capable of. You have tremendous courage within you. You are destined to achieve greatness."* He hesitated as if debating something. *"I will never lie to you, Deston, which is why I must tell you there will be more causalities."*

Deston's heart stalled for a second. "You can see the future? You know what's going to happen?"

Oberon held up his hand and shook his head. *"I am able to see a glimpse of what can be is all. But since every living being has free will, nothing is ever certain until it plays out. Only the Universe knows which path each life will take. That is because we chose the path ourselves in our previous plane of existence. The future is yours to direct and you can only fail if you do not try."* Oberon's loving smile made his face glow even brighter. *"I know you will not only try, you will succeed, because that's who you are."* He gave Deston a nod as he stood and his image began to fade.

Deston jumped to his feet. "Grandfather, don't leave. My powers aren't strong enough to do what I'm supposed to do. I'm not who everyone thinks I am."

Oberon's eyes softened. *"I've already told you, my son, I won't ever leave you. As far as your powers go, they are strong, but you have yet to release them. Until you take control and master your doubts and fears, your powers cannot become a subconscious part of you."*

"Yeah, but that's the problem ... I don't know how to do that."

Oberon held his hand in front of Deston's stomach and traced a symbol in the air over his root chakra. Deston involuntarily jumped as if he'd been shocked, even though Oberon's hand didn't make contact with his skin.

"Close your eyes and take four deep breaths. Each time, fill your lungs completely before blowing the air out through your mouth," Oberon commanded and waited for Deston to comply. *"Now visualize your body in your mind and tell me what you see."*

An image popped into Deston's head straight away—an okay looking boy with curly, dirty-blonde hair, violet eyes, and a deep dimple in his right cheek. It was the image he saw every time he looked into a mirror.

"I don't want you to focus on your outer appearance. I want you to look beneath the shell and tell me what you see inside," Oberon added, as if he could see the image Deston had brought up.

Deston's brow creased. "What'd ya mean? How can I see inside me?"

"You are trying to use your physical eyes, which can only show you the physical. Use your third eye. It is what you use to see beyond the flesh."

Deston took another deep breath and let his brain drift to his third eye. Slowly, his features muted and colors separated his body into sections from the top of his head down to his stomach.

"Can you see it? Your power?" Oberon asked, disrupting Deston's concentration.

The line between Deston's eyes deepened. "I don't know. I see colors."

"Good, that's good. What colors do you see?"

Deston listed off the colors, starting from the purple at the top of his head down to the orange at his stomach.

"That is all? You see no other?" Oberon questioned.

"Well ... there's sort of a dull brownish color that has a bit of red flickering in and out of it. Does that count?"

Oberon nodded. *"Ahh, I suspected as much. That is your Muladhara, the root of your consciousness that connects you to the earth's energies and to your ancestral memories. Its natural color is red; the color of energy, movement and development, but you can see for yourself that yours is buried under the layers of your doubt—thus, the brown color. As long as you continue to embrace that doubt, you cannot reconnect to the earth and you will not gain access to that which you so desire—your powers and the wisdom of your ancestors."*

"So ... what do I do? How do I reconnect?"

Oberon smiled sadly. *"It's really very simple. Have faith and believe in yourself. I know that is not going to be an easy thing for you to do. You have spent fifteen years harboring your doubt and it is well rooted within you. Everyone around you can see who you are, but it makes no difference. Only what you see counts and only you can reestablish the connection. You are a unique individual, Deston, but you try too hard to be like everyone else. Be proud of the individual that you are and know that your weaknesses are not limitations. They are opportunities to learn and grow. The Universe wasn't built in a day and neither will all things come to you in a day."*

Deston felt a stirring inside him. He squeezed his eyes together to hold onto the feeling, but a question came to mind. "If I uncover my powers, will my magic be as strong as Mordred and Grossard's?"

"You are not a sorcerer like Mordred, and you have not been schooled in the use of black magic as Grossard. You cannot compare your powers to theirs. Their energy is dark. Yours is light."

Deston mulled that over for a second. "So are you saying the light is stronger than the dark?" He looked up at Oberon with hope shining in his eyes.

"Stronger?" Oberon shrugged. *"Is day stronger than night? There is no answer to that question. The gods created the Crystal of Light to channel the light of the Universe for the benefit of this planet and everything and everyone on it. Erebus created the darkness that fills the Shard. It evokes chaos, destruction and death. For many millennia the Shard was buried under miles of ice and that held the darkness at bay. Now that it has resurfaced, the darkness is free to corrupt the entire world. But like the Crystal of Light, the Shard needs to reconnect with the energies of the Universe or it will weaken. That time of renewal is almost upon us. It will take place with the full lunar eclipse on the winter solstice. If Grossard has the incantation from the Book of Tenebris, he will be able to reverse the magnetic poles, which in itself will do great damage to this world. It will also open the portal allowing the darkness from the farthest corners of the Universe to enter. This world has not seen darkness of that kind since the gods exiled Erebus and locked his disciples in Tartarus. That was before the time of the fae, so it is unknown if They and the Crystal of Light will be enough to hold the darkness back."*

"There's no hope then," Deston mumbled.

Oberon's face softened. *"There is always hope, my boy. The fae have put Theirs in you, but that does not mean you have to fight this battle alone."*

Deston's shoulders sagged and his chin dropped to his chest. *They're wrong to put Their hope in me,* he thought. *Maybe Zumwald should just go ahead and find a new champion.* The sick feeling Deston had felt when he heard Zumwald say those words returned, and he wondered if Zumwald had already found someone else to take his place. He looked up, intending to ask Oberon, but Oberon was gone. He was alone again.

Confused and completely overwhelmed, he sank to the ground and buried his face in his hands. *All I've ever been is a freak. How do I change that and become a hero?* He rocked his head back and forth in his hands. *If I don't do this, more people are going to be hurt. Oh God, how did I get into this mess? How am I going to get out of it?*

Chapter 9

The sound of a wolf howl penetrated Deston's conscious. He reared up, instantly awake, and looked around in confusion at the dark shapes surrounding him. It took him another minute to realize he was lying on the ground beside a cold fire pit and was not in his cave.

What the hell? he thought as he wrapped his arms around his chest and rubbed his hands up and down his biceps to bring some warmth back into them. A wolf howled again, and then another much closer, which finally got Deston moving.

His joints were stiff with the wet cold and his muscles were sore, but he scrambled to the small woodpile, grabbed a handful of kindling and dried leaves and threw it on top of the ashes. His numb fingers could hardly hold the match and it took him several tries to light it, but he finally got a spark and the leaves caught fire. As the flame grew, he slowly added bigger branches until the fire was going strong and produced a good amount of heat.

He held his hands close to the flames letting the heat drive away the numbness, but his mind remained foggy and he couldn't recall why he'd been sleeping on the ground. He knew better than that, especially in the wild, where a bear or a wolf would relish a tasty treat like him for a midnight snack. But the only thing he could remember was Keir leaving after their argument and his grandfather appearing.

Ah crap! Was it all just another dream? Deston sighed in exasperation. He ran his fingers through his hair and closed his eyes, thinking back to the events of the previous day. His emotions volleyed back and forth like a tennis ball over a net: one minute, clarity—the next, despair.

As he sat, trying to put the pieces of his memory back together, a sudden cold shiver ran up his spine and the hair on the back of his neck stood on end. Every one of his senses came alive, but the only thing that moved were his eyes, as he scanned the area for the cause of his alarm.

The trees looked the same as they always did and nothing was out of place; but it was the middle of the night and the fire only provided a small ring of light that did not even reach to the edge of the campsite. But he didn't need to see to know there was another presence nearby. He sensed them.

Casually, he threw another branch on the fire as if nothing was wrong. Then he got up and walked to where he kept his bag. He bent over as if to retrieve something out of it, but he reached for Caluvier instead. His hand closed around the sword's hilt and in one swift move, he straightened, spun around, and brought the sword up to show whoever it was that he was armed.

"You can come out ... I know you're there," Deston yelled into the darkness.

There was a pause and then a soft chuckle came from within the thick underbrush and quickly dissolved into a raspy cough. Seconds later, Rellik ambled out of the foliage, his chest heaving with the effort to take in a full breath. Deston tensed and gripped the sword tighter at the sight of his old nemesis. Before leaving Tir na-nÓg, he had heard rumors that Rellik had forsaken Grossard and was helping the fae, but he wasn't as quick to believe Rellik's switch in alliance was genuine like the others apparently were.

"Look at this ... the Prince of Tir na-nÓg alone and unguarded in the wilderness once again, and as before, I am amazed at how foolish the fae can be." Rellik cocked his head and studied Deston with his one good eye. A knowing look flitted through that eye and he smiled. "There is something different about you," he stated. "You've grown some since I last saw you." His gaze roamed over Deston. "Your muscles have developed nicely, and you were able to detect me, so your powers are beginning to emerge as well." He nodded his head. "I'm duly impressed."

Deston pressed his lips together and held his glare, although his chest puffed out a little at Rellik's offhanded compliment.

Rellik's legs were trembling from the exertion of racing to the forest. Gritting his teeth, he ambled into the clearing, counting on the darkness to hide his weakness from Deston. Deston took a step backward and raised Caluvier, but Rellik walked to the fire and collapsed beside it without giving Deston a second look.

"You can lower that sword. I am not here to do you harm," Rellik said causally.

"Yeah? Then why *are* you here?" Deston responded without lowering Caluvier.

"May I have some water? It was a long run from the gateway and I'm still recovering from some recent injuries, as I know you are," Rellik replied, purposely darting a glance down at Deston's thigh even though Deston's trousers were covering the scar.

Deston's eyes narrowed, but the wheezing in Rellik's chest made him realize that at least part of what Rellik said was true. Upon closer look, he noticed the wolf did appear quite ragged and not at all well. Rellik was quite a bit thinner than the last time Deston saw him and the wolf had been thin to the point of being unhealthy then. Each of his ribs were clearly visible, heaving in and out with each breath and a drop of blood clung to his bottom lip from the earlier bout of coughing. Ugly reddish scars covered his left side, which made it look as if his skin was still raw, and there were only a few small patches of his once luxurious coat left.

Deston lowered Caluvier, but didn't put it back into its scabbard. His eyes stayed on Rellik as he bent, picked up his one and only bowl and went to the creek to fill it with water. He placed it on the ground in front of Rellik and stood back to let him drink.

"I doubt you came all this way for a drink, so I'll ask you again … if you don't wish me any harm, why are you here? Were you sent to spy on me?" he asked after Rellik had emptied the bowl.

"I am no one's spy. I came here to give you a gift," Rellik replied, raising his head and smiling his lop-sided smile.

"You came a long way for nothing then. I don't want anything you have to give."

"You shouldn't speak so impulsively until you know the facts, because you may be wrong about that. Unless I'm completely mistaken in assuming you would like to know where to find Mordred."

Deston eyed Rellik skeptically, but held his response.

The wolf let out a sigh. "Not interested? Well then …" He slowly got to his feet, "I guess I did waste my time." He walked to the edge of the clearing. "Zumwald may have put protection around you and this place, but Grossard and Mordred can most definitely figure out how to get through it. So if I were you, I would keep my guard up a lot better than what you are doing."

As Rellik stepped into the trees, Deston called out. "Why would you want to tell me where Mordred is? What's in it for you?"

Rellik paused and looked back. "Mordred is merely a means to an end. My only interest lies in Grossard, but I have not been able to locate him. Mordred has that information and I want it."

Deston stared at the wolf's one glowing eye, which was all that showed from the shadows. He didn't know whether to believe him or not. Ever since the temple incident, every fae had been searching for Mordred and Grossard, but no one had been able to find either of them. If Rellik really did know where Mordred was going to hole up, it would be a real break. It could also be a real-life test to see if he was capable of fulfilling his destiny. At the same time, it could be a trap.

"So you're saying you want me to go find Mordred and get him to tell me where Grossard is. And then I kill him … is that the way you expect this to go?"

"I never said anything about you getting the information from Mordred. I fully intend to do that myself. Once I get what I need, how you deal with the sorcerer is totally up to you. As I said earlier, I have no interest in him."

"What makes you think Mordred is going to hand that information over to you?"

"Mordred is a coward at heart and hates Grossard as much as you and I do. I have no doubt he'll do whatever it takes to save his own life. I'm only asking for your assistance because I don't have the ability to create a glamour, and I can't walk amongst the humans without one."

Deston stared hard at the wolf, his eyes showing his skepticism.

"I know Mordred has caused you and your family much pain. That is why I thought you, of all people, would want to find him as badly as I do. It looks like I was mistaken. You obviously aren't up to the task. I'm sorry to have disturbed you." Rellik gave a slight bow of his head and turned once again to leave.

"Wait!" Deston yelled. "I need to think about this. I mean, you were trying to kill me not that long ago. Now you show up out of the blue and want me to partner up with you to get rid of your former boss. Can you see why I might have a little trouble trusting that you are on the level?"

"I am my own wolf now. I follow no one's orders. Do you think you are the only one who has been hurt by that pair?" Rellik asked, turning back and stepping into the light of the fire. "Look at me. I am dying from the injuries Grossard has inflicted on me. My dying wish is to see him bleed before I go and my time is running out."

It was obvious Rellik had changed much from when Deston first met him, but Deston had no idea the wolf was dying. "I … I still want some time to think it over," he replied, more concerned with the issue of not having gained the full use of his powers than he was with the possibility of Rellik luring him into a trap.

Rellik nodded. "I understand, but there isn't a lot of time for you to make up your mind. I've spent much energy trying to locate Grossard. This is the first break I've had, but I only know where Mordred is going to be, not how long he'll be there. If I miss him, he and Grossard will be lost to me forever. You can have thirty-six hours, but that is all I can spare. If you make your decision sooner, you can send word through the wolves. They will see that I get it." He stared Deston in the eye. "This is the best chance you're going to get to catch the sorcerer. It might also be your only chance of finding Grossard and the Shard." He wanted to say more, but he didn't want to push too hard or seem too eager. Instead, he gave a slight nod and dissolved into the shadows, leaving Deston alone to debate what to do.

Deston had spent the four weeks he had been in the Great Bear Rainforest working out and getting in shape to face Mordred and Grossard again. He was pleased with what he'd been able to accomplish in his physical growth, but the fact that he still couldn't control his powers was a source of bitter disappointment. Sometimes his powers would manifest on their own without so much as a thought on his part. Other times, no matter how hard he tried to bring them forth, they would completely elude him.

Blowing a breath out through his mouth, he was suddenly very tired. Though Rellik had made some good points, Deston realized it was useless to try to think it through when he could barely keep his eyes open. With a heavy sigh, he transformed into a kestrel and flew up to the cave. Without even undressing, he crawled into his bedroll and, as if drugged, immediately plunged into the abyss of deep sleep.

Chapter 10

Deston raced as fast as he could across the marsh, looking back over his shoulder every few minutes to make sure Margaux was still right behind him. The soggy ground sucked at his boots and it felt as if he was dragging fifty pound weights with each step, but he didn't stop. He had to get Margaux into the cover of the forest before he would even consider resting.

"The trees are not much farther. How are you holding up?" he yelled back without turning around. When Margaux didn't answer, he threw a quick glance over his shoulder and stumbled over his feet as he came to an abrupt halt. Margaux had been right behind him the last time he looked, but now she was gone and a swirling gray fog was slowly stretching out across the landscape.

"Margaux? Where are you?" he called out frantically. He squinted into the fog, but the unnaturally dense cloud was impossible to see through. A cold chill ran down his spine as the fog inched its way closer. He staggered back a few steps, sensing if he let the fog overtake him, he'd never get out of it.

Suddenly, a muffled scream came from within the mist. The blood drained from Deston's face and he breathed, "Margaux." His heart thumped faster as his head shook back and forth. "No ... you can't have her!" he yelled out to the fog and blindly rushed in.

The air immediately closed in around him like a suffocating plastic bag, He could hardly breathe, but he kept on going, calling out Margaux's name. It had only been seconds since he last saw her, so he was sure she couldn't have gone far. However, with the fog as thick as it was, he could walk by her and not even know she was there. As his panic began to take over, he batted wildly at the air. His efforts had little effect on the fog. Then suddenly, and for no reason, the cloud thinned and he could make out a faint wavering shadow a few meters ahead.

Margaux, *he thought with relief; then realized the shape was way too small to be Margaux. His brow came together as he strained to see what it was. At that moment, a great gust of wind swirled the fog into a frenzy and carried it out over the marsh. Deston stared down at the enormous black crow with a strange white tuft under its beak that was standing on the ground staring back at him. The crow clicked its beak loudly and Deston jumped. It then spread its wings and took to the air. Deston craned his neck back and watched its jet-black body fly into the gray sky and disappear. When he turned his head back, there was a white deer standing in the exact spot where the crow had stood a moment before.*

Deston opened and closed his mouth, but it took him another moment to find his voice. "Lilika, is that you?" he asked tentatively.

Instead of answering, the deer took a wobbly step toward him and sank to its knees. A dark red liquid poured from its underbelly. Deston recoiled as the thick pool soaked into the dirt like paint on old wood. As he couldn't take his eyes off the red stain, he didn't see the squirming bundle tied to the deer's back until it slid off and a pitiful wail rent the silence. The sound sliced through Deston as swiftly as a knife blade and he choked on his breath.

"My baby!" Lilika cried out, struggling to get up, but she was too weak to even lift her head. Her eyes met Deston's and welled with tears. "Why?" she asked. "Why didn't you come? I was counting on you. We were all *counting on you."*

Deston took a step back, his eyes widening in horror. What was she talking about? If he had known she was in trouble, he would have been there. She knew that. He would do anything for her.

Margaux suddenly appeared and knelt at Lilika's side. She gently picked up the small blanket-wrapped bundle that had turned scarlet with the deer's blood and cradled it in her arms. Rocking back and forth, she cooed softly as Deston stood by and watched helplessly.

"I didn't know, Margaux. If I had known Lilika was in trouble, I would have gone to her. You have to know that I would."

Margaux lifted her head and he saw the disappointment on her face along with the accusations in her eyes. "You may want to believe that, but it's not true. You knew what was coming, but you only want to be fae when it suits you. That's not how it works, Deston. You either are a fae or you aren't. There can be no in-between."

Deston drew back as if Margaux had punched him hard in the stomach. "I ... I—" he started, but his words trailed off as he realized he didn't know how to respond to that. She was right, and it pained him to admit it. A bitter taste filled his mouth. Unable to meet her eyes another second, he dropped his head and racked his brain for something to say in his defense.

An annoying hissing sound entered his head and interrupted his thoughts. The sound grew louder and became more sinister by the second. He finally looked up and saw a black void creeping toward Margaux, Lilika and Macaria.

"Margaux, watch out!" Deston yelled, pulling Caluvier from its scabbard.

Before Margaux had time to look up, the blackness was upon her. A menacing laugh rumbled within the darkness and sent a chill deep into Deston's bones. His sword fell from his hand and he covered his ears to shut the laugher out, but it didn't help. The noise grew louder and reverberated inside his head until he couldn't stand it.

"Stop!" he yelled out, dropping to his knees. At his command, the sound instantly ceased and all went silent.

Hesitantly, Deston lowered his hands and looked around. The dark had completely enveloped him. All he could see was black. He brushed his hand across the ground until he found Caluvier. As soon as his fingers closed around the hilt, he slowly got to his feet. He stretched his free hand out in front of him and shuffled his feet forward to keep from stepping on Margaux or the deer. The air was heavy with the scent of decay and death. The once emerald green grass had turned brown and crunched beneath his feet.

"You called for silence, Prince of Tir na-nÓg, and your wish was fulfilled, as all your wishes will be, now that you have joined us," a hissing, snarling voice whispered on the breeze.

Deston's eyes swiveled right and left, searching for the speaker. "Who said that?" he called out loudly.

"You know who I am, Prince Deston. You were most instrumental in bringing me back."

Deston's stomach plummeted and he shook his head in denial as the name Erebus popped into his mind. "No," he murmured. "I didn't help you. I would never betray my friends."

Erebus chuckled. "Ahh, but that is exactly what you did and without even lifting a finger."

The malicious laughter filled Deston's head and he clamped his hands over his ears, but as before, it didn't help. "Nooo," he moaned, feeling sick and helpless.

"NO!" Deston shouted out and with a jerk, he was wide awake. His heart pounded in his ears as loudly as the thunder rumbling through the cave. Soaked in a cold sweat and shivering, he reached for the blanket, but during the night it had twisted around his legs and it wouldn't budge. With a sigh, he wiped his hand over his face and blew a breath out through his mouth, trying to calm his nerves. The dream was already drifting into the abyss of his mind, but the disquiet and guilt stayed with him.

He shivered again and with a disgusted breath, kicked his legs until the blanket was dislodged. He pulled it up around his shoulders and crawled out onto the ledge just as a streak of lightning lit up the sky. Thunder followed seconds later, but the rain held back. Goose bumps ran up both of his arms and he grimaced as he recalled the look of disappointment on Margaux's face from the dream. The bridge of his nose burned with a sudden buildup of tears, but he gritted his teeth and held them back. Never had he felt so alone or so empty.

He stepped out to the edge of the narrow ledge until half his foot was hanging over. With his arms opened wide, he lifted his face to the sky, daring the lightning to strike him down and end his misery, but the storm suddenly calmed.

Figures, he thought sourly, jerking his head to the side to flip the hair out of his eyes. He scowled up at the heavens once more and then turned and flew down to the ground.

Mechanically, he started toward the fire pit like he did every morning, but his steps slowed as a flash of white in of the corner of his eye caught his attention. With the dream still fresh in his mind, he twirled around, expecting to find Lilika there. To his disappointment, it was only the white bear sitting at the edge of the camp with its typical amused look on its face. Fresh guilt heated Deston's cheeks and he held his breath, waiting for Keir to show. He had just seen Lilika die in his dream, and though he knew it wasn't real, he still felt uncomfortable having to face Keir.

Every muscle in his body tensed up, but several long minutes passed and Keir did not appear. Finally, Deston wiped his hand over his face and walked to the pit to start the fire.

"So you're here all by yourself this time, huh?" he said to the bear, as he stirred the ashes. "Did they send you to spy on me, or are you here to talk me into going along with their plan?" He looked over at the bear, which just sniffed noisily and scratched its front leg, paying no attention to Deston.

Deston shook his head and grabbed some of the smaller sticks to build the fire. *Okay, fine. Ignore me and I'll ignore you.*

A streak of lightning lit up sky and the following clash of thunder echoed through the trees. As the memory of the dream came back full force, his hand stilled and his stomach twisted. He bit down on his bottom lip and closed his eyes to clear his mind, but Margaux's voice stayed in his head, and it sounded so real.

"Deston, can you hear me?"

A pain shot through his chest and he dropped his head. *It's only the dream,* he told himself. *But I wish you were here.* He suddenly missed her more than he ever thought was possible.

"Deston, where are you? Please answer. I have information you need to hear. It's important."

Deston looked up and his mouth curved down in a frown. Margaux had not said anything like that in the dream. *"Margaux?"* he hesitantly replied.

"Oh, Deston, thank the stars I found you. Are you alright?"

Deston sat up straighter. *"Yeah ... I'm fine. Where are you?"*

"I'm here. Or I will be in a few minutes. Stay right where you are so I can hone in on you," Margaux replied.

Deston lifted his face to the sky, still wondering if it was real or some weird trick of his imagination. He didn't have to wait long to find out, as a small blur came out of the gray and zipped by his face. The blur circled his head and came to a stop in front of him.

"Your Majesty, we've been so worried about you since you left Tir na-nÓg. Don't you know it is dangerous for you to be out here on your own?" Tiff was beyond excited and her voice came out as a squeak.

"Tiff?" Deston stared dumbfounded at the small sprite. "How did you get here? How did you find me?"

"I overheard Zumwald tell the king you were on Swindle Island. The birds led us the rest of the way. You must leave right away, Your Highness. It's not safe here," Tiff rushed on.

Deston bristled at Zumwald's name, however, before he could respond, a kestrel dropped from the sky.

Margaux transformed the minute her feet touched down. She rushed straight to Deston and threw her arms around him, burying her face in his shoulder before he could see the tears brimming in her eyes.

The second Deston laid eyes on Margaux, the empty cavern that had existed inside his chest since Keir's death shrunk just a bit, and for a moment, he forgot to breathe. He had wanted to talk to her so many times since that incident, but he always chickened out at the last second. After all, Keir was her uncle and Deston was responsible for Keir's death. He figured she would want nothing to do with him because of what he had done, or actually, what he had failed to do, and to save himself the heartache, he had chosen the easy way out and avoided her. But at the sight of Margaux's copper-colored hair blazing in the sun, the dam he'd erected to hold back his feelings burst open and his heart nearly stopped. Daring to hope, he tentatively folded his arms around her and hugged her back, savoring the sweet scent of her hair, which always reminded him of cherry blossoms. When Margaux didn't cringe or push him away, his heart started beating again. He pulled back just enough to cup her face in his hands and look into her eyes, hoping to find an answer to the question that had been eating at him; but all he saw was the same uncertainty he felt gleaming back at him.

Unable to resist, Deston lightly brushed his thumb over Margaux's lips. Her hand moved up his neck and her warm breath teased his mouth as she let out a soft sigh. That was all it took for the fire in Deston's stomach to explode and burn away all rational thought. His whole world shrunk down to fit inside of Margaux and he wanted her more than he had ever wanted anything else in his life. Leaning in, he brushed his lips across hers. Her lips parted and he hesitated not sure what to do, but she pulled him back to her. As their lips locked, he tightened his hold and everything else on the planet ceased to exist.

"Your Greatness," Tiff repeated for the third time as she tugged on his sleeve. "There is urgent news you must hear."

Tiff's voice finally broke through Deston's spell and he looked up in surprise as if he had no idea the sprite was there. It took him another second to realize Tiff had witnessed the kiss, and with a jerk, he released Margaux and took a hasty step back, his cheeks flushing an even deeper red than what they already were.

"Rellik is on his way here. He is coming to get you and take you to Grossard," Tiff continued, oblivious to Deston's apparent discomfort.

Tiff's words snapped Margaux back to the present and she too jerked to attention. "That's right," Margaux started, but her voice cracked and she stopped to clear her throat.

"That's why we're here. You're in danger," Tiff added, using Margaux's pause to pipe in again. "We came to escort you back to Tir na-nÓg before Rellik can find you."

Deston's brain was still in a bit of a fog and he looked from Tiff to Margaux, trying to comprehend what they were talking about. "Rellik's already been here," he said shaking his head to clear his mind. "I've talked to him and he has no plans to take me to Grossard. He doesn't even know where Grossard is. He just wants me to help him get to Mordred. He thinks Mordred has information as to where Grossard is hiding out."

Margaux's mouth dropped open and her voice raised an octave as her next words rushed out. "You can't be … you aren't going to go with him, are you?" She didn't need to hear Deston's answer, for the look on his face told her everything she needed to know. Her eyebrows shot up and she huffed under her breath, "*Se un blag!*"

Deston was more confused than ever and didn't understand why Margaux seemed to be so upset. "Yeah, I'm thinking about it. I mean, why not? When I left Tir na-nÓg, the army hadn't been able to locate Grossard *or* Mordred. Have they found either of them yet?" He looked at both Margaux and Tiff and their silence confirmed what he already suspected. "If Rellik can take me to Mordred, it may be our best and only shot of getting to the Shard. I don't see how that can be a bad thing."

Margaux took hold of both of Deston's arms and gave them a little shake. "Deston, this is Rellik we're talking about … Grossard's former right hand man. Remember? What makes you think he can all of a sudden be trusted? Grossard could be behind the whole thing and Rellik could be leading you into a trap," Margaux exclaimed, hoping to talk some sense into him.

Deston shook his head again. "I don't think so. If you had seen Rellik go after Grossard in the temple like I did, you'd know his relationship with Grossard was over. He was almost killed trying to stop Grossard from getting the Shard. And you saw yourself how he tried to put an end to Grossard at the monastery. I think he's proven more than enough times that he's no longer a friend of Grossard's."

"Please—" Margaux started, but Deston cut her off.

"Look, everyone has been looking for these two guys, but no one can find them. Rellik knows where Mordred is going to be. I can't turn my back on an opportunity like this. It's the closest anyone has come to finding Grossard and we're running out of time."

Margaux opened her mouth to respond, but Deston held up his hand and stopped her. "If you know of a better way, then let me hear it, 'cause I don't have anything else." He paused, but Margaux's mouth snapped shut.

"I'm the Prince of Tir na-nÓg." It still felt weird calling himself a prince and he had to swallow before he could go on. "It's my duty and my destiny to put an end to this before Grossard and Mordred destroy the world. No one else is going to suffer at their hands, not if I can help it."

As Deston's words trailed off, he watched Margaux's lips press into a thin line. Recognizing that look, he rolled his eyes. *Great, here we go. She's going to be stubborn about this*, he thought as a heavy silence grew between them.

"Fine," Margaux finally stated, breaking the tension. "If you feel Rellik is telling the truth, we'll go with him. But if I so much as get a hint that he's up to no good, I'm immediately calling in your father."

Deston's brow went up and then came down as he scowled. "What do you mean '*we'll go*?'" You are *not* going with me. This is between me and Mordred. And if you think I would let you get anywhere near that lunatic, you'd better think again. It's too dangerous and you are not going to put your life at risk again," Deston yelled.

Margaux shifted her weight to one leg as her hands went to her hips. "My life is no more important than yours, and you can't do this on your own. You know it. You should also know that you can't stop me from going."

Deston glared at her and then turned his back to keep from firing back something he'd regret later. He raked his hand through his hair, berating himself for telling Margaux about Rellik in the first place. He should have known she'd insist on going along—she always did. She had gone with him when he searched for his mother and then again when he searched for the Shard, but that was different. Back then she was just another girl to him. Now she was his whole world and she held his heart in her hand. Losing her was not an option he was willing to risk.

"Look, Margaux ..." he started, but his words trailed off as he turned back and saw the obstinate expression on her face. He exhaled sharply and pressed his lips together, knowing that he was in a losing battle. He had had very little experience with girls in the past and they were still a complete mystery to him, Margaux being the biggest mystery of all.

Biting the inside of his lip, he tried to think of a way out. Suddenly, a crazy idea came to him. He knew it was a long shot, and if it didn't work out, it could destroy him, but it was all he could think of and he had to do something.

Timidly, he looked up, licked his lips and blurted out, "Do you have any feelings at all for me?"

Margaux recoiled and her eyes went wide, which was not the reaction Deston was going for. She stared at him, her face turning several shades of red. Deston's heart moved into his throat and he swallowed hard. The silence that followed was the longest of his life, and the longer it went on, the more desperate he became to know the answer.

"Do you?" he pressed and held his breath.

Margaux blinked and ran her tongue over her lips. "Yes ... I do. You know that I do," she stammered, her voice coming out as a croak.

Deston stared into her eyes, not sure he heard correctly. As her words slowly settled over him like a comforting blanket, a goofy grin turned up the corners of his mouth before he could stop it.

Seeing the grin, Margaux realized he had been trying to manipulate her. "What do my feeling have to do with anything?" she asked, lifting her chin higher.

Her icy tone instantly derailed Deston's train of thought. He gulped back his guilt and squared his shoulders, determined to keep her from going, no matter the cost. "If it's true what you just said ... if you really do have feelings for me, then you'll do what I ask. You'll stay in Tir na-nÓg and be safe, so I don't have to worry about you." He watched Margaux's lips thin out and knew he was in trouble, but he held his stance and took a deep breath. "Please Margaux; can't you just do this one thing for me? If something happened to you, it would kill me."

A long silence followed as Margaux tried to take reign over her thoughts and emotions. But her anger only grew stronger. "How dare you use my feelings to manipulate me."

Deston reached out, but then let his hand drop. "I ... um—"

"Don't you say another word. Just because I have feelings for you does *NOT* mean I'm going to cave in and allow you to go off and do something stupid." She held her hand up and stopped him from interrupting. "Let me ask you this ... what do you plan to do once you find Mordred? Do you actually think he'll welcome you in with open arms, serve you tea, and hand over all the information you want to know about Grossard?" She hesitated to give Deston a chance to reply, but his jaw was set and he just glared back.

"You haven't thought that far ahead, have you? And what happens if it is a trap? How are you going to get help?" She shook her head when he remained silent. "You want to use my love for you against me and for your own purposes. I can do the same, you know. I can ask you to prove your feelings for me and not go."

The 'L' word didn't escape Deston's notice, but he didn't dwell on it, for he still had to convince Margaux to go back to Tir na-nÓg.

"We're a team now. We work better together. I'm not going to let you go alone. You're going to have to accept that's the way it's going to be, because I *am* going with you one way or the other," Margaux added, crossing her arms over her chest to show she wasn't going to budge on her stance.

Deston stared at her and realized there was no use in arguing. She had gone into her determined mode. But that didn't change the fact that he couldn't allow her to go along. There was only thing left for him to do, and that was to trick her into going back to Tir na-nÓg. He hated to do that to her and he knew he'd pay for it if he ever saw her again, but her safety was more important. Blowing out a heavy sigh, he put on his best-resigned look.

"Okay, you win. You can come, *BUT* you have to promise you'll stay back when we find Mordred. Rellik and I will handle it from that point on."

"If Margaux gets to go, I'm coming too," Tiff piped up.

"I don't think that's a good idea, Tiff," Margaux interjected before Deston could respond.

Tiff's chest puffed out and as the two quarreled about who was going to get to go, Deston used the time to figure out how to get both of them to go back to Tir na-nÓg so he could slip away with Rellik.

"I'm okay if Tiff comes," Deston cut in, shocking both Tiff and Margaux. "As long as you abide by the same rules as Margaux—that means not getting involved when we find Mordred. Also, I was just thinking that you should both go back to Tir na-nÓg ..." Margaux opened her mouth to protest, but Deston continued on before she could say anything. "... to get the spell that will protect us from Mordred's magic. You know, the one Keir used in the temple. I think we can all agree that Mordred can't be trusted, so it would be smart to have the spell just in case. While you're there, you can also grab a few extra weapons. We may not need them, but I think we should be prepared for whatever we might come across." He paused. "Do you think you can get the spell without letting on why you want it?"

Margaux and Tiff both nodded their heads at the same time.

"Good," he sighed, pretending to be relieved. "So ... you better get going. Rellik's supposed to be back here tomorrow and we'll leave as soon as he gets here." Deston stepped up to Margaux and put a hand under her chin, tilting her face up to his. "I really wish you'd reconsider and stay in the city where you'll be safe. I wasn't kidding when I said it would kill me if something happened to you." It took a great deal of effort to look her in the eyes, and he prayed his face didn't give away his deception.

Margaux put her hand over his and squeezed, and Deston almost lost it.

"Nothing is going to happen," she said matter-of-factly. "Don't you remember what Titania told us when we first got to Tir na-nÓg? She said my destiny was to help you fulfill yours. That means we're in this together to the end."

Deston's heart swelled and he pulled her into his arms. Margaux's strength and determination had never failed to amaze him and he loved her all the more because of it. He didn't know what was going to happen, but he did know sending her back to Tir na-nÓg was the right thing to do to keep her safe. "Be careful in the city and don't let anyone know you've seen me. Promise me that," he whispered into her hair.

"I promise," she said and leaned back to give him a quick peck on the lips. Before she could pull back, he caught her and deepened the kiss. When they broke apart, her face was flushed and she could hardly catch her breath. "Um ..." she swallowed. "We should get going if we want to be back before Rellik returns." She turned away to hide her red cheeks.

Tiff nodded her head, but she didn't look convinced that this was the right plan. Deston saw the look and reached out, catching her around the middle.

"Do *not* tell anyone what I've told you about Rellik and Mordred—*no one*, under any circumstances. Understand?"

Tiff quickly put her hands behind her back and crossed her fingers as she nodded her head.

"I mean it. I'm commanding you to obey me. You know you can't break your prince's command."

Tiff's shoulders sagged. "But Your—"

"No buts, Tiff. Give me your word or I'll tie you up right here and leave you behind," Deston replied, cutting her off.

Tiff stuck out her bottom lip in a pout and glared at him, but seeing he wasn't going to relent, she finally nodded her head. "I give you my word," she replied reluctantly.

Deston held back a smile and released her. "Okay then ... I'll see you both tomorrow."

Margaux had already changed into a kestrel and had taken to the sky. She let out a squawk and dipped low over his head, brushing his hair with her wing tip in farewell. Tiff caught up to her and together they streaked across the sky toward the gateway.

Chapter 11

Deston waited five torturous minutes to make sure Margaux and Tiff were clear before he raced into the trees to send Rellik a message. He prayed Rellik hadn't gone far, for he wanted to be long gone before Margaux and Tiff returned. He knew Margaux was going to be furious with him when she discovered what he'd done. Each time he thought about facing her again after having lied straight to her face, his stomach twisted into a knot. But he would do it all over again if given the chance, for he would rather she be mad than dead.

The forest was typically a buzz of activity due to the wide variety of wildlife that lived there and Deston never thought for a moment he'd have trouble finding a bird or animal to carry a message to the wolves. But for some mysterious reason, it was unnaturally quiet at the moment and there was not a single creature in sight. His heart started racing faster than a marathon runner and he began to worry that he might not be able to get a message off in time for Rellik to make it back before Margaux returned.

As the morning mist was still hovering in patches near the ground, Deston didn't see the fallen log in his path until he tripped over it and went down. He pushed himself up with a curse and caught a movement out of the corner of his eye. He turned his head and did a double-take at the giant wolf lying under a tree a few yards away, nonchalantly chewing on the remains of some kind of animal. He rapidly scrambled to his feet as Rellik smiled, showing no surprise at seeing him there.

"What are you doing here? I thought you were going back to ..." Deston's words trailed off as he realized he didn't know where he expected Rellik would go. But he certainly didn't expect the wolf to be hanging out so close to his camp. His eyes narrowed as the thought came to him that Rellik might have stayed to listen in on his and Margaux's conversation. "Have you been spying on me?" he snapped.

Rellik's amusement at seeing Deston's shocked expression vanished. "I told you already ... I'm not a spy. I believe I also told you I'd be nearby awaiting your answer. You were to send me a message by way of the wolves. Since you came yourself, I could ask you the same question ... what are you doing here and are you spying on *me*?"

"No, I wasn't," Deston sputtered, forgetting for a moment why he was there. "I, um, I was looking for an animal to tell you that I'd go with you and help you find Mordred. But we need to leave right now," he rushed out.

Rellik cocked his head and studied Deston, but said nothing more.

"You do still need my help ... right?" Deston added after the silence grew uncomfortable.

"Yes, I need your help, but I'm curious to know why the sudden change of heart?" Rellik replied.

Deston could feel his ears heat up, but he did his best to keep his voice level. "Well, you said it yourself—you're probably my best chance of finding Grossard. And I figured since you want to see him dead like I do, we might as well team up and help each other out."

Rellik studied Deston another moment before getting to his feet and sauntering off into the trees.

"Wait ... where are you going?"

"You said you wanted to leave right away. The gateway is this way. I imagine you'll take to the sky and will beat me there. Wait for me and do not go through until I arrive," Rellik replied without stopping or turning around.

"Which gateway are we going to take out of Tir na-nÓg?" Deston yelled after him.

Rellik halted and looked back. "Are you wanting to know that so you can leave me behind?" he asked suspiciously.

"No ... I—" Deston stumbled over his words, for that was the exact thought that had come into his head.

The corner of Rellik's muzzle lifted in a sly smile. "You only need to worry about one thing. That is how you're going to disguise us. I'll worry about where we're going." He flashed his teeth in an insecure smile and loped off as Deston's face turned red.

Chapter 12

Margaux kept her head down and walked stiffly across the palace grounds, hoping if she didn't look at anyone, they wouldn't notice her. It had turned out to be a lot easier than she thought to procure the protection spell Deston wanted. All she had to do was go to the group of ex-warriors, who played *latrunculi* in the gardens every day, and ask if they had ever had to use such a spell. As they all had a competitive nature, the men began recounting their encounters with dark magicians, each trying to outdo the other in their tale. Within minutes, the yarns had escalated into an argument over who could produce the most effective protection and all Margaux had to do was sit back and memorize the words as, one by one, they called forth the protection to prove they were the best.

After leaving the gardens, she took an obscure, out-of-the-way route to the armory to ensure no one would see her. There she loaded up with extra arrows and a few extra daggers. All that was left was to make it to the exit without being stopped or questioned and she would have plenty of time to get back to the rainforest before Rellik returned.

The palace yard had never seemed so big to her before and it was torture to walk and not run. When she finally made it past the guard towers and was sure she was in the clear, she ducked into the thick leaves along the side of the road. She knew that picking her way through the foliage would slow her down a bit, but she felt it was worth taking a little extra time to avoid detection. A strange anxious feeling had been nagging at her ever since she entered the palace and she was afraid it was because someone had noticed her.

The traffic on the road was light and whenever it dried up completely, Margaux raced along the shoulder to make up for going off road. So she was making better time than what she thought she would. But as she rounded the last bend, her stomach plummeted. Standing in the middle of the road a short distance ahead was Joliet.

"Se un blag," Margaux whispered, ducking back into the foliage. Of all the people she had hoped to avoid, Joliet was number one, as it was a well-known fact the queen had a bit of a psychic gift, especially when it came to Deston.

Crouching down to make sure she was well hidden in the underbrush, Margaux inched her way forward. When she got to the point straight across from Joliet, she stopped and peered through the leaves, curious as to why Joliet was just standing in the middle of the road all alone.

At that moment, Joliet's head flipped around and she looked directly at the spot where Margaux was hiding. Margaux's hand flew to her mouth to cover her small gasp of surprise, but she wasn't fast enough and Joliet heard the small sound.

"You can come out, Margaux," Joliet called out.

Margaux's heart nearly stopped, however, instead of rising, she crouched down further into the leaves and tried to disappear.

"There's no reason to hide. I know you're there," Joliet called out again and stepped to the side to give Margaux a clear view of Tiff, who was hovering in the air next to Joliet.

Ah Tiff, what have you done? Margaux thought and realized it was pointless to stay hidden. Reluctantly, she stood and walked up to Joliet. Her lips were pressed into a thin line as she threw Tiff a frosty look, but the sprite didn't even have the decency to show the least bit of remorse.

"I've been told Rellik has recruited Deston to help him find Mordred. Is that correct?" Joliet asked, doing her best to keep her voice steady, although her face showed she was peeved.

Margaux shot Tiff another frigid glare. "Tiff, how could you? You were ordered not to tell," she stammered, stalling to think of what to say so she wouldn't give Deston's whole plan away.

"Don't blame Tiff. She has never spent time in the human realm and has not learned to lie. I commanded her to tell me why she was loaded down with weapons. She had no choice," Joliet answered for Tiff and then tenderly put her hand on Margaux's arm to show she was not mad at her. "I know you're a loyal friend to my son. I'm so glad he has you. I want you to know you won't be betraying him by telling me where he's going, but you could be saving his life. There is no proof Rellik has broken all ties with Grossard. We only have his word on that. I, for one, do not think he can be trusted, so please, Margaux ... tell me what you know before it's too late to help Deston."

Margaux looked down at her hands and toyed with a silver band on her finger.

Joliet could see Margaux was torn over her allegiance to Deston, but there wasn't time to coddle the girl. Taking Margaux's hands in hers, she bent her knees and looked into Margaux's eyes. "I know you don't want to get Deston in trouble. But I'm sure you don't want him to get hurt, or possibly killed, either. Because of what happened to Keir, he feels an obligation to take on Mordred and Grossard by himself, but he doesn't understand the power those two control. He won't stand a chance going in there on his own. Please, I beg of you ... tell me what you know."

Margaux could feel tears building up behind her eyes. It wasn't that she disagreed with what Joliet said. In fact, she agreed wholeheartedly with her and felt certain Deston was headed into trouble. That was why she had been so insistent on going along. But she'd made him a promise and she wouldn't break it for anybody, not even the queen.

"I can't," Margaux finally said without looking up. "I promised."

Joliet was so frustrated she wanted to scream, but she clenched her teeth and held it back. "I understand," she said once she had regained her composure. "I wouldn't want you to break a promise. But you must understand that I too have made a promise to protect my son and I will not break it, either." She exhaled a breath and lengthened her neck. "Being the queen, I have the power to keep you from leaving the city. Do you realize that?"

Margaux's head jerked up and her eyes went wide. She took a step back, but Joliet tightened the grip on her hands and kept her from fleeing.

"I didn't say I would do that; I just want you to understand it is within my power." She gave Margaux's hands a squeeze. "But I think I have a better solution for us both. I'll not ask you again to tell me about Deston and Rellik's plans. That way you won't be breaking your promise. But I will follow you to your meeting place and wherever else Deston and Rellik intend to go. You can ignore me and pretend you didn't know I was there, or you can tell him I forced you to bring me along. However you want to handle it is up to you, but you are going nowhere without me. That is how it's going to be."

"Her Highness is right. Mordred is strong. Deston will need all of our help to defeat him," Tiff added, breaking her silence.

Margaux chewed on her lip and debated her options. Deep down she didn't mind having Joliet come along. Joliet was a great archer and if Mordred had his forces with him, an additional archer would come in handy.

"What's it going to be? If I understood correctly, Rellik will be coming back for Deston in one day, so there is no time to delay. I need your decision."

Margaux took a deep breath and swallowed hard. "Are you planning to tell the king about this?"

Joliet's face fell and her heart skipped a beat. "No," she stated bluntly, shocking Margaux. "Oseron has enough to deal with as it is. There is no need to distract him when we don't know for certain that Rellik can lead us to Mordred."

Margaux's relief was evident. "Do I really have a choice?"

"No, you don't," Joliet said, and then added a sad smile to soften the statement.

Margaux tried not to think of how mad Deston was going to be when he saw she had brought his mother back with her. "I guess we should ..." she started, but her words trailed off as a new thought suddenly came to her. Her head jerked up, and though she did a good job of keeping her face blank, she couldn't keep the excitement from shining in her eyes. "If we're going to get back to Deston in time, we'll need to fly and you can't shapeshift. You won't be able to keep up with us."

"Keeping up won't be a problem. I know a man in the valley who's been breeding the winged horses. We'll just need to make a small detour and pick one up," Joliet responded, promptly cancelling out Margaux's joy. "We should hurry. Follow me," she added and took off down the road without further delay.

Margaux stared after Joliet, feeling completely deflated. *What am I going to do? Deston will never trust me again.* For the briefest of moments she entertained the idea of sending him a warning, but she was afraid if she did, he would do something drastic, like take off with Rellik before they got there. That would be far worse than him being mad at her.

"Oh, Gaia, please tell me what I should do?" she whispered softly. Immediately, an idea came to her as if the goddess had truly sent the answer. As a kestrel, she could fly faster than both of them, and if she could get far enough ahead so that they lost sight of her, she could then call out to Deston and have him meet her in a different location. Joliet and Tiff wouldn't know what happened until they got to Deston's camp in the Great Bear Rainforest and found him gone.

"Come on, Margaux," Tiff called back, jolting Margaux out of her reverie.

Margaux looked up as the idea settled in her head. This was going to work, she just knew it. "Thank you Gaia. Now please help me fly fast," she whispered and sprinted off after the other two.

Chapter 13

Deston had worn down a path in front of the gateway into Tir na-nÓg by the time Rellik got there.

"My God, what took you so long? Don't you know Margaux could be coming back any second?" he lashed out and immediately felt guilty as Rellik collapsed to the ground and his sides heaved in and out.

A muscle in Deston's jaw twitched and he tried to stay calm, but too much time had passed and he really was worried Margaux and Tiff would come through the gateway at any moment. He clenched and unclenched his fist as he stood beside Rellik, waiting for the wolf to recover. After what seemed like an hour, but in reality was only five minutes, he cleared his throat.

"We really should get going … if you're ready."

Rellik glowered at Deston and pushed up to his feet, daring Deston to say more, but Deston was staring at the wolf's quivering legs.

"Dude, you really don't look all that great. Maybe I should go on by myself. You can stay here and rest," Deston said, and then winced as he looked up into Rellik's cold eyes.

Rellik straightened and stood as tall as he was able to, lifting his head up proudly. "I may not be as strong as I once was, but there is still enough life left in me to finish Grossard. No one is going to take away my joy of watching him die."

Deston wasn't sure there was enough life left in Rellik to finish the trip, let alone finish Grossard, but it wasn't his place to say anything. With a shrug of his shoulders, he turned and walked into the gateway. As soon as he stepped out on the other side, he stopped and looked out upon Tir na-nÓg. A lump formed in his throat as his gaze automatically traveled to the top of the giant tree where the crystal shrine sat. Directly below the shrine was the golden palace—his home. As he stared longingly at the palace, wondering if he'd ever see it again, Rellik came out of the gateway and butted into him. Caught off guard, Deston stumbled forward and almost fell on his face.

"Is everything all right?" Rellik asked, embarrassing Deston even more.

"Yeah, I um ..." He shook his head. "Never mind. We should get going before someone sees us," he muttered, ducking his head to hide his red cheeks. Without looking back, he scurried into the vegetation to make his way around the city.

～

Tiff zoomed over Margaux's head and then up and over the heads of the tall sunflowers.

"Stay down! Someone is going to see you," Margaux hissed telepathically for the third time. She had thought, and had hoped, the sprite would stay by Joliet's side, but Tiff either suspected Margaux was up to something or had just decided to be extra irritating today and was sticking to Margaux like peanut butter on the roof of a mouth. It was not only extremely annoying, but Margaux was beginning to worry she may not be able to get ahead of Tiff as she had planned.

Tiff looked down at Margaux, wrinkled her nose, and soared up above the flowers again.

"If you keep that up and someone sees you, the queen is going to be very angry," Margaux called out.

The mention of the queen finally brought Tiff around. She dipped down to zigzag through the flower stalks, pausing at the junction where several roads crossed. This was the spot they were to meet-up with Joliet, who, because of the horse, had had to take a route around the city to make sure she wasn't seen.

Margaux came up on the junction a second behind Tiff, transformed and batted the sprite out of the way to peer through the foliage. Due to a royal mandate that had instructed the habitants of Tir na-nÓg to stay close to the city, they had met no one on the roads up to that point, but Margaux wasn't taking any chances. She had enough troubles to contend with and didn't want to add any more on top of them.

Margaux's gaze roamed over the landscape. The roads were all clear for as far as she could see, but it didn't ease her anxiety. Time was running out for her to lose Tiff and she still didn't know how to go about doing that. Her plan would be doubly hard to implement once Joliet joined back up with them, so she knew she had to come up with something quick.

Tiff fluttered back and forth in the air, wringing her hands. "Where's the queen? I don't see her. Do you think she's been spotted?" she squeaked, visibly agitated.

Margaux scanned the sky and saw Tiff was right. There was no sign of Joliet. Her brow wrinkled in concern; then in the next instant, she perked up. This could be the just answer to her problem. A smile tugged at the corners of her mouth, but she caught it and replaced it with a frown before Tiff noticed.

"I don't know. I wouldn't have thought she'd run into anybody going over the woods, but maybe you should go check on her. It might just be that she's having trouble with the horse," Margaux whispered.

"Why are you whispering? There's no one around," Tiff stated the obvious.

"I know, but there could be ears listening just the same. Lilika says you have to be careful, because spies are everywhere," Margaux replied, hoping that would be enough to scare Tiff into going back to check on Joliet. But instead, Tiff cocked her head and narrowed her eyes.

"Are you going to wait here for us?"

"No," Margaux replied without thinking. Seeing Tiff's eyebrows shoot up, she hurriedly added, "I should probably go on ahead and make sure Deston doesn't leave before we get there. There's really no need for us all to go together. It might even be better if we don't. You know the way back to the rainforest the same as I, so you can lead Joliet there just fine. You'll probably only be a few minutes behind me."

For a moment, Margaux thought Tiff was going to object, but then the sprite's eyes crinkled up in the corners and her face lit up in a devilish grin. "Ohh, I see what's going on. You want to get to Deston first so you two can be all kissy again."

Margaux shrank back and her cheeks turned a deep shade of pink. "That is NOT it at all!"

Tiff tittered and flew up above the sunflowers. "Okay, if you say so." She cupped her hands around her mouth and whispered loudly. "Don't worry; your secret is safe with me. I won't say anything to the queen." She gave Margaux an exaggerated wink and headed toward the woods to find Joliet.

Margaux blew out her breath with a groan. *Ugh, she is impossible. She has no idea what she's talking about,* she thought, turning back to the road. With more force than was necessary, she thrust her hands through the stalks and parted them to check the way again. It was still clear, but as her gaze scanned the bushes across the road, she noticed them rustle and saw a dark shape moving between the leaves. She sucked in her breath and leaned forward, straining to see what it was. A second later,

Deston darted out of the bush and raced across an open space to the tall grasses.

Margaux's heart gave a small leap and her first thought was that the goddess had stepped in again and was helping them get away before Tiff and Joliet returned. She was so thrilled that her plan was going to work out after all; she didn't stop to think or question why Deston was there. She glanced over her shoulder to make sure Tiff was out of sight and turned back just as Rellik streaked out of the same bush Deston had and ran into the grasses.

Too stunned to move, Margaux watched the grass flutter in a wave as Deston and Rellik made their way through it. Even though she saw it with her own eyes, she couldn't believe it and her heart immediately went to battle with her mind over the obvious—Deston had lied to her and never intended to let her go with him.

"I thought you were going ahead so you could be alone with Deston?" Tiff suddenly spoke right next Margaux's ear.

Margaux's nerves were already on edge, and as she hadn't heard Tiff approach; she jumped a foot off the ground and automatically swung her arm out as she jerked around and accidently knocked Tiff back. "Oh!" she stammered, seeing Joliet helping Tiff up. "I'm so sorry. I ... I ..." Her mind was in such a jumble by what she had just seen she couldn't put the rest of her words together.

Joliet took one look at Margaux's face and knew something had happened. "What is it?"

Margaux turned and looked back at the grass on the other side of the road. So many questions were flooding into her brain, she was barely conscious Joliet and Tiff were there.

Joliet took hold of Margaux's arms and spun her back around. "What's happened? Is it Deston? Have you heard from him?" Joliet was trying to stay calm, but Margaux's blank stare was freaking her out. She looked over to see if Tiff knew what was going on, but Tiff shrugged and shook her head.

Grasping Margaux's hand in hers, Joliet closed her eyes and took two deep breaths to clear her mind. A second later a fuzzy image flashed through her mind. Her brows creased as she tried to focus in on the images that floated in and out. "Deston was here ... and Rellik too," she whispered. "You saw them. They ..." She reached for more, but something blocked it from coming through. She opened her eyes and searched Margaux's face for the answers. "He's already left to go after Mordred, hasn't he? He didn't wait for you." It was just a guess, but as a single tear drop coursed down Margaux's cheek, she knew she was right.

"He said Rellik wouldn't be back until tomorrow," Margaux stammered. "Maybe ... maybe Rellik got some new information and they couldn't wait." She was trying hard to grasp onto any explanation that would justify Deston's actions.

"He mustn't face Mordred alone. We need to go after him," Tiff squealed and started flitting back and forth in her anxious way.

Joliet shushed Tiff and turned her back to think. Seconds later, she whirled back around. "Which way did they go?"

Margaux's chest was so tight she could barely breathe, but she lifted her arm and pointed to the tall grass.

"Tiff, I want you to go back and tell Oseron that Deston and Rellik are tracking Mordred."

At the mention of Oseron, Margaux anxiously looked up, but she didn't say anything.

"Tell him to get a unit together and be ready. Margaux and I will follow Deston to see where he's going. As soon as I know the location, I'll send Oseron a message," Joliet continued.

Tiff stopped flitting and nodded her head so vigorously her whole body bounced up and down. "Yes, Your Highness. I will go faster than an arrow," she said. She gave a quick bow and zoomed off toward the palace.

"You may need to fly ahead if we lose their trail," Joliet stated, turning back to Margaux, and then had another thought. "Or do you already know which gateway they're headed to?"

Margaux was staring off into the distance, caught up in her own thoughts and didn't hear the question.

"Margaux," Joliet snapped. Margaux started and looked up. "Did Deston say what gateway they were going to take?" Joliet repeated.

Margaux blinked. There was so much going on in her mind she couldn't think.

"Look, I understand that you're upset. Deston took off without you and I know it hurts to be deceived, but you've got to move past it. I need you to help me find him before it is too late. You need to focus … Margaux!" Joliet yelled, seeing the far-a-way look in Margaux's eyes. "If this is how you're going to be, I'll send you back to the village. Is that what you want?" she added, giving Margaux's arms a soft shake to snap her out of it.

Margaux's eyes widened. "No, you can't send me back," she said, shaking her head vehemently. "I won't go. Deston needs me. Please don't send me back."

Joliet stared into Margaux's eyes, which had become bright and alert again. "I won't as long as you keep your emotions and your judgment separate. You don't know Deston's reasoning for leaving without you. There are two sides to every story. I'm sure he thought he was doing the right thing." She gave Margaux's arm a squeeze. "We need to get going before he gets too far ahead. If he makes it through the gateway before we catch up, we may lose him."

Margaux nodded in agreement and raced across the road and into the grass right behind Joliet and the winged horse. Deston and Rellik were far enough ahead she couldn't see them, but their passage had left a clear trail of trampled grass to follow.

A large black crow sitting high in a tree craned its neck to watch Margaux and Joliet run into the grass. Minutes later, when the two had become dark spots in the distance, the crow lifted into the air and sped toward the gateway, needing no trail to tell it where to go.

Chapter 14

Grossard closed his eyes and opened his mind. An image no bigger than a pinpoint immediately appeared behind his eyelids. He concentrated on the image until it expanded and gave him a clear view of a metal railing and a sea of water extending all the way to the horizon.

Ahh, Mordred ... where are you going? Do you really think keeping the book near water will ensure its safety? He stared at the wake of the boat and involuntarily shuddered. Then he smiled. Mordred had not only taken the bait, but was wearing the ring just as Grossard knew he would. *You say I'm the one without a brain, but you're the one that fell into my trap. You haven't a clue I'm following your every move and can see exactly where you are going.* His smug smile broadened. *So who's the smart one now?*

He leaned back and shifted his weight to get more comfortable. He didn't know where Mordred was headed yet and it could be a long wait before the boat docked, but there was time. The solstice lunar eclipse was still months away, and thanks to the ring, which was working perfectly, he would soon know where Mordred was keeping the book. His hands began to itch in anticipation of holding it.

∼∼

Gotland, the largest island in the Baltic Sea, was once a major Viking center of trade for Northern Europe. In present day, its long sandy beaches, rich history, and odd-shaped limestone sea stacks, which the locals call raukars, attract more tourists than trade, the majority of which was in the summer months. The rest of the year, the island was peaceful and quiet and the locals mostly had the varied countryside to themselves.

Deston stepped out of the gateway at the base of a limestone cliff on Gotland's western coast. Behind him the cliff rose forty feet straight up. In front of him there was nothing but water. A chilly wind whipped his hair across his face and a wave splashed up and over his boots, wetting them half way up his calves. He shivered and looked around. A thin strip of rocky beach was the only buffer between the cliff and the sea, and that bit of land disappeared with each new wave that rolled in. Overhead, dark ominous clouds hung low in the sky and looked ready to open up and pour down rain. Due to the cloud cover, there was no way to tell the exact time of day, but Deston could tell it was daytime.

He looked back as Rellik stepped out of the gateway, panting heavily. He could see the race to the island had taxed Rellik's strength, but he knew better than to point that out. If Rellik weren't so proud and so set on seeing this to the end, he'd suggest going on alone, but he knew what Rellik's response to that would be, so he saved his breath.

Another wave rolled in, splashing icy water up to Deston's knees. "We need to get away from the water. I think the tide is coming in." He stated that fact as much to himself as to Rellik.

Tilting his head back, he surveyed the cliff. Over the centuries, the weather and the sea had taken a toll on the limestone, carving deep channels and pockmarks into its face. It looked extremely unstable and there were numerous trails of rockslides to support his observation. More importantly, it was too steep to climb, even if Rellik was in tip-top form.

"Why don't you fly up to the top and have a look around. Find a place I can climb up. I can stand the cold, but I'd rather not stay here in the water for long," Rellik remarked.

Deston jerked around in surprise. The entire trip to the gateway Rellik had been adamant that Deston stay in human form. Deston argued he would be able to find Mordred a lot faster searching from the air, but Rellik was persistent and even made Deston swear an oath that he would not shapeshift or go near Mordred unless Rellik was with him.

Noticing Deston's shock, Rellik went on to explain, "It is a waste of time and energy to search for a way up from here. I'm not familiar with this island and neither are you. I don't want to go one way and then find out there was a quicker way." He turned his good eye on Deston. "I'm not worried you'll fly off and leave me behind. You gave me an oath that you wouldn't," he added, as a reminder of the promise.

Deston didn't bother to respond. He transformed into a kestrel in the blink of an eye and soared up into the sky. The wind carried him out over the water and he drifted on the current a few seconds before banking to the left to fly back along the cliff's edge. It never failed to amaze him the advantages he gained when he became a bird. For one, the cold no longer had an effect on him, and the enhanced sight enabled him to spot a section of the cliff a good distance down that had crumbled away. The sloping slide of dirt and rocks was the only place along the entire stretch that provided a half-way scalable way up from the water.

He squawked loudly to get Rellik's attention and dipped low over the slope to show the way. While Rellik climbed up, Deston used the time to determine which way to go from there. He circled the top of the cliff, going a little wider with each round, but the area was heavily wooded and if there was a sign of Mordred's passing, it was well hidden by the trees. In addition, a thick swirling fog was rolling in from the east and rapidly blanketing the landscape in a thick gray cloud, obscuring everything in its wake.

By the time Rellik made it to the top of the cliff, his breathing had been reduced to wheezing gasps and his legs were barely able to support him. Deston transformed back and pretended not to notice, directing his attention to the fog instead, which was moving toward the sea at an unnatural speed.

"There are a few houses and farms that way," Deston stated, tilting his head to the south. He then gestured to the north. "That way there's a city. I'm thinking we should start there. Mordred would need somewhere to stay and there would be more places in the city." He looked at Rellik to see if he agreed.

Rellik shrugged. "Seems like a logical conclusion," he said and ambled into the trees without further discussion.

The fog reached them before they had made it out of the trees. The air was heavy and pressed in on them, coating them with a fine film of moisture. It reminded Deston of the mist of Avalon that had overtaken the boat on Mirror Lake, with one major difference—this fog came with a faint scent of rotten eggs. The smell set Deston's senses tingling and he came to a halt, turning his head slowly to determine which direction the odor was coming from.

"I smell it too," Rellik remarked before Deston could comment. The wolf lifted his nose higher in the air and turned his head to the east. "He is this way," he said and loped off into the fog.

A chill that had nothing to do with the icy fog sent goose bumps racing up Deston's arms. He had spent many weeks preparing and planning for this day, but now that it was close, his old doubts returned. He just didn't know if he would be able to do what must be done, and the fact that so much was at stake and so many people were counting on him made it all the worse. He clasped the leather bag around his neck, feeling the lump of malachite that was inside, and took a deep breath. Then, gritting his teeth, he jogged off after Rellik.

They followed the scent for the next four and a half hours before the darkening sky and Rellik's fatigue forced them to stop. They spent the night in a sheltered spot within a cluster of pine trees and started out fresh at first daylight. The fog was as thick as it had been the day before and the scent of sulfur still infused the air, so they knew Mordred was still on the island.

It was not yet noon when they reached the eastern shoreline of Gotland. Rellik stood at the water's edge and stared off into the sea, the crease between his eyes deepening as he concentrated on hiding his breathing difficulties from Deston.

Deston's hand was resting on Caluvier, as it had been ever since the malachite in his leather bag had grown hot to warn him of nearby danger. He absentmindedly rubbed his fingers over the point of Caluvier's hilt as he stood stiffly beside Rellik and looked around. For as far as he could see, which wasn't far due to the heavy fog, there was nothing but pebbly sand, water, large rocks and the tall, strange shaped raukars. He breathed out a frustrated sigh. They had just traversed the width of the island and were no closer to finding Mordred than before. If the fog continued to stay with them as it had the whole way across the island, he wasn't sure they would ever be able to find the sorcerer.

He was just about to voice his concerns to Rellik when a strong wind blew in from the sea and swept the fog back from the shore along with it. For a few seconds Deston had a clear view of the area. His gaze darted from one raukar to the next, but the fog settled back in before he made it beyond them. Fortunately, the gusts of wind continued to blow in at regular intervals and each time it would push the fog back. After several gusts, he managed to piece together a good idea of their surroundings.

They were standing on a rocky beach on one side of a small bay that was rounded like the bottom of a cup. On the opposite side, the shoreline tapered to a point that extended out into the sea. Several yards off the point, one tall sea stack stood alone in the water. As Deston's gaze swept over that stack, he noticed a dark shape on the top of it. The shape kind of looked like a person sitting there, but the fog moved back in too quickly and swallowed up the stack before he could be sure.

Ahh, stupid fog. I wish you'd just go away, he thought. Immediately, the fog lifted, as if obeying his command, and there was nothing obstructing his view of the raukar and the person sitting on top—a person with pale blonde hair.

Mordred? The name slammed into Deston's brain like a cannonball, and for a moment, he couldn't breathe. Then, as quickly as if a switch had been flicked on, a dark rage engulfed him and his hand tightened around Caluvier. A burning desire to make Mordred pay for Keir's death took over his mind and only his subconscious picked up on the absence of Mordred's guards.

Nudging Rellik in the shoulder, Deston's hand shook as he pointed to the raukar. Rellik followed Deston's finger and his eyes narrowed, but he showed no other reaction. Deston, on the other hand, could hardly contain his emotions. He was near to bursting with a need to do something and small ominous voices inside his head egged him on with whispers of, "Kill him. Kill him."

Without a thought of the powers Mordred possessed or the danger he would put himself in, Deston dropped his backpack on the ground, drew Caluvier and took a step toward the bay as if in a trance. Before he could take another step, Rellik's paw slammed into his back. Caught off guard, Deston wasn't prepared to catch himself and went down hard, face planting on the wet, rocky ground. He jerked his head up, spit the sand out of his mouth and started to get back to his feet, but Rellik pushed him down again and placed two front paws on his back.

"Get off me," Deston sputtered, barely able to speak with Rellik's weight pressing him down.

"I never thought I would see a fae who was so anxious to kill. I won't allow you to ruin this for me," Rellik snarled, shifting more of his weight to his front legs. Deston squirmed wildly, trying to knock Rellik off, but Rellik had the advantage and Deston only swatted the air.

A wave rolled in at that moment and washed up over Deston. The shock of the ice-cold water snapped him back to his senses. He instantly went still. A second later, he shook his head, flinging water droplets in all directions. "Get off me," he growled once again.

"Not until you give me your word that you'll not do anything rash," Rellik replied.

Deston gritted his teeth, but as Rellik's claws and weight were becoming painful, he finally relented. "Okay, just get off."

"Say it," Rellik ordered. "I want to hear you say you will not go after Mordred if I let you up."

Deston curled his fingers into the lumpy sand. "I promise I won't go after Mordred. Now get off me!" he snarled.

Rellik hesitated another moment before stepping back, but he stayed close and kept a wary eye on Deston.

Deston scrambled to his feet with a groan. He gave Rellik a piercing glare as he brushed the sand from his tunic and turned his back, clenching his fists spasmodically as the last of the dark thoughts drifted out of his mind. He stared out over the water, taking in long, deep breaths until the urge to kill was gone and an empty feeling was all that remained.

It took some time before his humiliation faded. "So what's the plan? Are we going to sneak up on him or wait until he comes off of that rock?" he finally asked.

When Rellik didn't reply, Deston looked over his shoulder to repeat the question, but Rellik was gone. Cursing under his breath, Deston whirled around. "You stopped me from going after him so you could go after him yourself," he hissed under his breath, noticing the giant footsteps Rellik had left in the sand and mud.

With another curse, he sprinted off, following the trail to a cluster of tall bushes. He didn't slow down as he rounded the greenery and yelped in surprise as he almost tripped over Rellik, who had made himself a bed on a small patch of grass.

Stumbling to a stop, Deston gawked in disbelief. "What are you doing?" His voice cracked, but he plowed on. "I thought you wanted to get Mordred and the information? He's sitting out there all by himself, so what are you doing lying around here?"

Rellik rested his nose on his paws and let out a long sigh. "I have every intention of getting the information, have no fear about that. I also intend to rest and regain my strength first. The hard part is done ... we've located him. If he leaves that rock, he'll not go far and it will be easy enough to find him again." He looked up through his brow. "You look as if you could use some rest yourself. I suggest you take advantage of what little time there is to do that. You'll want to be sharp when the time comes to make our move."

"But—"

"I guarantee you Mordred *is not* going anywhere. Get some rest and remember your promise," Rellik cut him off and closed his eyes to end the conversation.

Deston opened his mouth, but he was at a loss of what to say. He stared down at Rellik for a long moment and then walked away. Too wired to rest as Rellik suggested, he picked out a spot behind a tree next to one of the larger raukars and watched the sorcerer as the sky darkened even more. A steady wind held the fog at bay and he had no trouble seeing Mordred sitting there all alone, staring out at the Baltic Sea as if he had no other care in the world.

Hours later, Deston was still there with his eyes fixed on Mordred.

"I told you our sorcerer wouldn't be going anywhere, didn't I?" A gravelly voice said from behind him.

Deston hadn't heard Rellik approach and automatically swung out as he whirled around. Rellik was quick and ducked to miss the blow that would have hit him in the throat.

Deston's eyes bulged when he saw who it was and he gulped back his racing heart. "What are you doing sneaking up on me like that?" he asked through clenched teeth.

Growing tired of Deston's accusations, Rellik snapped out, "I did not sneak up on you. I simply walked up. Your distraction has nothing to do with me, but it does lead me to remind you this is not Tir na-nOg. No white deer is going to come and save you here. This is hostile territory and you had better start staying alert if you want to survive."

The reproach brought two pink splotches to Deston's cheeks and he inwardly cringed. He turned his back so Rellik couldn't see his discomfort and glared out at Mordred. "He's just been sitting there. He hasn't even moved."

Rellik's gaze moved to the small figure on the top of the stack. "He knows we're here."

Deston jerked back to Rellik. "What? How could he know that?"

"He just does. Trust me."

Deston looked back at the raukar. "If that's true, why hasn't he come after us?"

Rellik squinted as he pondered the answer. "That's the question, isn't it? I guess he has something else planned." He eyed Deston with his one good eye. "And what do you have planned, young prince?"

Deston fingered the small bag tied to his belt. While he waited for Rellik to wake up he had poured some of the dirt from the bow into the bag to make it easily accessible for when he got close to Mordred. "I'm going to use this dirt from King Arthur's grave and take away his magic. Then I'm going to tie him up and make him talk."

Rellik let out a loud guffaw, which quickly turned into a hacking cough. His knees wobbled and his body rattled as he tried to suck in a breath. Deston pressed his lips together and his dimple sunk deeper into his cheek as he glared at the wolf.

"That's your plan?" Rellik finally asked after the coughing fit subsided. He swiped his paw across his mouth to remove the spittle hanging off his lower jaw. "And how do you propose to get close enough to him to throw that dirt?"

The corner of Rellik's muzzle lifted in amusement as he watched Deston blanch. "Ahh, I see. You haven't thought that far ahead, have you?" With a sigh, he turned and started down the path that led around the bay.

"Hey, wait. Where are you going?" Deston called out after him.

"I guess I'm going to divert Mordred's attention so you can get close."

Deston started after him. "How are you going to do that?"

"I'm going to go talk to him so you can fly in behind him. Unless you have a better plan," Rellik replied without looking back.

Deston came to a stop. *This is crazy,* he thought and looked up at the sky. *"Keir, I hope you're close by, 'cause I think I'm gonna need your help."* He fingered the bag of dirt on his belt, blew out a breath and bolted after the wolf.

Chapter 15

Oseron and a battalion of twelve men arrived at the junction of roads where Tiff had left Joliet and Margaux. From the minute Tiff told him what was going on, he'd been berating himself for not assigning a guard to Joliet. She had said she was going after Deston, but he never imagined she would be foolish enough to go anywhere near Mordred without backup. He felt helpless standing around and waiting for information, knowing that the two people he loved most in the world were in mortal danger; and for the first time in his life, he was actually worried.

"Oseron, we've followed Deston to the gateway that leads to Gotland." Joliet's voice suddenly broke through his thoughts. *"He has already gone through. Margaux and I are heading in now. I'll let you know more as soon as—"* her words abruptly cut off.

"Joliet? Joliet!" His jaw clenched when no answer came back. "I just heard from Joliet. She is following Deston into Gotland," he said to Torren, who was standing beside him.

"It is good to know where they are headed," Torren replied.

"Yes, but her message cut out before she finished," Oseron added.

"So Mordred does have communications blocked, as we expected he would."

Oseron and Torren had talked about the possibility of not being able to communicate, but talking about it and knowing it as fact were two different things, especially when Joliet and Deston were alone in the lower realm.

"It is fortunate for us that Mordred chose Gotland. The island is not large. We should be able to track Deston and Joliet down quickly once we get there," Torren added.

"True, but only if we get to them before Mordred realizes they are there. Contact every soldier available who is in the vicinity and send them to Gotland."

Oseron didn't wait for Torren to acknowledge the order, but transformed into a falcon and sped off toward the gateway into Gotland.

"Go with the king. I will catch up," Torren ordered the men, who immediately obeyed without question.

~~

Tiff grumbled her frustration under her breath as she flew back and forth in front of the palace entrance, kicking the banners that hung on each side of the wide double doors each time she passed by. She was passing in front of the doorway for her twelfth time when Lilika walked out of the palace and the two nearly collided.

"Whoa, Tiff, what are you doing? There are other people around here, you know. You should watch where you're going," Lilika scolded, rearing back to avoid getting smacked in the face.

Tiff mumbled a quick apology and continued across the courtyard. It was obvious she was upset about something, but Lilika had no desire to get drawn into the sprite's business. Smiling to herself, Lilika walked on; sure it was nothing more than a minor disagreement.

"He had no idea what was going on until *I* brought him the news. That alone should have been reason enough to let me go along," Tiff grumbled as she passed Lilika once again and continued on.

Lilika's gaze followed Tiff across the courtyard, her interest suddenly aroused by that small snippet she had heard. She waited for Tiff to start back her way and as Tiff drew near, she reached out and caught the sprite around the waist.

"Who were you talking about a second ago, and what news did you bring?" she asked, a touch of amusement creeping into her voice at the sullen look on Tiff's face.

Tiff wiggled in Lilika's grip, but once she realized Lilika was not going to let her go until she answered, she crossed her arms over her chest and glowered. "The king, that's who. If it wasn't for me, he wouldn't know Deston and Rellik are going after Mordred. He should have—"

Lilika jerked to attention and with lightning speed, clamped her finger over Tiff's mouth to keep the sprite from saying more as she quickly scanned the courtyard to see if anyone had heard. A few people were milling about, but none seemed to be paying attention to her or to Tiff. Tiff twisted Lilika's finger and pulled it off her mouth, but before she could say anything else, Lilika shushed her and stuck her under her cloak, then rushed into the palace. As soon as they were in the privacy of Lilika's chambers, she pulled Tiff out.

"How did you get this information?" Lilika asked.

Tiff's face was red with indignation. She clamped her lips together, lifted her nose in the air and turned her head away, refusing to say a word.

"Tiff, come on. I'm sorry if I offended you, but this is important … especially if it has to do with Deston. Please tell me what you know."

Tiff looked at Lilika out of the corner of her eye. "If I tell you, are you going to go after them?"

"I don't know what you're talking about, but if Deston's in danger … yes, I will go and do what I can to help. It is my duty."

Tiff instantly puffed up. "It is my duty too! I will tell you, but only if you swear to take me with you," she said, suddenly realizing she had a bargaining chip she could use.

Lilika's eyes darkened. "You know I can go to Joliet and have her command you to tell me what you know."

"No, you can't," Tiff replied with a smirk. "The queen and Margaux have followed Deston. They think Rellik is leading him into a trap. I think so too."

"They've *what*?" Lilika yelled. Tiff shrank back and her smug look slipped. "I'm commander of the queen's guard and if this has to do with the queen's safety, you best tell me what's going on, and I mean right now."

Realizing she had pushed too far, Tiff quickly relayed all that she knew. When she finished her tale, Lilika let her go and stormed to the closet. Without saying a word, she yanked her gown over her head and began changing into her traveling gear. Tiff stayed out of the way and watched, but it wasn't until Lilika began hauling out her chainmail that she realized what Lilika was doing.

"His Lordship told you to stay in the palace and take care of the baby. I heard him say so myself." Lilika shot Tiff a frosty look, but didn't stop what she was doing. "I understand how you feel honor bound to do your duty—I feel the same way. If you insist on going after them, then you must take me with you. I can cover your back. You know I can do it. I've already proven that to you."

Lilika stopped and looked over at the sprite, remembering how Tiff had taken on an ogre singlehandedly. However, that was one incident and Tiff was not trained or qualified to go up against a mad man like Mordred. "Yes, you have proven you're strong, but I'm sorry, you aren't trained for battle."

Tiff rushed up, hovering inches in front of Lilika's nose. "But I'm fast. I promise I won't get in the way. I could be the eyes in the back of your head. You'll need that to keep the baby safe." She saw Lilika's resolve soften at the mention of the baby and hurriedly added, "I give you my oath that I'll protect Macaria." She placed her right fist over her heart as she spoke. "From this point forward, my life is dedicated to keeping her safe. I will allow no harm to come her way as long as I am around."

At that moment, the baby kicked Lilika in the side, right in the spot where she'd been stabbed. Lilika gasped and hunched over, grabbing her stomach as the pain took her breath away.

"My lady," Tiff bounced around nervously, not sure what to do. "Do you want me to fetch you the healer?" She headed toward the door without waiting for Lilika's reply.

"NO ... wait," Lilika gasped just as Tiff was about to go through the door.

Lilika breathed in several long, deep breaths and then slowly straightened her back. Macaria's little foot pushed against her side again, showing a clear imprint of five tiny toes. Lilika winced; then squared her shoulders and lifted her chin. There was a fine sheen of sweat across her nose and her face was pale.

"It seems I almost forgot my own promise to keep Macaria safe. I shouldn't have to be reminded, but I guess ..." Her words trailed off. She took a deep breath and let out a heavy sigh. "I made that promise to Keir. I almost failed him once and that put our daughter in peril. Now that he's gone, I'm the only one left to protect her. It hasn't been easy for me." Her eyes were glassy as she looked back at Tiff. "Thank you for your oath ... I accept. It is a relief to know Macaria has more than one guardian watching out for her." Seeing Tiff's face light up, Lilika rapidly added, "However ... if I let you go with me, you must promise that you will do whatever I say. Even if I ask you stay to back and not get involved. Agreed?"

Tiff bobbed up and down in her excitement. "YES ... I won't get in your way. You won't even know I'm there."

Lilika forced a smile and then bent down and collected her weapons. "We'll exit through the side entrance. You can distract the guard while I sneak out. We'll meet up at the crossroads."

She paused at the door and stuck her head out to make sure the hall was clear. *"Be good little one, there is work to be done,"* she said silently to her child as she rubbed her hand over her belly. As if Macaria understood, she pulled her foot back and released the pressure on Lilika's side.

"Good girl," Lilika whispered, and with a smile, stepped out into the hallway.

Chapter 16

Deston and Rellik had already passed through the gateway by the time Joliet and Margaux reached it, but there was no mistaking it was the right one. The trail of trampled grass led straight up to the entrance. Unfortunately, their luck didn't hold out and once they stepped through into the lower realm the trail was gone. Joliet stayed optimistic, though, and held onto the hope they'd be able to catch up, for she knew Deston and Rellik would have to travel on foot since Rellik couldn't fly, and both she and Margaux could. However, as soon as she took to the sky and saw nothing but a thick gray carpet below her, she realized they just weren't going to catch a break.

By Joliet's calculations, Deston had gone through the gateway approximately ten minutes before her and Margaux, which equated to almost a full day in the lower realm. A day was more than enough time for Deston to find trouble, but her gut feeling told her he had not come to any harm. That, however, could all change in a heartbeat. There was a hint of sulfur in the air and the unnatural fog that hugged the land like a second skin confirmed Mordred was on the island, which made it imperative they find Deston quickly. Joliet was counting on the winged horse to help them do just that, as the horse could cover ground a lot faster than a person on foot. With that advantage, she thought they would be able to make up some of the time they had lost.

Joliet and Margaux started out riding double on the back of the winged horse, but when they came to a pasture with several horses grazing in it, they decided it would be better to borrow one of the horses and split up to cover more ground. Margaux had taken the north end of Gotland and Joliet had taken the south.

Joliet was conscious of each minute that was slipping by and her anxiety level increased with each one. After several unsuccessful attempts at getting a message off to Oseron, she came to the realization that Mordred had put up a spell to block communications. She didn't know if that was because Mordred knew Deston and they were on the island, or if he always took that kind of precaution, but either way, it was a hindrance to their search. Thankfully, she had sent Oseron a message before stepping through the gateway, so he at least knew they were in Gotland. He wouldn't arrive for some time yet, though, due to the time difference between realms, so it was still up to her and Margaux to find Deston before Mordred did.

She fretted over the fact that she had no idea which direction Deston had gone and she knew she was wasting valuable time. She had yet to find a single trace of his trail, and just as she was contemplating turning back, a local stopped her to inquire about her unusually large horse. In their brief conversation, he mentioned it must be the season for giant animals, for he'd seen an abnormally large dog with a boy the day before, heading east. Joliet had no doubt that boy and dog was Deston and Rellik. Overcome with relief at finally having a direction to go, she jumped off the horse and startled the man with a big hug. Then with renewed hope, she whipped the horse around to the east and rode off.

It was a little unnerving for Joliet, riding through the fog and not being able to see where she was going, but after hours of isolation, she had grown accustom to the silence; and when Margaux's voice broke through her thoughts, she was so startled, she unintentionally pulled back hard on the reins. The horse reared up, its front legs kicking the air, and it was all she could do to stay on its back. It took her several minutes to get the horse settled down before she could answer back.

"Margaux, is that you? Where are you?" Joliet asked breathlessly, completely forgetting that the island was under a communication-blocking spell and Margaux should not have been able to communicate with her.

"I've found them," Margaux's voice repeated. *"I'm in the woods near Ardre luke. It's part of the south section of the wall of Torsburgen close to the eastern coast. Follow the directional signs to Kräklingbo and you'll be able to find the way from there."*

"I'll find it. I'm on my way. Don't engage them. Wait for me," Joliet replied and spurred the horse into a full gallop.

∾

A natural cliff, rising thirty feet in certain areas, cordoned off the north, east and west side of the ancient castle plateau of Torsburgen. On the south side where Ardre luke was located, a two-kilometer long wall of limestone completed the fortification. After thousand years, the wall still stood, but not a single stone of the castle remained.

Joliet had no trouble finding Ardre luke, for as Margaux said, there were signs pointing the way, but locating Margaux was proving to be a different story. The fog had become quite a bit denser and visibility was down to a few feet. She followed the mound of grass covered limestone, shifting uneasily on the horse's back. There was something in the air that didn't feel right. The horse seemed to sense it too and its gait was a little more hesitant.

"Margaux, I'm here. Where are you?" Joliet called out for the second time.

When she received no answer, she pulled the horse to a halt and twisted in her seat to look around. The fog instantly wrapped her in its clammy clutches, shutting the rest of the world out. From the horse's back, she could no longer see to the ground and the heaviness of the air made it hard to breathe. Her stomach clenched in a tight knot as she swung her leg over and slid off the horse. She shrugged the bow off her back and pulled an arrow as a precaution as she walked beside the horse, bending over every few steps to study the ground.

"Margaux," she called out loud and waited. No reply came, but the horse suddenly whinnied and shied back several steps. "Shhh, I know," she whispered, placing a hand on its neck. "I'm uneasy too. It—" Her words abruptly cut off at the sound of crunching gravel. She looked from one side to the other, trying to detect the source, but with the fog it was like trying to see through a gray wall.

All of a sudden, she got a whiff of a foul scent of decay. At the same moment, the horse shook its head, snorted, and lifted its feet nervously. Joliet ran her hand up its neck soothingly, but it sidestepped and bolted for the trees.

"Come back," Joliet called out and started after the horse, but several dark shapes stepped out of the fog and blocked her way. Taken by surprise, she came to a halt and before she realized what was happening, rough hands with pointy, claw-like nails grabbed her arms from behind. In the next instant, a gunnysack, smelling of dirt and potatoes, slipped down over her head.

"Let me go," Joliet screamed.

Her unseen attacker's answer was to pull the sack tighter around her face and her voice was cut off as moldy soil filled her mouth. She gasped for air and kicked out, wrestling to get free, but the hands holding her were inhumanly strong. Another set of hands took hold of her legs and wrapped a cord around her ankles and then around her wrists, binding her hands behind her back.

"Oseron, I've been taken. You must hurry," she called out telepathically, praying that he was already on the island and by some

miracle could hear her. *"I'm by Ardre luke in Torsburgen. Come find me."*

Joliet could hear voices, but they were low and guttural and she couldn't make out what they were saying through the sack. Seconds later, she was roughly lifted up, as if she weighed no more than a feather, and thrown over a boney shoulder. She coughed and tried to shift her position to relieve the pressure on her chest that prevented her from filling her lungs, but whoever had her had a tight hold on her legs and she couldn't move but a fraction of an inch. She heard the sound of more crunching gravel; then something brushed by her arm and they started moving.

Her captor's gate was jerky, like that of an animal walking on two legs and each bounce forced out the little bit of air she could get into her lungs. Within a few minutes, she was lightheaded not only from the lack of air, but also from the smell of moldy potatoes mixed in with the putrid smell of rancid blood. She fought to stay conscious and just as she was about to lose that battle, her captor came to a stop. With a grunt, she was dumped unceremoniously onto the ground and the bag was yanked off her head. She gasped in a full breath of fresh, salty air and shook her head to get the hair out of her eyes. Her eyes had not had a chance to readjust when someone pulled her arms behind her back and her wrists were tethered around the trunk of a tree. Hearing a rustling noise to her left, she turned her head and saw Margaux sitting a few feet away. Margaux's face was pale and her eyes were filled with concern.

"Did they hurt you?" Margaux whispered.

"I'm fine," Joliet whispered back and quickly scanned the group of creatures surrounding them. There were seven cucubuths and four golems, but no sign of Deston or Rellik, which gave her a seed of hope.

"I tried sending you a message when they caught me to let you know, and to tell you to stay clear, but you never answered. I'm sorry you didn't get the message," Margaux said.

Joliet frowned and looked back at Margaux. "I did get a message from you, or it sounded like you. It told me to meet you at Ardre luke."

Margaux vehemently shook her head. "No, I didn't send that. It wasn't me."

Joliet pressed her lips together and swallowed back her exasperation. "Of course it wasn't, and it's my own fault for listening. I should have verified who it was. I was just ..." Her words trailed off as she suddenly realized what had happened. "It was Mordred. He sent that message to lead me into a trap. He also has communications blocked, so he must have known the minute we got here." Her heart suddenly clenched. "And if he was able to detect our arrival, he surely has to know Deston is here too. Did you find any of Deston's tracks?"

"No. But maybe Mordred hasn't found him yet." Margaux tried to sound positive, but her voice wavered a little too much to make it believable.

Joliet started to answer; then stopped as one of the cucubuths' heads jerked up. A second later, the same cucubuth shouted out an order to the others and turned to Joliet and Margaux.

"I hope you're right, and I think we're about to find out," Joliet answered under her breath as the creature came toward them.

The cucubuth sliced through the rope that had them pinned to the tree and roughly hauled Margaux to her feet. She tried to hold back her cry of agony, but a small squeal escaped as his sharp claws pierced her skin. Joliet was also yanked up, and before either of them could rub away the soreness, their wrists were bound together in the front of them. A long piece of rope was then attached as a lead. The cucubuth tugged the two prisoners along with him and walked to another on horseback.

As Margaux stumbled forward, she gave Joliet a quick sidelong glance. "I have a way to contact Oseron," she whispered in a rush. "He gave me and Deston a medallion that can contact him if we get into trouble. It will send out a message even if there's a spell blocking communication. But it needs to be held against a tree trunk for it to work. It's in the pouch on my belt and I think I can get to it if you can create a distraction."

Joliet's expression didn't change, nor did she look over at Margaux. She just gave a slight nod of her head to let Margaux know she understood.

The rider took the lead rope and looked over his shoulder with a vicious grin, showing his long, needle-sharp teeth. Then with a kick, he set the horse into motion. The rope pulled tight, leaving Joliet and Margaux no option but to follow along.

Joliet staggered forward a few steps and then pulled back; digging her heals into the dirt. The horse felt the resistance and came to a stop. Without bothering to turn around, the rider gave the rope a hard jerk and lifted Joliet clean off her feet. She flew forward into Margaux and they both went down.

"Hurry," Joliet whispered as she lay on top of Margaux, making no attempt to get up.

The cucubuth on the horse barked an order to one of the others on foot. That cucubuth took hold of the back of Joliet's tunic and lifted her up, placing her on her feet. He then grabbed Margaux up with his other hand.

"You walk or you be dragged," the cucubuth growled, thrusting his red, devil-like face into Joliet's.

Joliet lifted her chin regally and glared back, showing no fear. The cucubuth's lip lifted in a sneer as he raised his hand to strike her, but before he could, the rider yelled out a harsh command. With a snarl, the cucubuth's hand dropped to his side. He gave a hard tug on the ropes, cinching them painfully tight around Joliet and Margaux's wrists and went back to the front without saying anything more.

"Did you get it?" Joliet whispered as they started up again.

"Yes," Margaux confirmed. "But the medallion has to be held against a tree trunk for it to work."

They were traveling through a heavily wooded area, so finding a tree to use was not an issue, but stopping long enough to hold it against the trunk was. As they trudged along, the two threw ideas back and forth on how to get the cucubuths to stop long enough for Margaux to send a message. It was Joliet that finally came up with a plan that she hoped would work.

"We both need to walk faster and pull up as much slack in the rope as we can. When we get to a narrow spot, you run to the left and wrap the rope around a tree trunk. I'll do the same on the right. You may only have a few seconds to get a message off. Will that be enough?" Joliet asked.

"I don't know. Oseron never said anything about how long it would take to get through to him. But it sounds like a good plan," Margaux replied.

They both increased their pace, pulling up the excess rope as they went, and Joliet stretched her neck to keep an eye on the path ahead. When she saw an area coming up where the trees closed in on both sides, she gave Margaux the signal and waited until they were in just the right spot before calling out, "Now!" Joliet ducked to the right at the same time Margaux dodged to the left. The rope was only long enough to wrap around the tree once, but it was enough to pull the horse up short. Margaux wasted no time pressing the acorn-shaped medallion against the trunk.

"*Oseron, we've been captured by Mordred's guards. There are eleven of them. We're on the eastern side of the island, near a place called Torsburgen. We haven't found Deston yet and haven't been able to make contact with him, because Mordred has blocked communications. So we don't know if Deston has been taken or not. I'll try to get another message to you if we hear anything more. Just hurry and get here, and watch out for Mordred's guards, because there might be others on the island.*"

Margaux held the medallion pressed against the tree trunk until one of the cucubuths grabbed her by the hair and tore her away. He yelled something unintelligible to the others as he roughly dragged her to a horse and threw her over its back like a sack of potatoes, her feet dangling off one side and her arms over the other. They hoisted Joliet up next to her in the same awkward position. Then their two lead ropes were passed under the horse's belly, stretching Margaux and Joliet's arms under the horse, and the rope was tied around their ankles to ensure they could not throw themselves off and cause further delays.

Margaux turned her head and looked sideways at Joliet. She knew better than to say anything in front of the cucubuths, but her expression showed her uncertainty. Joliet gave a weak smile back in understanding. They had done what they could. Their fate and Deston's now rested in the hands of the gods.

Chapter 17

Oseron's thoughts were on getting to Gotland and finding Joliet and Deston, and he didn't pay attention to the extra falcon or the tiny sprite riding on its back, tailing a short distance behind his men. He did not miss the high frequency murmur of the trees calling out to him, though, and he came instantly alert. It had been a long time since he had received a message through the tree medallions and until he heard the persistent ringing, he had forgotten he had given one to Deston and Margaux. He thanked the gods one of the two had thought to use it and went into a dive for the ground.

Torren, who had been flying at Oseron's flank, saw Oseron streak downward and followed. *"What news?"* he asked as his feet touched down.

Oseron lifted his wing to silence Torren. Every bird and animal in the vicinity, even the wind, went perfectly still as Oseron closed his eyes and listened to Margaux's message, which had traveled through the roots of the tree into the earth to get to him.

When the message finished, he looked up at the men who had gathered around him and opened up a channel to speak to them all at once. *"Joliet and Margaux have been captured."* His tone had a hard edge to it. *"The message was short, but Margaux was able to tell me they are being held near Torsburgen. I believe you are all familiar with the location and the woods in that area. That's where we'll start. Margaux has also confirmed Mordred is on the island and communications are blocked, as we suspected. Eleven of Mordred's guards are holding Joliet and Margaux. I am sure there are more scattered around the island, so stay extra alert and be prepared to fight if we must."* His gaze roamed over the group of men. This was always the hardest part for him— knowing he was leading them into danger and there was a possibility that some of them wouldn't make it back. *"First priority is to rescue Joliet, Deston and Margaux and get them back to Tir na-nÓg. As soon as they are safely away, we'll go after Mordred. I do not want him harmed. He has information we can use."* He struck his heart with his right fist. *"Go with speed and may the gods be with you."* Without further ado, he lifted into the air and raced toward the gateway.

~~

To stay out of sight, Lilika had perched in a tree several yards from where Oseron and the others had landed. As she wasn't officially part of the group, she wasn't privy to what Oseron was saying, but she could tell by the men's reaction they had received some jarring news.

"Something has happened," Tiff stated, coming to the same conclusion.

Lilika didn't reply as she was fully immersed in thoughts of how she could find out what was going on. She had already tried reaching out to Margaux and Joliet, but neither of them was answering.

As the falcons took to the sky and sped off, she flapped her wings and trailed behind. She could sense something was seriously wrong and it exasperated her to be left out. Macaria, feeling Lilika's tension, kicked out with her own frustrations. Lilika winced at the jar to her side, but kept going.

"Shhh, little one," she cooed silently, *"now is not the time."* Macaria ignored her mother and continued kicking against the walls of her womb as if she was practicing karate. *"Yes ... I know. You're bored and you want something to do, but please—"* Lilika's words trailed off as a thought suddenly came to her. Macaria was the perfect excuse to use to contact Torren. The second Lilika latched onto the idea, Macaria went perfectly still.

"You little devil ... you planted that idea in my head, didn't you?" Lilika smiled a knowing smile. *"You are becoming more like your father every day."*

In response, Macaria turned over and a gush of tears sprang to Lilika's eyes. She never imagined she'd lose Keir and it was still hard to believe he was gone. When he left, he took a piece of her heart with him and she knew that hollowness would remain with her for as long as she lived. But each time Macaria kicked or moved, it reminded her that Keir was still with her and always would be watching out for her and their daughter.

"So let's try this idea of yours," she said and opened the channel to Torren. *"Torren, Macaria is being overly active today. I think she is tired of sitting around. Do you have something I could do ... something to take my mind off this drudgery?"*

Several long seconds later, Torren's rushed voice answered back. *"I'm sorry Lilika, but I don't have time right now. Why don't you check with the palace guard?"*

"Oh, is something wrong?" Lilika asked innocently.

"No ... Joliet has run into a bit of a problem is all and I need to help her out," he answered after another long pause.

"Isn't Margaux with Joliet?" Lilika made a concerted effort to keep the panic out of her voice.

"She is, and I'm sure we'll be able to resolve the issue quickly. You have nothing to worry about. But like I said earlier, I need to attend to this matter and I don't have time to talk." He tuned out before she could say anything more.

Lilika had too much experience to buy Torren's attempted reassurance. *"Joliet and Margaux are in trouble,"* she told Tiff and gave a strong push down with her wings to increase her speed.

"Oh, no, it was *a trap then,"* Tiff cried out.

"I think you might be right this time," Lilika replied. *"But I don't think Mordred will hurt them. He'll want to use them to draw Oseron in,"* Lilika added and then took in a shuddering breath, hoping she was right.

Chapter 18

Mordred looked out at the sea from the top of the raukar. He'd been sitting in the same position for hours, still his spine remained rigid and no part of him moved. Not even his cloak or a single strand of his hair stirred with the great bursts of wind that blew in from the sea. It was almost as if he'd become part of the stone.

"So you came after all," Mordred said calmly. He had not looked around, but he knew Rellik was standing on the point of land five yards behind him. "And I see you did bring me a present as you said you would."

"Yes, the boy accompanied me and the girl followed as I suspected she would," Rellik replied.

Mordred's body gave a barely noticeable twitch. "The boy, you say?" He'd been informed that Margaux and Joliet had arrived on the island, but this was the first he heard of Deston.

Mordred was facing out to sea, so Rellik couldn't see the shock on the sorcerer's face, and by the time Mordred unfolded his legs, stood, and turned, a maniacal smile had replaced it. He adjusted the pair of glasses up on his nose and looked down on Rellik standing alone on the cliff.

"You don't look well," Mordred stated, and then his gaze swept the area. "Where is the boy? I thought you said you had brought him with you. Are you trying to pull some kind of trick on me?" For just a second his face darkened, and then he brightened and smiled. "Or is it supposed to be a surprise?" he whispered and giggled like a young girl. "You know how I love surprises." He clapped his hands together in glee and pretended to be unaware of the kestrel swooping down behind him.

The second Deston landed on the sea stack behind Mordred, he shifted back and his hand went to Caluvier's hilt. He was close enough to end Mordred's life at that very moment. His pulse raced as his hand tightened on the sword, but somehow logic made its way through his dark thoughts and he realized if he killed Mordred, it would reduce his chances of ever finding Grossard. Reluctantly, his hand moved off the sword and to the bag attached to his belt.

At that precise moment, Mordred vanished from the raukar. In the next instant, he was standing next to Rellik and had a dagger pressed to Rellik's throat.

"Once again it seems you have stepped into a situation you aren't fully prepared to handle. Did you actually believe I'd be that easy to sneak up on?" Mordred's eyes gleamed with insanity as he addressed Deston.

Deston's hand closed around the bag and he took a step forward. Mordred responded by pulling Rellik's head farther back and pressing the knife in, drawing a fine line of blood across Rellik's taut neck. "Tsk, tsk. Are you that anxious to cause the death of another one of your allies?"

Deston went pale and his hand froze around the bag. His eyes remained locked on Mordred, but he could still see the fur on Rellik's neck turning dark with blood in his peripheral vision.

"Ah look at that, Rellik ... and you thought he didn't care," Mordred chortled.

"You seem awfully anxious to get to that bag there on your belt," Mordred added to Deston. "What do you have in there? Could it possibly be ... dirt?"

Deston's pupils dilated and Mordred's smile vanished.

"I suggest you drop that bag on the ground at your feet unless you want me to finish this," Mordred added.

"I'll put the bag down, but only if you give me your word you won't use magic," Deston countered.

Mordred gave a snort. "Not use magic? Silly boy, why on earth would I want to do that?"

"Because we're not here for you. We want Grossard. Just tell us where we can find him and we'll leave. There'll be no harm done."

"Oh ... is that all?" Mordred snickered and paused. "Okay, let's just say, hypothetically of course, I give you this information. What are you going to do with it?" He was purposely taunting Deston and enjoying every minute of it.

"I'm going to take care of Grossard so he won't be able to hurt anyone else." Deston answered simply.

Mordred couldn't hold his amusement back another second. "You're going to take care of Grossard? All by yourself?" He threw his head back and let out a hearty laugh. "You really are naïve." He looked down at Rellik. "Did you hear that? The boy is going to *take care* of Grossard, just like that."

He turned back to Deston. "I must say, your confidence and fortitude is to be applauded, even if it is a bit misguided."

With a small twitch of Mordred's fingers, the bag of dirt on Deston's belt came loose and dropped. Lightning quick, Deston swooped down and grabbed it up before it hit the ground. In the next instant, he was standing behind Mordred on the rocky shore.

Mordred twirled around and yelled out, "*Ostende te!*"

At his command, the fog parted, showing a group standing a short distance away on the top of another very tall sea stack. Deston did a double take and his heart clenched as he looked upon Joliet and Margaux, bound and gagged and standing between two red-skinned creatures.

"Mom," Deston gasped and started forward, but Mordred held up his hand.

Instantly, two golems jumped forward, grabbed Joliet and Margaux by the back of their necks and held them over the edge of the raukar so that their feet dangled above the ragged rocks two stories below. Deston gulped in a breath and froze.

"I'm glad to see you're beginning to understand the situation here. If you'd like to see your mother and girlfriend shattered on those rather nasty looking rocks down there, go ahead and open that bag." Mordred rose up on his tiptoes and stretched his neck as if looking over the edge of a cliff, even though he was too far away. "They could, I suppose, survive the impact and maybe only break their spine—be paralyzed for the rest of their lives. There is that possibility. But I, for one, would not want to take that bet." He smiled as he watched the variety of emotions play across Deston's face.

"Put down the bag ... *now*," Mordred reiterated.

Deston's eyes locked with Margaux's. *"What are you doing here? Why couldn't you just stay in the city like I asked?"*

"I suggest you do as Mordred says. He's not a patient man," Rellik added.

Deston's gaze shifted to Rellik, who was calmly standing beside Mordred, the knife no longer at his throat. Deston's brow creased in confusion and then rose up as reality set in.

Mordred couldn't contain his mirth at Deston's stunned expression and giggled again. "Please tell me you at least had an inkling that you were walking into a trap?" He cocked his head and raised his right eyebrow mockingly.

Deston held his tongue and glared back.

"Indeed ... how have you managed to stay alive as long as you have?" Mordred asked. "Do you actually believe just because you have that sword there at your side, you're invincible? Arthur thought the same, but ... well I guess you probably know how that turned out for him." Mordred tilted his face to the heavens and closed his eyes. "I wish you could have seen the expression on Arthur's face when I buried my sword in his chest. It was how you say … priceless." The corners of his mouth turned up and he sighed in ecstasy before opening his eyes. "I'll have to tell you all about it one of these days. If you survive this little encounter, that is."

"What are you going to do with Mom and Margaux?" Deston demanded.

"Hmm, that's a good question … I've actually not come to a decision on that as yet. I suppose the answer depends on you." Mordred's gaze lowered to the bag in Deston's hand and then back up to Deston's face.

Deston's hand tightened around the bag as he looked at his mother. If he threw the dirt and took away Mordred's powers, Margaux could shift into a bird and fly away before she hit the rocks. But Joliet didn't have that power. *"Mom?"*

The communications spell prevented Joliet from hearing Deston, but she had no trouble reading the uncertainty in his eyes. She gave him a slight shake of her head, which was all she could manage as she was gagged and the golem had a firm grip on her neck.

"You can save your energy. They can't hear you any more than you can hear them. I made sure of that. I know how you fae like to talk behind peoples' backs even when that person is right in front of you. It is quite rude, actually," Mordred remarked.

Deston's gaze moved back to Mordred. "Release them and let them return to Tir na-nÓg and I'll drop the bag."

"You're in no position to barter, my friend, but I'll make you a deal anyway. Drop the bag and surrender, and I promise I won't kill them."

Deston took a deep breath and weighed his options—none of which sounded good. As he looked over at Margaux, it suddenly occurred to him that Tiff wasn't with her. It wasn't like Tiff to let Margaux come by herself, so either Tiff was out there hiding somewhere, or Joliet had sent her to get Oseron. He looked directly at Margaux, his brow raised in question, hoping she'd give him some sign, but all he could see on her face was worry.

Damn, he thought, realizing he had no choice but to do as Mordred asked. Without raising his arm, he opened his fingers and let the bag drop to the ground. As the bag fell, a small sound came from either Joliet or Margaux, he couldn't tell whom. Then someone grabbed his arms from behind and wrapped a cord around his wrists.

Mordred beamed in triumph as a guard pushed Deston down to his knees. "You see, Rellik … I told you it wouldn't be difficult to get the boy to cooperate."

Deston glared up at Rellik, but the wolf didn't have the decency to look at him.

"Take Deston back to the farmhouse and secure him in the storage room off the kitchen. The women will stay in the camp with you," Mordred told his men. He then whirled and strode away, his cloak billowing out behind him.

Rellik looked over his shoulder and met Deston's glare for a brief moment. The wolf's eyes held no remorse, no emotion of any kind, but there was a strange gleam in them. Then, without saying anything more, he trotted after Mordred.

Chapter 19

Grossard woke with a start and blinked the room into focus. He had watched the bow of Mordred's boat ram into the waves for hours, until the monotony had lulled him to sleep. His mouth stretched in a wide yawn and he rolled his neck to work out the kinks. As there were no windows in the room, he had no idea how long he'd been asleep. His gaze drifted to the table in the corner where the remains of a bloody carcass lay and his stomach growled with hunger as his mouth filled with saliva. He smacked his lips together, but resisted the urge to partake of the snack and instead closed his eyes and whispered the words to bring up the ring's view.

Lights and shadows shifted behind his eyelids, then little by little a table covered with a cloth and several-high back chairs came into focus. A dried flower arrangement, six candlesticks and a wine glass filled with a few sips of dark liquid was all he could see on the table. Only three of the candles were lit and their dim light was not enough to reach to either end of the table. However, a reflection of the flames flickering at the edge of the shadows, suggested a window or a mirror beyond.

"Hmm, where are you, Mordred?" Grossard whispered, trying to identify the fuzzy images within the faint light.

~~

Rellik lounged on a rug in the dining room, his back against the wall, giving the impression he was perfectly content. But in truth, his muscles were tense and ready to react at the first sign of trouble.

"You don't seem to be too concerned about the possibility of Oseron coming to rescue his family. Grossard made the mistake of underestimating him once. It didn't work out well. I suggest you not follow in his footsteps," Rellik commented casually.

"One thing you are going to learn about me right away is that I'm not Grossard. There was never a question in my mind that Oseron would fight to get his family back. But as you well know, I am extremely skilled at keeping my whereabouts a secret. He has no idea we're on Gotland. I appreciate your concern, but have no fear; I will be long gone before the fae get word of this island."

"Oseron may not be able to track you, but he can track his own. He has a surprising number of resources, more so I would say than Grossard. If it were me, I'd take advantage of this small leeway and head for a more secure location—a place where the fae and Grossard can't go."

Mordred finished off the wine in his glass, pushed his plate back, and took his time patting his lips with a cloth napkin. Two weeks had passed since Rellik found him on St. Michael's Mount and offered to produce a member of the royal family in exchange for information on Grossard's location. Mordred accepted the deal, but never imagined Rellik would be able to deliver on the bargain.

"You aren't me, though, are you?" Mordred said, leaning forward on his folded arms on top of the table to look down on Rellik. "Trust me; I don't underestimate Oseron's talents or resources. I and the prisoners will be gone before he arrives. However, no one is leaving until I take care of the unpleasant task of dealing with Grossard."

"There is something else I don't understand. I was under the impression you two had joined forces and were working together."

Mordred tutted. "Our relationship has only ever been one of necessity. He had what I wanted ... I had what he wanted. He betrayed me at the temple, which I should have expected, but that is neither here or there. I still hold the bargaining chip. And now, thanks to you, I have two bargaining chips—the book and the boy. Grossard will be mine for the taking in no time at all." His giggle sounded like a demented child.

Rellik shuddered. He knew Mordred felt he was superior to Grossard, but in Rellik's eyes they were both the same, and he wanted to be long gone before Grossard proved Mordred wrong.

"I've held up my end of the deal. The time has come for you to hold up yours so I can be on my way," Rellik stated, watching Mordred through half-closed eyelids.

Mordred's pale eyes studied Rellik for a moment. "I'm curious ... how did you do it? How did you get both the prince and queen to accompany you here?"

Rellik had no idea the queen had accompanied Margaux until he saw her standing on the raukar, but he wasn't about to let Mordred know that. "How I managed it makes no difference. All you need to know is that I delivered what I said I would, and in fact, even more than what the bargain was for. I expect you to do the same."

Mordred grinned and shook his head. "Rellik, Rellik … your lack of patience reminds me a lot of your former master." His grin widened as Rellik bristled. "Don't worry; you'll have your time with Grossard soon enough. I give you my word on that. I'll even do you one better—I'll deliver him to you. Save you the effort of trekking across the globe and wearing yourself out to get him. He will be all yours to do with as you please as soon as he hands me over the Shard."

Rellik let out a harsh laugh. "If you really believe Grossard is going to hand the Shard over to you, you're as insane as they say."

Mordred's face turned dark. "Mind your tongue or you'll find yourself without one," he sneered and then straightened his back and adjusted the silk ascot at his throat before flashing Rellik a heartless smile. "What little common sense Grossard does possess disintegrates when it comes to matters of the boy. He wants Deston as much as he wants the book. In that respect, he's single minded." His eyes twinkled. "I can't wait to see his face when he learns I've succeeded where he has failed so many times. What do you think … shall we invite him in to have a little peek right now?"

Rellik tensed. "What are you talking about? Is Grossard here?"

"No, but I have resources and can summons him in an instant," Mordred replied, centering the pink diamond on his finger.

Rellik jumped to all fours and his lips pulled back to expose his yellowed teeth. "If this is a setup, be warned, you'll go down with me," he growled.

Mordred waved his hand in dismissal. "Relax, I haven't betrayed you. I don't expect him to show up here. He is too far away to pull that off. But as I told you, I understand how he thinks. He believes he's clever, but very little gets by me. I discovered his little scheme and I just want to tease him a bit with a glimpse of the boy. His ego will take over from there, and as always, it will be his undoing." He motioned to the guard standing behind him. The guard made a small sound of acknowledgement and left the room.

Mordred breathed a self-satisfied sigh and flicked his hand in the air. "So … let the show begin!"

Seconds later, Deston appeared in the doorway, a foot-long rope binding his ankles together. At the sight of Rellik, he stopped short, but the guard gave him a shove from behind. He stumbled forward and fell to the floor, wincing with pain as his kneecaps hit the hard wood.

Mordred turned his head to the side, faking a look of concern. "Now, now … is that any way to treat royalty? Help the boy up," he ordered.

The guard hauled Deston to his feet and dragged him around to the end of the table to face Mordred, who was sitting at the head. One by one, the three unlit candlesticks flickered to life, bathing the room in a soft yellow light. Deston stood in the glow, his head bent and his face obscured by his hair, which hung down over his eyes.

Mordred leaned back and laced his fingers over the top of his stomach. He said nothing, just stared down the length of the table until Deston finally looked up. It was a prodigious moment for Mordred and his smile was stretched wide, showing off his extraordinarily white teeth.

Deston gave a defiant jerk of his head to flick his hair out of his eyes and glowered back.

~~

Grossard's brow creased as he tried to make out a feature in the room that would help him determine where Mordred had landed. He wished he had used a spell that provided sound as well as picture, but at the time he prepared the ring, he hadn't thought sound was important.

"Come on. Move," he muttered under his breath, straining to see more detail, but the room was too dark and shadows distorted a lot of what he could see.

He winced as the unlit candles on the table unexpectedly flared to life all at once. The brighter light momentarily blurred his sight, but when his vision cleared, he noticed a person standing at the end of the table. He sat up straighter and the crease between his brows deepened. There was something familiar about the curly mop of hair and the slump of the shoulders, but the head was bent so Grossard couldn't see the face. Then the head snapped up and flicked the hair out of its face and Grossard stared into the violet eyes that he had come to despise.

"Damn you, Mordred!" Grossard screamed, springing to his feet. "If you think you can win at this game, you have underestimated who you are playing with."

With his eyes open, Grossard could no longer see what was going on in the room, but it didn't matter, for he'd seen enough. He paced across his chamber and back, his fury distracting his thoughts of how to deal with the unforeseen turn of events. His men had been searching for Deston ever since word came down that the prince had left Tir na-nÓg. However, to date, they had not been able to discover as much as the section of the world Deston was in. Could that be because Mordred had already captured the boy? *Impossible! Mordred isn't that smart.* Yet, he couldn't deny what he saw—Mordred had Deston in custody.

Unable to hold back, Grossard let out a thunderous roar, which rattled the furniture in the room. "You have gone too far this time, sorcerer!"

He never should have let Mordred see how badly he wanted to get his hands on Deston. That had been his first mistake, and he hated making mistakes almost as much as he hated Mordred, Oseron and Deston. His gaze roamed the room, taking in the treasures he had accumulated over the past two years—treasures any man, any nation would pay millions for, possibly even die for, and not a one of them could compare to the Shard. That one piece of crystal could alter the world and its powers were all his. Yet, he was still hiding out instead of taking his rightful place as ruler of both realms—all because of two men: Mordred and Oseron.

With a strangled yelp, he threw his arm in the air and the furnishings in the room exploded. The sound of the blast echoed throughout the compound as fragments of wood and stuffing rained down on him. Hearing the commotion, the guards shifted uneasily and looked from one to another. It took only a second for the first one of them to head toward the exit and then the others quickly followed suit and scurried to safety as fast as their legs would carry them, wanting to get away before Grossard emerged from his chambers.

Grossard stood in the midst of the rubble, panting heavily. It was time to show Mordred and Oseron his powers and regain control of the situation. Mordred was nothing more than an obstacle, the same as Oseron, and it had been a couple of years since he had a good challenge.

He picked up his pacing again as he contemplated his options. Mordred didn't know he had seen Deston, which gave him the upper hand, but he would need to be very careful how he executed his next move. He couldn't let Mordred learn the ring's true purpose, for if Mordred took the ring off, he would have to start all over and there wasn't time for that.

He still couldn't believe Mordred had succeeded where he had failed and the thought sent another surge of rage coursing through him. He looked around for something to take his wrath out on, but the entire room had been reduced to rubble and there was nothing left to destroy. Growling his frustration, he strode to the door and flung it off its hinges with a twitch of his finger. His breath whistled through his bared teeth as he stormed through the empty compound and out into the sizzling heat of Dasht-e Lut, the hottest place on earth. He took one look around at the barrenness that surrounded him and let out an ear-splitting howl that shook the landscape and sent a cascade of sand rolling down a nearby dune. The intense glare of the sun burned the back of his retinas, but he stood there seething and stared into the brilliance just the same.

He had chosen the Lut Desert for his compound not only because it was the opposite extreme of water, but because of its isolation. No living thing could exist on its own in this part of the world. That was one of the factors that had drawn him to the area, but it now irritated him. What was the point of obtaining all the treasures he had, if no one knew he had them?

Grossard stared unblinking at the seemingly unending ocean of sand, yearning to wipeout the constant hunger that consumed him, but he didn't know how. From an early age he had envisioned himself being the one that changed the world. He'd had several opportunities to do just that; but each time he'd been cheated out of his just reward and he was tired of coming in second best.

Moving his lips silently, he beckoned the wind and watched dispassionately as it shot across the sand and swirled the miniscule granules into a cloud. Within seconds, the air was thick and brown and the sun turned an eerie red. He stood still, letting the stinging sand batter him until his rage began to dissolve. This wasn't a failure; it was just a small setback. He was still in control and the situation was salvageable. He would take his place in the winner's circle at long last and the whole world would know his name.

Lifting his chin in grim determination, he swept his arm through the air, sending the dust storm rolling away. *Mordred has nothing over me and I think he needs a reminder of that*, he thought, watching the storm move toward the city of Kerman. Without giving a second thought to the destruction the storm would cause the city, he turned and strode back into the compound and straight to his chambers. He stood in the center of the room beneath the large Murano glass chandelier, the only item in the room still in one piece, and held his hand out, palm side up. With his eyes closed, he whispered a spell, using the language of the gods. A single crystal at the very top of the light fixture pulsed to life like a burning star. The blinding red glow showed through his eyelids and in the next heartbeat, he felt a weight in his outstretched hand. He closed his fist around the Shard and savored the burn of the dark energy seeping through his skin. Mordred may have the book and Deston, but he, Grossard, had the Shard and that would ensure him the victory.

With his confidence bolstered, he brought up the ring's view and whispered, *"Kūtasendo."*

Chapter 20

Looking at Deston across the table, Mordred's face was a picture of delight, as if he'd just been reunited with a long lost friend. "I do hope you're finding your room and bed to your liking," he said sincerely. "I gave you ..."

"What did you do with my mom and Margaux?" Deston snapped.

Mordred continued as if Deston hadn't interrupted. "... the best mattress to ensure you would be comfortable, and to make up for that little mishap back at the temple." He pointedly looked down at Deston's thigh.

Deston breathed out an exasperated huff and curled his lip. "Oh, yeah? If my comfort is that important to you, why don't you remove these ropes around my wrists and ankles?"

Mordred was too pleased with the outcome of the day to rise to Deston's taunts. "Tsk, tsk. You and I both know if I removed those ropes, you'll go and do something that will cause you more pain." He scrunched up his nose in mock sympathy. "The bindings are there for your best interest—trust me."

"I won't do anything ... I swear," Deston stated, crossing his fingers behind his back to cancel out his lie.

Mordred studied him for a brief moment and then shrugged. "Never let it be said I wasn't a hospitable host." Deston's ropes loosened and dropped to the floor. "But heed my warning ... do not abuse my generosity."

Deston's muscles convulsed as he brought his arms around and rubbed the raw strip of skin on each of his wrists, but he held back the wince. "What about Mom and Margaux? When do I get to see them?"

Mordred let out a sigh and looked over at Rellik. "I guess it is true what they say ... give a child an inch and they'll want a mile."

Dealing with children had never been one of Mordred's strong suits, and teenagers were twice as trying, but he did his best to produce a semblance of a smile, though it was weak and strained and did not reach his eyes. "Why don't you take a chair while we wait?"

"What are we waiting for?" Deston asked belligerently.

"Why Grossard, of course."

Deston visibly flinched and his eyes went wide, even though he thought Mordred was kidding. But when Grossard appeared at his side a few seconds later, he discovered he was wrong. He reared backward at the same time that Rellik leapt to his feet, but Mordred didn't even flinch. The sorcerer knew without a doubt the sight of Deston would get a reaction out of Grossard, and seeing he was right brought his jovial mood back.

"Grossard ... so glad you got my invitation and were able to join our little party," Mordred said, his voice bubbling with excitement.

To Grossard's credit, the only sign of shock at the realization that Mordred was expecting him was a slight wince and the squaring of his jaw. "You're playing a dangerous game, Mordred. I hope you've taken into consideration there's more than a good chance you'll be the loser," Grossard growled. His gaze moved over to Rellik. "And you," he sneered, "you best lie down before you fall down." He scoffed in disgust. "Surely you don't believe this sociopath can save you from my wrath?" He shook his head. "Nothing on this earth can save you now. You'll soon be ruing the day you betrayed me."

Rellik's ears laid flat and his hackles rose as a low growl rumbled in his throat. His lips were pulled back to expose his four inch long fangs and no words were needed to get the point across that he accepted the challenge and was ready for the fight to begin.

It took Deston a moment to recover from his shock and realize Grossard was not physically in the room, but was only a hologram. Still, he unconsciously backed into the corner, getting as far away from the monster as he could.

"No game." Mordred beamed. "Just some good, honest negotiating. I sensed you weren't overly anxious to cooperate with me the last time we spoke, and so I thought adding a little incentive might help you come to terms. What do you think? Was I right?"

"Your little show has gained you nothing. If I had wanted the prince, I could've taken him at any time," Grossard countered.

Mordred crossed his arms on the table and leaned forward. "That lie *might* be convincing if you hadn't just popped in as soon as I let you have a glimpse of the boy."

Grossard's upper lip lifted in a smirk. "He is a foolish boy and won't bring—"

"I have more than just the boy. Look behind you ..." Mordred cut Grossard off and pointed to the back of the room.

Grossard's eyes narrowed in doubt, but he turned just the same and stared into a large, ornate mirror. From the time Oseron had put the curse on him and transformed him into a hideous looking monster, he'd made a conscious effort not to look in a mirror. Seeing his reflection again after such a long time caught him off guard and his hatred for Oseron multiplied tenfold. He sneered and started to turn away, but paused as the mirror faded to black and a wooded scene replaced his image. The details were difficult to make out as the only light was coming from a campfire, but the red-skinned creatures huddled around the flames stood out plain as day.

"What does this ..." he began; then stopped as he noticed something else. There were two others at the edge of the light. Prisoners it seemed, as their backs were up against a tree and their arms were pulled behind the tree trunks. Grossard leaned in and squinted, curious to see whom else Mordred had captured. One of the larger logs in the fire suddenly cracked and fell into the embers, sending up a bright flame, which briefly bathed the prisoners in light. Grossard's spine went stiff and he straightened as he instantly recognized Joliet and Margaux. *You fool,* he thought. *What have you done? Oseron will have your head for this and you've put the book and Shard in jeopardy with your stupid move. This could ruin everything.*

Mordred watched Grossard's reaction and giggled. "If you're wondering if that image is a hologram, too, let me assure you, it is not. The queen and the girlfriend are indeed my prisoners and they complete the package that will bring Oseron to his knees." He gloated for a moment while Grossard smoldered. "Do I have your attention, now?"

Grossard forced his anger down and turned to face Mordred. On the wall directly behind Mordred's head was a plaque that Grossard had not noticed before. Printed across the top of the plaque in bold letters were the words, 'Njut av din vistelse på Gotland—Enjoy your stay on Gotland.' Grossard's eyes widened slightly before he caught himself and hurriedly scowled to hide the fact he'd seen the plaque and knew Mordred's location.

"I believe our previous negotiations involved the Shard *and* the book. You say you have it, but once again you fail to produce that evidence. There isn't much time left for you to retrieve it from your 'secure' location." He added air quotes around the word 'secure.' "Or are you not worried because the location is on the way to Viroconium?" He posed the question to get a reaction out of Mordred and try to get an idea of the proximity of the book, but Mordred didn't take the bait. "I doubt I need tell you how upset I will be if you fail to bring the book with you. You don't want me to get upset," Grossard added. His voice was tinted with bitterness, though his face remained a blank mask.

Smile wrinkles appeared around Mordred's eyes and without breaking eye contact with Grossard, he turned his palms upward. A bright flash washed out Mordred's pale face, but it was brief and when it was gone, the book was sitting in his hands.

Rellik and Deston could see the book was only a hologram, but to Grossard, who was a hologram himself, the book looked real. His brow shot up in disbelief and his pulse quickened. Baring his teeth, he breathed in and out through his mouth.

"Are you insane? You have the book there with you when you know Oseron could be there at any moment to rescue his wife and son? He'll destroy you with the snap of his fingers and then he'll destroy the book. All my work will be for naught!" Grossard screamed.

Mordred's smile didn't waver. He flicked his hand and waved Grossard off. "Oseron has no clue what is going on here. Other than those I brought with me, no one knows where I am, and precautions have been put in place to ensure no communication can leave this island. I doubt he has even learned his wife and son are missing yet. But you're right to be worried about the book, for if you're not in Viroconium on the stroke of midnight—" Mordred pulled his pocket watch from his vest pocket and studied the face for a brief moment. "—that's a little less than twenty-eight hours from now," he looked up through his brow, "you will *never* get access to the book, and I'll be forced to come after the Shard with every resource and power that I have at my disposal."

Grossard tore his gaze away from the book and glared daggers at Mordred. "I told you before I don't like to be threatened. You think you're powerful enough to win a battle against me, but I can assure you, you are not. The Shard has increased my powers more than you can imagine, even without the spells in your precious book."

Mordred shrugged and pointed at Deston. "You're forgetting our little friend here. The fae will do whatever it takes to get *Their* beloved prince back. I dare say, *They* would even join up with me. And once Oseron's powers are combined with mine, you'll go down—Shard or no Shard."

Mordred's insanity gleamed in his eyes and the two stared each other down, neither of them wanting to be the first to look away. Finally, Mordred brushed his hand through the air in dismissal.

"This is just silly and a waste of valuable time. We both have something the other wants. I'm willing to be the bigger man and offer you an added bonus. You can have the queen and the girlfriend in addition to a look at the book ... all for the small price of allowing me to hold the Shard and gain a small portion of its powers, as I'm entitled to."

Grossard narrowed his eyes and a long tension-filled pause followed. "I want the boy, too," he finally replied.

Mordred sat back and folded his hands together, knowing he had won the round. "Of course, I have no attachment to the LaForesters. You can have them all. My only interest is getting my fair share of the power."

"Then I'll see you at Viroconium," Grossard sneered and twirled his arm over his head. A thick cloud of yellow smoke rose up, whirling about him like a tornado. Mordred rolled his eyes at the dramatics, which was the exact reaction Grossard wanted, for as Mordred looked away, he removed the protection spells Mordred had put over Gotland. Then with a pop, he vanished.

The silence in the room that followed was broken by an unsettling snicker, which started low and rapidly rose to a sinister rolling laughter, raising the hairs on the back of Deston's neck. An involuntary shiver ran up his back, and he bit the inside of his lip to keep from cringing.

A smug grin remained on Mordred's face as he removed the ring from his finger and shoved it inside the pocket of his vest. He then let out a sigh and turned to Rellik. "That went well, don't you think?"

Rellik eyed him as if he was crazy. "You won't be able to fool him with a hologram of the book in person," he stated instead of answering Mordred's question.

Mordred shrugged. "It won't be a hologram, but it won't be the real thing, either. All I need to show him is a replica that is convincing enough that he will produce the Shard. Because you see, one touch is all it will take, for unlike him, I *do* know the words that will unlock its power."

Rellik suddenly realized why the book was so important. He stored that knowledge away in the back of his mind to dwell on later. "Grossard has a knack of getting what he wants, you know. It wouldn't surprise me if he knew that book you just showed him was a fake. I would even wager he is on his way to get the real one as we speak. I think it would be in your best interest to check and make sure it's still safe before meeting him in Viroconium," Rellik said calmly.

Mordred smiled smugly and gestured to the guard to take Deston back to the storage room. The guard grabbed Deston by the arm and dragged him toward the door. Deston did his best to resist, but he was no match for the guard's strength.

"Where are you keeping Mom and Margaux?" Deston shouted at Mordred as he was pulled out of the room. "You better not have hurt them, or I'll—" His words trailed down the hall and were abruptly cut off as the door to the storage room slammed shut.

Mordred stared silently out the window until the commotion had quieted down. He then turned to Rellik. "I never knew you to be such a worrywart, Rellik. But let me put your mind at ease—it is highly unlikely Grossard has discovered where I'm keeping the book. I purposely chose the location with him in mind, and if I do say so myself, it was a rather ingenious choice."

Rellik's lips automatically curled back, exposing his teeth. Mordred's arrogance was wearing on his patience. "It surprises me that you're being so reckless. You of all people should know Grossard better than that. If he wants something as badly as I believe he wants the book, he'll find a way to get to it. You can bet on it." He cocked his head. "And if you think stowing it inside a church or a holy place of some kind, which I assume you have, will stop him, you're wrong. He can always send someone else in to get it for him."

"Rellik, Rellik ... have you no faith in me? I'm not a simpleton born yesterday, you know. I put a great deal of thought into choosing the right safe house for the book. You are correct in assuming I placed it in a place of worship, and yes, Grossard does have minions who can enter such an establishment; but do you have any inkling of how many holy places there are in the lower realm?" He paused, but Rellik didn't offer up a guess. "More than you can count and definitely far too many for Grossard to find *the one* in time. He could go out and smash every church, every cathedral, every abbey to the ground, but it would take him years if not decades to do so. By then the Solstice will have long passed."

Rellik opened his mouth, but Mordred held up his hand and stopped him. "That's not all. I have other precautions in place. The book has been left in the hands of one of most influential men of all time—a man I truly admire despite the fact he is human. I did this because I know how much Grossard hates humans, and how little he knows of them and their history. He won't understand the significance of my placing the book inside this man's sarcophagus, nor will it ever enter his mind to look for it there." He smiled broadly at Rellik's confused look and pushed his chair back and stood. "Let's just leave it to say that your concerns are unwarranted. Put your mind at ease and get some sleep." He walked to the door and then added as an afterthought, "We'll be leaving before dawn, so tomorrow will be a very long day."

Rellik stared at the door long after Mordred exited, repeating Mordred's words over and over. He was sure there was a clue in them as to the location of the book, but they meant nothing to him. He had no intention of sleeping as Mordred suggested, but despite his valiant efforts, his head bobbed with fatigue and his eyelids soon closed on their own accord. Minutes later he fell into a deep, dreamless sleep.

Chapter 21

Margaux shivered in the damp air and winced as a jolt of pain jetted through her shoulders. Mordred's men had taken her and Joliet deeper into the woods to a different camp than the one they had been in before. For hours, she had been sitting with her arms tied behind a tree trunk with no relief and her arms were cramping badly and her fingers tingled as if a thousand pins were pricking them. Every little shift or movement sent sharp, burning pains across her shoulders and down her arms. Still, she religiously held the acorn medallion against the bark of the tree and suffered in silence.

As soon as the guards had left her, she sent a second message off to Oseron, letting him know Deston had been captured. That was the only new piece of information she could pass on since Mordred had separated them and she had no idea where he had taken Deston. She also didn't know the location of the new camp where she and Joliet were being held. A gunnysack had been put over their heads before they were taken away from the sea and it was too dark to pick out any landmarks by the time the sacks came off. All she knew was that they were in a wooded area, but as a good portion of Gotland was wooded, that bit of information wouldn't help Oseron out much.

The one hope she had left was that the medallion would somehow lead Oseron to them. She had no idea how it worked, but she had noticed a high-pitched hum in her head each time she pressed the medallion against the tree. Thinking that if she could hear the hum, then Oseron should be able to hear it and she hoped it was something he could hone in on and follow to find them. Knowing it was the only thing she could do and was probably the best chance they had of being rescued; she endured the discomfort of the awkward position and kept the medallion in place. Her muscles were starting to seize up, though, and she didn't know if she would be able to hold the position for much longer, so she prayed the fae would get there sooner rather than later.

Joliet's arm wasn't as twisted as Margaux's was, but she was just as uncomfortable; although her mind was so occupied with wondering what was happening to Deston, there wasn't room left to worry about her discomfort. She didn't like that Mordred had separated Deston from her and Margaux, and her greatest fear was that the sorcerer had already sent Deston off to Grossard. She had tried to keep that thought from taking hold and poisoning her optimism, but since she'd been unable to connect with Deston psychically, it was hard not to think the worst. And if Deston had already been sent off the island, she might never see him again. Grossard had managed to elude the fae for almost two years, so the probability of *Them* finding him quickly to get Deston back was slim, if not nil. But as hopeless as it all seemed, she still had faith in Oseron. And she held onto the belief that he would arrive in time to rescue them all as tightly as a miser held onto his gold.

∾

Lilika went through the gateway at the same time the other falcons did, even though she knew it put her at a greater risk of exposure. But the time difference between realms concerned her more than getting caught. If she had waited even a few seconds, it would have allowed the others to get far enough ahead she might not have been able to catch up.

She exited the gateway and flew into a sky that was as black as the inside of a cave. That was good in one respect; because it was less likely Oseron would see her in the darkness. But bad in another, because following him would be equally difficult.

She circled with the others above the cliff, trying to get her bearings, but even with her falcon's enhanced vision, she could barely see past a few meters. It had been early afternoon when they left Tir na-nÓg, but in Gotland it was the middle of the night. The heavy darkness was not just due to it being nighttime, though. There was a sinister vibe in the air. Lilika could sense it. Macaria could feel it too and shifted uneasily in her womb.

Oseron heard the trees calling out to him as soon as he came through the gateway, and without hesitation, he turned toward the cliff's edge to listen to Margaux's second dispatch. His piercing eyes darkened to a steely gray as he listened to the news that Deston had been taken and his cry of frustration came out as a loud squawk, which hung eerily on the dense air. He had known all along that Mordred would likely find Deston before he could get there, but it was still a blow to hear another one of his loved ones had been taken and he had not been there to stop it. An icy cold band squeezed his heart, but he only let it stay a nanosecond before he pushed it away and morphed into warrior mode. He couldn't afford to let his emotions control his actions. There was too much was at stake. To win the battle he would need a clear head.

He listened through the entire message before he realized he had not caught the location of where Joliet and Margaux were being held. He played it back and listened to it a second time. When it ended without giving direction, he grimaced, but then noticed the hum of the medallion was still ringing in his head, which meant the medallion was still connected to the tree. As long as the connection remained intact, it was as good as a homing beacon and he'd be able to follow it right to them.

You're a smart girl, Margaux, he thought as he transformed and gathered his men around him to pass on the information.

"Mordred has captured Deston." There was a bit of a rustling amongst the men, but they all held their silence and waited for Oseron to go on. "The message didn't give a location of where they're being held, but the medallion is still sending a signal. We'll follow it and pray the connection holds out long enough for us to get to them.

"It's safe to assume Mordred is expecting us and has created this fog to hinder our progress. But my guess is he doesn't know about the medallion. If he did, Margaux wouldn't have been able to use it and the connection definitely wouldn't still be open. I'm not ruling out the possibility it's a trap, so we'll need to proceed with caution. Susane and Caer, I want you two to stay here and guard the gateway in case Mordred tries to use it to escape. The rest of you follow me and stay in tight formation. Time is of greater essence now. We'll need to fly swiftly. That will be dangerous in this fog, but we can fly above the trees as long as we have the signal. Since Mordred had blocked communication, we will have to use vocal signals. If you come upon danger, call out once. If you locate Mordred or any of the others call out twice. I'll give a distress call if I receive any other information. Keep your eyes open for anything out of the ordinary and may the gods guide your flight."

He didn't give the warriors a chance to discuss the situation or ask questions, but immediately transformed back into a falcon and took off after the high-pitched hum that rang in his ears.

When Lilika saw Oseron's warriors land, she landed in a tree several paces back. Luckily, the others were as eager as she was to hear what Oseron had to say and no one paid her any attention.

Her talons tightened around the branch when she heard Oseron report that Deston had been captured. She felt Tiff tense on her back at the same time, but neither of them made a sound.

As the others lifted off and sped away with Oseron, Lilika did the same. Getting caught was no longer her main concern as she had reverted back into her role of commander of the queen's guard and the only objective on her mind was locating Deston and Joliet.

Oseron's sight was restricted to a few feet, sometimes less, and he was flying way too low and way too fast for those kinds of conditions. Torren kept an even pace alongside Oseron, forsaking his own safety to make sure he'd be at the king's side if trouble arose. They'd already had several near misses when the tip of a tree they had not seen coming suddenly appeared in front of them. Torren lost a few feathers on one such occasion when his wing snagged a branch, but that didn't slow them down.

The magnetic hum of the medallion led them across the island, gaining strength the closer they got to the source. At long last, Oseron sensed he was close to the vicinity of the camp and sent out the distress call to alert the men as he dove toward the ground. The minute he touched down, he transformed and listened for a new message. The connection was intact and humming loudly, but there was nothing more from Margaux.

"We will go on foot from here. The signal is coming from that direction." He pointed the way. "My best guess is it's no more than three kilometers." He paused to allow the men to transform back. "Stay alert. We know—" His words suddenly cut off and his head jerked over his shoulder. At the same time his hand came up, telling the men to wait.

The others stood silently, assuming Oseron was receiving more information, but as he turned back, they saw the dark expression on his face and reached for their weapons, knowing something was wrong.

"The signal is gone. It is possible Mordred discovered the medallion or they could be on the move. If they are on the move and preparing to leave the island, it's vital we catch up to them before they depart. Let's spread out to cover as much area as possible and hope they don't get past us. If you come across anything, or see anyone, use your signals to alert the rest of us. Margaux mentioned eleven men, but I am sensing more. We'll likely run into some patrolling the outer perimeter."

Lilika could tell Oseron's mind was already on the upcoming battle as she watched him nod to the men one by one, because he didn't notice her, the lone falcon sitting in the tree to the side of the group. As the men sprinted off in different directions, she stayed where she was, concerned only with where Oseron was headed. The second he took off on foot, she lifted up and flew as high above him as she could and still keep him in sight.

She knew they must be getting close to the camp, for the fog had become so thick she felt like she was flying through a bubbling chowder. Once she lost Oseron in the soup and could no longer see the obstacles in her path, she rose higher and picked up her speed, hoping there would be a break in the cloud a little farther ahead, but it seemed to have settled in and she saw no way to get around it. Clicking her beak in frustration, she descended until she felt the brush of the leaves against her feathers. She was virtually flying blind, but that wasn't her only problem. She also had no idea which direction to go. Afraid of getting too far off course, she set down on a branch to do a quick look around. The cloud of mist immediately moved in and swirled closer about her as if it knew she was an intruder and she could see nothing other than the gray, roiling fluff.

Tiff wiggled impatiently on Lilika's back and then shot into the air and came around Lilika. "I'm going ahead to see if I can find the others," she yelled and streaked off into the cloud before Lilika could respond.

"Wait!" Lilika shouted after her. The call came out as a loud squawk and whether Tiff didn't hear it or just chose to ignore it, Lilika didn't know.

Ugh, I should have known she would not follow orders, Lilika thought, straining to see through the fog. With a shake of her head and a flutter of her wings, she took off after Tiff, flying through the murkiness faster than she knew she should. The thick, moist air rushed into her face and the trees were a blur of dark shadows whooshing past her. Then suddenly, a mass of limbs and leaves sprang up out of the gloom. She instinctively banked sharply to the side, only to discover too late that it wasn't just one branch; it was several branches from two different trees that had become entwined. Before she could correct her flight a second time, she careened into a web of thin, wispy branches and her right wing became thoroughly entangled. She let out a loud squawk and thrashed about to get free, which only made matters worse. Finally, realizing there was only one way out, she transformed without taking into consideration what the added weight of her human form would do. The thin branches that had caught her up immediately snapped in two and she fell into a pile of pine needles on the ground. Fortunately, the fall was a short one and though her breath was knocked out of her, she landed on her rump and no major damage was done. Still, her hand pressed against her belly and she held her breath until Macaria answered her with a soft kick.

Exhaling a sigh of relief, she gingerly got to her feet and turned in a complete circle as she looked around, wincing and rubbing the spots on her body where the sharp little pine needles had pricked her skin. It was hard to believe, but the fog seemed to be getting thicker by the minute and she could barely see a few feet in front of her. Yet strangely, she felt exposed. The detached sounds that drifted in and out of the murk didn't help that feeling. She pivoted this way and that, trying to detect where the murmurs were coming from, but she couldn't tell.

Tilting her head back, she called out to the only person she knew could hear her—Keir. *"My love, I need your guidance. Show me the way and help me find Oseron or Joliet and Margaux. You're the only one who can help me. I know you're here with me, so please, my love, don't let me wander needlessly."*

As if in answer, Macaria flipped over and jammed her foot into Lilika's left side. The jarring kick almost keeled Lilika over. She rubbed her hand over the perfect imprint of the little foot and five small toes and looked down in awe as it suddenly occurred to her it was a sign. *"Is this your way of telling me which way to go?"* She turned her head in the direction Macaria's foot was pointing and a smile tugged at the corner of her mouth. *"Have I ever told you how ingenious you are?"* She lifted her eyes to the heavens and added, *"Thank you, my love."* Sure that Keir was leading her in the right direction; she sprinted off into the fog without a second thought.

Lilika could feel the air pressure of the fog weighing her down and her stomach clenched tightly with every shadow she passed. Macaria pushed back in protest, but Lilika couldn't help it. The fog had her completely disoriented and as she began to question the probability of finding anything within the cloud, a puff of air blew by her right ear. A second later, another puff blew by her left and she came to a startled halt as Tiff appeared in front of her.

"I found them ... Joliet and Margaux. They're tied to a tree about one hundred fifty meters ahead. I didn't see Deston. Mordred's not there, either, but his guards are in the camp and there are more hiding in the branches of the trees," Tiff squealed. In her excitement, her words came out in one long sentence, but Lilika was able to grasp most of what she said.

"What about Oseron? Did you come across him or any of our warriors?"

Tiff stopped flitting about and shook her head. "No, I didn't see anyone else but Mordred's guards, hiding in the trees. I only saw them because I was flying through the branches. If I hadn't been, I would have missed them in the fog cover." She suddenly stopped and her face took on a look of horror. "Oh, no! The king is traveling on foot, so he won't see the guards in the trees. He'll be ambushed. We have to do something."

Tiff's nervous fluttering about was distracting. Lilika turned away and closed her eyes to think. Before she had become pregnant, she wouldn't have hesitated to storm into the middle of the camp and fight whoever got in her way. But doing that now would be too big of a risk, and she had an obligation and promise to keep. If only there was a way to get a message off to Oseron. Her eyes shot opened as she realized there was a way.

"Take me to the camp. We need to hurry," Lilika said in a rush. In the next blink of an eye, she transformed into a ruby-throated hummingbird.

For once Tiff didn't argue. She looked at the small bird hovering beside her, nodded her head, and took off toward the camp.

As a tiny hummingbird, Lilika had no trouble maneuvering through the tree branches and around obstacles and she was able to zip along at a much greater speed than before. Still, she feared they wouldn't make it to the camp and get a message off to Oseron in time.

After flying a good distance, Tiff suddenly swerved to the left and hovered behind a tree, motioning vigorously at the cucubuth sitting in the branches up ahead. Lilika gave her a nod of acknowledgement as she passed, but she already knew it was there. Its red skin was like a beacon to her hummingbird vision, as was the red skin of the four other cucubuths sitting in nearby trees.

She had been mentally throwing around the idea of picking the guards off with arrows as she came upon them, but seeing how many there were and how close they were to each other, she changed her mind. Though she was a competent archer in normal circumstances, taking down this number of targets in one fell swoop would require the kind of speed Keir had. She did not have that kind of speed, and once she started firing, all the guards in the vicinity would know she was there. If even one of them got away and alerted the others, their whole mission would be in jeopardy. So as before, she pushed back her natural instincts and flew on, taking solace in the fact that the cucubuths would be dealt with when the other fae came through.

Lilika kept a mental count of the red-skinned creatures as she flew over their heads, even though she was aware there were probably many more she couldn't see. She counted a high density of creatures within a thirty meter-wide band. Then there were no guards at all for the next thirty meters up to the edge of the camp.

She smelled the smoke of the campfire before she saw the flickering light through the branches. She landed on a branch just outside the radius of the light and Tiff landed next to her. It took her less than a second to spot Margaux's red head. Margaux was sitting on the ground with her back against a tree and her head slumped over at an odd angle that only someone lost in the abyss of slumber could endure. Joliet was tied to a tree next to Margaux and was wide awake and staring straight at the spot where Lilika was perched, as if she knew Lilika was there. The eleven guards Margaux had mentioned in her message were all present. Four were positioned at interval points around the perimeter of the clearing and the other seven were lounging close to the fire.

"What are we going to do?" Tiff whispered.

Lilika started to respond telepathically before remembering Mordred had blocked communications. She gestured toward a tree behind them with a jerk of her head and flew back until she was sure they were outside the limit of the light before transforming.

"We need to get a message off to Oseron with Margaux's tree medallion first and foremost. I didn't see any guards patrolling the last thirty or so meters, so we should be able to circle around through the trees and come up from behind to cut Joliet and Margaux free. I'll have Margaux send Oseron a message and warn him of the ambush. Then Joliet and I will take care of the guards in the camp. I want you to stay with Margaux and help her keep the medallion pressed to the tree so Oseron can follow the signal."

A sound came out of Tiff's mouth as she sharply sucked in her breath. Her hand flew up to her mouth and both she and Lilika looked back at the group of guards to see if any of them had picked up the sound. The four standing guards had not moved and still wore the same bored expression on their faces. The others appeared just as disinterested and also had not stirred.

Tiff sagged in relief and then jerked around to Lilika. "You can't fight the guards. There are too many. The baby might get hurt and you made a promise to protect her. We should just wait for Oseron to get here and let him take care of them." Tiff whispered louder than she had intended to, but she was so agitated she couldn't hold it in.

Lilika's eyebrows rose in shock at Tiff's insolence. Then she cringed as the words hit home. She loved Macaria more than she ever imagined was possible, but at the same time, she hated that her pregnancy was keeping her from doing her duty. Her own safety had always been second to that of the king and queen's for as long as she could remember. It wasn't easy to switch from that way of thinking. She stared into the crackling flames and unconsciously rubbed her stomach as a jumble of emotions swelled within her.

Oh Keir, why did you have to leave me? I don't know what to do without you. You're so much better at this than I am. You know I would die before bringing harm to our daughter, but what am I supposed to do about my oath and obligation to the queen? If you were in my position right now, you wouldn't hesitate to do what must be done. You gave your life for Deston's without a second thought. So tell me what you want me to do. I can feel you in my heart and I know you are watching out for us, but I need more than that. I need you here beside me, guiding my hand and arrows and helping me protect our daughter. Please, please my love, let me know you understand and will be here with me. It's the only way I can do this, and you know I must do this.

The flames of the campfire suddenly bent sideways as if a strong wind had blown through, although the air was still. In that brief moment, the silhouette of a tall man was illuminated within the swirling cloud of fog at the edge of the camp. Lilika's heart jumped to her throat and she leaned out, straining to see through the gloom, but the dark shape wasn't there long enough for her to verify who it was. "Keir," she muttered under her breath, needing no verification. Her heart gave a little leap and tears blurred her vision.

"Lilika? Are you alright?" Tiff whispered, sensing something had happened.

Tiff's voice right next to Lilika's ear jolted her back to the present. She sniffed and swiped her knuckles across her eyes before she turned and nodded. "Yes, everything's fine. It's all going to work out. Keir is with us. He'll see that no harm comes to Macaria," Lilika stated with conviction.

Tiff's brow creased and she flew backward a few paces, putting a little more distance between her and Lilika. "You know Keir is—" she started, but Lilika abruptly cut her off.

"Let's go. We have to get word to Oseron before he gets ambushed." Lilika changed back into a hummingbird and flew off before Tiff could say anything more.

"Oh dear," Tiff said, wringing her hands and looking over her shoulder, debating whether to follow Lilika or try to find Oseron herself. She had told Lilika she would do whatever Lilika said, but she'd also given an oath to protect Macaria. Logic told her Oseron was the only sure way of doing that. "Oh dear," she repeated, her gaze roaming over the guards in the camp. "Oseron better get here fast," she added under her breath and took off after Lilika.

Chapter 22

The sound of silence woke Rellik with a start. He blinked repeatedly until his eyes adjusted to the brightness of the room, however, his mind remained fuzzy and his head felt like it was underwater. His legs also didn't seem to want to respond to his brain's command to stand and it took a great deal of effort to force them up under him and rise. However, as soon as he got to his feet, a spasm seized his left leg and he crashed back to the floor. He winced as stabbing pains buzzed up and down his left leg like a thousand stinging bees had been set loose on him, but it wasn't anything new to him. He'd been having attacks like that for over two years. Gritting his teeth, he pushed up and stood on three legs, adding weight to his left leg little by little until the quivering stopped. When he was sure it would not buckle under him again, he blew out a puff of air and looked around the room.

He immediately sensed something wasn't right, but his mind was still too groggy to pinpoint exactly what. He turned his head toward the door. The movement, though small, sent the room spinning again. He closed his eyes and held his breath, listening for sounds in the house, which was oddly quiet, except for a ticking clock.

Tentatively, he opened his eyes and realized for the first time that every light in the room was on. The candlesticks, vase of flowers, and dishes from the table were gone, though he couldn't recall seeing or hearing anyone come in and take them away. He then noticed a thick layer of dust covering the furniture as if no one had been the room in a long time. His mouth went suddenly dry and his legs wobbled as he lumbered through the door that led into the largest room of the house. Just like the dining room, every light in the room was on. The weapons that had been piled up against the walls, as well as the mud the guards had tracked all over the floor and rugs were all gone, along with the guards themselves.

The sound of his beating heart drummed in his ears as he turned to the doorway of the main floor bedroom, the room Mordred had claimed as his own. The door was wide open and the lights were on so he had no trouble seeing it was as empty as the other two rooms.

"No," he breathed, his ears falling flat against his head. "He wouldn't do this to me." He rushed toward the kitchen. As his feet hit the cracked linoleum, which had been oiled to give it a shine, his legs flew out from under him. He slid across the room on his back and slammed into the door of the storage area where Deston was being held. The door sprung open from the impact and swung on its hinges. Rellik moaned loudly, rolled to his stomach and stared inside.

The storage area was a small, narrow room with several rows of shelves stacked high with various small appliances, cooking utensils, food staples, tools, and cleaning supplies, but other than that, it was empty. Deston was gone just like everyone else.

Small globs of foam dripped from Rellik's muzzle as he stared into the empty closet. It didn't matter that he had planned to double-cross Mordred and help Deston escape. All that mattered was that he had been betrayed and Grossard was going to get away from him again.

His hackles were up and his teeth were bared as he raced out into the cold night air. It took him no time to pick up a fairly strong scent of the cucubuths, so he knew the group had not been gone long. Narrowing his eyes, he stared off in the direction the scent led. Mordred had made a mistake thinking he could discard Rellik that easily. Grossard had made a similar mistake.

"Not this time," he growled through his teeth, and with a silent curse, raced across the lawn and into the trees to follow the scent.

Chapter 23

Margaux had done her best to keep the acorn medallion pressed against the trunk of the tree, but as the hours dragged on, exhaustion set in and no matter how hard she tried, she couldn't keep her eyes open. When she finally nodded off, the medallion slipped from her hand and the signal that was keeping Oseron on track abruptly ended.

Joliet, on the other hand, was wide awake and watching every movement the guards made as she rubbed the rope up and down against the rough bark, trying to fray and weaken it enough that she could break it and get free. From time to time, the four cucubuths that were standing watch around the perimeter would switch out positions with those lounging by the fire, but other than that there was no interaction between the guards, and they showed no interest in her or Margaux.

She had started working on the rope the moment they tied her to the tree and she figured she had scraped as much skin off the heels of her hands as she had fibers off the rope. At first her eyes watered from the pain, but the tenderness had left her long ago. Now her hands were mostly numb and all she felt was a dull ache and the sticky wetness of her blood running down her fingers. But she didn't stop, for she knew their chance of getting away would greatly decrease once the light came, and the dark was already beginning to fade, which meant dawn was getting close.

She had finally accepted that Oseron was not going to get to them in time, and she was determined to get them out of there herself, whether it was breaking through the ropes or some other way.

As two new cucubuths walked out of the trees, Joliet's hands stilled and her gaze followed them across the clearing to the group by the fire. For the first time since their arrival, the guards engaged in a lively discussion. As she strained to hear what they were saying, she felt a weight on her shoulder. She automatically reacted; bringing her shoulder up at the same time she cocked her head to the side and knocked the weight off.

Tiff quickly recovered, but didn't land on Joliet's shoulder again. "We're here to rescue you, Your Highness. Lilika is going to cut the ropes, so please hold still," she whispered urgently as she hovered next to Joliet's ear.

Joliet went stiff and resisted the urge to look behind her to verify Lilika was there. She could feel the pressure of the blade against the rope and a second later, the restraints fell away. She breathed a soft sigh of relief as the tension in her shoulders released. She would have given just about anything to wrap her arms around her chest and stretch her muscles, but she didn't want to alert the guards and so she held her arms behind her as if she was still tied to the tree.

Lilika moved behind Margaux, who was asleep. As Lilika cut through the rope, Margaux stirred and automatically started to raise her hand to rub her eyes. Lilika caught her hand in the nick of time and held it down. "Be still, *a leanbh na páirte,*" Lilika whispered to keep Margaux from crying out in alarm.

Margaux came wide awake in an instant and darted a sidelong glance at Joliet, who formed a silent, 'shhh' with her mouth and gave a subtle shake of her head. At the same time, Margaux felt Lilika squeeze her hand in reassurance. The corners of her mouth lifted up in a relieved smile, but only for a brief moment before she replaced it with a blank mask in case one of the guards happened to look over.

"I need you to send Oseron a message. Do you still have your acorn medallion?" Lilika whispered in Margaux's ear.

Margaux gave a slight nod of her head, but as she clenched the fist that had been holding the medallion, her eyes went wide. "Oh, no, it's gone! They must have taken it while I was sleeping," she squeaked in alarm.

"That's not possible. I've been alert the whole time and no one has come close," Joliet protested.

A moment of silence elapsed; then Margaux felt a small object pressed into her palm.

"You dropped it is all, but it is here. Now hurry and send Oseron a message. Let him know there are cucubuths, and possibly others, hiding in the branches of the trees and preparing to ambush him. When we came through just now, they were only watching the ground. We were able to fly over them with no trouble. He should be able to as well." She waited for Margaux to send the message off and added, "Keep the medallion pressed against the trunk for as long as you can so that he can follow the signal here."

Lilika turned to Joliet. "Take my bow and bring down the four standing guards. I'll go in and take care of the ones around the fire."

Joliet frowned and shook her head. "That's not a good plan. There are too many. We'll have a better chance if you get up in the trees and fire down on them. You're a faster draw and a better marksman than I."

"I cannot do that. I cannot leave you here unguarded. What if they rush you once I start firing? You'll be safer in the trees."

"Leave me your sword then. I can deal with any who storm us, and Tiff can help as well," Joliet replied.

"I agree with the queen. You can't take on nine guards on your own. Not in your condition," Tiff piped in.

Lilika opened her mouth to protest, but Joliet cut her off.

"Lilika ..." Even though Joliet was whispering, her tone was sharp and commanding. "I'll not allow you to put your life in that kind of danger. You shouldn't even be here right now."

Lilika was tired of hearing that, but before she could counter, a strong spasm squeezed her stomach and wiped out what she was going to say. She clamped her teeth down on the inside of her cheek and went stiff as she concentrated on keeping her face blank so the others wouldn't know what was going on.

"No, Macaria, this is not the time or the place. Please, my sweet girl, wait a little longer. I promise I won't fight if you'll be good," she silently said and held her breath, waiting for another contraction, but all that came was a small flutter, like that of angel wings drawing back in. *You're a good girl. I'll go to the trees and abide by your wishes.*

She sat back on her heels and took in a deep breath, blowing it out through her mouth to release the tension she'd been holding in. "All right ... we'll do as you say," she said, trying to sound put out so Joliet wouldn't suspect anything was wrong. "Are you sure the message has gone?" she asked, addressing Margaux.

Margaux nodded in reply.

Lilika did a quick survey of the clearing and trees surrounding it, looking for a spot that would give her the best advantage. Reluctantly, she pulled her sword and placed it in Joliet's hand. She felt naked and lopsided without it at her side, and she still wasn't overly comfortable leaving her queen and niece alone. But at the same time she knew she was in no condition to enter a fight. She flexed her hand back and forth to loosen it up and gave Joliet's arm a squeeze. "Don't let them see that you're free until they come at you," she added and then disappeared into the fog, praying Oseron would get there before all hell broke loose.

As Joliet waited for the first arrow to fly, she studied the guards and tried to guess which one would come at her first. Her main concern was that one of them would get by her and get to Margaux. She didn't have long to contemplate what she'd do if that happened, for she heard the first whoosh of an arrow and saw one of the standing guards crumple silently to the ground. In rapid succession, two more guards fell without even realizing what was going on. The fourth, however, caught a movement and saw the cucubuth on his right go down. He yelled out a warning as he ran for cover behind a tree. In the blink of an eye, the cucubuths around the fire were on their feet with their swords drawn and their heads swiveling in every direction, looking for the threat. The golems stood silently beside them.

Lilika let another arrow fly. As her target went down, the remaining cucubuths snatched up their bows and dove for cover behind whatever they could find. The golems, however, remained standing in the open like giant statues and waited for instructions. Lilika didn't waste her arrows on those clay creatures, for she knew the only way they could be brought down was by severing their heads from their bodies. Instead, she aimed into the trees and low to the ground.

With the next arrow she let loose, a volley of arrows fired back at her, but she was one-step ahead and had already vaulted to another tree. The branch she landed on wasn't as sturdy as it looked and dipped precariously with her weight. Several of the cucubuth noticed the jostling leaves and took aim just as Lilika leapt to another branch. One of their arrows sliced through her leggings, leaving a deep gash in her thigh. She felt the stinging pain, but ignored it, and rapidly nocked another arrow to take the creature down before he had a chance to get back under cover.

The arrows were flying at her fast and furious and it was all she could do to dodge them and stay out of their path. As she was using her instincts and not her eyes, she didn't see the arrow that was whizzing toward the branch she was about to jump on. The arrow was on a straight track to her heart, but at the last second it miraculously veered and buried deep into the tree trunk right above her head. She didn't even flinch at the close call. She just grabbed hold of the arrow and used it to pull herself up so she could climb higher.

On the ground two of the golems suddenly jerked to life and moved toward Joliet and Margaux. As they drew near, Joliet jumped to her feet. The golems weren't expecting this and halted as if they were unsure what to do. Joliet used that moment of indecision and swung her sword in an arch, severing one of the golems' heads from its body. The head plopped to the ground, but the body remained standing for several seconds before imploding into a pile of dust. The second golem then made a lunge for her. She ducked and spun behind him, whipping the blade across his upper arm, which did nothing to stop him. He came around surprisingly fast and lifted his arm to block her next attack. He was much stronger than she was, but she was light on her feet and danced around him, jabbing and thrusting at every opportunity as she ducked out of the way of his swings.

Tiff rushed out as two more golems lumbered across the clearing toward Joliet. She zipped around their heads and darted back and forth in an effort to distract them and draw them away. One of them stopped and swatted and grabbed for her, but the other continued on for Joliet.

The minute Joliet jumped up; Margaux got to her feet as well and skittered behind the tree to be out of the line of sight. Her breathing was heavy, but she could still hear every whoosh of every arrow. For a half-second, she thought about going for her bow, which was lying with Joliet's weapons across from the fire, but she knew she wouldn't be as much help as Oseron would be, and for him to find them, she had to keep the medallion in place.

There were only two of the guards left standing, and they were shooting arrow after arrow into the trees as fast as they could pull them. Margaux was a bundle of nerves, knowing it was only a matter of time before one of those arrows struck Lilika. Sure enough, moments later, a cry came from within the leaves. Hearing the cry and fearing her aunt had been hit; Margaux dropped the medallion, bent in half to become a smaller target, and bolted for her bow in the pile of weapons. She ran faster than she ever had in her life, but it still felt as if she was moving in slow motion and each second pounded in her ears like a ticking time bomb.

She made it to the pile of weapons and grabbed up her bow, just as a blur streaked past her cheek. It was so close the fletching left a welt on her cheek. She dove for cover behind a clump of bushes and waited a heartbeat before rising up and peeking out over the top. The two archers were both concentrating and shooting into the trees and neither seemed to realize she was still a threat.

Another man suddenly appeared at the edge of the clearing and ran toward Joliet. Margaux's hand shook only a little as she brought her bow up. Just as she pulled the string back and locked in on the man, she recognized the green tunic and blonde curly hair. She instantly dropped her arm without firing.

Oseron had caught a glimpse of Joliet battling the two golems as he approached the clearing. He landed and didn't even break stride as he transformed and rushed to her aide. He was just a blur as he swung his sword with such force one of the golems' heads disintegrated on impact. He then whirled around and cut the second golem down before Joliet even realized what was happening. In the next heartbeat, Oseron took a flying leap, flipped once in the air and came down in front of the last clay monster. The golem had just taken a swing at Tiff and his fist caught Oseron on the side of the head instead. Oseron was lifted off his feet and throw a few feet back. The golem lunged at him, but Oseron rolled out of the way and jumped to his feet behind the monster, and with one final swing of his sword, the golem's head flew into the trees.

Joliet's chest rose and fell and her arms quivered with fatigue. She stared down at the pile of dust and her legs suddenly went weak. She swayed to the side, but Oseron was there and caught her in his arms before she collapsed. She lifted her gaze to his face and saw the uncertainty in his eyes and the fine lines of worry around his mouth. She tried to smile to let him know she was all right, but she was too physically and mentally spent to manage even that small gesture. With a half sigh and half sob, she melted into his arms.

The golems had made no sound when they went down, but the two cucubuth archers flipped around to Joliet and Oseron as if someone had called out a warning. Their faces showed no sign of shock at seeing Oseron there. They each just reached back for another arrow. Margaux rose up out of the bushes and brought her bow up to eye level. Seeing that both archers were aiming at Oseron's back, she stepped out into the open to make sure she had a clean shot. Her hand was surprisingly steady as she took aim and let the arrow fly. At almost the exact same instant, a second arrow shot out of the trees and the two cucubuths collapsed to the ground simultaneously.

Oseron heard the whoosh of the arrows and whirled around, pushing Joliet behind him to shield her with his body, but his sword lowered when he saw it was Margaux standing across the clearing with her bow at her side. His gaze followed her stare down to the cucubuths and flicked right back up. His eyebrows rose in question, which was answered a second later when Lilika swung down from the tree and landed lightly on the ground. She walked straight to him, dropped to one knee and bowed her head.

"What are you doing here? I believe I ordered you to stay in the palace. Purposely disobeying my—" Oseron started, but Joliet put a hand on his arm and interrupted him.

"You wouldn't have found us if it hadn't been for Lilika. And remember she *is* commander of my guard and has taken the oath to protect me. Are you going to fault her for doing her duty and rescuing us?"

The dimple in Oseron's cheek deepened as he looked down on Lilika who was being uncharacteristically silent. "That may be so, and I'll be eternally grateful that she had your best interest at heart. However, that does not take away from the fact that she disobeyed a direct order. A good soldier, especially a commander, knows better and also understands there will be repercussions for such action."

Joliet gave his arm a soft squeeze and he made the mistake of looking into her pleading eyes. Almost immediately his resolve began to soften. She then leaned into him and wrapped her arm around his waist and he realized he wasn't experienced enough to win the battle.

"We'll deal with it when we get back to Tir na-nÓg. We still need to get you all out of here," he said, in an effort to regain control of the situation. The sudden sound of metal pinging off metal rang through the trees to prove his point. The fae soldiers had found Mordred's men and the battle had begun.

Lilika sprang to her feet as the others turned in the direction of the clamor. Within seconds, the noise level escalated, making it clear additional men and swords had joined in the melee, though they didn't know if those extra men were Mordred's or fae.

Oseron hurriedly turned and surveyed the trees behind him. Mordred's communication block had been a nuisance, but it would act in their favor now, for the guards in the battle wouldn't be able to alert those on the other side that the fae had arrived. He still had to figure out how to get Joliet past the guards without being detected, though. The rest of them could transform into birds and fly high above the guards' heads, but Joliet didn't have that luxury.

As his mind raced to formulate a plan, he felt the presence of another coming their way. He spun around as a large falcon streaked across the clearing and came to a skidding halt.

Torren transformed the second his feet touched down and he quickly took in the downed guards and the women standing with Oseron. His eyebrows rose ever so slightly at seeing Lilika in the group, but he gave no other acknowledgement of her and spoke only to Oseron. "The fog lifted without warning. We were forced to engage," he stated.

The fog had been the least of Oseron's concerns and he didn't realize it was gone until that moment. His eyes flicked to the sky and he frowned.

"From what I've seen, I don't believe Mordred has his entire army with him. Six more of our men arrived right before I left them. Together with those that came with us, they should be able to neutralize the situation. But I believe we should take the women out a different way." Torren said and then leaned in closer to Oseron. "I caught a glimpse of Rellik heading this way. He should be arriving momentarily."

"Yes, I sensed him coming," Oseron replied.

Without warning, Oseron disappeared and reappeared at the edge of the trees just as Rellik emerged into the light. Once again he moved so fast, Rellik was pinned to the ground before the wolf knew what was going on.

Oseron's eyes gleamed like steel and his dimple was a deep hole in his cheek as he leaned down and murmured in Rellik's ear, "Give me one good reason why I shouldn't turn you over to Grossard this very minute."

Rellik made no effort to escape. The threat of death was becoming commonplace to him. "For one, you don't know where to find Grossard. Two, I know where Mordred is taking your son and how to get him back," he replied, his tone reflecting a confidence he wasn't fully feeling.

"Why should I believe anything you tell me?" Oseron replied, jabbing his knee into the middle of Rellik's back.

Rellik grunted. "I have no quarrel with you or the fae. My only interest lies in finding Grossard."

Oseron scoffed. "If that is true, why did you turn Deston over to Mordred?"

"I wasn't going to let Mordred keep Deston. I was only using him to get the information I needed. I had planned to help your son escape as soon as I got that information, but it seems Mordred discovered my intentions. I don't know how he did it, but he did, and I was drugged. When I woke up, I found he had left and taken Deston with him. But I do know where they are headed."

"Where?" Oseron demanded.

Rellik made a noise through his nose. "I am not one to make the same mistake twice. If I tell you, what's to keep you from taking off and leaving me behind, like Mordred did?" He tried to shake his head, but Oseron had too tight of a hold on him. "I'll tell you nothing, but I will take you to where you can find Mordred and your son. That's my offer. If you don't like it, go ahead and kill me now, but then you may never see your son again."

"Oseron ..." Joliet began, but the rest of her words trailed off.

"He is not to be trusted," Torren interjected.

A loud caw suddenly echoed through the trees and broke the tension. Oseron looked up, his gaze going straight to the branch where a large black crow with a white tuft under its beak was perched.

"Oseron, you promised," Joliet pleaded, even though she knew he wouldn't be able to hear her. To her surprise, Oseron flinched and looked over at her, his eyebrows raised in question.

"Can you hear me?" she asked telepathically, her voice rising in question.

"Yes," he replied out loud, releasing Rellik and getting to his feet. "It looks like the spell has been lifted."

Rellik gave a fierce shake of his body and looked up at Oseron. "Mordred must have left Gotland then. I assume you took precautions and have someone guarding the gateway." He was already sure of the answer, so he didn't phrase it as a question. "If Mordred can't use the gateway, he'll have to go by air. If we hurry, we can catch up."

"Where's Mordred going?" Oseron and Torren asked simultaneously.

Rellik ignored them and turned toward the trees. "Follow me. I know how to get past the guards. It's a bit longer way around, but it will be faster than fighting our way through," he said and ran off without waiting to see if they were going to follow.

Oseron and Torren exchanged looks.

"I don't see we have a choice. We have to go with him," Oseron stated. "I'll take the lead, you bring up the rear. The rest of you stay between us and keep your weapons at the ready ... you may need them."

With that said, he took off after Rellik and the others followed at his heels.

Chapter 24

Deston filled his lungs with air and held it in for as long as he could before slowly blowing it out through his mouth. Just concentrate, *he told himself, squinting into the trees in front of him. His fingers twitched on the grip of the bow and his muscles were taut, waiting for a target to appear. Ever since Keir had taught him how to shoot a bow, he'd been spending a good part of each day practicing his marksmanship. He'd gotten to where he could hit the center circle of the target about eighty percent of the time, but only when he was alone. When Keir was present, it was an entirely different story. Then his hands would shake and his strikes would be all over the target. But this was the day he was going to prove to Keir and to himself that he was worthy to stand side-by-side with the fae.*

"Locate the target and lock in on it, but don't let it take over your mind. You need to stay conscious of all that is going on around you. It is essential, especially in battle, to listen to your other senses. They will alert you to the dangers coming at you from different directions. You should never lose yourself to one objective or you'll find yourself completely lost," Keir said.

Deston pressed his lips together and nodded unconsciously. I can do this, *he told himself again for at least the tenth time.*

"Are you ready?"

Deston nodded his head again and before he could blink, a large ape-like creature with white hair, glowing eyes, and yielding a sword ran out from behind a tree. Deston's heart leapt to his throat. He had never seen a morlock before, but it was not only the creature that had his heart racing. He had expected the targets to be the round paper type, like what he'd been practicing with. He'd never fired at a living, breathing being before, and even though he knew the morlock was an apparition, it was still a little unnerving.

He fumbled a little getting the first arrow nocked, and he didn't dare look over at Keir to see if he noticed. The arrow made a soft thud as it hit the morlock. A heartbeat later, the arrow fell to the ground as the morlock vanished in a puff of smoke. Before he had time to think about it, three more morlocks appeared a nanosecond apart. At the same time, the woods came alive with the sounds of birds chirping and animal calls. The sounds quickly melded together to become one loud whine hammering in Deston's ears. It was incredibly annoying and took a great deal of willpower for him to keep his focus.

His heart was also pounding in his ears, adding to the noise, but he managed to pull one arrow after another and released them faster than he ever had before. To his surprise, he hit every target that appeared, but instead of feeling proud, a strange heavy sadness swelled in his chest. He swallowed hard to push it back, but it returned and grew stronger with each morlock that went down.

Deston was so engrossed with the morlocks and hitting every one, his internal alarm warning of another danger went unnoticed and he was not conscious of a dark shadow emerging from the trees behind him. The shadow inched its way across the ground, growing longer until Grossard stepped out into the open.

Grossard had looked forward to seeing Deston's reaction at his appearance, but Deston continued to fire arrows at the wind and didn't even turn around. Grossard took a few more steps forward and stopped when his shadow had overtaken Deston.

The morlocks had begun appearing two and three at a time and Deston was so engaged in making sure none of them got away, he didn't pay attention to the heavy breathing behind him. He also ignored the sudden chill that ran down his back. But when Grossard pulled his sword and lifted it into the air, Deston did see the movement of the shadow on the ground and finally realized there was someone behind him. He looked over his shoulder, but the sun was sitting right above Grossard's shoulder and he was blinded by the glare until Grossard shifted and blocked the rays.

As the white circles the sun had branded on Deston's retinas dissolved and Grossard's grotesque face came into focus, Deston shrank back, but he didn't run. He was sure Grossard was just another apparition like the morlocks. "You're not real," he mumbled with a shake of his head, but unconsciously took a step backward.

Grossard raised an eyebrow and the corners of his mouth turned up in a leer. He advanced another step, closing the gap between him and Deston.

Deston's nose wrinkled in revulsion at the smell of Grossard's foul breath, and the longer he stood there the harder it was to hold onto the belief that he was imagining the whole thing. As doubts began to dance through his mind, he glanced to where Keir had been standing seconds before. Keir was no longer there and standing in his place was Zumwald.

Zumwald's face was dark and cold and he held himself stiff. A jagged flash of light streaked across his right eye as he shouted, "Do it!"

Deston recoiled and his brow creased. He'd never heard Zumwald speak in such a tone before.

"You've slipped through my fingers one too many times, boy. This time it will come to an end," Grossard hissed, bringing Deston's attention back to him.

"DO IT!" Zumwald called out even louder.

Deston's eyes shot open, but as his head was still in the dream and Zumwald's voice was still echoing in his head, he was confused by what he saw. He blinked repeatedly at the wood grain paneling and red and tan carpet, which blurred in and out and spun in circles, adding to his dizziness. His head felt like a balloon that had been blown up way too much and the pressure was pushing against his eardrums. He squeezed his eyes shut to keep from getting sick and let his head fall back against the soft leather headrest. His neck popped loudly as he moved it side to side and his stomached pitched back and forth. He concentrated on taking in long, deep breaths to keep from throwing up and the scent of lemon oil filled his head.

After several minutes, his stomach settled down enough that he risked opening his eyes again. The room was no longer spinning, but it took several blinks before his eyes adjusted to the bright glare coming in through a small oval window at his side. Even after his vision cleared, he still wasn't sure he was seeing correctly.

Next to him was an empty leather captain's chair, just like the one he was sitting in. Across a narrow aisle there were two more identical chairs, one empty and facing him, another turned around facing the other way, so all he could see was the high back. He stared at the chairs in confusion. The last thing he remembered was sitting on a thin mattress inside a cramped utility closet.

All of a sudden, the chair that was turned in the opposite direction whirled around and Mordred beamed up at Deston in delight. "So glad to see you're finally awake. I was afraid I'd be left to talk to myself the whole trip," he squealed in his girlish voice.

Deston winced at the sight of the sickly pale face and supercilious smile and slumped back into the seat, digging his fingers into a sudden spasm that seized his neck.

Mordred snapped his fingers and a young woman dressed in a navy suit and a silk scarf tied around her neck instantly rose and stuck her head between the seat backs.

"May I help you, sir?" she said in a heavy English accent.

"Our guest is in need of a hot pack," Mordred ordered, and turned his attention back to Deston. "A little heat will make that feel much better."

Deston pressed his lips together and continued to rub his neck, ignoring Mordred and wondering how he'd gotten on the plane.

In less than a minute, the young woman was back and offered him a small square pack. The heat went to work the second he held it up to his neck and the ache was quickly forgotten in lieu of the deluge of questions that rattled around in his brain. He hated the idea of asking Mordred anything, but some of his questions needed an answer.

"How did I get here? Did you drug me?" he finally blurted out.

"Oh good heavens, my boy, I wouldn't dream of wasting good money on such primal practices," Mordred exclaimed. "Drugs have such nasty side effects and you never know how a person will react to them. A simple spell, on the other hand, is clean and leaves no lingering residue. And since it doesn't involve dark magic, it can be used on anyone ... even those under a protection spell." He smiled haughtily.

Deston couldn't bring himself to look at Mordred, so he didn't see the smile, but he heard the gloating tone in Mordred's voice and it irked him. Gritting his teeth, he swallowed back his retort and fumed. *If he's so powerful, he should be able to tell I'm not under a protection spell.* His spine went rigid with that thought. *Ohmigawd, Margaux! She must have put one on me.*

He yanked the release of the seat belt buckle and reared up, scanning the interior of the small Learjet. Other than the seats he and Mordred were in, there were two others, a jump seat where the attendant was sitting, and a short, leather couch along one side of the wall behind them. He could also see the backs of the two pilots through the small door of the cockpit. Other than the five of them, there was no one else on the plane.

"Where's Margaux? Where's my mom?" Deston demanded, turning back to Mordred. It was all he could do to stay put and not run over and punch Mordred in the face.

Seeing Deston's struggle to hold back his anger, Mordred's smile grew larger. "Why don't you sit down and put your seat belt on. The turbulence over the North Sea can be unpredictable and rather bumpy at times. I'd hate for you to be thrown about and get hurt," he said with an edge to his voice.

Deston ignored Mordred's request and continued to stand. "What have you done with them?" he reiterated, his voice rising in pitch.

Mordred picked up his cup of tea and looked at Deston over the rim as he took a sip. His pinky finger stayed upright as he set the cup back on the tray and cocked his head to the side. He let out a soft sigh. "I understand you were raised in America, but that is no excuse for rudeness," Mordred said, impatience creeping into his voice.

Deston blushed deeply, but didn't back down.

Leaning back in his chair, Mordred folded his hands over his stomach. "I was hoping we could work out a beneficial treaty, you and me, before we reach Viroconium." He looked up questioningly to judge Deston's reaction.

Deston's fists were clenched so tightly, his knuckles had turned bone white. "What have you done with Mom and Margaux?" he yelled.

Mordred's calm appearance slipped for the briefest of moments and his face twisted into an ugly mask of rage. "I SAID, SIT DOWN," he screamed.

Deston's legs immediately gave way against his will. He fell back into the chair and sat in stunned silence for a moment. Then, with his mouth set in a grim line and the dimple in his cheek twitching, he grabbed hold of the armrests and tried to push up, but an invisible force held him in the seat.

Mordred cleared his throat and pulled on the lapels of his suit jacket, smoothing away the creases in the cashmere. "You may not be aware of the advantages my partnership would bring you, so let me enlighten you. Together, you and I could create a whole new world where both fae and humans live together as one. Imagine being the supreme ruler of your own little universe, revered as a god, and having no other power on earth that could challenge you." He paused and watched the stubborn set of Deston's jaw as Deston squirmed to get up. "I find your loyalty to the fae commendable; especially in light of the indifference *They've* shown you from the time you were a wee babe."

Deston's pupils dilated, leaving only a small ring of violet visible.

"Let me ask you something … how many times did your father, or any of the fae for that matter, checkup on you to see how you were fairing in the lower realm during all those years when it was just you and your mother struggling to survive in the world of humans?"

Deston pressed his lips tightly together and didn't answer.

"I thought as much," Mordred replied with a knowing nod of his head. "You're not significant enough for the fae or your father to bother with. Even now … your mother, a mere human, was the only one who came to rescue you. That right there should tell you your father doesn't care about you or think you're important enough to worry about. If you need further proof, let me assure you, no loving father would ever allow his only son to run off and play in the woods on his own when there's a savage killer stalking him. Tsk, tsk," Mordred shook his head sympathetically. "It's a damn shame you're treated in this fashion after all you've done to help the fae."

The deep red of Deston's cheeks expanded to the tips of his ears.

"I would never do that, but unlike Oseron, I've always wanted a son." Mordred paused to let his words sink in.

"I've been around a long time and I've witnessed many a travesty at the hands of the inhabitants of the higher realm, who think *They're* infallible just because *They* have special powers. *They* treat humans as dispensable playthings and refuse to acknowledge the magnificent innovations humans have contributed to the world. But imagine for a moment, if you will, what it would be like if the fae didn't have special powers and the barrier between the realms was destroyed, leaving only one realm? That's what I'm talking about—a world where humans are allowed to be on the same plane as the fae. The gods did make us in their image, after all. Would they have done so if they hadn't planned for us to follow in their footsteps? It's the fae that have held us back and haven't given us the chance to live up to our full potential." He reached over and patted Deston on the knee. "You and I could change that, because we would have the power and the means to do so."

Deston shrank back as far as he could go in the seat, his face expressing the repulsion he felt for Mordred's insane words.

"Come on … let me show you what it would be like to have a real father," Mordred continued. "A father who cares about you and who will proudly stand by your side, teaching you everything you need to know. Together we could make this world a better place. What do you say? Wouldn't you like to live in a perfect world?" He paused to give the seed he had planted a chance to take root.

"Say something … anything," Mordred exclaimed after several minutes of silence.

Some of what Mordred said about his father not caring had struck a nerve with Deston, but most of it was just plain scary. His jaw ached from clenching his teeth together to keep from telling Mordred how ridiculous he sounded. But he was afraid what Mordred would do and he needed to find out what had happened to his mom and Margaux.

When it became obvious Deston wasn't going to answer, Mordred sighed and reached into his vest pocket, retrieving his pocket watch. He looked down at the face and then snapped the lid closed. "Time is running out for you to make a decision. The wise choice, of course, would be for you to join me," Mordred said, his eyes glinting with madness. "The other is—well, I turn you over to Grossard and let him determine your fate, along with the fates of your dear mother and girlfriend." Mordred shrugged and locked eyes with Deston. "You're a smart boy, or at least that's what I've been told." He pushed the button on the armrest and slowly reclined back. "I have no doubt you'll be able to analyze the options and calculate the best outcome for everyone concerned," he added and closed his eyes.

Unable to stand the sight of the smirk that seemed to be tattooed on Mordred's face, Deston turned away and stared out the small, oval window at a sea of white. His stomach was twisted into a tight knot of worry over what had happened to Margaux and Joliet. It didn't bode well that they weren't on the plane. His biggest fear was that Mordred had sent them straight to Grossard, and as Rellik wasn't on the plane with them, it could be that the wolf was delivering them.

The thought of Rellik brought a sour taste to Deston's mouth. Margaux had warned him not to trust the wolf, but he'd been so sure Rellik was the answer to finding Grossard, he hadn't listened.

A sense of hopelessness weighed down on him and he laid his forehead against the cool glass. *What do I do?* He stared at the clouds, but all he saw was Margaux's face and he couldn't concentrate on anything else. He rocked his forehead back and forth on the glass and opened the channel to her even though he knew the line of communication was blocked and she'd never be able to hear him.

"Margaux, I should have told you the real reason I didn't want you to follow me. I just didn't know how to tell you that I think I'm in love with you. I've never felt anything like this before." He sighed, knowing that was a lousy excuse. *"But I swear I'm going to get you out of this. I'm going to do whatever it takes. Just hold on until I can figure it out ... please, just hold on."*

He swallowed back the panic that was constricting his chest. He didn't care so much about himself, but he had to come up with a way to get Margaux and Joliet out of the mess he had gotten them into.

Chapter 25

With no warning, Margaux stopped short and Joliet nearly ran into her.

"What is it?" Joliet asked, as she came around and saw the strange look on Margaux's face.

Margaux held up a finger and stared off into the trees, indicating for Joliet to wait. *"Deston, I can hear you. Where are you?"*

Deston jerked up at the sound of Margaux's voice in his head. Then, realizing what he had done, he shot a quick sidelong glance at Mordred. Mordred's eyes were closed and his chest was slowly rising and falling as if he was asleep, but Deston had already learned he couldn't trust Mordred with even the smallest of things. He let his head fall back against the headrest and closed his eyes, doing his own imitation of sleeping to play it safe.

"Margaux, is that really you?" he replied.

"Yes, it's me. I'm here. Oh, Deston, where are you? Are you still in Gotland?"

Deston glanced at Mordred through a slit in his eyes. He could totally see the sorcerer disguising his voice to get Deston to go along with his crazy plan.

"If you're really Margaux, tell me who was in the tunnel when we went back to get Zumwald's clue?" he asked, knowing that there was only one person who would know the answer to that question.

"What? Deston, we don't have time for this. Where are you?"

Deston's heart was racing. It certainly sounded like Margaux, but he couldn't see how she was able to get through the spell. *"I know, and I'm sorry, but I have to be certain this is you. Just answer the question ... who did I meet in the tunnel the second time we went there?"*

Margaux breathed out a frustrated sigh. *"It was Nimue. She pulled you into the ice wall and tried to get you to release her. You almost didn't make it out,"* she replied, a tinge of impatience coming through in her tone.

Deston smiled at her answer, but sobered just as fast and turned back to the window in case Mordred actually was spying on him. *"I'm on a plane with Mordred. We're headed to some place called Viroconium. Are you okay? Did they hurt you? Is Mom there with you?"*

"I'm fine. Your mama is fine too. Oseron is here and rescued us. Rellik is here with us too, and he is going to take us to where you are going."

Deston bristled at the mention of Rellik's name. *"Don't believe a word Rellik says. You were right all along. I shouldn't have trusted him. You shouldn't either."*

"What is it, Margaux?" Oseron asked, rushing back to the small group surrounding Margaux.

"It's Deston. He was able to get through to me. He says he's on a plane with Mordred," Margaux replied, looking up into Oseron's deep blue eyes, but Oseron was looking at Joliet. There were tight lines around Joliet's mouth, but he put his hand up before she could say anything.

"I'll take it from here," he said to Margaux, his eyes staying on Joliet.

"Deston, are you all right, son?" Oseron called out.

Deston jolted again as the unexpected voice came through, and he again looked over at Mordred. The sorcerer still had his eyes closed, seemingly unaware of Deston's communication.

"I'm fine. Mordred's taking me to Viroconium to meet up with Grossard. The meeting is set for midnight tonight."

"Viroconium?" Oseron said out loud, looking over at Rellik for confirmation. Rellik didn't respond, but his pupils dilated, which was all the confirmation Oseron needed.

"We're on our way there now. Don't let Mordred know you've spoken to me," Oseron added.

"Dad, wait ... Mordred has a book that Grossard really wants."

"Yes, the Book of Tenebris. We're aware Mordred has it."

Deston frowned. *"I don't understand. That's the book that had the Shard's location in it. Why would Grossard want it, he's already got the Shard?"*

"Yes, but like the Crystal of Light, the Shard has to have its energy renewed from time to time. It's been buried for millenniums and its powers have weakened. Grossard has exhausted more of its power with the chaos he's been creating around the world. The Shard's powers can only be renewed on a total lunar eclipse on the winter solstice. That particular event will take place at the end of this year. If Grossard has the incantation from the Book of Tenebris that opens Erebus' portal at that time, he will have the power to extinguish all the light from this

world and destroy our realm. That is why he is desperate to get his hands on the book."

Deston was gripping the armrest of the chair so tightly he left deep impressions in the leather. *"Then we've got to stop him. Mordred and Grossard are supposed to be doing an exchange at this meeting tonight. Grossard is supposed to get a look at the book and Mordred gets to hold the Shard. But Mordred is planning to double-cross him. Grossard showed up at the house on Gotland as a hologram and Mordred showed him a fake book, but Grossard thought it was the real thing. Afterwards, I overheard Rellik arguing with Mordred and saying Grossard knew it was a fake and was probably on his way to get the real book."*

"Where did Mordred say he was keeping the real book?" Oseron asked, looking back at the wolf.

"I didn't hear him say. I was taken out of the room and didn't get to hear the whole conversation. But if Rellik is there with you, ask him. He might know, but be careful, because he probably won't tell you the truth."

"I'll ask him, but it seems highly unlikely Mordred would give such important information to the likes of Rellik. See if you can learn more about where Mordred is keeping the book. Just be careful. Mordred is insane, but he's also very shrewd. I don't want you taking any unnecessary risks; just try to get him to talk about the book."

Deston shot a sidelong glance at Mordred. *"I'll try."*

∿

Mordred yawned and looked across the aisle to the back of Deston's head. In the short time he'd spent with the boy, he'd come to realize Deston was as stubborn as his father. But Deston was also young, inexperienced with the powers of magic, and had a tendency to wear his heart on his sleeve, which was just the right combination to make him susceptible to Mordred's powers of persuasion. He was confident he could turn Deston to his way of thinking, but he didn't know if he could accomplish the feat within the timeframe he had to work with.

Mordred reached into his vest pocket, glanced down at his watch, and clicked the lid closed. The sound, though barely discernible amidst the noise of the jet engines, made Deston jump. He jerked around as Mordred pushed the seat button and resumed his upright position.

An amused expression crossed Mordred's face as the two locked eyes and Deston quickly looked away. Since his conversation with his father, Deston had been racking his brain for ways to get Mordred to tell him where the book was. Most of what he had come up with, he didn't figure Mordred would fall for, but one idea had possibilities—that was convincing Mordred he'd join him. He worried that Mordred might be able to see through his deception, especially if Mordred was anything like his mother and NiNi and could read Deston's thoughts, but he had no other options and time had just run out.

Deston cleared his throat. "I, um … I've been thinking about what you said." His mouth was so dry he could barely spit out the words. He swallowed hard and ran his tongue over his teeth. "The stuff you said about my father is true. He could have found me if he wanted too, but I guess he didn't want to." Even though he was only saying what he thought Mordred wanted to hear, the words stabbed at his heart. "But Mom and Margaux are different." He swallowed again to unstick the next words from his throat. "If you let them go and promise not to ever hurt them, I'll join you … *in Viroconium*," he added under his breath, so he wouldn't be held to his promise beyond that point.

Mordred remained silent for what seemed like an eternity and then jumped to his feet and clapped his hands in glee. "I knew you were a smart boy and would come to your senses," he exclaimed and let out a loud whoop.

Deston pressed back into the seat and watched Mordred dance and twirl up the aisle of the plane. *He really is insane*; he thought as Mordred danced back to the chair directly across from him and flopped down in it.

"You've made a wise choice, son," Mordred gloated.

Deston's stomach turned over at Mordred's use of the word 'son,' and he pressed his fingernails into the palms of his hands to keep from letting his disgust show. "So you promise to let Mom and Margaux go?" He forced himself to look up at Mordred.

Mordred waved his hand in the air as if brushing off an annoying gnat. "Already done."

Deston sat up straighter. If Mordred had made contact with his minions on Gotland, he'd know Oseron was there and had already rescued his mom and Margaux. Squirming uncomfortably in his seat, he studied Mordred's face, but the sorcerer gave nothing away. "Are they still on Gotland?"

Mordred cocked his head and his eyebrows rose. "Are you hoping they're on their way to rescue you?" Deston's ensuing blush put a twinkle in Mordred's eye. "I'm sorry to disappoint you, but you see, they have no idea where you are. And the cucubuths I left behind will be keeping them occupied for a while longer. That's one thing you're going to learn about me very quickly … I like to err on the side of caution."

Deston struggled to keep the relief from showing on his face. "So what about Grossard?" he asked after a long pause.

Mordred sighed and rolled his eyes. "Yesss … Grossard. We should probably keep our arrangement a secret from him for the time being. I doubt he'll be happy about it."

"No, that's not what I mean. I heard him tell you that you wouldn't get to see the Shard unless you showed him the Book of Tenebris. But you don't have the book, so—"

"Oh, I have the book, all right, and I will show it to him," Mordred cut in as he turned his hands palm side up. The book instantly appeared in his hands with a soft pop.

Deston frowned as he looked down at the red scaly cover with the strange unfamiliar symbol debossed in the center. It looked just like the hologram Mordred had produced back at the farmhouse, but this was definitely no hologram. "How did it get here? I thought ..." he stammered. His words trailed off as his brain tried to grasp the implications of what he was seeing. When he overheard Mordred and Rellik talking earlier, it sounded like the book was hidden away and Mordred wasn't planning on letting Grossard have it. But if this was the actual book, it changed everything and there was a lot bigger problem than he thought. He lifted his gaze to Mordred, who was grinning like a little kid who had just gotten away with a fistful of forbidden candy.

"Ahh, your reaction is exactly what I was hoping to see." Mordred beamed radiantly. "You think this is the real book, don't you?" He lifted the cover and flipped the blank yellowed pages over. "It's a fake, you see, and it has just passed its first test. If it could fool you, seeing it here in full light, it should most definitely fool Grossard in the black of night."

"Are you kidding? All Grossard has to do is open it to know it's a fake. What do you think he's going to do then?" Deston's voice came out an octave higher than he would have liked, but he couldn't help it.

"You certainly don't expect me to give him the real thing, do you? Lord, we'd all be doomed if I did that."

Deston shook his head, the expression on his face making it clear he was not following Mordred's logic.

"You have nothing to fret about. Over the centuries I've been able to pick up a few tidbits of knowledge. The fact that I'm alive to talk about it should be more than enough to give you comfort. The book is in a safe place and that's where I intend it to stay until Grossard is out of the way. All I need from this," he hefted the fake book, "is to fool Grossard long enough to get my hands on the Shard. One mere touch and a few spoken words and my powers will be equal to his. He'll be at *my* mercy then, for only I know the incantation to open the portal and unlock the Shard's full potential."

"But what if he kills you when he sees you've double-crossed him?" Deston asked.

Mordred put a hand to his chest. "Your concern for me is touching." He sniffed back a nonexistent tear. "That's not going to happen. He won't kill me. He knows better. He's way too greedy and wants to destroy Tir na-nÓg too badly to throw it all away, and he knows the only way he can do that is with the incantation in the book, which, as I just stated, is in a safe place."

Deston frowned and looked down at his hands. Mordred seemed pretty confident of his plan, but he wasn't so sure that Grossard wouldn't kill Mordred just for the fun of it. He also couldn't imagine a place the book could be that Grossard couldn't find.

"I've learned a great deal since coming to Tir na-nÓg, and a lot of things have happened that I never thought could. Like, I didn't think Grossard could live after being thrown into the chapel, but he did. And after I got to the Shard first, I thought it was all over and he'd never get it, but he did that too. I don't know how he does it, but he has a crazy way of always coming out on top and he's pretty good at accomplishing the unexpected. I don't think you should count him out and assume he's not going to find where you have the book stashed," Deston mumbled after a long silence.

Mordred bristled. For the second time in just twenty-four hours he was arguing Grossard's intelligence and it was becoming quite tiresome. "You're giving Grossard too much credit. He barely has enough brains to tie his shoes."

"That's not what my dad says. He—"

"Your dad is wrong!" Mordred sneered as he jumped to his feet, turned on his heels, and strode toward the back of the plane. Halfway down the aisle he twirled around and stomped back to Deston. Putting a hand on each of the armrests, he leaned in until his face was inches away from Deston's. "I was the one who figured out the Shard's location. I'm also the *only* one who can read the ancient language to reverse the poles and open the portal to bring Erebus back." His breath, smelling strongly of curry and garlic, was enough to turn Deston's stomach. "Grossard was a necessary means in the beginning, but I see now that I should have listened to Mother and not involved him. If I had known you would get to the Shard first, it would have saved me a whole lot of trouble. I'm still curious to hear how you accomplished that little feat. You'll have to enlighten me one of these days." He glared into Deston's eyes. "I can assure you this—me not having the Shard is a temporary situation, but Grossard getting his hands on my book is a definite *never!*" His nostrils flared in and out, daring Deston to contradict him.

Deston shrank back as far as he could, his eyes wide. He could tell Mordred was barely hanging onto a tiny fragment of lucidity, but he needed to find out where the book was. The only way to do that was to press him further. He licked his lips and swallowed hard.

"You may want to think Grossard won't find the book, but you didn't think he knew where Olcas had hidden the Shard. He showed up at the temple, though, didn't he?"

Mordred gnashed his teeth and stepped back, throwing his hands in the air. "ENOUGH! I am a hundred times smarter than Grossard could ever hope to be. I took every one of his weaknesses into consideration when I chose the location for the book." He lifted his hand and ticked off on his fingers the safeguards he had put in place. "We all know Grossard can't tolerate water, so I picked an island that is in a lagoon. Ingenious, yes?" He nodded his head, affirming his own statement. "That's not all. I placed the book inside an iron box with iron chains and locks, because, like all species of faeries, Grossard cannot handle iron." He held up his index finger. "Wait, there's more ... my pièce de résistance. Faeries, both solitary and fae alike, have never deemed it necessary to keep track of what goes on in the lowly human realm. They know virtually nothing of those who have shaped the human race. In fact, I could come right out and tell Grossard that I put the book in the hands of one of the most influential humans in the history of the world, a man who was never defeated in battle, a man who is legitimately called great, and he still wouldn't have a clue as to whom I'm talking about. So trust me when I say the only place the book could be safer is in Tartarus. And I do *NOT* want to speak of it again."

Mordred's hair, which usually didn't have a strand out of place, was hanging down over his eyes and his chest rose and fell as he glowered down at Deston. Then in the blink of an eye, his superior demeanor returned. He smoothed his hair back in place with his hand and pulled on his lapels to straighten his jacket. He strutted back to his seat and snapped his fingers. The flight attendant's head instantly appeared in the gap between the seats.

"Bring us the Dom Pérignon ... and some strawberries, too, I think. We're going to celebrate a very special occasion."

Deston turned back to the window and missed the victory grin Mordred flashed at him. Mordred hadn't said where the book was, but he gave plenty of clues in what he did say. The problem was the clues made very little sense to Deston.

Chapter 26

Mordred stood in front of a short, stone brick wall—a small piece of the once impressive bath basilica complex of Viroconium—and stared at the archway of the largest surviving section of a Roman wall in all of Britain. At one time, Viroconium was the fourth largest and most secure city, in Roman Britain, but at some time in the fifth century it fell to ruins. To date, only a small fraction of the ruins have been excavated, leaving the majority of the 200-acre site buried under fields of pasture and grazing sheep.

Mordred stared at the structure with a far-a-way look in his eye, not seeing the sparse remnants and crumbling stone bricks, but the magnificent city of his youth. Memories of the time he'd spent in the city were some of the few happy ones of his childhood; the time before his father denounced him and forced him and his mother into exile. After that, his life was not an easy one and he quickly learned that power was the only true way to achieve respect and happiness. He'd been striving to obtain that power ever since, but there always seemed to be someone, like his father, Arthur, getting in his way. In the end, he got his revenge on Camelot and on Arthur, and there was no question in his mind that it would be the same with Grossard. He realized it would be a bit more challenging than it was with Arthur, due to the involvement of the Shard; but it was a foregone conclusion that he, Mordred, would come out as victor in the end, for he had intelligence and the book, two things Grossard would never have.

Pushing his glasses higher up on his nose, he looked out over the countryside and past the Roman townhome that had been resurrected across the road from the ruins to give tourists a taste of what life had been like back in the day. It was a new moon and without moonlight to obscure their brilliance, a thousand stars twinkled like miniature Christmas lights pushed through the back of a black velvet painting. The lack of light and his old memories were part of the reason he had chosen this date and this place for the meeting. The enhanced darkness would help him detect the tale-tell silvery glow of magic when Grossard and his army arrived, and his personal knowledge of the old city gave him the advantage to initiate a sneak attack.

He had instructed Grossard to come alone, but he harbored no illusions that Grossard would; any more than he, himself, had. In fact, Mordred was counting on Grossard bringing his minions, and counting on the clash of the two armies coming together to help distract Grossard and ensure he didn't notice the book was a fake.

"Stay alert and let me know if you see anything," Mordred called across the yard and looked over his shoulder to make sure Deston heard him.

Deston had been tied to a metal guardrail at the top of the mound that bordered the excavation site to give the appearance that he was still Mordred's prisoner. He was sitting on the ground, slouched over with his chin resting on his chest, looking very much as if he was asleep. Mordred opened his mouth to wake him, and then closed it again without making a sound. If by some chance Grossard figured out the book was a fake, there was still the possibility that Mordred would have to resort to plan B and hand Deston over to get the Shard. If that was the case, it would be better for the boy to be asleep and not hear the negotiations.

Sighing contently, Mordred turned his head to the west. The river Severn was not visible from where he stood, but he knew it was not too far away. Just as he knew the entrance to the secret underground tunnels was well-hidden on the banks of the river, and that the tunnels ran all the way to the castle that was still buried beneath the layers of earth. He and his mother had used the tunnels to make their escape from Arthur's men when the army had come for them. Only a handful of people had ever known about the tunnels, and, of them, Mordred was the only one still alive.

He reopened the tunnels a little over a year ago, and wasn't surprised to find several long sections had completely collapsed in. It took his men the better part of the year to dig them out, fortify them to make them usable, and complete multiple passages, connecting the tunnels to the surface. His army was concealed in the tunnels now, awaiting his signal to emerge. He tingled with anticipation at the thought of Grossard's reaction when the soldiers stormed out of the earth. With an extra flounce in his step, he moved to one of the short stone walls and settled on top, confident his long wait to hold the Shard was about to come to an end.

Deston's head was down, but not because he was sleeping. He was stressing out over what was going to happen when Grossard arrived. He was also worried that the fae wouldn't get there in time, and if *They* did, where *They* would go to keep their presence hidden. Viroconium was not at all what he had expected. He thought there would be an actual city, not just a maze of stone brick walls, some as short as three-courses high, showing the footprints of buildings long gone. A wood picket fence cordoned off the ruins on one side and a tall hedge ran along two other sides, which he supposed could provide some cover for the fae, but it was definitely not ideal.

"*We're here.*" Oseron's voice broke through Deston's thoughts.

Deston reared up, his back ramrod straight. Realizing what he had done, he shot a quick glance at Mordred to see if the sorcerer had noticed. To his relief, Mordred was facing the other way.

"*Where are you?*" Deston called back, hurriedly scanning the shadows.

"*We're in a copse of trees near the river southwest of the ruins,*" Oseron replied. "*Where is Mordred's army? I haven't seen any sign of them.*"

"*They're in an underground tunnel, waiting for Mordred's signal to attack.*"

"*How many did he bring?*"

"*I'm not sure. There were a lot ... like hundreds,*" Deston replied.

All at once, silence dropped over the ruins and the air pressure changed. Deston tensed and felt a rush of heat as a sense of dèjá vu settled over him. After his mom's disappearance in Pennsylvania, he had had a repetitive dream in which the air would rush out of the room the moment Grossard would appear, as if even it didn't want to be in the same space as that monster. He could still vividly recall that feeling and he didn't have to think twice about why his palms were suddenly clammy or why he couldn't breathe. He knew it was because Grossard had arrived. The heat coming from the leather bag around his neck confirmed his assumption.

Deston glanced up through his brow and then tilted his head back to take in the full view of the faint, silvery outline of a hulking shape that looked to be floating in the sky. Soft green balls of light suddenly blinked to life and hovered around the top of the two-story stone wall of the Roman bathhouse upon which Grossard stood. He looked as big as a giant with his cape whipping wildly around him as if a strong wind was blowing, though the air was still and heavy. In his right hand, he held a long staff, topped with a horned serpent's head, the eyes of which threw out sparks of red as the light of the green balls bounced off them.

Mordred had also felt the change in the atmosphere and knew Grossard had arrived, but he took his time turning to face his nemesis. He looked up at Grossard standing on top of the tall structure and scoffed, "No one's impressed or intimidated by this spectacle, Grossard. Come down and let us talk like civilized men."

Grossard held his theatrical pose for several long seconds more and then disappeared with a soft pop. He rematerialized a nanosecond later on the ground in front of the sorcerer. The two stood face to face, glaring at each other, neither saying a word.

The crushing pressure that had enveloped Deston ceased the moment Grossard landed on the ground. He straightened his back, keeping his eyes locked on the immense figure. He hadn't seen Grossard in the flesh since the temple and he was ill-prepared for the powerful emotion that came over him and the deluge of dark thoughts that immediately infested his mind. His breath wheezed in and out through his clenched teeth as he slowly got to his feet.

The total stillness of the ruins amplified Deston's heavy breathing and Grossard heard it. He whipped around, but it took him a moment to spot the boy tethered to the railing at the top of the grassy knoll. In his excitement of knowing he was minutes away from obtaining his life-long dream, he'd forgotten all about the extra prize Mordred had promised to bring him. His face lit up in a sadistic smile, which was still in place when he turned back to Mordred.

"Have you heard the saying, imitation is the sincerest form of flattery?" Grossard asked and paused to let Mordred answer. "Well," he continued when Mordred didn't comment. "Not all of us are as well-educated, I guess. But you should be extremely flattered in learning that I have imitated you." Mordred opened his mouth to speak, but Grossard hurried on. "Just like you, I got in contact with an Oracle."

Mordred's back went a little straighter and his chin rose a little higher.

Grossard could see he'd struck a nerve, which was exactly what he had intended to do— make Mordred squirm a little. Though he hadn't actually contacted an Oracle, he knew the mention of it would be enough to set the sorcerer off his game. Chuckling, he turned away and started across the yard, stepping around the footings of the old Roman columns.

Mordred's gaze followed Grossard's progress and then darted to Deston. Was it possible Grossard had learned of his deal with the prince? He didn't see how that could happen. He had acted on an impulse after the idea came to him out of the blue. His entire life he had worked alone, but age had finally caught up to him and the thought of having someone at his side to share in his many triumphs had held a certain appeal. The added bonus of knowing it would infuriate Grossard if he brought Deston into his fold had helped him make the final decision. He was, however, a firm believer in the old saying, 'agreements are made to be broken', and the only loyalty he cherished was his own. If it became necessary to turn Deston over to Grossard to get hold of the Shard, so be it. But he wasn't going to rush into that move until he learned exactly what Grossard knew.

"If you did seek out an Oracle, then you know my word is my honor and the boy will be yours as soon as you let me see the Shard—just as I promised," Mordred called after him, attempting to provoke Grossard into telling him more with his lie.

Grossard ignored Mordred and squatted down on his haunches in front of Deston. Deston lowered his eyes and refused to look at him, but Grossard took hold of Deston's chin and forced Deston's head back so he could look into his eyes.

Deston glared back defiantly as a strange prickling sensation moved through his left hand. He tried not to fidget, but it was hard to hold still. It felt like a thousand fire ants were crawling under his skin. He balled his hand into a tight fist and seethed with a scorching hatred that took over his thoughts. Ever so carefully, his hand inched toward his belt, forgetting that Mordred had kept Caluvier. When his fingers reached the empty scabbard, he glanced down and jerked fiercely against his restraints.

Grossard cocked his head to the side and narrowed his eyes. "All this time I thought there was something special about you. But now I see the truth. You aren't special at all. I would wager I have more power in my little finger than what there is within the whole of you."

"I'll show you how special I am when I rip your heart out," Deston hissed back.

"Wah ho!" Grossard called out in delight. "Is that any way for the prince of the fae to talk? What would the real fae think if *They* knew you were so eager to kill?"

Deston recoiled in horror at Grossard's words. At that exact moment, a loud caw pierced the night sky and a jagged streak of light shot through Deston's right pupil. Deston's whole body gave a small jerk and the urge to kill Grossard evaporated faster than it came, leaving behind a deep heaviness on his heart.

"You brought the Shard with you?" Mordred cut in, anxious to take Grossard's attention off of Deston.

Grossard's smile vanished and his nostrils flared, but before he rose he gave Deston's chin a hard squeeze. "We'll finish this later." Then with his teeth bared, he rose and turned back to Mordred.

"And you brought the book?" Grossard responded, popping back to where Mordred was waiting.

It flashed through Mordred's mind to demand to see the Shard first, but instead of quibbling over the details, he shrugged and lifted the flap of his cloak to give Grossard a glimpse of the top of the book sticking out of an inside pocket. Grossard's eyes lit up as he took a step forward, but Mordred let the cloak fall back in place and put his hand out.

"There, there ... I showed you mine, now you show me yours," Mordred said and giggled at the innuendo he knew Grossard wouldn't understand.

Grossard's gaze lifted to Mordred's pale face and their eyes locked. "You say that as if you expect me to believe it to be true."

Mordred visibly tensed.

"But I know better and I know you haven't shown me all of yours yet, now have you?" Grossard sneered.

Though Mordred blanched, it was too dark for Grossard to detect that small display of shock. "I don't know what—" Mordred began.

Before he could say more, Grossard lifted his staff and brought it down hard, pounding the end into the ground.

Mordred squared his shoulders. "I dare say," he started, but was again interrupted by a muffled underground sound that rapidly rose like an on-coming train. He looked down at his feet and stepped back in alarm as large cracks radiated out from the end of the staff and quickly veined across the ruins to the surrounding mounds of earth. The earth shook with wave after wave of energy and the mounds began to crumble away. Within minutes, additional stone ruins appeared; then collapsed in the dust and exposed a long gaping trench that snaked toward the river.

The startled faces of Mordred's army gaped up from the trench, and before they had a chance to recover from the shock of being revealed, a volley of arrows rained down on them. Loud shrieks and curses echoed through the air as the combatants scrambled over each other to get out of the line of fire and mass confusion took over.

Mordred, being the narcissist that he was, believed no one was capable of outwitting him, especially not a dim-witted solitary faerie like Grossard. For a long moment, he just stood and stared aghast at the carnage. In the next heartbeat, his face turned a peculiar shade of scarlet and a vein in his temple began to pulse like a time bomb ready to detonate. He whirled to face Grossard, his cape bellowing out around him like a pair of wings, and let out an unearthly wail as he hurled a fiery ball of energy at his archrival.

Grossard had fully expected Mordred to retaliate and was ready with the tip of his staff lowered and pointed. Mordred saw a flash of light and then his world turned red as Grossard's ball of energy absorbed his. The burst struck him mid chest, lifted him off his feet, and sent him careening backward through two wood, picket fences and into the side of the Roman townhome replica. All the air was forced out of his lungs and he was barely conscious as he slid down the wall and slumped to the ground like a marionette without strings.

~~

Deston was as surprised as Mordred to see that Grossard knew about the tunnels. As the arrows rained down on Mordred's army, he turned his head, unable to watch the slaughter. His gaze landed on Grossard just as the monster lowered the head of his staff at Mordred. Deston's breath caught in his throat as he watched the serpent's mouth open wide, as if it were alive, to reveal the Shard.

At the sight of the Shard, a strange stirring flickered to life within Deston. Mesmerized, he stood and gawked until the loud whoops and war cries of Grossard's army breaking through and trampling down the large hedge bordering the property jolted him back to reality. He reeled backward, but only a few steps, for he was still bound to the railing. He jerked hard on the cord and felt it give, but it didn't break as Mordred assured him it would. Cursing Mordred under his breath, he squatted down to make himself as small as possible so he wouldn't draw attention and wiggled, pulled, and plucked at the cord until he worked his hands out of it.

By the time he got free, the first of Grossard's soldiers were nearing the bathhouse wall. From the sound of it, more were coming in from behind him. A handful of Mordred's army had made it across the road and had flattened the wood picket fence that enclosed the ruins on the other side. And there he was, caught right between the two armies without a weapon.

Deston looked toward the townhome where Mordred had gone down, but all he could see was the red glow of the Shard. Another round of arrows streaked across the ruins and fell on Mordred's forces. The soldiers were more prepared for the assault and fewer of them went down, but masses of bodies still littered the ground. As his gaze roamed over the field, it suddenly dawned on him that there would be weapons amongst the bodies. He took off in a sprint without a second thought and raced along the top of the raised mound, dodging the sheep that had broken free and were running here and there in a frantic attempt to get out of the way of the horde.

As soon as he spotted the first body, he dropped and slid the last couple of feet across the damp grass. He grabbed up the fallen sword just as a wave of arrows came from the southwest. The arrows flew straight into the swarm of Grossard's soldiers who had just reached the tall bathhouse wall and were rushing through the archway. A unit of fae followed the arrows out of the grove of trees and raced toward the battle.

The three armies came together in a clash of swords, grunts and cries. By the time Deston realized he had inadvertently put himself in the midst of the action, it was too late.

Chapter 27

Grossard's gaze swept over the battlefield. Everything was working out just as he hoped—better, in fact. The look on Mordred's face when the tunnels were exposed had filled him with a sense of satisfaction he had not experienced in a long time. He fixed his eyes on the spot where Mordred had gone down. "I warned you not to underestimate me, sorcerer," he sneered through clenched teeth, and with a small pop he disappeared.

~~

Mordred came to with a jerk and reared up, gulping in a big breath as if it was his last. He staggered to his feet just as Grossard appeared in front of him.

"You are so much like your mother, thinking you're smarter than everyone else," Grossard scoffed. "That's what did her in, you know. And now, here you are in the same predicament." He flashed his razor sharp teeth in a fiendish grin. "Go ahead ... I want to hear you beg me for your life like she did."

Mordred swiped away the blood dripping from his nose with the back of his hand and glared up through his brow. "No matter how much you want to, you know you can't kill me. You need the book and incantation and I'm the only one who can give them to you."

Grossard laughed out loud and lifted the staff. Mordred rose several feet in the air, his arms extended out to the sides as if he was hanging on a cross. His lips moved feverishly with a counter spell, but nothing happened.

Grossard cackled even louder. "Save your breath. Your powers are not strong enough to counteract the power of the Shard." He strutted forward. "And they never will be," he added, spewing his putrid spittle over Mordred's face.

Mordred could feel his powers draining away and knew there was nothing he could do. He glared at Grossard, gritting his teeth as the monster reached inside his cloak. A small charge of energy from the protection spell he'd put around himself sent a tingling sensation through his chest, but the spell fizzled out as his powers did and Grossard pulled the book out with no resistance.

"I've waited too long to claim what should have been mine in the first place." Grossard's solid-black eyes gleamed triumphantly as he pressed the book against his chest and stepped back. "Would you like to retract your statement about my infinitesimal brain now, because I believe I have just outsmarted you once again." He leered down at Mordred, thoroughly enjoying the moment. "I told your mother that victory would be mine in the end," he added and slowly lowered the head of the Shard to point at Mordred's heart.

"Wait ... that's not the book," Mordred squeaked.

Grossard's gaze flicked down to the red scaly cover and right back to Mordred. "Your lies do not sway me. You are transparent and I know how deep your desire is to get the Shard. You wouldn't jeopardize that, not after all you've gone through to get it."

"It is a fake, I tell you. Look for yourself and see."

Grossard studied Mordred. The sorcerer was shrewd, but Grossard couldn't imagine Mordred would risk losing everything on such an easily detected deception. His fingers rubbed the rough texture of the book's cover, as several disturbing questions diluted his elation. He wasn't aware of a spell that would trigger and destroy the works when a book was opened, but that didn't mean there wasn't one. He also wasn't sure if Mordred would be stupid enough to enlist such a spell, for it would be as devastating to him as it would be to Grossard.

Grossard's upper lip lifted in a sneer and a growl rumbled in the back of his throat. "No more attempts at manipulation. I'm done with you." He took in a deep breath, preparing to finish Mordred off, but the smug look on Mordred's face stopped him and a small doubt took root in his mind. If he killed Mordred and the book turned out to be a fake after all, his plan to overthrow Oseron and take over the world would be ruined forever. His fingers tightened around the book, trying to gain some kind of insight as to its legitimacy, but it was an inanimate object and gave off no kind of vibe.

Damn you, Mordred! he silently cursed. He hated letting Mordred have even a miniscule speck of victory, but he had to know for sure. Reluctantly, he held the book away from his body and magically lifted the cover. Deep creases formed on his forehead as he stared down at a blank page. He turned the page over, and then the next, and the next. The air became thicker with the scent of sulfur as his anger spiraled and the blank pages began flipping over at an increased speed. When he reached the last page, he threw his head back and let out a bloodcurdling howl.

～

Rellik crept unseen along the roof of the front portico of the Roman townhome, the pads of his paws making no sound on the roof tiles. His strength was failing faster than he expected and he had come to the realization that this would more than likely be his last chance to destroy Grossard. But he was still determined to take Grossard with him when he took his last breath.

He made it to the corner edge of the roof and crouched down to wait for the right moment. He harbored no illusions it would be easy, especially in his weakened state, but knowing that Grossard's ego was his greatest weakness, Rellik was confident he'd succeed.

His muscles quivered in anticipation and when he saw Grossard flipping through the pages of the book, he knew his time had come. Rellik rose up out of the shadows and leaped at the moment Grossard threw his head back and howled.

Blindsided, Grossard staggered backward and with Rellik's heavy weight on top of him, he lost his balance and tumbled to the ground before he could recover. Grossard's bulk padded Rellik's fall and he wasted no time getting to his feet to make a second lunge for Grossard's throat. But Grossard's thick wool cloak was in the way and his bite caught more fabric than skin.

Grossard heaved up, threw Rellik off to the side and looked around for his staff, which had been knocked out his hand when he hit the ground. Rellik rolled to his feet and leaped again. Grossard dropped his chin in defense and Rellik's long fangs sank into the side of Grossard's face and jaw instead of his neck. He clamped his teeth together with all his strength and held on, even though it wasn't the lethal strike he had intended.

A curse rumbled in Grossard's throat as he stretched out his hand, feeling for his staff. The tips of his fingers brushed over it, but he couldn't quite grasp hold.

The metallic taste of blood flowed into Rellik's mouth, but he knew he hadn't gotten a clean shot at Grossard's throat and hadn't done any real damage. He clawed at the cloak that had twice prevented him from finishing Grossard off. The fabric shredded, along with Grossard's tunic, and four deep, red streaks cut across Grossard's chest.

Grossard didn't feel the pain, but he had had enough of Rellik's interference. He had planned a slow torturous end for Rellik, but it was time for the wolf to be gone and out of the way. Grabbing Rellik's head, he pressed his palms against each side of the wolf's temples, and hissed, *"Eay peoh de ahfee duweema."*

Rellik's body jerked spasmodically and the whites of his eyes turned red. Then blood began to ooze out from the corners of his eyes and also from his nostrils and ears. As his whole body bounced about uncontrollably, he lost his grip on Grossard's jaw. Grossard's eyes sparkled with delight as he pressed his palms harder against Rellik's temples. Rellik coughed and went stiff. Then with one long, shuddering breath, he went limp and fell to his side, his tongue, which was coated with Grossard's blood, lolling out of his mouth.

Chapter 28

Deston looked about frantically at the creatures of every shape and size, slashing at one another mercilessly. They had completely surrounded him and he saw no way out that didn't involve joining in the melee, which he knew would be certain death with his lack of experience.

Mordred's army had been instructed not to harm him, but that was little help, because Deston couldn't tell them apart from Grossard's army. To him, they all looked like monsters. The fae were somewhere in the mix, as well, though he couldn't see them from where he stood; and if he couldn't see them, they couldn't see him, so they weren't any help, either.

Jagged bolts of lightning suddenly sliced through the blackened sky and Deston jumped with the resounding clap of thunder that followed almost simultaneously. He didn't see where the lightning struck, but it was close enough that he could smell the ozone and his hair stood on end. Another flash of lightning crackled from the sky, lighting up the battlefield and he saw a number of korrigans fighting not too far away.

Deston gulped back his heart at the sight of the goat-legged creatures—not because they were scarier than the others, but because he knew the korrigans were part of Grossard's forces. If Grossard's soldiers had already made it this far through Mordred's line, his window of opportunity to get out unscathed was closing faster than he thought it would. As the sky was littered with arrows and lightning, he didn't have the option of transforming into a bird and flying out of there, which pretty much narrowed it down to the only way out was through the masses.

With a feeling of dread, he looked down at the sword in his hand. The only sword he'd ever wielded was Caluvier and this sword was definitely not Caluvier. It felt heavy and foreign in his hand, but that wasn't even the issue. He had no skills or experience in fighting in open combat. Deston adjusted his grip on the sword and bit his lip. He was out of choices and the sword was better than nothing. He blew out a breath and murmured, "Now would be a good time for you to share some of your know-how with me, Grandfather, 'cause I'm going to need all the help I can get."

Adrenalin pumped through his veins as he started into the mob, dodging and ducking around the swinging swords, clubs, battle axes and flails. He slashed out at anyone and any weapon that got too near, but only with defense moves, for he did not want to get caught up in a one-on-one swordfight. His feet slid on the slick blood and slimy entrails of the fallen and he knew the liquid running down his face was more than sweat, but he tried not to think about it. The rancid smell of the creatures mixed in with the smell of rotten egg from the dark magic and the pungent odor of ozone was nauseating, and he had to constantly swallow back the bile that rose to the back of his throat.

He was panting heavily from the exertion of swinging the heavy sword, but it didn't seem as if he was making much progress. For every creature he got by, it seemed two more took its place and the battlefield was becoming so congested, he could hardly move. Time was slipping away from him and he knew it. As he ducked to avoid another flail that was on course with his head, he noticed a big gap between the legs of an ogre. Without a second thought, he dropped to the ground and crawled through the space, coming up on the other side just as a korrigan turned his way. The korrigan's red eyes lit up in recognition and he shouted out to another. The second korrigan turned Deston's way and when a third followed, Deston knew he was in trouble.

The first korrigan, who had a huge, bulbous nose, let loose a bone-chilling laugh and flashed his pointed, blackened fangs as he and his two companions threw those standing in their way to the side, as if they were giants walking through a crowd of toddlers.

Deston looked left and then right for an escape route, but there was no way out. As the korrigans drew nearer, he planted his feet and gripped his sword with both hands. He knew he didn't have much of a chance, but he couldn't just stand there and let them take him to Grossard without at least trying to resist.

A malicious grin twisted the face of the first korrigan as he swung the flat side of his broadsword at Deston's head. Deston ducked at the last possible second and the blade whizzed over him, taking with it only a few strands of his hair. The other two lunged forward and swung their giant clubs simultaneously. Deston brought his sword up to block, but at that same moment, the creature behind him stumbled backwards and its bony elbow caught Deston in the side of his ribs. Deston lurched over with a groan and the first club missed him completely. But the second one slammed into his left side, lifted him off his feet and hurled him into the back of an ogre. A searing pain shot through his left shoulder and raced down his arm like a wildfire. Before he could even gasp out a moan, the ogre whipped around, punched him in the ribs and gave him a hard shove. The air whooshed out of his lungs and pain like he'd never experienced before exploded in his chest. When he hit the ground, the jolt knocked his sword out of his hand. He feebly reached out for it, but it was swiftly swept away in a scuffle of feet.

His vision blurred in and out, and it felt like the earth was tilting, but he knew he had to get up or be trampled to death. Gritting his teeth against the mind-numbing pain in his shoulder and mid-section, he pushed up to a sitting position with his right arm. The korrigans were a few feet away, but they couldn't see him in the confusion of bodies. Digging his heels into the ground, he scooted backwards to get through the legs of the ogre that was behind him before the korrigans found him again. The korrigan with the big nose suddenly let out a yell as he rushed forward and stomped down on Deston's ankle.

"Going somewhere, little prince?" the korrigan taunted.

Cradling his aching arm, Deston looked up into the hideous face, thinking it was going to be the last thing he ever saw. He closed his eyes so he wouldn't have to watch the final blow come and end his life. The clamoring noise of metal clanging upon metal and the grunts, roars, and shrieks of the creatures rang in his head, but through it all he heard the piercing caw of a crow.

"You said I'd never be alone, Zumwald, but it looks like you're wrong," he whispered.

Suddenly, his mind was filled with images of his life, flicking from one to another as fast as they could go. He saw his mom kiss his knee after he'd fallen off his bike when he was a toddler; her dancing around the kitchen and singing *Come What May* from Moulin Rouge as she cooked his favorite dinner; his father rise up from the dead after the Light Crystal was renewed; and the first time he saw Margaux; their first kiss. His whole life flew by in chronological order and winked out as fast as it came, leaving a vivid image of Zumwald stamped onto the back of his eyelids. Though, it wasn't the Zumwald Deston was used to seeing. It looked more like what he had always imagined Merlyn from the King Arthur days to look like. A dark, foreboding face with angry eyes, and the jagged line that had previously only shown as a fleeting flash in his right eye, stayed constant and shined brightly.

Altogether, the images of Deston's life took no more than a nanosecond and his mind barely had time to register the flashes before he was ripped out of his memories by a heavy weight falling on top of him and a sharp point cutting into his skin. His eyes flew open with a gasp and he tried to pull in some air, but one of the korrigans had fallen on top of him and he couldn't expand his lungs.

Wheezing and coughing, he tried to push the bulk off, but with only one arm he couldn't get the leverage he needed, and the pain and lack of air was draining his strength. He lifted his head to see if there was any other way to get free and saw the arrow protruding out of the back of the korrigan's head. Lying a few feet away, the other two korrigans had identical arrows sticking out of the back of their heads. As he stared and tried to comprehend what he was seeing, a giant foot landed in the spot where his head had been a second before. The ogre who belonged to the foot hopped back another step to get out of the way of a blade and nearly tripped over the korrigan's body that was lying on top of Deston. In a fit of rage, the ogre gave the korrigan a kick, the force of which lifted the body into the air. It came back down on top of Deston's legs.

With the weight off his chest, Deston drew in a gulp of fetid air and then another. His head was swimming, but he wiggled and pulled until he got his legs free. He felt cold and clammy and his breathing was labored, but that was nothing compared to how he felt when he looked out at his collapsing opportunities. Bodies were piling up and being trodden on as more of Grossard's forces were getting through the lines. It was just a matter of time before someone else recognized him. Without a sword and no use of his left arm, he didn't hold much hope for his odds of getting out.

In desperation, he called out to Oseron, *"Dad, I'm trapped. Can you send help?"*

Whether Oseron answered him back or not, he never knew, because a blood-curdling shriek pierced his eardrums. He whirled in the direction of the sound and saw another korrigan hacking his way through a line of creatures to get to him. He unconsciously took a step back, but a solid wall of bodies prevented him from going any farther.

The korrigan's teeth were bared in a vicious snarl as he swiped viciously at the cucubuth who stumbled into his path. The cucubuth agilely jumped to the side, missing the blade, but the korrigan was lightning quick and swung his sword back around, slicing the cucubuth's chest open right down the center. The cucubuth went rigid and then shuddered and crumpled to the ground, leaving a wide-open space between the korrigan and Deston. The korrigan's eyes glinted with malice as he took a step forward, but he didn't take another. His mouth drooped open and his red eyes fixed on a space above Deston's head. A small trickle of blood dribbled out of the corner of his mouth and down his chin and the sword slipped from his hand. He swayed to the side, back to center, and teetered forward, landing on top of the cucubuth he'd just killed.

Deston's gaze followed the korrigan down and he didn't see Torren standing behind the creature.

"Deston, look out," Torren's voice suddenly shouted in Deston's head. Deston jerked up, but another creature had already jumped into the space between him and Torren.

Deston dove to the ground just in time to miss being struck by a giant club. *"Torren, where are you? I'm caught in the middle of the fighting and I can't get out,"* he called back.

Suddenly, the creatures on all sides of him fell, but Deston's mind was fixated on how to get out and he didn't realize what was happening. He grabbed up one of the creatures' swords that had dropped beside him and scrambled to his feet with a loud, "EEE YAAHH."

His vision was fuzzy and sweaty strands of hair hung down over his eyes, so all he saw was a large, dark figure appear before him. He slashed out without realizing who it was. Torren deflected the blade, but Deston deftly whipped the sword around for another strike. The two blades met in the middle and formed an X.

Deston's eyes went wide as he looked through the blades and recognized his friend. "Torren?" he whispered, dropping the sword to his side. "Torren, I ... um ..." His mind was so jumbled he couldn't put any more words together.

Torren looked at the blood covering Deston from head to toe. He could see it wasn't all Deston's, but the dilated eyes and the pain etched on Deston's face told him the prince had incurred significant injuries.

"We must get you out of here. Are you able to walk on your own?" Torren asked.

Deston blinked and swayed slightly. "Torren?" he questioned again, still unsure if the warrior was real or if he was imagining him.

"Are you able to walk?" Torren repeated, taking hold of Deston's left arm.

The fresh surge of pain brought Deston back to his senses. He nodded his head and mumbled, "Yes."

"Okay, stay close to me. We'll get you out of here," Torren replied.

Eight fae warriors immediately appeared and surrounded Deston. In a tight group they slowly moved through the fighting, fending off anyone who tried to stop them. As they neared the outer edge, more fae joined in and minutes later Deston broke free.

"Run," Torren shouted to Deston, as arrows flew from the trees to cut down any creature that tried to follow.

It seemed as if the field went on forever. By the time Deston got to the cover of the trees he was trembling as much from the adrenaline rush as from the exertion. His breathing was labored as it hurt too much to take in a deep breath, but he made it to a tree, leaned his right shoulder against it and looked back. As the dawn was still hours away, all he could detect was distorted shapes and silhouettes moving about through the ruins and out over the fields. Another lightning bolt cut the sky in half and hundreds of swords sparked with the reflection of the light. In that flash, Deston combed the faces for Grossard, but the light was too brief to pick out one individual within the mass of bodies.

"Deston," Joliet called out behind him. He was just starting to turn when a pair of arms encircled him and squeezed him in a tight hug, sending another round of pain surging down his arm. Hearing his gasp, Joliet instantly drew back. "You're hurt!" she cried, stepping around him to get a better look. Her face paled at the sight of all the blood. "Oh honey, what have they done to you? Get the healer," she called over her shoulder. To Deston she said, "You need to sit down."

She gently put her arm around his waist to help him over to a fallen tree, but as she shifted her position, Deston got a glimpse of Margaux and the all too familiar fire sparked to life in the pit of his stomach. His eyes lit up, but then he realized that she was there in the middle of the battle and his fear for her safety shattered his joy of seeing her. Pulling away from Joliet, he marched over to where Margaux was standing.

"What are you doing here? Can't you see there's a war going on right out there? You've already been taken prisoner once. Isn't that enough for one day? You should be back in Tir na-nÓg." He rambled on without giving her any chance to respond between questions. He blew out a breath of frustration and added, "Why won't you ever listen?" He was so overcome with emotion he didn't realize he was shouting, or that Joliet, Lilika, and several other fae were watching them.

Margaux's relief at seeing Deston vanished the second he started in on his tirade. Her cheeks flamed a deep pink and her lips thinned to a line, but she held her response until he finished. "Might I remind you that you were taken prisoner, too, and I just helped save your life, so don't you shout at me. You're welcome, by the way." Her hands went to her hips. "And in case you hadn't noticed, I'm a fae, which gives me as much right to be here as you." Her nose burned with the tears that were building behind her eyes and not wanting him to see, she spun on her heel and walked away. After only two steps, she whirled back around. "I tried to warn you Rellik was leading you into a trap, but you didn't listen. Maybe you should take your own advice," she fired back, and with a huff, stomped away.

Deston's nostrils flared as he watched Margaux melt into the shadows. However, the second she was out of sight, his anger dissolved and an empty cavern opened in his chest. He blew out the breath he'd been holding in and ran his fingers through his hair that was stiff with sweat and blood. His mind was totally occupied with Margaux and when a hand softly touched his shoulder, he twisted around without thinking. Fresh pain sliced through him and he grabbed onto Lilika's arm to keep from falling over.

"You sounded like Keir just now," Lilika said, her eyes bright with unshed tears. "He always wanted me to stay in the village whenever there was trouble about. But that's not who I am any more than it's who Margaux is. Gender doesn't dictate how capable a person is, you know. Margaux has trained hard and she just wants to show you that she is your equal." She took his hand and gave him a sad smile. "I know you care for her, so let me give you some advice ... don't hold her back. Accept her for what she is and let her learn and grow along side of you. You will both become stronger for it." She wanted to say more but tears clogged her throat and she couldn't go on. She gave his hand a squeeze and walked off.

Deston bit his lip. Everything Lilika said was true. Somewhere along the line, Margaux had stolen his heart without him realizing it, and with his heart, went his brain. He was always saying and doing stupid things around her and pushing her away, even though in reality he wanted her with him and felt more confident when she was. At the same time, it made him crazy sick with fear to think she might get hurt, and his heart would go into arrhythmia at the thought of losing her. When it came to Margaux, he just couldn't do anything right.

Gawd, I'm such an idiot, he thought, afraid he'd gone too far and she wouldn't forgive him this time.

Caught up in his misery, he wasn't conscious of the healer tending to him until a burning pain ripped through his arm. He gulped in a breath to scream, which only amplified the pain in his side and in the next instant, his worries fled into a red haze of agony.

168

M.J. BELL

Chapter 29

Grossard shoved Rellik off and got to his feet. After seeing Rellik in Gotland and seeing the pitiful condition the wolf was in, he hadn't expected Rellik to accompany Mordred to Viroconium. Even at Rellik's strongest he was never a match for Grossard, and Rellik knew that, but obviously, the wolf's body wasn't the only thing that had become severely weakened. But Grossard was never one to turn away from good fortune when it presented itself on a silver platter.

"You could have been great, Rellik," Grossard sneered, his black eyes gleaming with rapture as he looked down on his former second in command.

He turned his head as he caught a movement out of the corner of his eye and his bliss fled as he looked upon the serpent's head on the top of his staff and saw that its mouth was stretched wide. He frowned as he stared at it, wondering what had caused it to open on its own, and suddenly he felt a shift in the air. An icy chill engulfed him. He pivoted on the spot and gazed out at the battle, noticing a number of fae fighting amidst the others. His gaze paused on one particular fae that had a familiar stance. *No ... it can't be.* As if the warrior knew Grossard was staring at him, he turned and stared Grossard in the eye.

"Oseron?" Grossard uttered in total disbelief and unconsciously took a step back. "What? ... How did you know?" His brain froze, and for once in his life, he was at a loss for words. Mordred had told him that Oseron wouldn't find out about their meeting until it was long over. He knew the sorcerer was a conniving sociopath and a habitual liar, but he couldn't imagine Mordred would risk everything and bring the fae in. But no one else knew the place and time of the meeting, except for the two of them, so it could be no one other than Mordred. Grossard blanched and threw his head back. "MORDRED!"

~

The second Rellik knocked Grossard to the ground, the spell holding Mordred was broken and he dropped like a stone, landing with a strangled cry on the hard ground. There was a loud ringing in his ears and his head felt like he'd been twirling non-stop on a merry-go-round. He could barely put two thoughts together, but his self-defense mode was fully aware and screaming at him to get moving. It took him several attempts to get his weak, shaky legs under him, but he finally made it to his feet. He didn't bother to look around to see where Grossard was, for he was afraid even that small movement would bring on another bout of dizziness. Leaning heavily against the side of the building, he forced his limbs to move and inched his way along.

Once he had made it around the corner, he paused to catch his breath. His eyes darted from left to right, for the ringing in his ears drowned out all other sound and that left him vulnerable for someone to sneak up on him. He could feel that his powers had been almost completely depleted, but there wasn't time to replenish them. Grossard could come around the corner at any moment to finish him off and his only hope of surviving was to put as much distance as he could between the two of them.

Gritting his teeth, Mordred summoned what little power he still possessed, which took more energy than what he could afford. With a faint pop, he disappeared and reappeared at the edge of a copse of trees. He had no idea where he was, but all he cared about was that he was away from the battle and Grossard. He wobbled a few feet, wanting to get farther into the cover of the trees, but his strength was gone and his legs gave out. He crumbled to the ground and rolled to his back. Closing his eyes, he breathed in the damp, mossy smell of the trees. The ringing in his head wasn't nearly as bad as it had been, but red and white blobs swirled and shifted crazily behind his eyelids and then darkness slowly moved in.

~~

The hair on the back of Oseron's neck suddenly rose and a cold sensation crept up his back. He turned and saw a red glow highlighting a large imposing figure near the building across the road. He didn't need the surge of energy he felt from the Crystal around his neck, to know it was Grossard.

"I've spotted Grossard," he called out to his men. In the next blink of an eye, he appeared in front of his nemesis.

The Crystal of Light and the Shard reacted to their close proximity and both flared brightly, lighting up the area like a stage. As one, the armies turned to see what was going on and a dead silence settled over the ruins.

With a barely discernible movement, Grossard replaced the staff in his hand with a sword just as Oseron lunged. He blocked Oseron's thrust with a bellow of outrage, which sent his soldiers back into action and the fighting resumed with a vengeance throughout the ruins.

Grossard glared through the crisscrossed blades. "You no longer have an advantage now that I have the Shard, and you will not win the battle this time around," he spat, his double row of serrated teeth gleaming in the light of the crystals.

"You may have the Shard, but that does not give you the advantage. Not as long as I have the Light Crystal and Mordred has the book," Oseron responded.

Grossard jerked back in surprise. He had no idea Oseron knew about the incantation. Oseron lunged again and Grossard dodged to the right, but his moment of distraction cost him and Oseron's blade laid a slice across his bicep. Grossard gnashed his teeth as blood gushed from the wide gash and he slashed back with as much force as he could muster.

Sparks flew and Grossard hissed through his teeth. "Don't you worry. I'll have the book soon enough, and once I do; your world will be the first I destroy and your whole family along with it."

Oseron scoffed. "Mordred has hidden the book well. You haven't found it up to this point and I doubt you ever will."

Grossard's upper lip curled up and his nostrils flared. "Mordred will give me—"

"No, he won't. But as he is presently in our camp, he may give it to me. He has always been more than willing to do whatever it takes to save his life."

Grossard's eyes narrowed and his face turned a purplish hue as he swung his sword in a vicious downward strike. The descending blade narrowly missed Oseron as he whirled and parried Grossard's next swing. Again and again, Grossard slashed out, getting more reckless with each thrust, as he pictured Mordred's face before him and strove to erase the smirk off the sorcerer's face.

Chapter 30

Deston sat on the ground with his back against a tree, taking shallow breaths to keep the pain of his broken ribs down to a manageable level. A tight bandage had been wound around his middle to help, but certain movements and deep breaths would cause the fire in his chest to erupt again. His dislocated left shoulder had been put back in place and his arm was loosely bound to his side to keep it stationary, which held the pain down to a throbbing ache. That was all the healers could do for him until they got him back to Tir na-nÓg and could tend to him properly.

He rested his head against the tree trunk and closed his eyes. He was so very tired. Torren, along with several other select warriors, had stayed with him in case there were more attempts to capture him. Their low murmurs of battle reports reached his ears, but he was too drowsy to pay much attention until one of them called out, "The king has found Grossard!"

At that, Deston's eyes flew open and he lurched up, sending another shooting pain through his midsection. Gingerly holding his side, he eased back down, trying not to move in any way that would cause him more discomfort. He blew short breaths out through his mouth and closed his eyes. Instantly, the vivid image of Grossard driving a sword into Oseron's chest back at the monastery appeared behind his eyelids, making the pain of his injuries nothing compared to the pain that sprang to his heart. The Crystal had saved Oseron back then, but that was before Grossard had gained the powers of the Shard.

A torrent of thoughts bombarded his brain at the same speed as his heart was beating, and in that second, it finally dawned on him that denying his destiny had done nothing but bring him and everyone around him heartache and pain. He had spent so much time and energy dodging the truth and what had he accomplished by doing so? Taking a shuddering breath, he looked up through the tree branches. As if a veil had been lifted, everything suddenly looked much clearer. It was his destiny to put an end to Grossard and the Shard. That was the whole reason he had been born and it was pointless to fight the fact.

"All right, I'll do it." He felt a stirring in his chest. *"But Grandfather I'm going to need you now more than ever. You said you'd always be there for me. I hope you meant it."*

He gulped back the knot in his throat and cautiously peeked through a slit in his eyes. The warriors were huddled around Torren, but within seconds, the others rushed off, leaving Torren standing alone. Torren's hand twitched on the hilt of his sword as he stared out through the trees. Deston could see the warrior wanted to be out there with the others, fighting for his king, but he couldn't because of him.

As Deston pondered the best way to sneak away, he saw Torren suddenly tense and turn his head. The grim look on Torren's face and the hard lines around his eyes and mouth were a sure sign that something bad had happened. It took all Deston's will power to stay still and not jump up to find out what, but he needed Torren to think he was asleep to execute his plan. It was agony not knowing what was going on, but he squeezed his eyes shut and held his breath.

Long torturous seconds ticked off inside Deston's head before he dared another peek. Torren was no longer there. In his place there were two others, who had their backs turned to him as they stared out at the battle.

Biting his lip, Deston stifled a groan and got to his feet. The warriors didn't even flinch. His heart was pounding so hard, he couldn't believe it didn't do more damage to his ribs. He held his breath and darted to another tree. Once behind it, he counted to ten before leaning around the trunk to see if the warriors had noticed he was gone. Seeing that they were still watching the battle, he hustled to the next tree, and then the next.

～

Torren had allowed Tiff to stay with Deston, but only after she promised she would stay out of sight and not bother him. So she was there, sitting on a tree branch above Deston's head, when the news came in about Oseron and Grossard. From her high perch, she watched Deston slink from one tree to the next, knowing all the while she should alert Torren, but also knowing Deston would never forgive her for snitching him out if she did.

"What do I do? What do I do? What do I do?" she muttered under her breath. It was such a monumental decision for one little sprite to make— help the prince or help the king. She had never had to make a choice of such importance before and she was terrified she would choose wrong.

Fluttering anxiously between the branches, she watched Deston get closer to the boundary of the trees, knowing she couldn't delay making a decision much longer, because in another minute, Deston would be gone.

"Tiff, are you still with Deston? He's not answering me," Joliet's voice suddenly intruded on Tiff's thoughts. Tiff jumped as if she'd been caught doing something wrong and flew straight up into the branch above her.

"Where are you? Why is no one answering me?" Joliet called out, her tone edgy with anxiety.

Tiff blinked and rubbed the bump on her head. Joliet was the queen, which meant Tiff couldn't just ignore her. Wringing her hands together, she bounced from one limb to the next; trying to convince herself that Deston would understand that she didn't have a choice. But at this point, whether he got mad or not didn't make a difference. She was duty-bound to answer Joliet.

"Yes, I'm with Deston. He's leaving to go back into the battle. You should come quickly," Tiff called back.

There was hardly a pause before Joliet answered, *"I'm coming. Stay with him, and don't let him out of your sight."*

Chapter 31

"It's Mordred. Over here!"

The voice drifted into Mordred's subconscious and a point of light appeared within the blackness. As the point of light slowly expanded, he floated toward it and a sense of peace settled over him. *It's just like they said,* he thought, recalling the tales of near-death experiences and the white light every one of them mentioned. But a small nagging in the back of his mind broke through his tranquility, telling him something was wrong. He most certainly would never be going toward the light.

Suddenly, voices saying his name blasted through his head and the illusion of heaven dissolved. His body gave a jerk and his eyes shot open to a ring of faces staring down at him. One of the faces looked vaguely familiar, although in his confused state, he couldn't quite grasp onto the girl's name—or how he knew her.

As he stared into girl's honey colored eyes, a small voice in the back of his mind prodded him to get up and get out of there. He still wasn't thinking clearly, but that advice sounded like a good idea. However, as he tried to move, his muscles locked and refused to cooperate.

The familiar face leaned in closer and spoke to him, but she was not making any sense. He frowned in confusion and watched as her hand rose up in slow motion. Then a stinging blow connected with his cheek. His head snapped to the side and a burst of light detonated in his head. His cheek burned from the force of the blow, but thankfully the ringing in his ears stopped. He moved his jaw back and forth and blinked Margaux's face into focus.

"Where am I?" he asked. Before anyone could answer, his memory came back. "The Shard!" he said under his breath and held out his hand to be helped up to his feet. Two strong hands took him by the arms and heaved him up so fast his head swam for a moment. Several others swiftly stripped him of his cloak and weapons. It was then he realized he had transported himself into the midst of the fae.

Mordred hid his trepidation and turned his most charming smile on Margaux, as one of the fae handed her Caluvier. "You're as resourceful as your boyfriend, I see."

"Where's the book?" Torren interrupted.

The smile slid off Mordred's face and his gaze slowly turned to the tall warrior. "You think after all these centuries I'm going to turn the Book of Tenebris over to the fae?" He snickered. "I'd die before I'd let a one of you touch it."

"My mama used to say, 'be careful what you wish for.' I always thought that was a silly saying, but I can see the wisdom of it now," Margaux replied. "Unless you really do wish to die, you better tell us where the book is."

Mordred locked eyes with Torren and a sly grin lifted the corners of his mouth. "That might be a good threat if I wasn't aware that you fae are not cold blooded killers." He wrinkled his nose. "So is that really all you have?"

"It may be true we won't kill you," Torren replied. "But we can make the rest of your life one of misery, isolation, and poverty so that you wish you were dead."

Mordred lifted his chin and tried to hold onto his smug look, but it had lost a lot of its vigor.

"Or we could just turn you over to Grossard. I doubt he'll be as lenient with your life as we are. From what I hear you two are not exactly on the best of terms," Torren added.

Mordred clenched his jaw and glared at Torren as his mind whirled. He was a master of schemes and there had to be a way he could turn this around. He just needed time to think it through. If that meant swallowing his pride to get time, so be it. It wouldn't be the first time he'd lose face to get what he wanted.

"Now, now," he said, holding his hands up in surrender. "I'm sure we can come to some terms that will benefit both of us. After all, your prince and I have agreed on a deal, so I see no—"

"Deston would never make a deal with the likes of you," Margaux cut in and stepped forward, but Lilika was faster and got between Margaux and Mordred.

"None of us are going to believe your lies. So just tell us where you've hidden the book," Lilika hissed, grabbing hold of Mordred's hair and pulling his head back until his neck was stretched taut.

Mordred looked down his nose at Lilika. "You're too late. Grossard has already taken the book. He is the one you should be concentrating your efforts on, not wasting your time harassing me."

Margaux stepped into Mordred's space. "We already know all about the fake book you brought Grossard. And we know you still have the real one hidden somewhere."

Mordred's eye widened and then narrowed. "Ah, I see you've been talking to Rellik. I should tell you, he'll say anything and do anything to get what he wants?"

"Ha! Unlike you?" Torren interjected. "It wasn't Rellik who told us of your devious plan. It was Deston."

Mordred looked at Torren out of the corner of his eye. The fae weren't liars; but Deston couldn't possibly have told them about the book, not with the spell he'd put in place to block communications. But how they found out was inconsequential. They knew, and it was another development he hadn't expected and was going to have to deal with.

"Not that I doubt you, but I don't see how that is possible." He looked over the group standing around him. "I don't see the prince here amongst you."

"Never you mind about Deston. He's doing just fine," Margaux answered. "Now quit stalling and—"

"Torren, Deston has left," a warrior called out as he came running up to the group.

Torren and Margaux both turned at the same time with the same shocked expression on their faces. Torren quickly took the warrior by the arm and guided him away from the others. Margaux followed right behind him.

"Deston left? Where did he go?" Torren asked, keeping his voice low so Mordred couldn't hear, but unbeknownst to him, Mordred had enhanced hearing.

"He went to help the king fight Grossard."

Torren tensed and his jaw twitched with the effort to hold in the expletive he so wanted to shout out. Margaux, however, gasped out loud and without saying a word, she turned on her heel and took off at a dead run.

"Margaux! You've been ordered to stay out of the battle," Torren yelled after her. She ignored him and transformed into a falcon and flew off into the darkness.

Lilika turned her head. "What's happened? Where's Margaux going?"

"Your prince is a foolish boy with dreams of grandeur. He thinks he can defeat Grossard. It's a pity that by the time he realizes he's wrong, it will be too late for him," Mordred replied with a smirk.

"What do you know?" Lilika said through gritted teeth, giving his hair a yank.

Mordred let out a small yelp and replied, "I know that the boy believes the gods are on his side, but in reality the only thing that has kept him alive up to this point is luck and Caluvier. But with the Shard in play, I'm afraid it cancels out both of those advantages."

Lilika shoved Mordred into the arms of the fae standing behind him and hurried after Torren. "Is it true? Has Deston gone to fight Grossard?"

"That is ..." Torren began, but as Lilika put her hand up, he stopped.

She could see he wasn't going to impart any information to her and it infuriated her. "Torren, do not treat me like an invalid. You know me. I can deal with this. Just tell me what is going on."

Torren shook his head. "I do know you and what you're capable of, but right now Deston is not your concern. The baby is the only thing you should be worried about. We have everything handled. Stay here and help guard Mordred. Do not leave the trees and do not get involved in the battle—that is a direct order from Oseron."

"But—" Lilika started, but Torren cut her off.

"There are no buts about it, Lilika. Obey this command or be taken back to Tir na-nÓg. Those are your two options."

Lilika glared at him, but Torren refused to waiver. Keir was one of his best friends, and with Keir gone, he felt the same responsibility as Oseron to watch over his friend's family. He gently laid his hand on her arm in an attempt to soften her disappointment. As he felt her tense and saw her eyes fill with tears, he took a step back and shook his head, mistakenly assuming the tears were her way of getting him to relent.

"I'm sorry, but the order stands," Torren said gruffly and walked away, too preoccupied with all that was going on to realize it wasn't like Lilika to let the matter drop, or that there might be another reason for Lilika's tears.

Lilika stood, clenching her fists and grinding her teeth together to fight off the pain that had ripped across her belly in the midst of the argument. Her insides felt as if they were being torn apart and it was all she could do to hold back her moan so Torren wouldn't know.

As Torren walked away shouting out orders, the warriors immediately went into action and no one paid attention to Lilika. She turned her back and blew out the breath she'd been holding. Just when the pain began to subside and she thought she had made it through, another stabbing cramp streaked across her abdomen. It was just as intense as the first and she almost doubled over. It took all her willpower to stay upright, but she still hunched over slightly as she fought back the pain and blew short breaths out through her mouth.

"Oh, my sweet girl, now is not a good time," she whispered, rubbing her swollen stomach. "I still have one more thing I must do before you come. Please hold on just a little longer. Your mama gave an oath and this is important." She inhaled deeply several more times until she could stand straight. She then squared her shoulders and turned her attention back to what was going on.

Torren and all but five of the warriors were gone. Of the five, two were securing Mordred to a tree and three were milling close by, throwing curious glances her way. With her head held high, she walked stiffly to the men guarding Mordred, keeping her stride purposeful even though it was painful with Macaria pressing hard against her pelvic bone. Dirt from Arthur's grave dusted Mordred's shoulders, but his pale blue eyes glinted with amusement as he looked up and opened his mouth to speak.

"Gag him," Lilika ordered before Mordred could get a word out. "We don't need to listen to any more of his lies." One of the men pulled Mordred's ascot up over his mouth and tightened it as Lilika added, "Since you do not need me here, I'm going to check on the archers."

As she started to walk away one the men stepped in front of her. "Torren told us you were not to leave."

The amber flakes in Lilika's eyes sparked and she lifted her chin in indignation. "Are you challenging me, the commander of the queen's guard?" The man blushed, but he held his ground and she could see he was not going to back down. "The king ordered me to stay off the battlefield, but nothing was said about me helping the archers, who are *not* on the battlefield. I suggest you step aside unless you'd like me to report your insubordination," she added, using a tone of authority.

The warrior hesitated and then bowed and stepped aside. Lilika's face was blank, but inside she was smiling in relief as she hurried into the shadows. She headed straight to the archers as she told the warrior she would. However, as soon as she made sure everything was under control there, she transformed into a hawk and flew straight for the light at the north end of the ruins. She had no trouble picking out Oseron and Grossard; they were illuminated in the light of the Crystals, but she did not see Deston or Margaux. Fearing what that could mean, she ignored the ache in her stomach, flapped her wings and sped across the sky.

Chapter 32

Deston's eyes were fixed on the light of the crystals and his feet barely touched the ground as he sprinted toward it. He was counting on finding Mordred near the front, north corner of the building where he saw the sorcerer go down. He was also counting on Caluvier being there with Mordred. If it wasn't, he had no backup plan, so he wouldn't even let the thought of that possibility enter his brain.

He slowed his gait as he reached the back of the Roman townhouse and vaulted over the half brick wall of the rear portico. The battle was being fought across the road from the front side of the building and the glow of light coming from the north end told him that's where Oseron and Grossard were. There was no one at the backside of the building, but he ran close to the wall and stayed within the shadows of the portico's roof just to be safe. When he got to the northwest corner, he halted and sucked in a breath before daring a peek out.

The light from the crystals extended to the road that separated the townhouse from the ruins. Just beyond the light he could see a few dark shapes of soldiers battling it out. In the center of the light were his father and Grossard, whirling around each other in a macabre kind of dance, their swords moving so fast only the sparks of the blades clashing together were visible.

By Deston's calculations, he figured Mordred was near the front portico, but once he rounded the corner he'd be in the light and there'd be no place to hide. If anyone spotted him, Grossard being his biggest concern, he'd have little chance of escaping.

Pressing his back against the rough brick wall, he let his head fall back and looked up at the stars, willing his heart to slow down. *I can do this. I just need to get Caluvier and then go for Grossard. It'll be a piece of cake,* he told himself, although his gut told him that wouldn't really be the case.

Cautiously, Deston peeked around the corner of the building once again. Grossard's attention seemed to be focused on Oseron and only Oseron and it didn't look as if the monster was even taking a breath between swings. For one second, Deston thought about reaching out and asking his father to keep Grossard turned the other way so he could get to Caluvier, but he threw that idea out as quickly as it came in fear the distraction would give Grossard an advantage.

Nervous sweat ran down between his shoulder blades and his stomach was a hard knot. He inhaled deeply, blew it out through his mouth and wiped his clammy palms against his tunic. *This is it.* He inhaled again, held it in and darted around the corner.

Deston crouched as low as he could and crept along the side of the building, his gaze sweeping wide as he went in case Caluvier had been flung away in the blast. He made it to the opposite corner of the building where he thought Mordred had gone down in no time at all, but there was nothing there—no Mordred and no Caluvier. He stared at the trampled grass and then back the way he had come. He was sure it was the right spot; he'd watched it happen with his own eyes—Mordred had been standing at this corner of the building. Completely confused and nearing a state of panic, he stretched up to scan the area, forgetting all about the need to stay low.

At that moment, Grossard sidestepped to avoid one of Oseron's thrusts and caught Deston's movement out of the corner of his eye. He did a double take, and then quickly looked back at Oseron, who appeared to be unaware his son was there. A thin smile tweaked the corners of Grossard's mouth and with precise moves; he slowly maneuvered Oseron around so that Deston was at Oseron's back.

Deston's brain was racing double time, desperately trying to think of where Caluvier could be. He looked back along the building, wondering if he had missed something, but before he could start back to retrace his steps, a dark object streaked by his head so close, the breeze ruffled his hair. He jerked around and then reared back as Margaux landed and skidded to a stop beside him.

"Are you completely mad standing out in the open like this? You don't even have a sword to defend yourself!" she shouted inside his head, trying to tug him toward the shadows of the front portico.

He blinked at her, his mouth agape. "What are you doing here?" he stuttered and then looked over his shoulder as he suddenly remembered Grossard. "You shouldn't be here," he added, taking her arm and guiding her into the same shadows she had been trying to steer him to.

"You shouldn't be here, either," she fired back as they squatted down in the shadows together. "Especially without Caluvier." Her hand trembled as she held out the sword she had brought him. A blue spark ran along the cutting edge of the blade, highlighting the runes engraved down the center.

Deston's face brightened as he reached for Caluvier, but his delight didn't lasted. "How did you get this?"

"Mordred had it. He appeared outside of our camp badly hurt. I guess he couldn't get any farther than the trees. *They're* going to take him back to Tir na-nÓg to make sure Grossard can't get to him."

Deston gripped Caluvier tighter. "Go back to the camp with the others," he said as he stood, a grim look of determination etched on his face.

Margaux stood along with him and grabbed his arm as he turned away. "I'm not going anywhere unless you are."

Deston gave her an incredulous look. "Margaux, this is danger ..." His words trailed off as he saw her lips thin to a fine line. He blew a breath out through his mouth and ran his hand through his hair. "Please, just ... this ... once ... do as I ask," he whispered.

"No," she hissed back without hesitation.

A vein in the center of Deston's forehead popped out and his mouth opened and closed, but he was so frustrated he couldn't think of what to say. As he glowered at Margaux, a soft breeze blew across the back of his neck. In the next second, Tiff's small voice yelled inside his head, *"Watch out."* He sucked in a sharp breath and flipped around just as Grossard materialized behind him.

Margaux screamed as Grossard reached out for Deston. Deston instinctively reacted and flung his arm out, knocking Grossard's hand aside. He then twirled and kicked out, planting his foot into Grossard's stomach with all the strength he could muster.

Grossard bent in half and staggered backward, coughing as though the punch had actually hurt him in a ploy to get Deston to lower his guard. Then, without warning, he sprang. Deston sidestepped and flipped around behind, but Grossard spun, too, and rushed at Deston, slashing out with his sword.

"Deston, watch out!" Oseron called out as he rushed to intervene. Deston threw a glance at his father just as Grossard reached out. The next thing he knew, Grossard's hand had closed around his waist and he was lifted him off his feet. He choked back a cry of pain and the color drained from his face as Grossard squeezed him against his chest, crushing his broken ribs.

Grossard whipped around to face Oseron, putting Deston between the two them. Oseron pulled back his thrust and his ice blue eyes turned to steel at the sight of Deston dangling in Grossard's grip, but he didn't back down or lower his weapon. Grossard and Oseron glared daggers at one another and time stood still.

"I'll not let you take my son," Oseron ground out through his teeth.

Grossard let out a loud guffaw, making Deston grimace as he was bounced up and down with the laughter. "As long as I've known you, you've been arrogant and sure of yourself—the handsome, enchanting hero always arriving to save the day. Too bad that's not the way it's going to work out this time," he snickered.

Grossard reached inside his cloak and retrieved his staff in a motion so quick no one saw him move. The serpent's mouth at the tip opened wide, displaying the blood red Shard inside. In answer, the Crystal of Light flared a white blue against Oseron's chest. Grossard's face twisted into a vicious snarl and his eyes gleamed like polished black onyx as he pointed the Shard at Deston's chest.

"Nooo," Margaux screamed out, and without thinking about whom she was facing, she pulled an arrow and let it fly.

With a slight flick of his staff, Grossard batted the arrow out of the air and turned the staff toward Margaux without taking his eyes off of Oseron. His lips barely moved as he whispered a curse.

Oseron lunged for the staff, but Tiff appeared out of nowhere and slammed into it first, knocking it to the side. A thundering boom shook the building as the end column of the portico exploded behind Margaux. A second later, there was a loud creak and the corner of the roof sagged, then came down with a resounding crash, along with several dozen hand-made clay tiles that splintered into pieces as they smashed into each other on the ground.

Grossard didn't so much as flinch at the boom. He whipped the staff back at Margaux and hissed, *"Seeah zahfeae."* As all eyes immediately shifted to Margaux, no one saw him reach up and pluck Tiff out of the air.

The blast from the Shard silently tore through Margaux's protective shield as if it were made of air. One small squeak escaped her lips as her eyes rolled to the sky and her bow fell to the ground with a soft thunk. A small gray stain blossomed out from the middle of her chest and rapidly spread over her clothes, skin and hair. In a matter of seconds, she was frozen in her pose, a perfect statue of horror.

"What did you do to her? Leave her alone," Deston yelled and kicked out wildly to get free.

Grossard looked down in amusement, but his chuckle never made it out of his throat, for out of the corner of his eye he saw Joliet rushing in from the shadows. At the same moment, Oseron brought his sword up. Grossard whipped Deston around to stop Oseron at the same time he cast a spell to send Joliet sailing backward across the road and into the picket fence.

In the next heartbeat, a sword replaced the staff in Grossard's hand and with renewed confidence, he went on the attack, hammering and hacking at Oseron with all his might as he drove the king backward. Oseron parried and blocked the blows to defend himself, but did not make an attempt to strike back in fear of hitting Deston.

Deston felt as helpless as a rag doll being jerked this way and that with each of Grossard's movements. His arms were pinned down in Grossard's crushing grip and Caluvier dangled uselessly from his hand. The only thing he could do was watch in horror as the monster struck out at his father again and again. Seeing that Oseron wasn't fighting back and knowing it was because of him made it all the more terrifying.

Just as Deston began to wonder how much longer Oseron would be able to hold out, Torren and three other fae appeared with a pop and hurriedly spread out to surround Grossard.

Grossard's head swiveled around the circle, his eyes gleaming with hatred. He would gladly take them all on if he had both hands available, but doing so one-handed would put him at a grave disadvantage. Cursing the fae for interfering, he vanished from his spot and reappeared at the edge of the light. The fae all whirled to face him, but none of them advanced for Grossard had the Shard pointed at Deston's chest.

Grossard smiled a mocking smile. "I'm glad to see you understand the gravity of the situation," he gloated, feeling confident he had recouped the upper hand.

Oseron held his hand up, indicating to his men to hold back as he took a step forward. Grossard's smile slipped and he moved the Shard in until it was almost touching Deston.

Deston could feel the dark energy radiating from the Shard and his skin crawled. The raspy voices he'd heard earlier started up again with a vengeance, murmuring more hateful thoughts. Gritting his teeth, he turned his head, hoping that if he didn't look at the Shard, it would make a difference. His gaze landed on the trees that bordered the townhouse property just as a tall figure stepped out of the shadows and into the light. Shadows obscured the figure's face so he couldn't see who it was, but the stance reminded him of Keir. He squirmed and craned his neck as Grossard shifted and blocked his view. When Grossard moved again and Deston could see, the figure was gone. So were the voices in his head, but as his mind was on Keir, he didn't notice. He also didn't notice the large black crow with a white tuft under its beak sitting on a branch of the tree.

"Keir?" Deston called out telepathically, desperately wanting to confirm it was the warrior. He received no response, but it didn't quell his belief that it was Keir. Keir had said he would be there as long as Deston needed him, and Keir always stood by his word.

"I told you I would not let you take my son," Oseron yelled, jerking Deston's attention back to the scene in front of him.

Grossard's chest was puffed out like an Olympian gold medal winner. "And I told you that you wouldn't win this battle. You will watch your son die, or you can trade your life for his—either way you lose."

"What makes you think you have the power to kill either of us?" Oseron replied, his voice somber and deadly.

Grossard shook his head and chuckled. "You think you're the only one with special powers, eh? You have no idea the power I've gained from the Shard, but I will be happy to give you a small sample." He lifted the staff high over his head and swirled it in a counter-clockwise motion. The wind instantly picked up and circled around the small group in the same rotation as the Shard. A shrill keening started out low and escalated quickly as a dozen tendrils of dark smoke seeped up from the earth. The tendrils writhed and stretched as if they were being sucked up by a vacuum. The disgusting smell of rotten eggs permeated the air and Deston's eyes watered, so he wasn't sure if he was seeing things or if the smoky shapes really did have eyes and a mouth.

"Do you doubt my powers now?" Grossard sneered. *"Jiri vi Izvara,"* he called out, rapping the staff on the ground. The smoky demons stopped their squirming and as one, turned toward Oseron.

Lilika could see that Grossard was completely engrossed in Oseron and the demons and she had a perfect window of opportunity to initiate an attack. She focused her sights on Grossard's arm—the one holding Deston. She would get only one chance to hit the pressure point just above the elbow. She had used the technique before in hand-to-hand combat, but never when she was in the form of a hawk, and she prayed her talons would do just as good of a job as fingers.

"Deston, get ready," she called out at the last minute before extending her feet and pulling up behind Grossard to punch her powerful talons into his arm.

She came in so fast Grossard didn't know what hit him. One second he was watching the demons, the next, an agonizing pain shot through his arm and it went limp, and Deston slipped out of his grasp. With a startled yelp, he dropped his staff, as well, and clutched his now useless arm.

As the Shard hit the ground, the demons let out an ear-splitting screech and streaked toward Oseron. They whirled around him, moving faster and faster, tightening the circle until they had completely enclosed him inside a smoky cocoon. He slashed out with his sword, but the cloud only ruffled a bit and the blade did nothing to disperse them. Thin tendril like arms stretched toward him, but pulled back when light of the Crystal turned upon them. The second Oseron noticed this; he raised the Crystal over his head and called out the words to make it flare as he held it high.

The demons broke apart with a tormented wail as the Crystal's light burst forth and they raced upward with great speed. They rose several meters into the sky and then jerked to a sudden halt, as if having reached the end of a chain. There they froze, suspended in the air for a moment, before they plummeted back to earth, struggling and clawing against an invisible pull. Just as the wind had sucked them out of the dirt, the earth sucked them back in.

All Deston wanted to do was curl up and let the black fog that hovered at the edges of his eyes take him away into a pain-free abyss. But a small voice in the back of his mind reminded him he hadn't finished what he started and he knew his chances of success would be a lot greater if he struck before Grossard recovered the use of his arm. With a moan, he pushed up to a sitting position and staggered to his feet. Once standing, he removed the sling from his left arm, so there would be nothing hindering him. He then closed his eyes and attempted to call up the darkness he had felt on Gotland to help him finish his mission.

Lilika had circled around and soared back across the sky to Deston. As soon as she touched down on the ground, she transformed, rolled in a somersault and came up on one knee next to him. "Get out of here, now," she yelled as she pulled an arrow and nocked it.

Deston butted Lilika's bow aside and yelled back, "No, you get out of here. This is my destiny and I'm going to take care of Grossard."

Lilika looked over at Deston with a retort ready to fire back on the tip of her tongue, but when she saw his face, which was dark with hatred, her mouth just dropped open. In her moment of hesitation, Deston charged forward with a white knuckle grip on Caluvier.

Grossard had moved away and was standing at the edge of the light as he opened and closed his hand and rubbed his arm to get the feeling back. In his peripheral vision he saw Lilika hit the ground and then he saw Deston charge. He jumped to the side in the nick of time to avoid being skewered, but his cloak got tangled up in Caluvier's blade. Deston gave the sword a yank and sliced through the fabric as if it were paper. The momentum whirled him around and he took another swing. Grossard reared backward, but he wasn't quite quick enough and Caluvier sliced a wide gash in his arm, crisscrossing over the one Oseron had made earlier. Snarling through his teeth, he dove; twisting his body at the same time he reached out to summon his staff. It flew to his hand and he flipped around just in time to bat Deston's next assault away. Deston came right back with another thrust, but Caluvier struck nothing but air, for Grossard had evaporated and reappeared several meters away.

Grossard's face screwed up with rage. He couldn't use the Shard against Oseron as long as Oseron had the Crystal around his neck, but as he glared out over the fae, he realized he could use it on those Oseron cared about. His eyes glinted with malice and reflected the red glow of the Shard as he tilted it at Lilika, and hissed, *"Kad raeg truh yafor."*

Deston opened his mouth to scream as he leapt to intercept, but nothing came out.

At the same moment Grossard raised the Shard, Oseron appeared behind Lilika with the Crystal in his hand. Its light leaked between his fingers as he moved his lips in conjunction with Grossard's. The bursts of the two crystals collided, sending a shock wave through the air that lifted Deston and Lilika off their feet. They were blown backward straight into Oseron, and all three of them went down.

Deston rolled to his back and laid spread eagle on the ground, feeling as if he'd been hit by a train. Every inch of his body ached and his head was ringing. With a great effort, he pushed himself up to a sitting position and groped around for Caluvier. The light was softer than it had been and it took his eyes a second to readjust to the darkness. Still, he couldn't see much.

A few yards away the last lingering tendril of gray smoke rolled away on the breeze. Beyond that, he could see several mounds littering the ground. He squinted through the darkness, trying to piece it together, but not quite able to grasp onto what he was looking at. Then he suddenly remembered Lilika. He twisted around with a jerk, fully alert. It took him a moment to pick her out of the darkness, as she was lying on the ground and Oseron was beside her, bent over her body.

Deston scrambled to his knees and crawled to the pair as fast as his trembling legs would take him. As he looked down at Lilika, his heart sank. Her eyes were closed and he couldn't tell if she was breathing or not. Tentatively, he reached out and touched her leg. Feeling it wet and sticky, he jerked his hand back, assuming it was blood, although he couldn't see for sure as his vision had gone blurry and Keir's disapproving look swam before his eyes.

"I didn't mean for Lilika to get hurt," he whispered, the words came out sounding hollow. Whether he meant it to happen or not, Lilika was dead just like Keir, because he had failed them once again. It suddenly hurt to breathe, and not because of his broken ribs. The tears dammed up behind his eyes and his nose burned, but he refused to release the pain and let them fall.

"Deston!"

He heard Joliet's voice call from a distance and a whole new wave of guilt washed over him. He dropped his head into his hands to hide his face. In the next minute, Joliet's arms wrapped around him and she gently pressed his head against her shoulder. "Oh, baby," she breathed. "Are you okay?"

Deston felt her life beating against his cheek and realized she could be the next one lying on the ground dead. He choked on a sob that suddenly clogged his throat and pushed Joliet away. She started to reach out for him again, but Oseron came up behind her and knelt down. Deston looked into his father's blood splattered face and seeing the grim look, the tears he'd tried so hard to hold back came very close to spilling over.

"I'm so sorry," Deston whispered, dropping his eyes in shame.

Oseron put his hand on Deston's shoulder. "You have nothing to be sorry about. If you hadn't come between Lilika and Grossard, she wouldn't have survived. Your protective shield combined with hers made all the difference and kept you both alive."

Deston looked up with a jerk. *Lilika survived?*

"Lilika ..." Deston's mouth was so dry the words stuck to his lips. "She's alive?"

Oseron nodded his head and tried to smile to ease Deston's anxiety, but the worry lines around his mouth cancelled out the effort.

"Is she hurt bad?" Deston asked and bit down on his lip. He wanted to know, but at the same time, he dreaded the answer.

"She has a small bump on the head. I didn't see any other substantial injuries, but I'm not a healer."

Deston frowned. "But there was so much blood."

Oseron shook his head. "I think you're mistaking her water breaking for blood. It seems Macaria is anxious to see what all the commotion is about. I'm afraid she is going to be just as headstrong as her mother is."

Oseron's words tumbled around in Deston's mind, but he couldn't quite grasp hold of them. "She's alive?" Once he repeated the words they finally sank in. He inhaled sharply, feeling as if he had just come up from being underwater too long. The corners of his mouth started to lift, but before it turned into a smile he sobered. "What about Grossard? Did he get away?"

Oseron glanced at Joliet and Deston's stomach plummeted.

"What? ... Did something happen?"

Joliet took Deston's hand, but he pulled it back.

"What's going on? What aren't you telling me?" he added, wincing as he scrambled to his feet.

Joliet let out a sigh. "Grossard got away," she said softly and paused to rise.

Deston knew her well enough to know she was holding something back. He turned to his father. "And?"

"He took Margaux with him," Oseron said bluntly.

Deston reared back as if he'd been slapped and pivoted to where Margaux had been standing. Her bow was on the ground where she'd dropped it, but there was nothing else. He dropped to his knees and gasped for air as his whole world came to a stop. For several seconds, he couldn't think and couldn't breathe. Then a boiling rage flickered to life in the pit of his stomach and his face turned dark.

"He won't hurt her," Oseron said, putting a hand on Deston's shoulder. "He'll want to use her as a bargaining tool. We'll find a way to get her back."

Deston shrugged Oseron's hand off, got to his feet, and faced the trees, his rage running rampant within him.

"Tiff is also missing," Oseron added. "No one saw what happened to her, but I think she might have jumped onto Grossard before he disappeared to try and help Margaux."

A slight twitch of Deston's shoulders was the only indication he heard what Oseron said. He wanted to scream, he wanted to yell, but all he did was stand and stare into the darkness, trying to think of some way to get Margaux and Tiff back. A jagged light flashed through his right eye and without saying a word, he transformed into a falcon and flew off for the fae camp before Oseron could stop him.

Chapter 33

Deston's weak shoulder slowed him down, giving Oseron the opportunity to get to the camp before him. Upon hitting the ground, Deston transformed and in the next instant he was standing in front of Mordred, who was slumped against a tree. Deston squatted next to the sorcerer, tugged the gag down and leaned in close. The action startled Mordred and he almost smacked Deston in the nose with his head as he jerked up.

"I want to know where you've hidden the book," Deston whispered so no one else could hear.

Mordred's eyes lit up and he looked thoroughly delighted. "I knew I made the right choice when I chose you," he squealed. "Now cut me loose."

Deston cringed at the sound of his girlish voice and at that moment he would have given anything to be able to knock the superior look off Mordred's face, but he needed Mordred's cooperation. "Tell me where the book is first."

Mordred paused and looked hard at Deston, sensing something had changed. "We had a deal, you and me. You're a fae ... you cannot break your word."

The dimple in Deston's cheek deepened. "Yeah, I remember our deal. We were going to be partners and you weren't going to turn me over to Grossard, because you're a man of your word. Isn't that right?"

"I *am* a man of my word ... when I deal with reputable men," Mordred replied, looking up through half-closed eyelids.

Deston's patience was gone. He pulled Caluvier and pointed the tip of the blade at Mordred's chest. "I'm not as naïve as you think I am. I'm also half-human, as you pointed out on the plane. My human side has no qualms about breaking our deal or running this sword through your heart, so tell me where you put the book, because I'm done messing around."

A hand came down on Deston's shoulder and squeezed hard. His gaze jerked up, but he didn't say anything. Neither did Oseron.

"Your timing is impeccable, as always, Your Highness. Your son and I were just discussing the matter of fae honor," Mordred quipped.

The tips of Deston's ears turned pink, but he didn't look away from his father's stare. *"Dad, I can—"* he started to say telepathically, but Oseron gave his shoulder another squeeze.

"I believe the prince asked you the whereabouts of the Book of Tenebris," Oseron said, his words directed at Mordred.

Mordred sputtered for a moment. "You know perfectly well I would never give you the book," he spat.

"No one asked you to *give* it to me. You were merely asked where it currently resides."

Mordred snorted. "Why would I tell you that? So you can go get it and destroy it? Where would that leave me?"

"You seem to be missing a very important factor here," Oseron explained calmly. "The only bargaining tool you have right now, and the only one that will give you your life back, is telling us where the book is. You do that, we go get it, use it to bargain with Grossard to get Margaux back, and you go free. If you don't like that option, there's option two— we trade you to Grossard for Margaux. I don't see the second option playing out so good for you in the end, though."

"You would never turn someone over to Grossard, not even me. You would also never give Grossard the book for the life of one silly girl," Mordred whispered, his eyes showing the first real hint of panic.

Deston bristled and pushed the tip of the blade through the fabric of Mordred's vest. "She is *not* a silly girl," he snarled.

"I absolutely would turn you over," Oseron stated without hesitation. "And it is well known that I *am* a man of my word."

Mordred's head rocked side-to-side in utter shock. "You would allow Grossard to bring Erebus back and destroy the high realm?" he muttered unable to fathom Oseron's reasoning.

Oseron watched Mordred flounder for a moment. "All right then ... I guess option two it is." He turned and walked away.

"Wait," Mordred called out after him. Forgetting about Caluvier, he leaned forward to get to his feet and the blade pierced his skin. With a sniveling yelp, he flopped back against the tree and whined pitifully, "Pleassse ..."

Oseron halted, but did not turn around.

A dozen thoughts raced in and out of Mordred's mind as he stared at Oseron's back. He wasn't worried about losing the words to reverse the magnetic poles; he had memorized that incantation centuries ago. However, there were so many other useful spells, enchantments, and curses within the book that were not found anywhere else in the world. Curses he would need to control and diminish Grossard's powers, as well as the one that would do away with the barrier between the realms. Without the book, he wouldn't be able to accomplish half of what he dreamed of doing and he'd been waiting so long to bring those dreams to fruition. He closed his eyes and tried to think. He knew there had to be a way. There was always a way. He just needed to buy some time to figure it out.

"I ... I need some time to think about your offer."

"We don't have time," Deston snarled, adding pressure to the blade until Mordred squeaked again and a small round circle of red appeared on the sorcerer's vest.

Oseron slowly turned. "You can have twenty-four hours."

"What? NO! We have to get Margaux back now," Deston cried out at the same time Mordred stammered, "I need more time than that."

"Twenty-four hours is what you get," Oseron replied. As he walked away, he added, "Deston, walk with me." His tone made it clear it was not a request.

Mordred put his head back and looked up through the branches. He hadn't noticed until that moment that the lightning had stopped, which meant Grossard had left the area. And from what he'd just learned, Grossard had taken Margaux with him. A smile split his face for real. The girl was apparently more valuable than he thought if Oseron was willing to give up the book for her. That was just the kind of information he could use to turn the situation around to his favor.

Deston had to sprint to catch up with Oseron. "Why—" he started, but Oseron's voice came into his head and cut him off. *"We'll speak once we're alone,"* Oseron said.

A belligerent response sat on the tip of Deston's tongue, but he knew it would do him no good to disregard Oseron's command. It wouldn't get him any closer to getting Margaux back, either, so he followed Oseron in silence through the trees and along the bank of the Severn River for a good forty-five meters. In the dark, the water looked more like a wide band of black asphalt than it did a river. If it weren't for the occasional ripple, and a fish jumping up and splashing back down, it would be easy to confuse it for a highway.

Oseron finally came to a stop and stood on the bank staring out across the water. He could feel Deston's turmoil and it stabbed his heart like tiny blades. He would give anything to be able to take away that turmoil and the heavy burden Deston was carrying, but it wasn't in his power to change what the gods had set in motion. Merlyn had made that clear. The gods had personally shaped Deston's destiny, which intertwined with Grossard's. However, there was one thing Merlyn and the gods hadn't taken into consideration—that the burden of the son becomes the burden of the father.

Once Oseron came to a standstill, Deston waited all of one second before he opened his mouth to speak, but his voice faltered as his father's hand came up and it was glowing with a faint pink light. Oseron moved his hand through the air in an arc and the black water lit up like a movie screen with the image of a beautiful sunlit meadow with trees that were just beginning to bud and small bunches of crocus intermixed in the grass that was just turning green. As Deston watched, the buds on the trees rapidly swelled into small leaves and the crocuses shriveled away and were replaced with a field of yellow daffodils, which then became a field of multi-colored tulips. The time-lapse movie traveled on to a field of strawberries and then to a field of purple lavender, a waterfall plunging into a river far below, and to a country road lined with trees. There it paused and the leaves of the trees turned to red, gold, orange and yellow. It looked just like the autumns in Pennsylvania that Deston remembered and for a second he felt a twinge of homesickness. But the scene didn't last long before it flashed to a close up of an evergreen tree that had each of the needles individually and perfectly coated in a fine layer of ice. Next, a snow covered mountainside sparkled in the sunrise as if dusted with diamonds and a sky that was such a rare color of blue it could never be duplicated on canvas. At last, the scene came back full circle to the sunlit meadow and the trees just beginning to bud.

"When the gods first came to this planet, it was nothing but a rock orbiting a small star. They spent centuries transforming this rock into a world of wonders that no other in the universe can compare to. The gods were and always have been quite proud of their accomplishment. They went to a lot of trouble to see that it stayed pure and protected. That is the reason our people were brought here—to watch over and keep the earth in balance. We have managed fairly well up to this point, but the darkness we have had to face in the past is a tiny seed of what we are facing now. If the poles are reversed and the magnetic shield taken down, the full strength of darkness will be let in. The gods' masterpiece and everything we cherish and love about this world will be devoured and it will be made barren." He paused and the river went back to being a river.

"I know what Margaux means to you," Oseron continued. The knot in Deston's stomach twisted and he lowered his eyes. "I know you want to save her. I do too, so we must figure out a way to do that without jeopardizing the whole planet."

Deston twitched and his brow creased. Did he hear right? He looked up, searching his father's face. "You're going to help save Margaux?"

Oseron squeezed Deston's shoulder and tried to smile, but his eyes remained sad. "We'll do all that we can within our limits."

A rush of elation sped through Deston and he could hardly contain himself. "Then let's go back, 'cause I know I can get Mordred to give me the location of the book—"

His words trailed off as he suddenly remembered the talk he and Mordred had on the plane. He closed his eyes and thought back to that conversation, trying to bring up the clues Mordred had ticked off on his fingers, but they stayed just beyond his reach, and the more he tried to reel them in, the more scrambled his thoughts became.

Deston felt the light pressure of Oseron's hand on his shoulder and with it came a comforting warmth that seeped into his body. The warmth rapidly traveled down to the tips of his fingers and toes and into his muscles, dispelling the tension that had been building up over the past weeks. The feeling that he was sinking in quicksand fled, and for the first time in days, he didn't feel scared. Splotches of white slowly merged together in the blackness behind his eyelids and formed an image of his grandfather. Deston looked into in Oberon's silver eyes and saw the wisdom of the ages and something in his brain suddenly clicked. He jerked up.

"While we were on the plane, Mordred gave me clues to where he's keeping the book. I just remembered what he said, and I think I might be able to figure the clues out," he said, looking up at Oseron.

Oseron looked impressed and gave Deston's shoulder another squeeze. "Tell me what Mordred told you and we'll figure them out together."

∿∿

The minutes were ticking by faster than Mordred would have liked, but he had managed to come up with a plan. He knew it might not be easy to pull it off since Oseron didn't have the ego Grossard had and wasn't as easily manipulated. But he, Mordred, had one special play up his sleeve, or rather in his pocket—Grossard's pink ring. With the ring, he was sure he could turn the situation around. But first he had to convince Oseron he was willing to go along with the fae, which would take an Academy Awarding-winning performance on his part.

∿∿

"... a man who was never defeated in battle. I'm sure there are probably several men who have earned that recognition, but the first one I thought of, and the only one I know for sure, is Alexander the Great. I learned all about him in history class. He never lost a battle, and I can totally see Mordred admiring someone like him. What do you think?" Deston asked.

None of the clues Deston listed off about the man that was holding the book meant a thing to Oseron. The fae were not and never have been allowed to get involved in human affairs unless the actions threatened the welfare of the world and the balance of nature. "I can't say. I know very little about human history. Once the gods divided the realms, we were instructed to let the humans deal with their own issues."

Deston sighed. "I wish I had a computer and internet access so I could look it up. I really think it could be Alexander the Great, but I don't know where he's buried. And I kind of remember something about no one knows where he's buried."

Oseron looked out over the water, trying to recall the names of the humans that had come to his attention in the past, but a voice entered his head and interrupted his thoughts.

"Your Highness, the sorcerer has asked to speak with you. He says it's important," the voice said.

Oseron's brow rose at the news. If Mordred was giving in so readily, it could mean only one thing—he thought he could outsmart them. That wasn't really a surprise. Oseron had witnessed many of Mordred's schemes over the centuries, but Mordred had never attempted to scam him. As he got to his feet, he couldn't help but wonder what Mordred had in store. "I just received word that Mordred is ready to deal. Shall we go see what he has conjured up for us? It should be interesting," he said, offering his hand to Deston.

As Oseron and Deston walked back into the trees, the circle of fae parted, clearing a path up to the sorcerer.

"Follow my lead," Oseron instructed Deston as they came to a stop.

Mordred lifted his head and looked up pathetically, giving his best dramatic performance, but the effort was wasted, for neither Oseron nor Deston bought into his act. Oseron towered over him and looked down; waiting for Mordred to say his piece, but Mordred wasn't done with his show yet.

Laboring to his feet with a great deal of grunting and moaning, Mordred sagged against the tree trunk, panting as if the effort cost more than what he had to give. He glanced up through his brow after a few seconds time, hoping to see a little softening in Oseron's expression. To his chagrin, Oseron's face remained hard and the deep indentation in the king's cheek was further proof he wasn't falling for Mordred's antics.

Mordred let his chin fall to his chest to hide his snarl. He knew it wouldn't be easy, but he had hoped Oseron would show some sympathy. He wasn't done yet, though. Heaving a heavy sigh, he looked up again with puppy dog eyes. "You have no idea how hard this is for me." There was a catch in his voice. "My own dear mother gave up her life to keep that book safe and ensure it never left the family." He looked Oseron in the eye and paused. "You drive a hard bargain, Oseron, and you have an unfair advantage over me. You are, however, the lesser of two evils and at least I know I can trust you to keep your word. Whereas Grossard ..." he snorted, "well, it's no secret that he would lie to the gods' faces if given the chance."

Mordred doubled over and coughed, playing his part again to make it look as if he was indeed in a great deal of pain. Oseron stood stoically with the same steely expression and Mordred finally accepted his theatrics weren't going to work. Straightening up, he swiped the sleeve of his jacket over his mouth.

"All right ... you win. I will lead you to the book. All that I ask is that you unbind my hands and leave the gag off. They aren't necessary, as you and Grossard have quite successfully taken all of my powers from me. You know there is no way I can get away, and to be bound up like a common criminal in public would be rather embarrassing. I do have a reputation to uphold, you know."

Oseron studied Mordred's face, wishing he could get inside the sorcerer's head to see what he really had in mind. For centuries Mordred had been causing trouble, but as none of it had affected the high realm, Oseron had not had to deal with him personally. But he was fully aware of Mordred's reputation and knew that very little of what Mordred said could be believed. In Mordred's entire speech there was only one statement Oseron knew to be true—that Mordred's powers were neutralized and there was no way he could run.

"Cut his bindings," Oseron silently commanded his men.

A smile tugged at the corners of Mordred's mouth as he rubbed his wrists to get the circulation back into his fingertips, but he knew better than to let the smile show. Oseron noticed the glint in Mordred's eye, however, and leaned down to whisper in the sorcerer's ear.

"There are no second chances, sorcerer. Exploit my trust and you'll spend the rest of your pathetic life incarcerated in the most dismal prison the human world has to offer, just like every other *human* criminal."

Mordred's chest puffed out, but he held back the snide remark that lodged in his throat. "The agreement is I show the location where you will find the book. That is all I'm obligated to do. You will then let me go free and we will part ways. Deal?" Mordred held out his hand to shake.

Oseron ignored Mordred's gesture. "You'll be released when the book—the real book—is in our possession."

"So where is it?" Deston cut in, unable to stay silent a moment longer.

Mordred's gaze flicked to Deston and went right back to Oseron. "Bring me a map of the British Isles. I'll show you."

A man immediately appeared with a yellowed parchment scroll and unrolled it on the ground. Oseron sat back on his haunches and stared down at the map. Mordred leaned over the map and pretended to examine it as well, as he causally stuck his hand into the pocket of his vest and slipped the pink diamond onto his finger. He pulled his hand out of the pocket and pointed to the dot labeled *London*. "There," he said.

"London?" Deston said excitedly, knowing that London was very close and they could get there in no time at all. He looked up at his father, expecting him to start gathering the men, but Oseron didn't move.

"Where exactly in London do you have the book?" Oseron asked, standing tall.

"Dad, we—" Deston started, but Oseron held up his hand and stopped him from saying more.

Oseron looked down on Mordred and right away noticed the large ring on the sorcerer's finger. His brow furrowed. "*Where* in London?" he asked a second time, his tone insinuating he didn't believe Mordred.

Mordred cleared his throat. "Where else ... the renowned Westminster Abbey."

Oseron's steel blue eyes drilled into Mordred's. "You're lying."

Mordred's chin raised a notch as two thoughts went through his mind at the same time. How dare Oseron call him a liar, and how did Oseron know he was lying? As Oseron squared his shoulders, Mordred unconsciously took a step backward.

"If you already know the book's location, what's the point of going through this charade?" Mordred challenged.

"Tell me again what Mordred told you on the plane, Deston," Oseron said without taking his eyes off the sorcerer. To Mordred's credit, the only sign of alarm he gave away was a slight rise of his brow.

As Deston looked from Mordred to Oseron, it hit him all at once why Oseron was questioning Mordred's statement. "He said the book was on an island in the middle of a lagoon. England is an island all right, but it's not in a lagoon ... you *are* lying!"

Mordred's lips thinned as he glared at Deston. "I just told you those things to pacify you," he hissed.

Deston shook his head. "No ... you told me 'cause I egged you on. You spilled more than you intended to, didn't you? And I remember all of it—the iron box, the man who never lost a battle that you left it with— so don't try to pull any more of your tricks, 'cause I'll know."

Mordred's nostrils flared and this time he didn't try to hide his sneer. "We had an agreement."

"Oh, so now you want to talk about agreements? How about the agreement you just made with my dad? You know ... the one where you agreed to take us to the real book for your freedom?"

Mordred had the decency to blush, but he clamped his lips together and didn't take the bait.

"Turn him over to Grossard," Oseron ordered and walked away as two warriors rushed forward.

"Wait. You can't do this. You gave your word," Mordred screamed as the men took hold of his arms. Oseron kept on walking. "All right ... all right. You win. The book is in Venice."

Oseron paused and then slowly turned back. "What do you think, Deston? Is he telling the truth this time?"

Deston thought about it for a moment and shrugged his shoulders. "It could be. Venice is an island and it's in a lagoon, I think."

"Bring me a map," Oseron ordered.

Again a parchment with a map of Italy appeared within seconds. They all gathered around it. Oseron swiped his hand over the northern section where Venice lay. That section instantly filled the page, showing the Laguna Veneta. In the center of the lagoon were the islands that made up Venice.

Mordred straightened the ring on his hand, leaned in closer to the map and slowly drew his finger under the word Venice.

Oseron frowned. The city fit the criteria of the clues, but it bothered him that Mordred had given in so easily. "Show me where," he said as he again swiped his hand over the map and filled the page with an enlarged layout of the city of Venice.

Mordred drew in a deep breath. "It's rather hard to pinpoint on a map. It would be best if I just take you there personally."

Oseron's dimple twitched. "Show me."

Mordred pursed his lips and lengthen his neck, but said nothing until Oseron turned to one of his men. Then, he hurriedly jabbed at a spot on the south shore of the city and snarled, "Here."

Chapter 34

Grossard paced back and forth across the entrance to the cave, replaying the events of Viroconium through his mind. He wasn't overly surprised Mordred had betrayed him. He had expected Mordred to try something, and his rage wasn't so much about Mordred's betrayal as it was about the unexpected arrival of Oseron. When Grossard saw Oseron on the battlefield, the first thing that went through his mind was that Mordred had been the informer. Now that he had some time to think about it, though, he remembered Rellik and Deston were both in the room in Gotland when the meeting was discussed. It made more sense that one of them had somehow gotten a message to Oseron. From the moment Mordred was born, he had been a whinny, sniveling pain in Grossard's neck, but the sorcerer was too much of an opportunist, not to mention a coward, to risk such a bold move. However, when it came down to it, it didn't matter how Oseron heard about the meeting. He had, and once again the fae had robbed Grossard of his victory.

"DAMN YOU, Oseron," Grossard cursed, throwing his hands in the air. Outside the cave, a sharp crack rumbled through the cliff and an avalanche of small boulders and dirt rolled down into the angry wave that had surged up the side of the precipice at the same moment. The wave swallowed up the rocks and dirt like a hungry sea monster, and barely had enough time to recede back into the sea before the next wave crashed in, sending an even bigger cloud of spray skyrocketing into the air.

Grossard stood at the cave's entrance, wheezing in and out. He should be on his way back to his compound in the sweet, hot desert with book in hand, not hiding out in a god-forsaken cave, which he hated almost as much as he did Oseron. When he left the cave after procuring the Shard, he thought he would never have to step inside its dank, cold cavity again. But just like when Oseron banished him from the high realm, his choices were limited, for he needed to be close to the fae, Mordred and the book.

The cave was not only much closer than his desert compound, it was the only other place he knew that Oseron, or anyone else who might be searching for him, would never be able to breach. The former owner, Morgane le Fae saw to that, and the two decades he was forced to live in the wretched place attested to the fact that it was indeed impenetrable.

Too agitated to stand still, Grossard began to pace again. Each time he spun on his heels to retrace his steps across the wide-open entrance, the wind gave a mournful howl and whipped the water into frothy swells that grew higher as his anger spiraled. The only thing that held him together and kept him from exploding and destroying the countryside was that there was still a chance for him to procure the book.

He had brought Margaux back to the cave with him on a whim, thinking only that he wanted to take something that mattered away from Oseron and Deston. However, after ruminating on the situation, he realized the girl might be useful in helping him get Mordred back. Deston obviously had feelings for her, and seeing how the prince was impetuous and let his emotions control his brain, he might be persuaded into exchanging Mordred for the girl. The hard part would be keeping Oseron unaware of the trade, for if Oseron got word of it, it would never happen. Fortunately, Deston had a propensity to run off on his own, and as soon as he did so again, Grossard would make his move.

With that in mind, he had sent Nolef back to Viroconium to keep an eye on Deston and follow him wherever he went. The korrigan had also been instructed to send word back by way of the black quartz, verifying the fae had indeed captured Mordred as Oseron claimed; because if the fae didn't actually have Mordred, it would change everything.

Time was creeping by at a snail's pace, as it always seemed to do for Grossard in the lower realm. Nolef had been gone less than an hour, but to Grossard it might as well have been twenty-four and his temper was reaching the exploding point. To occupy his time, he sat by the flames and sent small charges into a rat he had pinned flat to a rock. Each time the charge hit the rat, it let out a high-pitched squeal and its body writhed and jerked pitifully until its heart stopped, at which point Grossard brought it back to life and started all over.

After what seemed like an eternity, Nolef slunk into the cave. The korrigan made no noise, but Grossard sensed him and looked up through his brow. A tick in Grossard's jaw twitched furiously, but he said nothing. He just glared at Nolef, waiting to hear an explanation of why the korrigan was there and not following Deston as ordered.

"*They* do have Mordred," Nolef said.

The news was not at all surprising, but after such a long wait it was enough to set Grossard off. He jumped to his feet with a thunderous roar that ricocheted off the walls like a bullet. In the same instant, Nolef sailed through the air and slammed into the wall by the entrance. Before the korrigan could get his breath back, he was lifted and slung into the back wall.

Nolef sagged to the ground and shook his head. As he blinked Grossard into focus, his hand moved toward his sword. His fingers had just touched the hilt when Grossard appeared in front of him, hefted him up with a hand around his throat and hissed through his teeth, "I don't think I would do that if I were you."

Nolef's red eyes glared defiantly into Grossard's, but he let his hand drop. "Kill me and you won't know what else I learned," he managed to croak.

Blinded by his fury, it never occurred to Grossard that Nolef might have more information to impart. His upper lip curled as his fingers sprung open. Nolef dropped to the ground, but Grossard didn't move back from where he stood.

Nolef's hand went to his throat as he boldly got to his feet and stepped out from between the wall and Grossard. "*They* want the girl. Mordred agreed to take *Them* to get the book so *They* can trade it for her," he said, without looking up at Grossard.

Grossard stared unseeing at the wall as he digested the unexpected news. It had to be some kind of trick. Oseron would never give him the book for the girl. His head started reeling with paradoxes.

"Mordred was wearing your ring," Nolef added as a side note.

Grossard visibly flinched and whipped around, drilling the korrigan with his piercing eyes. "The ring?"

Nolef nodded. "It was on his finger."

Grossard hesitated, wondering if this was part of the trick. Could it possibly be that Mordred and Oseron were in this together? He shook his head, unable to make that reach. Mordred was a sociopath, but he was also a survivalist. And Oseron had seen the power the Shard could deliver and would surely not want to engage in another confrontation at this point. That left only one explanation—Mordred was up to something and there was only one way to find out what.

Grossard closed his eyes and whispered the words to activate the ring. An image appeared behind his eyelids no bigger than a dot, confirming that Mordred was indeed wearing the ring. Grossard concentrated until the image began to expand and come into focus. All of a sudden, Oseron was in front of him as big as life, staring directly at him. Grossard flinched and his eyes flew open, forgetting that he was just seeing Oseron through the ring and the king wasn't physically there. With a muttered curse, he hurriedly shut his eyes to bring the image back.

As before, there was no sound, but he didn't need sound to know that Oseron was calling Mordred out as a liar. He smiled a bit on the inside, but sobered as the image focused in on a map of Italy. He unconsciously leaned forward, even though that did nothing to help him see any better. However, seconds later, as Mordred lowered his hand and pointed, Grossard clearly saw the word Venice printed across the map.

Venice? He has the book hidden in Venice? he thought, a true smile spreading across his face.

"You said Mordred was going to take Oseron to the book," Grossard asked, flipping back to Nolef.

"Yes."

"What was Mordred going to get out of the deal?"

"He is to be set free."

"Hmm ..." Grossard walked to the fire and sat down. The rat was still pinned to the rock where he had left it. He picked it up by the tail and let it swing and flail in front of his face. "What are you playing at, Mordred?" he mumbled to himself, knowing full well Mordred was aware of the ring's true purpose, which meant he had intended for him to see where he was taking Oseron—but why? Was Mordred attempting to get back in his good graces? That thought barely entered his mind before he threw it out. More likely Mordred was trying to save the book. The sorcerer was smart, but he didn't have the power to defeat Oseron on his own. For that he would need the Shard. Letting Grossard know where they were headed, would ensure Grossard would step in, save the book, and take care of the predicament Mordred had gotten himself into.

The corners of Grossard's eyes crinkled in amusement. "You think you can manipulate me, sorcerer, but you've underestimated me again. Lucky for you, I never tire of seeing the expression on your face when I outwit you. But this time will be your last. There will be no happy ending for you once the real book is out in the open," Grossard muttered under his breath.

With a chuckle, he threw the rat into the flames and ignored its squeals as he got to his feet. "Mordred is leading the fae to Venice. We will need to hurry to get there before they do."

"What about the girl?" Nolef asked in reply

Grossard looked over his shoulder. "Bring her. If by chance the fae get to the book first, I might still need to use her to negotiate."

"And the sprite?"

Grossard didn't answer. He grabbed his cloak, swirled it over his head and let it settle around his shoulders. He then looked back at Tiff, who had been put under the same curse as Margaux. The sprite was one more inconvenience he really didn't have time to deal with. Lifting his hand, palm side up, he slowly cupped his fingers into a fist. Tiff vanished from her spot next to Margaux and Grossard's eyes lit up as he felt the small weight land in his hand. He clenched his fist tighter until his fingernails cut into his skin and his knuckles turned white. He gave it one more squeeze and then opened his fist and looked down at the mound of dust sitting on his palm. Spreading his fingers wide, he watched the dust stream through his fingers into a small pile on the floor. His eyes blazed brightly with a rush of ecstasy as he wiped his palm down the side of his cloak and scuffed the toe of his boot through the dust, scattering it over the floor. He turned to the doorway, feeling much better, and stormed out into the night without a backward glance.

Nolef picked up Margaux, hefted her up under his arm, and followed in Grossard's wake.

Chapter 35

Oseron had told Deston to fly at a speed that was comfortable for his shoulder and not to push it, as the ligaments had not had proper time to heal and his arm could easily pop out of its socket again if he overtaxed it. But Deston was determined not to slow the others down and pushed past his comfort level to keep up. A tail wind picked up about halfway to their destination, which helped ease some of his strain, and they were making good time despite the fact he suspected the others had slowed their speed to accommodate him.

They were headed to the Birmingham airport with plans to take Mordred's plane to Venice. Deston had suggested it, and though Oseron and the others weren't overly excited about the idea, they all saw the logic, as the plane would take less time than going back to Tir na-nÓg and through another gateway. And since Oseron suspected the ring on Mordred's finger was somehow connected to Grossard, he didn't want to waste a single minute in getting to the book.

Joliet and Mordred were on the way to the airport in the car Mordred rented to get to Viroconium. Mordred had assured them the plane would be refueled and ready to go the minute they arrived. The only issue was that the plane could only carry seven passengers. Joliet insisted on being one of the seven, and with Oseron, Mordred and Deston taking up three other seats, that left only three available for the warriors. Oseron wasn't thrilled with the thought of having only three warriors accompany them, especially with the possibility that Grossard might also turn up in Venice, but the need to beat Grossard there superseded his apprehension. So he relented and prayed the additional warriors that were already on their way back to Tir na-nÓg would make it to Venice before any trouble broke out.

Once they got to the airport, Oseron and the fae hung back and eyed the plane warily. They had all seen planes before, but none of them had any desire to fly in one and never planned to. A fine sheen of sweat glistened on Oseron's forehead as he walked around the metal tube with wings, inspecting every inch of it.

Joliet had witnessed her husband facing monsters that would give any other man terrifying nightmares, and never had she seen even a hint of panic in his eyes like there was as he walked back to her. With a knowing smile, she reached up, pulled his head down to her level and whispered reassurances in his ear. She then gave him a long, sensual kiss and tugged him up the stairs and into the plane while his head was still buzzing. Once Oseron was onboard, the others followed without delay. Ten minutes later, the plane was rolling down the runway.

Deston spotted the onboard computer equipment as he entered the plane and as soon as the pilot flipped off the seat belt sign, he plopped down in front of it and began an aggressive search of the internet. Twenty minutes later he threw his hands in the air with an exuberant '"yes!" and rushed up to the seat next to his father.

Oseron's spine could have been a steel rod for as straight as he was sitting and his fingers were clutched tight around the armrest, but Deston didn't notice. Leaning over the arm of Oseron's chair he whispered in a low tone so Mordred couldn't hear, even though Mordred was sitting at the very back of the cabin and the hum of the plane's engines was loud enough to cover the sound of Deston's voice.

"I think I've discovered where Mordred has hidden the book. You know how I thought the man that Mordred mentioned might be Alexander the Great? I'm pretty sure I'm right." His whole face shined with excitement as he went on to explain his discovery. "I found this article on the internet where some researchers say they have proof that the remains in the sarcophagus in San Marco Basilica in Venice are not the bones of St. Mark, but are Alexander the Great's. There's a whole big story about how the bodies were switched and everything. Most people don't know anything about it and believe St. Mark is in the sarcophagus under the high altar, so it's really kind of brilliant for Mordred to put the book there. No one would think to look for Alexander the Great in that tomb."

Oseron barely heard any of Deston's ramblings and what he did hear made no sense to him. Being in the confines of the small metal cylinder was extremely uncomfortable for him. His mind drifted in and out of the conversation as he fought to keep his queasiness at bay, but when Deston suddenly stopped speaking, he looked up and the excitement shining on his son's face jolted him back. Deston obviously had no comprehension of the sacrifices he may be required to make when they reached Venice. As much as Oseron hated to be the one to burst Deston's bubble, he knew it would be better if Deston went into showdown knowing the truth.

"You do understand I cannot allow Grossard to obtain the incantation that will reverse the magnetic fields, don't you, son?"

The light instantly drained from Deston's face and he stopped breathing for a second. His brain did know that, but his heart hadn't been listening to his brain much lately.

"I'm obligated … every fae is obligated to prevent the darkness from taking hold. It's the sole reason we were brought to the earth. Going against our nature like that would be the same as cutting out our hearts."

Deston stared at his father. "But … I thought …" His stomach plummeted and he couldn't go on.

Oseron put his hand on Deston's knee. "I told you I would do whatever I can to save Margaux. I'm still working on a way to do that without jeopardizing the world. I just wanted you to understand that giving Grossard the book is not an option."

Deston bit down on his lip and gave an almost imperceptible nod of his head. There was nothing else to say.

Joliet, sitting in the seat facing Deston's, overheard everything. She leaned over and took his hands in hers. "Your father is the greatest man I've ever known. He's one of the smartest too. Don't give up on him. He'll find a way to rescue Margaux." She gave his hands another squeeze as she flashed Oseron a look that said he'd better prove her right.

Chapter 36

The rest of the flight was a blur to Deston. He wasn't even aware they had landed until Oseron and the other three fae hurriedly got up from their seats, grabbed Mordred, and sprinted off the plane before the pilot even flicked off the seat belt sign. He had spent the last ninety minutes of the trip trying to think of a way to get Margaux back that didn't involve using the book as a bargaining tool, but he had come up with nothing. Grossard wasn't the type to let Margaux go unless he could get exactly what he wanted, and what he wanted was the book. But Oseron had made it very clear he would not allow that to happen. Deston understood the reasoning behind his father's conviction, but he also felt there had to be some way to make the exchange work without going against his duty as a fae to protect the world.

He stared at his hands and once again went over the few ideas he had been throwing around in his head; one: he'd tear the page out of the book that had the incantation on it before giving it to Grossard; two: he'd change the text of the incantation so it wouldn't work. According to Mordred, Grossard didn't know the ancient language the incantation was written in, so he wouldn't be able to tell that it had been changed. The problem with plan two was Deston didn't know the ancient language, either, and didn't know how difficult it would be to change it or even if it *could* be changed. By the time they landed in Venice, he was certain of only one thing—he had to sneak away and get to San Marco Basilica before his father caught up to him. And after he found the book, he would figure out how to handle the rest.

When the seat belt sign dinged off, Deston mechanically unbuckled the belt. As he started to rise, Joliet put her hand on his leg. He looked up into her eyes and immediately regretted it. *Damn!* he cursed silently, knowing he was caught. His mother had always been able to read his face, especially when he was up to something. He felt the heat rise to his cheeks and started to get up again, but she pressed down on his leg and leaned across the aisle between them.

"You're going to go after the book, aren't you?" Joliet said in a low tone to keep any listening ears from hearing.

Deston's mind froze and he couldn't think of a thing to say, but Joliet squeezed his leg and continued, "I know you are, so don't try to deny it. I'm not going to stop you. But I'm not going to let you do this alone, either." Deston pulled back. "I want to help," she added quickly as he started to protest. "I have a plan to get Margaux back and keep Grossard from getting the book."

Deston wasn't prepared for the rush of emotion that swelled inside him. He never for a moment thought his mother would side with him against Oseron. He didn't know what to say, but there wasn't time to quibble. He leaned forward until his head was nearly touching hers and she began to lay out the plan.

"You really think Dad will go for this?" he asked when she finished.

"I'll take care of your father. That's not your worry," Joliet assured him and took both of his hands in hers. "I never wanted you to be involved in any of this, but no matter how hard I tried, I couldn't keep you out." Her eyes grew glassy, but her chin stayed strong. "Titania told me you were born for this; it's your destiny, but that doesn't mean you have to do it alone. I'll be with you and I want you to promise me you won't take any unnecessary risks. All you need to do is lure Grossard out and then get out of the way and let your father take care of the rest. Promise me you'll do that, please. I couldn't bear to have anything happen to you."

Deston pulled his hands out of her grip and put them on top of hers. "You're not the only one who's had a hard time accepting my destiny. I tried to ignore it myself, but I think I finally understand what I have to do. It actually makes it a whole lot easier knowing that you understand that too. I know you'll worry no matter what, but you have to trust me, Mom." He leaned forward, kissed her on the cheek, and got to his feet. "Everything's going to work out the way it's supposed to."

The sky was still dark when Deston and Joliet walked down the steps of the plane, but it wasn't the deep dark of midnight and the airport lights made it appear as bright as day. Mordred had not bothered to mention the Venice airport was on the mainland and they would need to cross the lagoon to get to the city. That wasn't so much a problem for the fae, they could shapeshift and fly into Venice, but Mordred and Joliet didn't have that luxury.

Though adding a leg to their journey was an inconvenience, it also helped Joliet with her plan and gave her an excuse to get Oseron away from the others by insisting he go with her to secure a water taxi. Deston watched his parents walk into the hangar and took a deep breath of the salty air as he steeled himself for what he was about to do. He could hardly believe the obstacle he thought would be one of his biggest challenges—sneaking away unnoticed—had been taken care of without him having to do a thing. Nothing was in his way now, other than a bad case of nerves.

He knew very little about Venice or San Marco Basilica, but as it was one of the city's main attractions, he assumed it wouldn't be too hard to find. He was counting on his bird's eye view to help in that respect, but he was still a little worried, because he couldn't afford to spend a lot of time searching for the right place.

The fae warriors stood in a tight circle around Mordred, giving the sorcerer no chance to escape. All were experienced warriors and had been in the king's service for decades. They were also well aware of Mordred's reputation and their eyes didn't deviate from him for a second in fear he might try one of his many tricks to get away. That made it quite easy for Deston to walk the few dozen meters to the end of the building and dart around the corner without being noticed.

The second he was out of sight, he transformed into a falcon and soared across the lagoon toward the lights of the city. The overcast sky looked as if it might split open and drop rain at any moment. A chilly wind blew, as well, but Deston didn't feel the cold. In fact, he didn't feel anything. With all he had been through the past twenty-four hours, and all the thoughts that were crowded inside his head, he was numb. He felt like some strange entity had taken over his body and he was just going through the motions.

The cloud level dropped even lower when he got to land, and in order to see, he also had to drop down, which left him flying just a few meters above the top of a sea of red tile-roofed buildings that were crammed so tightly together there was hardly a break between them. There were very few open spaces within the city and very little green, but there was an abundance of churches. Fortunately, he had looked up San Marco Basilica while on the plane and learned it was on the south side of Venice, which was the same general area that Mordred had pointed to on the map. He flew past one church bell tower after another and was just beginning to wonder if he would be able to pick out which one was San Marco when he caught sight of a tall tower rising above the other structures. Sensing that was the Basilica, he sped toward it with his heart pounding in his chest and his stomach filled with lead.

He had no doubt he had found the right place when he saw the five giant domes laid out in a Greek cross on the roof. He soared over the domes and then up and down the length of the piazza three times, inspecting more than one hundred archways that lined the front of the buildings that made up the historic square. Though the piazza appeared empty, he couldn't shake the feeling he was being watched.

At last, he came to rest on the round-arched portal over the main entrance to the Basilica, disturbing a dozen or so pigeons that were perched there snoozing away. From that high perch, he had a good view of the entire square. He didn't find it peculiar for the piazza to be vacant at this time of day, but something seemed off. For one thing, there wasn't a single light in any of the buildings, not even an exit sign. The antique luminaries that lined the piazzette—the walkway off the main piazza that led down to the lagoon—were also dark, though he had seen lights shining through the gloom throughout the rest of the city.

Lifting off from the arch, Deston flew down the length of the piazza once again and landed on a window sill at the opposite end. There was no evidence of life. In fact, the entire square was eerily quiet. He shivered involuntarily and flew back toward the Basilica, veering right onto the piazzette and down to the lagoon. A long row of gondolas lined the quay and gently bounced up and down in the tide. Evenly spaced between the flat-bottom boats were short wooden piers, extending out into the water just far enough to give patrons access to the gondolas. Farther down the quay, there was one pier that extended twice as far out into the lagoon.

Deston soared straight to the longer pier and landed on top of the support pillar at the far end that was over the water. The pier was where he was supposed to bring Grossard. He stared down the length of the wood planks and ran the plan through his head once again. Everything depended upon Grossard knowing they were in Venice and they were going after the book. Deston didn't wonder for a second how Grossard would get that information. The monster always seemed to know what was going on. He also didn't think about the possibility of Grossard not showing, or how mad Oseron was going to be when Joliet told him of their plan, for there wasn't anything he could do about either of those things.

~~~

Joliet held Oseron's steely glare and tried not to cower. He had stood stoically and had not said a word as she divulged her plan, but his lips were a thin white line and his intense blue eyes had turned so dark they were almost black, which was a sure sign of his smoldering anger.

"I could see in Deston's face he was planning to do whatever it took to get Margaux back. I had to do something. At least with this plan he won't take off and try to face Grossard on his own. You'll be there to step in as soon as he gets Grossard to the pier," she pleaded her case.

Oseron turned and walked away a few paces. He had sensed something was up, but he had not expected Joliet to set a plan in motion without talking it over with him first. Her proposal wasn't a bad one, in fact, if everything went exactly as she outlined, and if the book was in Venice as Mordred said, it actually might work. His concern was that Joliet was relying too heavily on her misconception that Grossard only wanted the book, when in truth; Grossard wanted him and Deston dead as much, if not more, than he wanted the book. Her plan also revolved around the ring that had appeared on Mordred's finger being an open communication line with Grossard. Oseron had thought the same when he saw it, but there was no proof to support that theory. All in all, there were too many unknowns for Oseron's comfort level. But the plan had already been set in motion, and he had no choice but to overlook his reservations and pray to the gods that the pieces all fell into place.

"I wish you would have confided in me before you took action," he said without turning around.

The hurt in his voice made Joliet cringe. She had been on her own making all the decisions for so long she'd forgotten what it was like to share the burden with a partner.

"I understand you were trying to keep Deston from getting himself into a situation he wasn't prepared to handle. I can accept that, even though I don't necessarily agree with it," he went on. "At some time in the future, I hope you will forgive me for not being there for you all those years. And I hope you will come to realize I love Deston and want to protect him as much as you do." He ran his hand through his hair and the dimple in his cheek twitched. "I will notify Grossard that we are willing to trade Mordred for Margaux, and I will send a man to prepare the pier in accordance to your plan." He turned and faced Joliet. "I will do whatever else it takes to keep Deston from getting hurt, just as I promised you I would."

A surge of emotion lodged in Joliet's throat and she rushed to Oseron. "I never doubted you would do anything but that," she choked out, throwing her arms around him. He hugged her back and laid his cheek against the top of her head.

"I should get going. We may not have much time," he whispered into her hair.

Joliet's eyes were red with unshed tears as she lifted her face and pulled his lips down to hers. She put all the love in her heart into that one kiss and he responded with the same.

"I need you both, so I don't want you to do anything stupid, either," Joliet whispered.

In answer, Oseron gave her another kiss, then turned and hurried out of the hangar.

Chapter 37

Deston shook himself out of his reverie and lifted into the air to head back to the Basilica. He landed on the ground in front of the three large arches of the central entrance into the building. He still hadn't seen another person, but he hopped into the shadows before whispering the words to become invisible on the off chance someone might happen into the square and he then transformed.

His palms were clammy as he stepped into the small alcove and reached for the handle of the large bronze door. He gave it a pull and was surprised when the door didn't budge. His heart pounded in his throat as he stared in bewilderment. Until that moment, the possibility of the church being locked never entered his mind. He'd always heard churches were open twenty-four hours a day. He gave the handle another tug to be sure before running into the square and looking back at the building. There were four other doors across the front of the church, two on each side of the central entrance. Starting with ones on the left, he quickly discovered both of the doors had bronze gates drawn across them. The gates were both locked. Feeling the first hint of panic, he hurried to the one that was directly right of the center entrance. It too was gated and locked.

There was only one door left to try. He trembled with trepidation as he ran to it. Seeing the gate pulled across it, he cursed out loud and rattled the lock in frustration. Dejectedly, he walked back to the main entrance and stared up at it, wondering what to do.

All of a sudden, the flock of pigeons that had been roosting on the second floor balcony rose up, their wings clapping loudly as they lifted off. The fluttering sound of their wings roused the hundreds of other pigeons nesting in the piazza and within seconds the square was a flurry of wings and feathers, but Deston's gaze stayed on the balcony. He remembered seeing pictures of people standing up on the balcony on the internet, so there had to be access into the building from up there. He focused on a spot next to the large, bronze horse statue and in the next blink of an eye; he was standing on the balcony.

"You've come for the book, I see." An unexpected voice came out of nowhere.

Deston jumped back and jerked Caluvier from his belt. He held the sword with both hands and quickly scanned the shadows, stopping when he saw a familiar form leaning against the wall of the Basilica.

"Zumwald?" Deston questioned to verify what he was seeing. Zumwald was the last person he had expected to show up. "What are you doing here?"

"I heard what happened at Viroconium and I thought you might come for the book to free Margaux." Zumwald folded his hands in front of him. "It looks like I was correct in my way of thinking."

Deston stood up straighter and adjusted his grip on Caluvier. "You aren't going to stop me from taking the book," he stated boldly.

Zumwald chuckled low. "Good heavens, why would I stop you? I'm only here as an observer—although I wouldn't be averse in providing a little help if needed."

Deston's brow puckered. "You're going to help me?"

"I believe you were looking for a way into the Basilica," Zumwald replied, swinging his arm around to the door he was standing in front of. "Shall we?" he added as it creaked open.

Deston stared at Zumwald, but it was too dark for him to read the old man's face. He had asked Zumwald for help once before and Zumwald told him at that time that he was forbidden to interfere in the goings on of this world. So why would the old man offer to help now?

"Come now. There really isn't time to loiter," Zumwald coaxed and stepped aside to give Deston clear access to the door.

Deston's gaze lingered on Zumwald another moment before he stepped forward. He had no idea what Zumwald was up to, but he had no worries that Zumwald would betray him or put him in danger. With just a bit of hesitancy, he walked through the door and down the steep staircase that led to the lower level, keeping a firm grip on Caluvier just in case.

The smell of moldy earth and old books assaulted his nose and he was engulfed in darkness as he reached the ground level and stepped out onto an uneven floor. He paused to let his eyes adjust and get his directional bearings. His search on the internet had told him the sarcophagus was beneath the high altar, but the Basilica was huge and he had no idea where in the building the high altar was located.

As he looked around, trying to decide which way to go, he heard a soft click and the lights flickered on. The sudden brightness blinded him and he brought his hand up to shield his eyes. When he looked out again his head automatically tilted back to the glittering golden mosaics that covered every inch of the walls and ceiling. He had never seen such opulence before, and for a moment, all he could do was stand and gawk as his gaze slowly traveled across the ceiling.

"This way," Zumwald said as he walked by and headed down the center of the room.

Deston's eyes narrowed as he stared at Zumwald's back.

"Hurry along, now," Zumwald called back.

Deston hesitated, but as he didn't know which way to go, he finally relented and started after Zumwald. Everywhere he looked glittered with gold. It made him feel small and uncomfortable and he hurried forward, wanting to find the book and get out of there as quickly as possible. As he closed the gap between him and Zumwald, he noticed the old man had stopped in front of a raised section that was partitioned off from the rest of the room by marble columns and a marble knee wall. Through the opening in the partition, Deston could see another raised platform on which sat the high altar. A velvet rope draped through metal posts stood at the bottom of the altar platform as a final warning that the area was off limits. Beneath the long altar, a stone sarcophagus was visible through a metal grate.

Deston rushed past Zumwald and irreverently jumped the rope without thinking and scurried up the steps, kneeling down on one knee behind the altar. He stared at the sarcophagus and his hand shook as he reached out and touched the cold stone.

"It looks like you might need some help with that," Zumwald said, joining Deston behind the altar.

Deston looked up, his face showing his uncertainty. "Are you sure the book is really in here?" he croaked, his mouth so dry he could hardly spit the words out.

Zumwald's eyebrows rose. "There's only one way to find out, isn't there?"

Deston looked back at the stone. He had never seen a real sarcophagus up close before, but he had seen them in movies. They didn't look anything like this one, though. In the movies, the tops of the tombs were thin slabs of stone that could be easily pushed aside. The top of this one, however, was equal in size to the bottom half, and they both looked extremely heavy. In addition, there was only a few inches of space on any side between the sarcophagus and the altar table. Even if he were strong enough to lift the top off, which he doubted he was, there wasn't enough room to do so. He took a deep breath to calm his thoughts. Mordred had gotten into it, so there had to be a way.

He dropped his head and stared down at the floor, trying to think. The floor was a mixture of mosaics and marble and in the geometric pattern he noticed deep scuff marks by the legs of the table that could only be made by something heavy sliding across it—something heavy like the altar table itself. He perked up. *Could it be?* Getting to his feet, he put his hands against the altar and pushed. It didn't move much, but it did move, which gave him hope.

"Help me push this," he called out to Zumwald and turned around to put his butt against the end of the table. Zumwald moved up next to him and together they pushed until the end of the altar began to slide. After they moved it back several inches, they went to the other end and pushed it back and continued in this fashion, switching back and forth from one end to the other until the sarcophagus was half way exposed.

Stopping to catch his breath and ease the ache in his back, Deston bent over and put his hands on his thighs. Through his brow, he could see Zumwald sitting on the steps. As tired and achy as he felt, he could only imagine that the old man must be really hurting, but it didn't look as if Zumwald was even breathing hard. Once again, the question entered Deston's mind of why the old man was there, especially after the rude way he'd treated Zumwald the last time they met. He had been so frustrated with Zumwald then and he didn't like how the old man kept information from him and the games Zumwald was always drawing him into. But if Zumwald hadn't shown up, he would never have been able to get inside the sarcophagus and possibly wouldn't have even gotten into the Basilica.

With a puff of air, he blew the hair out of his eyes. "I think I should apol—" he started, but that's all the farther he got before Zumwald cut him off.

"We should see if we can get that thing open, don't you think?" Zumwald said, getting to his feet and walking back to the stone box.

Deston looked at him and slowly straightened. "Yeah, sure," he replied, wiping the sweat off his forehead with his arm.

The two of them put their weight together again and slid the lid off the sarcophagus just far enough for Deston to reach inside. He could see the bare bones of the skeleton lying in perfect repose with its hands crossed over an iron box wrapped in chains, just as Mordred described. Deston smiled up at Zumwald. He could hardly believe it. He really had found it. He wiped his palms on his tunic and carefully, so as not to disturb the bones too much, lifted the heavy iron box out and set it on the floor. The chain around the box was one solid piece with no breaks in the links and no lock. Deston pulled on it to test it. It was strong and tight.

"Crap," he whispered, wondering how he was going to get the chain off to get the book out.

Zumwald silently knelt beside him and laid his hand on top of the box. He made no other movement and there was no sound, but when he took his hand away, the chain fell off and hit the floor with a loud clank.

Deston gave a slight jump at the noise and looked up into Zumwald's eyes. The old man gave him a nod and Deston tentatively reached out and lifted the top with trembling hands. The red covered book was inside. All he had to do was reach in and take it out, but he suddenly didn't want to touch it. He picked the box up and turned it over, tipping the book out onto the floor with a loud thwack that echoed through the dome over the altar. At the same moment, the lights in the church flickered and an odd, uncomfortable sensation washed over Deston.

"There you have it—the Book of Tenebris. Take it and do what you must," Zumwald said and turned his back.

Deston sat on his haunches and stared at the scaly cover. It was hard to believe that one book could be responsible for so much devastation. The future now rode on him and his next steps. He had to get Grossard to follow him out onto the pier. If he couldn't, and Grossard got his hands on the book, he would not only be responsible for Margaux's death, he'd be responsible for the destruction of the entire planet. He shuddered as doubts ripped holes in his fortitude

"Clear your mind of doubt and concentrate on the end result you want to accomplish," Zumwald said, putting a hand on Deston's shoulder.

At Zumwald's touch, the ache in Deston's shoulder vanished, but Deston was too overwhelmed with the task at hand to acknowledge it. His eyes reflected his uncertainty as he lifted them to Zumwald. "Do you know what's going to happen?"

Zumwald's lips pulled back into a smile that did not reach his eyes, and instead of replying, he gave Deston's shoulder another squeeze.

Deston lowered his head and looked back at the book. He hadn't really expected Zumwald to answer the question. He swallowed hard, knowing he should be going, but he couldn't bring himself to pick up the book.

Noting his hesitation, Zumwald took the altar cloth from the table, ripped it in half and wound it around the book twice. "It is time. It will be light soon and you'll want to get this over with before the innocent start making their way down to the square," Zumwald said, holding the book out for Deston to take.

Deston stared at the bundle of white lace in Zumwald's hand. After a long pause, he finally took it. The minute he touched it, he felt an uncomfortable weight press down on his shoulders. "Do I really have a chance of pulling this off?" he asked, turning his glassy eyes on Zumwald.

"You have as much of a chance as you believe you have," Zumwald replied. Without saying anything more, he walked away, holding his right arm stiffly against his side.

Chapter 38

Deston stepped out into the chilly air and walked to the railing of the balcony. The wind had picked up and the clouds looked ominous, but no rain was falling in the square, which was strange for it smelled like rain and he could hear the sound of rain falling out in the lagoon. A lump moved into his throat and a feeling of dread filled him as the leather pouch around his neck grew hot. Unconsciously, he clutched the book tighter to his chest and looked out over the piazza.

Mordred bristled when he saw Deston standing at the railing of the balcony with the book in hand. He couldn't believe the boy had pieced together the location from what little he said on the plane. He had intended to be the one to lead the way so he could stall them and make sure Grossard had time to get there first. But Deston had ruined everything, as he had a habit of doing. Glaring up at Deston's profile through half-closed eyes, Mordred finally understood Grossard's intense loathing of the boy.

"As you can see, Deston has retrieved the book. Per our agreement, my part is done. You must now let me go free," Mordred stated, trying to break away from the two warriors who had a tight hold on his arms.

Oseron and Joliet stood side by side on the corner of the piazza and piazzette, watching Deston through a slit in the construction tarp that had been draped over the front of the Biblioteca Marciana to cover the restoration work that was being done on the building. Neither of them acknowledged or answered Mordred, for they were sick of his whining and complaining, which had been going on nonstop ever since Mordred learned Deston had gone ahead to get the book. He had insisted Deston would not be able to get into the church without him, and when he demanded Oseron call Deston back, Oseron knew he had something up his sleeve.

Deston slowly scanned both sides of the square looking for the silvery glow of magic. He figured Grossard would be using a glamour since San Marco was a popular spot for humans to hang out, and all faeries, including solitary faeries, never let humans see their true selves. But just like before he entered the Basilica, everything was dark and the piazza looked empty. He walked behind the horse statues to the other side of the balcony for a different viewpoint. The hair on the back of his neck stood on end and the uncomfortable prickling feeling in his hand returned. He knew right then that Grossard and the Shard were close by.

According to the plan, he was supposed to go to the pier as soon as he had the book, but the weight of the book in his hand made him realize the gravity of the situation and it suddenly seemed like an awfully big risk to take. He loved Margaux with all his heart, but Oseron was right—he couldn't let Grossard get the book.

He squeezed the lace bundle tight and bit his lip, trying to decide what to do. His nerves were wound so tight his heart did a little flip at the slightest sound. When a pigeon shot out from one of the darkened doorways of the piazza, he flinched and his gaze followed it down to the square just as a figure step out into the open. He drew in a sharp breath and his eyes bulged. *Keir?* As the name flashed through his head, Keir vanished and another figure emerged from a different doorway. Deston's eyes went even wider. *Grandfather?* Just as Keir had, the apparition dissolved as soon as the name came into Deston's mind and he felt a stirring in his chest. Zumwald, Oberon, and Keir had all previously told him he was not alone, but until that moment he had not believed them, for he had always felt that he was. He pressed his lips together and took in a big breath.

"Okay ... I guess we're going to do this together then," he whispered. Holding his breath, he popped down to the ground and took off in a run towards the lagoon.

Deston was halfway down the piazzette when the smell of sulfur hit him and a giant figure carrying a tall staff materialized a few meters down the walkway. The serpent's eyes at top of the staff glowed red. The hood of the figure's cloak was pulled way down, but Deston didn't need to see the face to know it was Grossard. He skidded to a stop and transferred the bundle of lace to his left arm so he could pull Caluvier out with his right.

"What do you have in your arm there, boy?" Grossard sneered.

Deston took a step back and gripped the book tighter to his chest.

Grossard cocked his head. "That wouldn't be the Book of Tenebris would it? Surely Mordred isn't so desperate he would send a Halfling to fetch it for him. Or is this another one of his tricks?" He pondered the question for a moment, then lifted his head and called out loudly,

"Oseron, I've already been cheated out of the book once today. If you think you can play me the fool twice in one day, you are gravely mistaken."

Deston's eyes darted left and right looking for Margaux, but it appeared that Grossard was alone. "Where's Margaux?" he blurted out unable to hold back.

Grossard looked down his nose. "Where is Mordred?"

"Here," Oseron called out, as he, Torren and two other warriors who were holding Mordred between them appeared behind Deston. Joliet ran up to join them a few seconds later.

Mordred shot a quick glance at Grossard and cowered. "Let me go. You gave your word, Oseron, you cannot break it," he shrieked.

Oseron went on as if Mordred hadn't spoken. "I would also like to know where Margaux is," he said.

"The book you want is there in Deston's arms. Grab him before he gets away," Mordred called out. Joliet promptly pulled his ascot up over his mouth and gagged him so he could say no more.

Oseron gestured to the sorcerer, who was struggling to get free of the warriors holding him. "I know you are wiser than to believe anything this man has to say. He's lied to you about the book in the past; why would you want to believe him now? I told you earlier, I have no use for him— that is still true. I will gladly exchange him for Margaux just to get away from his sniveling," Oseron stated bluntly.

Grossard glowered and looked from Mordred to Oseron and back. Mordred's eyes were moving back and forth in a wild attempt to communicate, but the sorcerer had already betrayed Grossard too many times; and as Oseron said, he did know better than to trust anything Mordred said. All the same, he sensed something was amiss. He couldn't imagine Mordred would ever allow the fae to get *Their* hands on the book, which would indicate the book in Deston's arm was a fake. However, he also couldn't believe Oseron would make an offer to trade a dark, powerful sorcerer like Mordred for one insignificant girl, unless Oseron already had the real book and knew Mordred would be useless to Grossard. One of them was trying to make him look like a fool, but which one? Deceit was Mordred's typical modus-operandi, but Oseron knew that as well as Grossard did and could be using that to instill doubt in Grossard's mind so that he would believe Mordred still had the book. Gnashing his teeth together, Grossard glared from one to the other, uncertain which one to believe.

While Oseron had Grossard's attention, Deston had inched his way to the side. He was just about to slip into the shadows and take off for the pier when Grossard signaled Nolef. As the korrigan stepped out into the piazzette carrying Margaux under his arm, Deston gasped out loud before he could stop himself. Grossard heard the sound and looked over. Their eyes met and Deston took off at a sprint for the pier. Grossard disappeared from where he stood and reappeared in front of Deston before he could reach the quay.

"No more tricks, boy. If that is the book you have there, I will take it now," Grossard hissed, pointing the staff at the package in Deston's arm.

Deston looked down at the bundle of lace and back up at Grossard. "I don't think so," he said and lunged forward, thrusting Caluvier at Grossard's stomach.

Grossard's reaction was automatic and the staff came around to block Deston's strike. Deston was expecting that and jumped straight up, twisting and kicking out with a whirling sidekick. He had intended to plant his foot in Grossard's chest and knock Grossard backward, but his foot hit Grossard's wrist, driving the monster's hand into his own face. Grossard howled as blood gushed from his nose. Baring his teeth, he lunged for Deston, but Deston vanished with a small pop just as Grossard had moments before and all Grossard caught was air.

Oseron and Joliet ran toward Grossard, but he too vanished and reappeared far down on the walkway of the quay. It took him only a second to spot Deston out on the long pier.

Deston had run almost to the end of the planks and stood there with his feet planted in preparation for the wobble when Grossard joined him. There was no indication the pier had been altered in any way, but he trusted that it had.

Grossard was not anxious to step out onto the pier, but he was desperate to get the book. Placing the staff in its holder inside his cloak to free his hands, he braved a few feet out onto the wooden planks. A sneer remained plastered on his face, but Deston could see the discomfort in his eyes as he drew nearer to the water.

"You have no place to go now, boy," Grossard jeered, taking a few more steps forward.

Deston lifted his chin and smiled when he heard his father shout out, "Grossard, surrender now and I'll consider leniency in your punishment."

Grossard's teeth flashed as he vanished and reappeared on the end of the pier behind Deston. As he reached out for Deston with one hand, he grabbed for the book with the other, but Deston flipped around and all Grossard caught hold of was the tailing piece of the altar cloth. With a snarl, Grossard dug his fingers into the lace and pulled. The bundle flew out of Deston's grip, but Grossard only had hold of the cloth and not the book and it came unwound and plopped down on the planks between their feet. Grossard dove for it, but Deston kicked out with his foot and the book skidded across the wooden planks and over the edge into the water.

A piercing screech rose up from the quay. Grossard looked over from the floor of the pier and saw Mordred on his knees with his hands covering his face, wailing as if he was in a great deal of pain. At that moment, Grossard realized the book had been the real one. Letting out a thunderous roar that shook the pier, he pulled out his staff and lumbered to his feet.

"You!" he growled, glaring at Deston.

Deston's eyes locked with Grossard's and he gripped Caluvier tighter. He was finally at the moment the gods had been steering him toward his whole life, and surprisingly, his mind was perfectly clear. He stood with his head held high and his shoulders back, waiting for Grossard to make a move, so he could make his.

Grossard was in a pure state of rage and swung the staff out haphazardly before he found his balance. Deston easily ducked out of the way, but the power behind Grossard's blow rocked the pier precariously and the end section they were standing on broke away from the rest of the pier. Deston had been expecting it to happen and was somewhat prepared, but Grossard was not. The sudden dip of the section dropping down onto the floating drums threw him off balance. He bounced into Deston, which pushed Deston back to the very edge of the wood.

Deston teetered on the edge of the planks, his arms flailing as he strived to stay on the pier. But instead of helping, his actions only tipped the floating portion more his way and just as he felt he was about to slip off, he lurched forward and went straight into Grossard's arms, knocking the staff out of the monster's hand.

Grossard immediately brought his arm around Deston's chest and clutched him tightly. "I have you now, boy. You are now going to pay for what you've done," he hissed.

Grossard locked his eyes on Deston so he could watch the boy's terror as he reached down to his feet to retrieve his staff that was rolling back and forth with the rocking of the floating pier. Deston was forced to bend his knees and go down with him as Grossard's fingers felt along the wood planks. With a small exclamation, Grossard jerked his hand back and held it up in front of his face. He stared in disbelief at the huge, painful blisters bubbling up on the tips of his fingers and then his gaze dropped to his feet. Again he let out a cry of shock at the sight of several inches of water covering the wood. He released Deston and stumbled backward, lifting one foot in the air and then the other. The floating section dipped this way and that with his motions and each time more water lapped over the edge. Soon the water had risen up over the soles of his boots. Frantically, he looked around for help and it was then that he finally took notice that they had floated far out into the lagoon. He turned toward the quay and saw Oseron standing there.

"OSERON," he screeched and looked down for his staff, but it had rolled into the lagoon and was gone just like the book. His face was twisted into a hideous mask of rage as he lifted his hand to the sky and screamed out the words to call down a lightning bolt. Deston winced in anticipation of the hit, but the water had neutralized Grossard's powers and only a few sparks fluttered from his fingertips.

Grossard's shriek ripped through the sky and his eyes had a crazed look as he looked back at Deston. As Deston looked up into Grossard's savage face, his mind and muscle froze.

"You're finished," Grossard hissed as he lunged.

Deston tried to get out of the way, but the planks dipped with Grossard's weight and he was thrown off balance. Before he could get his footing back, Grossard caught hold of his arm and yank him into his chest and then stomped his giant foot down on top of both of Deston's feet, giving Deston no chance to get away.

Grossard looked back at the quay to make sure Oseron could see what he was doing and pulled a short dagger from his belt. "It seems we will both have a victory this day, Oseron. You were able to destroy the book after all, but I'm going to destroy your family," Grossard yelled. His eyes gleamed with malice as he lifted the dagger with a dramatic flair and brought it down.

Several things then happened at once. A burst of red exploded behind Deston's eyes as pain radiated through his chest. But it wasn't a sharp stabbing pain of the blade piercing his heart. It was an intense pressure pushing hard into his sternum, forcing the air out of his lungs. At the same time he heard Joliet scream somewhere off in the distance and a roar of a gigantic wave as it rolled over him and Grossard.

The wave swept the dagger out of Grossard's hand and slammed him and Deston to the wood. Grossard managed to grab hold of the edge of the floating planks, which saved him from getting thrown into the water. He frantically swiped his hands over his face, trying to wipe the water away, but everything was soaking wet and he could get no relief.

Deston landed on top of Caluvier. The force of the wave and his weight rammed the cross guard down into the space between two of the planks where it wedged. His death grip on the hilt kept him from being washed overboard.

Choking and sputtering, Deston rolled to his back and tried to draw in a breath, but his lungs were full of water and no air could get in. As a sense of weightlessness came over him, he gave up on his attempt to breathe and closed his eyes to let the blackness pull him in. He felt at peace and as light as a feather floating in the sea of black, but then he spotted a small rectangle far off in the distance. As soon as he took notice of it, it zoomed up to him, or he zoomed down to it, he didn't know which, but he was suddenly looking down upon himself lying on his back on the rectangle. Caluvier was lying next to him and Grossard was there too. He didn't find it strange to be floating over his own body, as he'd heard stories of near death experiences, but what he did find strange was that there was no blood on his chest from the stab wound that had killed him. There was only the leather pouch that he always wore around his neck. He moved closer for a better look and the second he saw the leather bag had a small cut down the middle, everything became crystal clear. The tiger's eye that was in the bag, the one the gods had sent to him, had stopped the blade from piercing his heart. He wasn't dead after all. The second that thought entered his mind, the pain returned with it. His eyes flew open and a violent cough racked his chest as a gush of water came up. He gasped and drew in a breath of air as he rolled to his side and coughed up more water.

When the water was all out and he could breathe regularly again, he wrenched Caluvier out from between the planks and staggered to his feet. He looked down at Grossard, who was lying on the planks, mewling and pitifully trying to wipe the water away. He could hear Joliet calling out to him, telling him to come back to the quay and let Oseron take care of Grossard's punishment, but her voice was drowned out by the words Zumwald had said to him back in the rainforest.

"You're a being of two worlds. This gives you the necessary means to do what the fae cannot. That is to draw on the darkness of your human nature and kill Grossard and Mordred."

The weight of Caluvier was suddenly heavy in his hand. He lifted it up in front of his face and stared as if he had never seen it before. A blue flash streaked up and down the sharpened edge, lighting up the runes in the center of the blade. This was the opportunity he'd been waiting for— he could kill Grossard and end the darkness for good. A shudder ran through him and a lump rose to his throat. He swallowed hard and gripped Caluvier with both hands and stepped up to Grossard. His hand was surprisingly steady as he raised the sword in the air over Grossard's heart, the tip of the blade pointing straight down.

"Deston!" Oseron shouted out. Deston pressed his lips together, but didn't lower Caluvier. "Don't do it, son. It is not the fae way. We do not kill defenseless beings no matter who they are or what they have done."

Deston's gaze darted to his father just as two shadows shifted at the back of the quay behind Oseron. He quickly looked away before he could see who they were, in fear it might be Keir and Oberon, for he knew if he saw them, he'd never be able to do what must be done.

His chest was tight and he felt hot, even though he was soaking wet and a chilly breeze was blowing over him. He shifted his grip on the hilt of the sword, and looked down at Grossard. With his powers gone,

Grossard had shrunk back to his normal size and looked nothing like the monster that had haunted Deston's dreams. He was actually quite pathetic, lying on the planks writhing in pain, his skin raw and bloated from the blisters that had virtually blinded him.

"Deston?"

The sound of Margaux's voice sent Deston's heart a flutter. He turned his head and sucked in a breath as his gaze landed on the redhead standing in the light of the luminaries on the quay. He hadn't known for sure if Margaux would be able to recover from the curse Grossard had put her under, but by some miracle she had. In the dawning light, he could just make out her face and the plea that was plainly written on it. She didn't want him to kill Grossard, even though the monster had nearly killed her. But she didn't know all that Zumwald had told him.

He turned back to Grossard and gritted his teeth. Zumwald had said something else to him back in the rainforest. *"One match is all it takes to drive away the darkness."* He was that match. He knew that now, and because his human side had always been stronger than his fae side, he also knew he could kill the darkness. Closing his eyes, he sucked in a gulp of air.

All of a sudden, he felt some give in his core and a flood of memories poured into his brain—memories from the beginning of time that were so real they actually seemed as if they were his own, although he knew they couldn't be. The memories broke loose a burning energy that pulsed to life just below his stomach. The energy flowed into every cell of his body and he tingled all over with a renewed burst of power. He opened his eyes and felt like an infant seeing for the first time. His fae powers had finally awakened and everything was crystal clear, but it was too late.

He shuddered and his gaze went to Caluvier, which was still pointed at Grossard's heart. His hands began to shake and he felt like he was going to throw up. He didn't want to kill Grossard. He didn't want to give up the feelings and the power he'd just found, but if he didn't, Grossard would hurt more people—people he loved.

He ran his tongue over his lips and tears pooled in his eyes. "I was born to do this," he whispered with a quivering voice. "I'm the Prince of Tir na-nÓg. It is my duty to save the fae."

"And you'll be a great king to the fae one of these days." Zumwald's voice suddenly came out of nowhere.

Deston jumped and blinked up at Zumwald, who was standing on the other side of Grossard. Thinking the old man had come to make sure he was going to fulfill his destiny, he opened his mouth to ask if he could change his mind. However, before he could get a single word out, a jagged spark streaked through Zumwald's right eye and the magician's hand reached out, seized Caluvier from Deston's grip and drove the blade straight through Grossard's chest in one fluid motion. At the same instant, a single ray of light cut through the clouds. It shined down directly on Zumwald and Grossard, washing away all color so they both appeared to be stark white. Deston reared back, trying to see through the blinding glare, and for just a second, he thought he saw the corners of Zumwald's mouth stretch into a sad smile. Another jagged spark of light flashed in Zumwald's eye. At the exact same moment, an identical spark flashed through Deston's right eye. Then the clouds closed up and the light blinked out—Zumwald, Grossard and Caluvier vanished with it.

A sharp pain seized Deston's heart the moment Zumwald disappeared. He fell to his knees, keeled over into the water, and sank into the blissful silence of the murky depths of the lagoon.

Chapter 39

Deston opened his eyes and stared at the splotches of blue, green and purple that swam before his eyes. He cocked his head and looked at them from a different angle, wondering why they looked so familiar.

"How are you feeling," Joliet asked, brushing his hair off his forehead.

Deston recoiled and his gaze jerked to her face. He hadn't realized she was sitting there. He opened his mouth to speak, but all that came out was a croak.

"Here, drink this. It will help," Joliet said, handing him a cup.

"How's he doing? Awake yet?" Oseron asked from the doorway. Deston lurched up at the sound of Oseron's voice and the sip he'd just taken went down the wrong pipe.

"Take it easy. Just small sips," Joliet said, patting him on the back as he coughed.

Deston's eyes were watering as he looked up at his father, who had joined Joliet at his bedside. "What happened? Why are you both here?"

Joliet gave Oseron a look that Deston knew well. It was the look that said 'watch what you say.' The emptiness in Deston's chest swelled and he pushed himself into a sitting position. "What is it? Tell me," he demanded looking from Joliet to Oseron and back.

Joliet patted him on the arm, and opened her mouth, but it was Oseron who spoke. "Do you remember anything about what happened in Venice?" he asked softly.

Deston's eyebrows came together. *Venice?* The word broke something loose in his mind and memories flooded in. His eyebrows rose and his gaze quickly scanned the room. "How did I get back here? Am I ..." It was hard for him to get the next word out. "... dead?"

"No, sweetheart, you're at home where you belong ... safe and sound," Joliet answered as she smoothed his hair back again.

He shrugged away and looked up at Oseron, his eyes begging for answers. Oseron sat down on the edge of the bed and recounted the events that took place, as Joliet looked on disapprovingly. All the missing bits and pieces that Deston couldn't remember were filled in and Deston was shocked to hear that two days had passed since it all went down.

"No one has seen or heard from Zumwald since the incident. We haven't seen or heard from Tiff, either," Oseron was saying. "But knowing her, she'll turn up sooner or later. Mordred disappeared in the confusion of the aftermath, but we were able to retrieve Grossard's staff along with the Shard from the lagoon. The book has not been located, but we'll continue to look for it until we find it."

Hearing that, Deston reared up and a sharp pain rocketed through his side, taking his breath away. He grimaced and held his breath until the pain subsided. Thinking Oseron had told Deston too much; Joliet scowled and put her hand out to stop him from saying more. Oseron saw the look and gave Deston's leg a pat as he rose to leave, but Deston caught Oseron's hand.

"The book didn't fall into the lagoon," Deston said in a rush.

Oseron frowned and sat back down.

"I took the book out of the sarcophagus, but Zumwald was the one who wrapped it in the lace altar cloth. When Grossard yanked on the cloth and the book fell out, it wasn't the same book. I think Zumwald switched them while we were still inside the Basilica. He has the real book."

Oseron rubbed his chin and slowly nodded his head. "I can see Merlyn doing that. He makes a big to-do about not interfering in the ways of this world, but if the situation demands it, he has always done what needs to be done. I can think of no better place for that book than in his hands. He will see that it is not ever used again."

"So do you think we'll ever see him again?" Deston asked after a short pause.

Oseron smiled and nodded his head. "I'm sure you will. He has a way of turning up every few centuries or so."

"What about Mordred?"

Oseron's smile vanished. "We will find him. It's only a matter of time. Without the Shard or the book, he is more of a nuisance than a threat."

Deston thought about that for a moment. "Do you think he'll try to find the Shard again?"

"The Shard has been taken care of. There's no chance it can ever spread darkness again. You don't need to worry about that."

Joliet cleared her throat and Oseron smiled down at Deston. "I think your mother is telling me I've stayed long enough. I better leave before she physically throws me out." He walked to the door and looked back. "The people are clamoring to pay you honor. I'm afraid you're going to have to endure a celebration soon." Deston's eyes widened and his cheeks turned pink. "That's what comes with being a hero. You might as well get used to it."

"But it wasn't me. It was Zumwald," Deston countered, stating the truth.

There was a hint of sadness in Oseron's eyes as he nodded his head. "Zumwald is not a fae or a prince … you are. And any way you want to look at it, you were greatly responsible for freeing us from Grossard's reign of terror." He smiled and added. "Therefore, like it or not, Titania and NiNi are planning an event in your honor. With those two heading it up, you have no chance of escaping." He chuckled at the horrified look that flitted over Deston's face. He then gave him a wink. "I understand you need some time. I'll make sure they hold off for a bit longer."

Deston stared at the door long after it closed, trying to process what he'd learned.

"Do you need anything, sweetheart?" Joliet asked, wanting to help him, but not knowing what to do.

Deston shook his head and didn't look at her. "Can I just be alone for a little bit?" His voice was so soft, Joliet almost didn't hear him.

"Of course … I won't be far away, though. Just call out if you need anything."

Deston nodded his head and suffered through Joliet fluffing up his pillows and setting out a fresh cup of water on the bedside table before leaving.

As soon as the door clicked closed, Deston replayed everything he had learned. The realization that Zumwald and Tiff were gone and he might never see them again hit him like a thunderclap. As he scrunched into a ball and hugged his stomach, he felt a tender spot on his side. He pulled his shirt up and looked down at a purple bruise in the shape of a half-moon that he got when he fell on Caluvier. Remembering that Caluvier was gone as well, he closed his eyes. *Why?* He didn't have an answer to that question and knew he probably never would. Tears sprang to his eyes and this time he didn't even try to hold them back. He buried his head in his pillow and let them pour out.

~~

A knock broke the silence of Deston's room and the door flew open before Deston had the chance to lift his head. Joliet strode in, walked straight to Deston and yanked his cover all the way back to the foot of the bed.

"MOM! Geez, what'dya doing?" Deston squealed, scrambling up, grabbing the blanket and pulling it back up under his chin.

"You've been sulking in this room for days now. That's long enough. The day is too beautiful. I will not allow you to waste another second of it."

"I don't wanna—" Deston began, but Joliet cut him off with a look.

"Either you get up and walk out of here on your own, or Torren will come in and carry you out. Now which would you rather it be?" she said, placing her hands on her hips.

Deston groaned and rolled his eyes. "*Fine*. I'll get up. But I'm not going to get dressed with you standing there."

Joliet's face softened. "It's for your own good, honey. You're not helping yourself by moping around and hiding out in here." She started to reach out to brush the hair out of his eyes, but her hand stalled and dropped back to her side. "I'll wait for you outside in the hall while you get dressed." She stopped at the door and looked back over her shoulder. "Don't be too long." The door then closed with a soft click.

Deston let out a heavy sigh and swung his legs over the side of the bed. He wasn't hiding out; he just wanted to be left alone. All everyone wanted to talk about was what had happened in Venice and he didn't want to talk about it anymore.

He took his time dressing in hopes that Joliet would get tired of waiting and leave, but to his dismay, she was still there when he opened the door.

"I was just about to come in and make sure you hadn't gone back to bed," she stated, stepping up and looping her arm through his to guide him down the hall.

"I'm up, okay," he said pulling away. "I don't need a babysitter." He saw the flicker of hurt in her eyes and his cheeks turned pink as he looked away. "I didn't mean it that way, but you've got to quit treating me like a kid. I'm perfectly capable of walking outside on my own. It's not like anyone's gonna hurt me here on the palace grounds." He threw a quick sidelong glance at her, expecting her to protest, but to his surprise, she didn't.

"I know you're not a kid, but sometimes I wish you still were. If you want to walk around the gardens on your own, I have no problem with that. I just want you to get some sunshine so you will start feeling better." She patted him on the cheek and watched him walk down the hall before turning and hurrying back in the opposite direction.

Deston gave a quick nod to the few people he met in the hallway and hurried on before they could ask him any questions. Just when he was beginning to think he was going to get out of the palace without having to talk to anyone, he turned the last corner and came face to face with

Lilika, who was just coming back from taking Macaria out for a stroll. He had not seen Lilika since she had the baby. The unexpected meeting sent his stomach plummeting and the blood rushed from his face and pooled down in his toes.

"I'm ... I'm," he stammered, but he didn't know what to say.

Lilika smiled. "I'm so glad to see you up and about. I've been meaning to stop by, but this little one has kept me pretty busy of late." She smiled down at the bundle in her arms.

Macaria gurgled as if she knew Lilika was talking about her. Deston looked down at the small pink face within the blanket. Her hair was the same fiery copper color of Lilika's, but the eyes staring up at him were definitely Keir's. Deston gulped and licked his lips. This was exactly what he'd been afraid of—seeing Macaria and knowing he was responsible for her growing up without a father. Macaria's small perfect mouth turned up in a smile and her chubby little hand reached out of the blanket. Deston couldn't stop himself from putting his finger in Macaria's tiny hand. She clutched it and squeezed harder than Deston thought was possible for an infant.

"Ah, look, that is her first smile. She likes you," Lilika said proudly and kissed Macaria on the top of her head.

Deston stood awkwardly and stared down at the baby. He didn't think he'd ever seen anything so small and so perfect.

"We should probably get going. It's time for her feeding and she has about as much patience as what can fit in her pinky fingernail."

Deston reluctantly pulled his finger back, but his eyes didn't leave Macaria's face.

"Come and see us soon, won't you, please? We'll have more time to talk," Lilika added, sensing Deston had something he wanted to say.

Deston nodded his head. "I will," he mumbled, still caught up in the infant's eyes.

Lilika laid a hand on his arm and waited until he looked up. "It's going to be all right." She gave his arm a squeeze and started back down the hall to her chambers.

Deston stared blankly at the empty hallway for a long time before he turned and headed out into the gardens. His step was a little lighter than it was before and he wandered aimlessly through the different levels of the garden for the next half-hour, paying little attention to what he was seeing or where he was going until he stumbled into a section he'd never been in before. The flowerbeds in the section were different than the others and reminded him of something, but he couldn't put his finger on what. He liked it, though. It felt peaceful and was quiet and empty, which was just what he was looking for. Climbing up into the crook of a tree, he laid his head back against the trunk and looked up through the leaves.

He hated to admit it, and he never would admit it to his mother, but it did feel good to be outside. As the sun warmed his skin, he could feel the tension in his shoulders begin to melt away. With a sigh, he sank into the branch and watched the clouds roll by, his thoughts wandering along with them.

"Mon dieu, Deston … is that you?" NiNi's voice suddenly broke through his daydream.

Deston jerked up and nearly lost his balance. He hadn't seen NiNi in months. In fact, he hadn't seen her since before he left for the Great Bear Rainforest, and until this moment, he hadn't realized how much he missed her.

"Come down here and give me a hug, young man," NiNi ordered with a smile.

Deston jumped down from his perch in the tree. His feet had barely touched the ground before NiNi's arms wrapped around him.

"I heard you were back," she said giving him a tight squeeze and then stepped back an arm's length to look him over. She reached up, brushed the hair off his forehead and cocked her head. "You look awful," she stated bluntly.

If anyone else had said that to him, he would have immediately felt defensive, but all he did was smile sheepishly and reply, "I haven't been sleeping so well."

"Humph," NiNi huffed knowingly. "From what I hear, that is all you have been doing."

Deston blushed and turned away. "Well … I've had some things on my mind."

NiNi walked around a tall flowering foxglove plant, sat down on a stump and patted the one next to her. Deston recognized the seats as ones from her cottage in France. "Would you like to talk about it?"

"No … not really."

NiNi's eyebrows rose knowingly. "You know I was just a young girl the first time I met Zumwald. He was the one who taught me everything I know about plants and herbs and how to use them to help others." She smiled at the old memory. "I did not always agree with his methods, but I always knew he had this world's best interest at heart. I could also tell he was quite fond of you."

Deston felt the all too familiar ache in his heart flame up. He looked down at his hands. "Do you think he'll ever come back?"

"Good gracious, of course he will. When the world needs him again, you will not be able to keep him away."

They sat in comfortable silence, each lost in their own thoughts until the crunching of the gravel announced someone else had arrived. Deston looked past NiNi just as Margaux stepped out from behind a lilac bush.

Both he and Margaux gave a quick start and blushed at the same moment.

Margaux timidly looked from Deston to NiNi and the pink in her cheeks deepened. "The queen said you wanted to see me," she stammered as she glanced back at Deston.

"No, I didn't," Deston replied without thinking what he was saying.

Margaux's face turned red. "Oh," she said and cleared her throat. "I'm sorry. I … I guess I got it wrong. I didn't mean to intrude." She turned to leave, but NiNi caught her hand.

"Nonsense, you are not intruding. I am glad you are here. I need to get back to something important, but I did not want to leave Deston sitting all alone. With you here now, I know I can leave him in your capable hands." She rose from the stoop and pushed Margaux down on it. "It is a beautiful day. You two stay out here and enjoy it." She gave them both a big toothy grin and winked at Margaux as she turned to leave.

"Oh, by the way, Deston, I have been meaning to share with you one of your *grand-mère's* favorite sayings. I know she would tell you this herself if she were here, 'If the past was what we were meant to see, then behind, not in front, our eyes would be.'" She paused to let the words sink in before adding, "She was a wise woman and knew what she was talking about. I hope you think about her advice and take it to heart." Without saying more, she waddled away, leaving Margaux and Deston in an uncomfortable silence.

Deston fidgeted with a blossom he pulled off the foxglove and Margaux twirled the end of a piece of hair around her thumb. They were both so caught up in their emotions neither of them noticed the large crow with the white tuft under its beak land on a high branch of the tree next to them.

Suddenly, they both looked up and started talking at the exact same moment.

"I'm sorry, you go ahead," Deston said, the tips of his ears turning pink.

Margaux looked down at her hands and right back up. "I just wanted to say I'm sorry … for everything."

Deston looked shocked and put his hand over hers, then pulled it back. "You don't have anything to be sorry about. I'm the one who should be sorry. If I had listened to you when you warned me about Rellik, you wouldn't have nearly died."

Margaux turned toward him and took his hand in hers. Their fingers automatically entwined. "That wasn't your fault. It was mine. I never should have fired on Grossard. It was a stupid thing to do and I don't know what I was thinking. But don't you see … everything that happened was supposed to happen. From the day you got to France, your destiny was sealed and so was mine. Even being kidnapped was part of it. If I hadn't been, you wouldn't have had to save me, and you wouldn't have gone after the book, and then Grossard wouldn't have come to Venice to get it. If none of that had happened, he'd still be alive and probably a bigger threat than ever. It all worked out like it was supposed to. Just like NiNi has said many times, there are no accidents in the Universe. I truly believe that's true."

Deston looked down at their intertwined hands. As usual, everything she said made sense, but he was tired of thinking. He had fulfilled his destiny and even lived to talk about it. That was enough. He was ready to take his *grand-mère's* advice and look forward rather than back.

He pulled his hand out of Margaux's and put his arm around her shoulder. She tensed for just a second and then relaxed into him. He tightened his arm around her and as she snuggled in, he laid his cheek against her hair. He never imagined he could feel such love for another person. There was so much he wanted to say to her, but there was no longer a need to rush. They were both home to stay. As he made a silent vow that nothing would ever come between them again, a faint jagged spark of light flashed through his right pupil and then was gone.

Lost in each other, neither Deston nor Margaux heard the flutter of wings as the large crow lifted off and flew away toward the sun.

A Note From the Author

Thank you for reading **How Dark the Light Shines**, the final installment of the *Chronicles of the Secret Prince*. It has been so much fun sharing Deston's journey with you. I hope you enjoyed it. If you would take a few minutes to rate and review this book online, I would very much appreciate it. It's a thrill for us authors to read our readers' thoughts.

And please tell your friends about the *Chronicles of the Secret Prince*, for word-of-mouth is an author's best friend.

For more information on MJ Bell and to get updates on new projects, please 'like' my Facebook page, **MJ Bell Author**, or check out my website at **mj-bell.com**.

~~

Other Books by MJ Bell

Before the Full Moon Rises,
Book I of the Chronicles of the Secret Prince

Once Upon a Darker Time,
Book II of the Chronicles of the Secret Prince

Acknowledgements

Writing the Chronicles of the Secret Prince has been quite a ride for me—a lot of sleepless nights with different storylines running through my head, a lot of time spent alone writing, and a lot of worry that it might turn out as good as I hoped. I don't think I could have gotten through it all if I didn't so many people supporting and encouraging me on. Here are just a few who have made my long journey worthwhile. I love you all and thank you from the bottom of my heart.

First and foremost—to all those who read my books and go out and tell their friends. That's what it's all about. You inspire me to keep the stories coming.

Tim, who has stood by me since I was thirteen-years-old, and never ever complains when I interrupt his reading to ask him for a word I can't seem to find.

Tiffany, my beautiful daughter, who is also my biggest fan. You were the first to believe in me and you never let me give up.

Aria Keehn, an amazing and incredibly talented artist who's imagination brought my books to life in spectacular color.

Jeff, my amazing son, who keeps my website looking incredible. You make me so proud.

Brandy, my great editor. Your suggestions, time, and effort made this book the best it can be. You are the best!

With special thanks to my close friends (you know who you are) for never losing faith in me. You always knew the right things to say and were always there to help me find my way whenever I got lost.

About the Author

M.J. Bell's love of reading and everything magical is what motived her to jump head first into a writing career. Her first novel was honored with a Gold medal in the Mom's Choice Awards' Fantasy category in 2009. From there she has gone on to write a new fantasy trilogy, Chronicles of the Secret Prince.

M.J. grew up in Iowa, but now considers Colorado her home and lives there with her husband, Tim. Her growing family has always been her pride and joy and provides her with a great source of inspiration to write and bring a little more magic into the world. She loves to hear from readers through her FB page at **MJ Bell Author**. Or contact her through her website at **mj-bell.com**.

Made in the USA
San Bernardino, CA
22 May 2018